Malcolm Bradbury is Professor Emeritus of American
Studies at the University of East Anglia. He has written
several novels including THE HISTORY MAN, EATING
PEOPLE IS WRONG, CUTS and DOCTOR CRIMINALE, as
well as works of popular literary criticism including THE
MODERN AMERICAN NOVEL, THE MODERN BRITISH
NOVEL and DANGEROUS PILGRIMAGES. He has also
adapted the novels PORTERHOUSE BLUE and COLD
COMFORT FARM for television.

SCEPTRE

Class
Work

The Best of Contemporary Short Fiction

EDITED BY MALCOLM BRADBURY

SCEPTRE

First published in 1995 by Hodder and Stoughton
A division of Hodder Headline PLC
A Sceptre Paperback

10 9 8 7 6 5 4 3 2 1

British Library Cataloguing in Publication Data

Class Work: Short Fiction by UEA Writers
  I. Bradbury, Malcolm
  823.0108 [FS]

ISBN 0 340 64935 6

Typeset by Palimpsest Book Production Limited,
Polmont, Stirlingshire
Printed and bound in Great Britain by
Cox and Wyman Ltd, Reading, Berkshire

Hodder and Stoughton
A division of Hodder Headline PLC
338 Euston Road
London NW1 3BH

CONTENTS

INTRODUCTION ∫

To start at the start: just over twenty-five years ago, Angus Wilson and I – we were both professors of literature at the very new University of East Anglia, a then gleaming concrete monument set in a windy green field just outside Norwich – began discussing an idea. We were each growing ever more depressed by the general state of serious fiction and the short story in Britain. At the end of the Sixties, the bright excitements of the postwar generation and the anger of the Angry Young Men had already died down, and publishers, editors and critics were all beginning to doubt the future of literary fiction. In the diminishing band of literary periodicals and little magazines, articles on the Death of the Novel appeared constantly, as they still do today. One memorable issue of Ian Hamilton's *The New Review* actually had a symposium in which some sixty-odd good novelists announced that nobody was writing good novels any more. Meantime the magazines that printed short stories were shutting down (*The New Review* itself closed shortly thereafter), publishers were beginning to limit their fiction titles, and post mortem thoughts were widespread.

One odd fact struck us. Though everyone was announcing the Death of the Novel, no one was announcing the Death of Literary Criticism. In fact (as was clear from the climate in our own university) criticism, stimulated by the new thoughts of France, was undergoing a vivid resurrection, emerging in the new guise of Literary Theory. In Paris Roland Barthes had lately published his essay on 'The Death of the Author'. Marshall McLuhan had not much earlier pronounced the End of the Gutenberg Galaxy, the closedown of the era of the book. Since Angus and I were both novelists as well as teachers of literature, and took our profession seriously, it seemed somewhat strange for us to be announcing the Death of the Author in the classroom, then going straight back home to be one. What seemed even more grievous was that the practice of criticism and the practice of writing were splitting ever further apart. Where once writers and critics had been much the same people, now the practice of writing and the theory of its study seemed ever more to divide.

What's more, the prevailing cultural gloom largely contradicted the evidence of our own eyes. The new universities, founded in the great educational dreams of the early 1960s, had attracted a new generation of vigorous and creative undergraduates, who were looking for a new and 'contemporary' approach to literature. Many of them were writing themselves. At UEA these included Rose Tremain, Clive Sinclair, the playwright Snoo Wilson, and Jonathan Powell, later to ascend the commanding heights of television. Angus and I began working informally with them and other writers on campus; we were both also in touch with young and unknown writers elsewhere whose talents and originality we admired. What's more, we had both been involved, on the other side of the Atlantic, with that distinctive and peculiar American institution, the creative writing course. These had existed in the United States for generations; Frank Norris, for instance, took the famous course at Harvard taught by Professor Lewis Gates in the early 1890s. It seemed reasonable enough to transform what we had been doing informally into a formal programme, and in 1967 (as I see from some old and weary files) we began proposing to the university the starting of a postgraduate, MA course in the writing of fiction: otherwise known as the MA in Creative Writing.

What neither of us entirely recognized was the degree of suspicion in which creative writing had come to be held in Britain. It was generally regarded as a dangerous American invention, like the vacuum cleaner and the hoola hoop – and certainly not one that had a place in the literature department of a British university. A good many of our colleagues doubted the idea. Some thought writing couldn't be taught. Some thought, if it could be, it shouldn't be. Some thought it couldn't be properly examined. And some thought that even if it could be taught with propriety and examined with rigour it still had no place in a university, which was devoted to the disinterested study of literature, not the practice of it. Happily, there were a good many others who took the opposite view. UEA had made a point of appointing writers to its literature faculty, including Vic Sage, Lorna Sage, Jonathan Raban and others with clear creative sympathies. It had also developed a strong commitment to contemporary writing, and soon there was an invaluable writing fellowship, which has since been held over the years by a wide variety of leading writers. By the end of the Sixties the course had struggled its way onto our postgraduate programme – as a possible small supplement to an academic MA degree.

I doubt, though, if it would have come seriously into existence had it not been for a remarkable turn of fortune. In the summer of 1970 I was telephoned by a recent graduate of Sussex, Ian McEwan (he gives his own account of the events that followed in this book), who asked to take the so-far non-existent course. And, on the strength of a remarkable bundle of short stories he quickly wrote to support his application, we admitted him as the sole and trial student in 1970–71. Angus and I met him in pubs and teashops, and we discussed his work. Though he had other heavy academic requirements to fulfil, over the twelve months of the course he wrote over twenty stunning short stories, and they subsequently became the contents of his first two volumes. By the time the year was done, the whole situation was transformed. The doubting parties were convinced; the MA course in Creative Writing was now effectively born.

The twenty-five years since have seen the course pass through many guises. It started off slowly and haltingly, with a few blank years – either because no suitable candidates appeared over the horizon, or because one or other of us was off on a writing sabbatical. Gradually the numbers admitted enlarged: from one to three, three to six, six to eight, eight to twelve. Other writers occasionally appeared to supplement the group – like Clive Sinclair, who had returned to the university to do a PhD in American literature. When Angus Wilson retired from the university in the Eighties, I went on teaching the programme, first with Angela Carter, then with Paul Bailey. Then came Rose Tremain, herself a graduate of the university, and most recently she has been followed by Russell Celyn Jones. As time passed, the success of the early graduates had considerable impact on the numbers of applicants (it peaked crazily when Kazuo Ishiguro won the Booker Prize for Fiction in 1989) and brought us new and remarkable students – who soon began making their mark in their turn. The course expanded in various ways – into screenwriting, playwrighting, and publishing – and added a PhD programme. In the late 1980s, the students themselves began a self-edited annual anthology of their work, and seven of these volumes have appeared to date.

Twenty-five years on happens to mark the point of my own retirement – and the appointment of Andrew Motion as Professor of Creative Writing at UEA, to carry forward the programme in the future. As is well known, there's nothing like retirement for encouraging a few moments of fond looking back. And what I see back there are something like 200 former students, along with a very large pile of several hundred stories and drafts of novels. Of those 200, perhaps a third have become published writers (others have gone into publishing, journalism, television production, teaching, arts administration and so on). Some of them are internationally famous, some are well known, others are just beginning their careers, and others have yet to make the breakthrough. Looking back through all of these, across the twenty-five years, I have selected, not without many agonies of choice, the stories that make up the contents of this book.

The stories that follow come from the full twenty-five years of the course, and, as a matter of archival interest, I have entered the dates when these writers actually took the course (save for Rose Tremain and Clive Sinclair, both former UEA undergraduates who returned to take part in the programme). Of these stories, a good many – like Ian McEwan's 'Solid Geometry' and Kazuo Ishiguro's 'A Family Supper', Glenn Patterson's 'Flag Day' and David Rose's 'An Ugly Night' – were actually written for and discussed in the formidable workshops, some of them as famous for bloodshed as the Charge of the Light Brigade. Several of the stories had quite a complicated genesis. For instance 'Iguana Hunting', an early piece of writing by Hernán Lara Zavala (now a well-known Mexican novelist and story writer) was first written in Spanish, then translated and reworked with another member of the course, Andrew Jefford. A number of stories here started life in the course but have been much reworked since, generally for publication. Some is more recent work (it seemed only fair to let the chosen writers indicate their own preferences). The course has always contained as many novelists as short story writers; and for that reason two of the pieces chosen, 'Killing a Pig' by Deirdre Madden and 'Cutting' by Martha Perkins, are self-contained sections from novels. From the start, the course was very deliberately international – which is why, of the writers that follow, several are American, a number Irish, one is Anglo-Japanese and one Mexican; a reasonably typical grouping.

A few other things are also interesting when seen in the hazy light of retrospect. It's now apparent that the literary and cultural gloom of the late Sixties was decidedly premature. For a wide variety of reasons – a profound change in the entire cultural climate, a new burst of energy and expansion in publishing, the growth of a new and young reading public, the birth of good new bookstores, the shift of literary interest away from theatre and back into fiction, the emergence of literary prizes, the habit of writers giving readings, the rising interest in creativity, even producing perhaps an increased tolerance for creative writing – the period soon after the course started was one of a new energy and vitality in serious fiction. New novelists were welcomed and at times even adulated or turned into glowing celebrities. New magazines started, and new outlets appeared. The conventions of fiction, and the culture and the multi-cultures underlying it, changed and expanded; and the idea of an age of new writing no longer seemed so absurd. It actually now seems possible to see the last quarter of the twentieth century as a highly creative period, perhaps reaching its peak in the 1980s, but still retaining much of its energy in the 1990s – and no doubt beyond, as the great millennial transition takes us onward into a new and different world.

It's never too wise to generalize about the characteristics of the writing of a period, and certainly the stories that follow are as various as the very various authors who wrote them. The one generalization probably worth offering is that this is self-conscious fiction – more or less by definition, since most of these stories have been through a much-discussed and much-analysed process of composition. But there was never any attempt to fix a method, lay down a rule-book, prescribe a direction, create a school. Writers were encouraged to develop their own creative methods and preoccupations, to follow out the line of their own writing – but to do it in a shared environment where writing and its problems and possibilities were taken seriously. Admittedly, reading through the stories, it's possible to glimpse many of the twists and turns of the literary generations that are a visible feature of any creative writing course, as they are for that matter in any longish-lived literary magazine. Ian McEwan describes how in the early years of the course 'everyone was keen on Borges and Julio Cortazar'. A few years later, the influence of Raymond Carver passed like a pandemic through the writing courses of the world, to be followed by such figures as Jeannette Winterson, Will Self and T. Coraghessan Boyle. Feminism, too, made its powerful mark, and, amongst other things, it helped dissolve the approved narrative voice and consciousness of previous fictional convention. And the international mixture of students ensured that influence from many sources fed all activities, and multiplied the sense of formal possibility.

No less potent than these things, though, have been the changes in writing technology. The age of the ballpoint pen and the notebook, or the clattering portable typewriter in the lonely bedroom, has given way to the age of the Apple Mac, the word-count, desktop publishing. No less than the great changes in the texture of contemporary culture, all this has broken open the old frame of fiction and allowed the visual appearance of the text to be transformed. And another potent influence has been the power of the visual media, and the screenplay. This has changed narrative pace and economy, and had its own powerful impact on the techniques, themes and genres of fiction. Technology and the age of internationalism and multi-culturalism alike have altered the spirit of contemporary writing, and dissolved or extended the once familiar literary voice of 'good' fiction into something much wider and more various.

Another great change, it seems, has been in the general attitude towards creative writing itself. It is, generally speaking, no longer held in suspicion, but regarded with, possibly, too much adulation, and the programmes now proliferate. After twenty-five years, I am still not totally convinced myself that writing can be taught – if by that is meant that writers of small talent can be transformed, by the touch of a hand or the aid of a handbook, into significant authors and great moral guides. But what certainly can be created is a significant climate around writing, in which talented and promising authors are taken through the problems, general and specific, universal and personal, of their form and their ambitions, shown the options and the possibilities, challenged, edited, pressured, hastened, treated as members of a serious profession. It is, after all, fair to assume that the problems of writers are just as interesting, just as complex and just as discussable as those of painters, actors or musicians – and that means treating the writing of fiction, or any other literary genre, as a professional, a demanding, a transmittable, a serious and an ever-changing art.

Teaching in the MA course at UEA has been the third greatest pleasure of my life. The second is writing itself, and the first you know what. I've been enormously grateful for an experience that has let me watch writing grow, generation by generation, style by style, temperament by temperament. Teaching writing, or rather working with the workings of writers, is the most intense and rewarding form of teaching I know, and has left the indelible imprint of many remarkable workshops (those at which the stories of Kazuo Ishiguro appeared, for instance). If I've tried to teach, I've also tried to learn. One way of expressing the consequential debt is the making of this book; I can only be sorry that many excellent stories and many fine writers are absent from it because of scarcity of space. And another debt is to Carole Welch at Hodder and Stoughton, for commissioning the volume, and to her colleagues Miles Hutchinson and Jeremy Page. Rose Tremain, Ian McEwan, and Clive Sinclair have also been wonderfully helpful. Another bow of gratitude is due to colleagues like Chris Bigsby, Lorna Sage, Vic Sage, and Jon Cook, head of the Centre for Creative and Performing Arts at UEA, for the longstanding support they have given. The course also depended heavily on the secretarial and moral input of Muriel Utting, a memorable figure in all its counsels, as well as of Aileen

Davies. In the formidable task of tracing writers who are now scattered worldwide, I am, as ever, deeply grateful to my wife Elizabeth Bradbury – who made not only this volume but so much else come out. Finally my direct thanks to the writers who agreed to contribute. Here it is, then, their class-work. And I hope it gives as much pleasure to the contemporary reader as it has to me over the last quarter century.

Malcolm Bradbury
Norwich, 1995

CLASS WORK ∫

In 1970 in England it was still possible to feel, if not to argue, that the chief concern of serious literature was moral and that its riveting complexities, especially in novels, were mediated by choice; what imaginary people chose to do or failed to do marked their destiny, and settled their hash by way of a kind of ascribed moral valency. At the age of twenty-two I considered myself to be five years into a scholarly apprenticeship that had come adrift, and I was feeling restless. I had had an intense sixth form at a boarding grammar school – I am one of those writers who feels his conscious adult life began under the magic spell of his English master – and had continued more vaguely and eclectically at university. Now all that was over, and I had a degree, and I was beginning to understand that unlike Oedipus or Coriolanus or Lord Jim, I myself had never really chosen anything at all. I hadn't even made a really interesting mistake.

I had been accepted at a couple of universities to do a PhD but the relevant government department mercifully refused to fund me and offered instead a year's grant to study for an MA anywhere I wanted. I liked the 'anywhere' but I was tiring of academic work. If literature was a stately conversation conducted down the generations, then I was bored with merely listening. I wanted to join in. I had the usual idle dreams of being a writer, though I had no urgent subject matter. I had made a few stabs at greatness during my final undergraduate year: I proudly kept a notebook, I wrote a long Yeatsian poem about circus animals, though whether they deserted or revolted I can no longer remember. I composed one of the worst radio plays ever written, about a saint who is so good he stinks, and everyone who came across him, what with the world being so corrupt, was compelled to vomit. I had started a novella with the title *The Man Who Hated Pain*.

The summer began and I still had not made an application for an MA. I went to the Aldeburgh Festival on a scholarship, worked in an ice cream warehouse in Brighton and spent the remaining weeks of the summer in Italy with my girlfriend. By the time I came back in September all my friends were fixed up with jobs or further study. It was time to make a choice. I went to stay at my parents' house on an army base near Middle Wallop and tried to think myself into a job. Teaching? I couldn't face it. Advertising was supposed to be 'creative' work, but I had absorbed a little of Arnold and a lot of Leavis and I loathed adverts with a high-minded passion. The Diplomatic Service? The support of the Wilson government for US policy in Vietnam had more or less finished off that possibility for me, though I still had lingering fantasies of myself, fluent in Arabic and desert lore, a gentleman scholar and man of the world.

I had brought with me a dozen university prospectuses and I thumbed them sceptically, fully aware that a course description is a literary sub-genre, impacted with unfalsifiable half-truth and unredeemable promise – in short, an advert. For all that, I was struck by the offer of a full immersion, in Norwich, in postwar American and British fiction, with a little literary theory on the side, a dose of comparative European nineteenth-century literature, and the option of handing in at the end of the year twenty-five thousand words of fiction in place of an academic mini-thesis. Norwich sounded perfectly like anywhere, American novels suited me fine, and there was the extraordinary offer of the fiction, so out of place in a university prospectus. I knew and liked Malcolm Bradbury and Angus Wilson's work. In a single unprominent paragraph my discontents and longings were addressed. It looked like a dream life was on offer. I made the first important conscious choice of my adult life and picked up the phone. Within a minute I was talking to Professor Bradbury himself (the world was emptier, things were easier then) who told me that in this its first year the fiction side of the course had been closed down due to lack of interest. In the same breath he invited me up for a chat. Essentially, I was in.

Norwich was further away in those days. There was no motorway, the train took forever, and even the phone connections were
unreliable. The car-owning revolution was years ahead, so the
city I moved to in October 1970 appeared peaceful, clean and
gratifyingly obscure. I arrived with my ambitions focussed; I
would do the academic work, for it accounted for four-fifths
of the course, but I was here to write fiction. I knew no one in
the city, I had chosen to be here, real life could begin. I moved
around as a character in my own novel, not Lord Jim perhaps,
but my own man at last, in control of a narrative that murmured
incessantly in my inner ear and went something like: 'he moved
to a forgotten town and took a room in a big house. That night
he put fifty sheets of paper on the table, took up a pencil and
promised he would not leave until a short story was written.' In
fact I worked until dawn, so excited by the romance and heroism
of it all that at intervals I could not write at all. 'He paced the
narrow room, biting on his knuckle.'

The following day I typed up the completed story and delivered
it to Malcolm Bradbury's office. A week later we met up in the
Maid's Head. He did not immediately inquire whether I was
deeply deranged, or whether I was out to shock him, and I
took his equanimity entirely for granted. His remarks were
mostly technical, and vaguely encouraging. I told him I wanted
to spend the year writing short stories. He said, 'that's fine by
me'. I said I might try out a number of deranged first-person
narrators. He said, 'why not'. I said one of them might trick his
kid sister into incest. He sucked on his pipe and said, 'try and
let me have it before the end of the month'.

Informality, complete lack of interference and carefully muted
judgment were the principal elements of Malcolm's pedagogic
style. Behind it was an unspoken but intensely radiated assumption that there was nothing quite so exciting or essential as the
writing of fiction. To be the 'product' of his writing 'course' was
to be the beneficiary of an absolute artistic licence. That there
was nothing that could not be said never needed saying. I don't
think I fully understood the extent of my privileges until five
years later, when I published the stories from that time in book
form and in the press took on the form of the ghoul I have never
quite managed to cast off.

A good deal of my time was taken up with the academic requirement. Lasdun's brutal dream was only a quarter realized, but the University of East Anglia was an optimistic, lively place. The seminars were intense and combative, and we probably showed off a lot. We read Bellow, Nabokov, Burroughs, Mailer, Updike, Roth, Barth, Gaddis and so on, a reading list whose rubric now would be Men's Studies. Everyone was keen on Borges and Julio Cortazar. I think we managed to avoid the postwar British novel, and if we did not, it made no impression on me. I heard the words 'post-modern' and 'fictive' and 'faction' for the first time. I 'compared' *Middlemarch* to *Anna Karenina*.

There were plenty of writers and would-be writers around, and a good deal of writing talk. Jonathan Raban had given up his academic career to write but still returned from London regularly. Victor Sage, who had just been appointed lecturer, was starting to write stories. John Webb with whom I shared a house was planning travel pieces. Snoo Wilson and Clive Sinclair had graduated the year before and put in appearances. Rose Tremain was living in Norwich. In the summer Alan Burns, the lawyer turned novelist, was the university's first writer-in-residence. After reading my stories he told me to read Beckett's trilogy because I appeared to be 'unconsciously influenced'. I took his advice, and immediately understood what he meant. Such are the tricks of memory that when I think back on those times the people I knew appear in perpetual good moods, their voices unusually loud, their gestures wildly exaggerated. The city itself was in a good mood. By 1971 the Sixties had spread up across the fens to take the town. I still have a hand-out inviting the citizenry to attend a smoke-in in Chapelfield Park where, it was comfortably predicted, clouds of cannabis smoke would envelop and confound the 'fascist pigs'.

After Christmas I met Angus Wilson and his friend Tony Garret. They were an incongruous couple on the concrete walkways with their pale, well-cut suits and carefree air of being globally well-connected. They had a trick of remembering even undergraduates' names, and they collected people with a passion. I don't recall anything so structured as a session about my fiction. I was invited to dinner at their cottage in Suffolk and Angus did imitations, gossiped and told outrageous stories spiked with comic cruelty. He called me 'dear boy' and when it was time to leave I overheard him mention in passing to another guest that I was a writer. For a long time afterwards I lived in the glow of that remark. On a later occasion he took me to task for homophobia, another new word.

Towards the end of my year Malcolm sent a story – the one I had written in a single night – to *Transatlantic Review*. It is easy for writers who make a living by their work to forget the thrill of first acceptance. I held on to the ten pound cheque for months. Publication led me in a roundabout way to Cape and my first volume of stories. It was a lucky year for me, though I like to think that I made my luck with an act of choice. For twenty-five years the course that Malcolm and Angus began and which Malcolm has continued to shape has offered to dozens of others the chance to try their luck and discover what it was they thought they needed to write, and whether they could do it well.

I know very few novelists who have not been to the University of East Anglia to read, and it is largely through Malcolm Bradbury that Norwich has gained its international reputation as a place where writers and would-be writers alike are treated well. To create round the business of writing a community that is essentially friendly is an extraordinary achievement. His retirement marks the end of an era in our literary culture. His genius as a teacher was to provide generous opportunities with minimal interference, as the variety of this collection eloquently testifies.

Ian McEwan

Will and Lou's Boy

Rose Tremain

Rose Tremain is the author of six novels: SADLER'S BIRTHDAY, LETTER TO SISTER BENEDICTA, THE CUPBOARD, THE SWIMMING POOL SEASON, RESTORATION, which won the *Sunday Express* Book of the Year Award in 1989 and was shortlisted for the Booker Prize, and SACRED COUNTRY, which won the 1993 James Tait Black Memorial Prize and the 1994 Prix Femina Etranger. She has also written three volumes of short stories: THE COLONEL'S DAUGHTER, which won the Dylan Thomas Short Story Award in 1984, THE GARDEN OF THE VILLA MOLLINI and EVANGELISTA'S FAN.

Will and Lou's Boy

This was an average dawn in the early summer of 1948, the year I got to be eighteen.

'Eat your fishcake, Dougie,' said Lou.

They were barracouta fishcakes. Awful. They tasted like it was the fish's seaweedy liver you were eating.

'Yes, eat your fishcake, Doug,' said Will.

Will and Lou. I thought of them as one: *Willou*. I was their son, Douglas. I was their only child.

Chief in our household was Lou's obsession to win the Queen Mary Gardening Cup. In 1947, we'd entered for the Princess Royal Gardening Cup, but we hadn't won it and Lou had turned her disappointment into rage. Until then, she'd been a moderately contented woman. Now, she was raging and cooking barracouta. Poor Will. Poor me. The world was funny those years.

We had a pre-fab. They'd built the row we were on in about one day. Only pre-fab dwellers were allowed to enter for the gardening cups. Rain had knocked down a lot of Lou's gladioli the night before Cup Day. It hadn't rained in Wandsworth, where the winner lived, and this was one among lots of things that didn't seem fair to Lou. 'Soddin' Wandsworth!' she'd say. She never normally swore much. She'd learnt 'soddin' from my Aunt If, who'd learnt it from my Uncle Pepino who sold ice-cream and illegal nylons meant for export. My Uncle Pepino was Italian, but pretended not to be during the war. 'Call me Pep,' he'd ask. 'Yes, call him Peppy,' said Aunt If, who, at the age of sixteen, had rebaptized herself Iphigenia. Her old name, which my father still used sometimes, was Gladys. She could get as angry about being called Gladys as Lou could get about Wandsworth. The men in our family, including me, seem to be calmer people than the women. Peppy was arrested that year, but he stayed calm.

The best thing about dawn in that pre-fab was knowing you'd be out of it all day. We were all out, even Lou, who worked in a rayon factory. Will was a wireless assembler. He had the same reverence for wirelesses as some people have for God. He relied on the Home Service to tell him who or what he was. He'd polish our wireless, this fount of understanding, with Min Cream and old stockings. Lou said a man like him ought to have a secure future. And she'd look at me. Sometimes, this sideways look of hers made me think she was thinking I didn't have a future of any kind, let alone secure. Lou and Will. Will and Lou. *Willou*.

I was a park attendant. My wage was four pound ten a week, not bad for then. Bits of my park had been ploughed up and sown with barley. This barley spoilt the atmosphere of the park, made it somehow noisier. Also, the kids used the barley to piss in. I'd see the heads of the girls, squatted down. But despite or notwithstanding the barley, I loved that park. That year, all the benches were getting painted and the fishpond was restocked with goldfish. We had a new Head of Parks called Mr Dowdswell, who wasn't like a clerk, but more like a visionary. The day they ploughed up his lawns for cereal, he developed the habit of tugging out hanks of his hair.

For my eighteenth birthday, Lou said, 'You ask a friend, Dougie.' I didn't have any friends really, as Lou perfectly well knew, so I asked Knacky Mick, who sold matches and empty boxes and tins of bootblack on the corner by my park gates. Knacky Mick was a Wicklow son, blue-pale in that way only the Irish are in winter. He must have been fifty. 'I'm an orphan, you know, Doug,' he often said. I liked him. When he heard I had an uncle getting black market stuff, he began to take an interest in me and sneak me matches for Lou, 'For the gas fire, like.' We didn't have a gas fire in the pre-fab. We didn't have a fire at all, but a paraffin heater Lou christened Old Smoky. But Lou liked getting matches. She grew to expect it. Free anything, in those peculiar days, was appreciated – a rubber band, a safety pin, a half yard of knicker elastic . . . and one afternoon, Lou won second prize in a raffle, one solitary brown egg. The first prize was three bananas. Lou didn't complain. She scrambled the egg with a lot of milk and we shared it on toast. She dreamt about the bananas, though. She dreamt someone gave us a banana tree for the pre-fab garden.

Two things were coming: the party for my eighteenth birthday and the day of judgment in the Queen Mary Gardening Cup. There was a long heatwave. The barley in my park started to ripen. Courting couples began the habit of lying down in it and I was supposed to shoo them away. 'I'm sorry, Sir, I'm afraid you're spoiling our crop,' Mr Dowdswell told me to say. One day, I said by mistake, 'I'm sorry, Sir, I'm afraid you're *soiling* our crop,' and I was so miserable at getting the wrong word, I left the couples alone after that, and the barley, which had once been a kids' lavatory, now became a field of iniquity.

The most iniquitous person in our family was my cousin, Patricia, daughter of Aunt If and Peppy the Italian. In the war, she'd fallen in love with a G.I. called Wedderburn C. Wicklens, a Southern, beefy man, raised with his gut full of corn pone and his brain full of cotton. He was from Louisiana State. Patricia could just imagine the kind of wooden house she'd own on the New Orleans delta, and when Wicklens left her in '46, she cried herself almost into the grave. Now, two years later, Wedderburn C. Wicklens was back and cousin Pat was made a bride. Peppy's son-in-law was exactly one foot and four inches taller than him, as witnessed to this day by the wedding photograph. In this picture, everyone's grinning except me. I'm standing to attention. 'God!' Lou sometimes used to say, staring at the photo on Aunt If's tiled mantelpiece, 'just look at that nincompoop!'

Preparing our garden for the Cup and preparing for this grand meal we'd have when I was eighteen took a lot of resourcefulness. We nicked bricks from the bomb site on Weatherby Road to make a garden 'wall' that never got higher than two feet. I nicked bedding antirrhinums and nemesia from the park and stakes for the gladioli, over which Lou was taking no chances. I would have got the sack if Mr Dowdswell had caught me, but Mr Dowdswell was a man who saw vistas of things, not small transactions. Uncle Peppy, not yet in prison, figured big in our planning, so did Wicklens, whom we now addressed as 'Wed'. 'In more than one sense Wed,' I said. But no one laughed. 'Shame Dougie was too young to see combat,' I heard Wed say to Lou one evening. 'Yes,' she said, 'it might have been the saving of him.'

They thought being eighteen might be the saving of me. If we could just scrimp together enough ration cards, if Peppy could just do a nylons deal with the butcher, if Wed could just get whisky and chocolate powder and margarine from the PX, if If could just run me up a new tweed jacket. If, if, if . . . 'You'll feel better when you're eighteen, Dougie,' Lou lullabyed as she tucked me in. 'You'll feel more like a man.' So I lay and thought about this. I didn't think I'd grow up like Will – to be good. I knew I wouldn't grow up like Peppy – to be smart. When I imagined my future, it was exactly the same as my present. The only thing that changed wasn't me but the park. They harvested the dirty barley. They ploughed in the stubble and back into the soil went the sweet papers and the used johnnies and the hairpins, and the land was resown with grass and everything in the park became orderly again. Mr Dowdswell's hair grew back. We were allocated some new shears. The thing I wanted to say to Lou was, 'I'm not unhappy.'

Then we heard about the housing lottery.

The coming of the news about the housing lottery was like the coming of malaria. Lou began to sweat. It was like the jungle had suddenly surrounded her. She'd fan the air with her knitting patterns. 'You can't breathe in this place,' she'd say, making our barracouta cakes. 'Help your mother,' Will would say accusingly. So I'd set the table and get out the tea strainer and stare at Lou's arms, white and moist above the greasy pan. Love for Lou has always been something I've suffered from. Even in my imagined future, I still suffered from it. 'I don't mind the pre-fab,' I'd say to Lou's arms preparing our seaweed meal. Without looking up at me, she'd say, 'Don't be silly, Douglas.'

It was me they sent to get our lottery number. The Housing

Office had women queuing right down the stairs and into the street. I missed an entire afternoon's work standing in that queue, risking my job for Lou's malaria. 'You're not eligible if you've got a pre-fab, love,' someone told me, but I hung on. There must have been a thousand people there, not counting babies, two thousand upper and lower jaws all wagging about hardship and eligibility and fairness. Our number was 879. Aunt If said this was auspicious because 879 was a close-together group of numbers. I thought of the number as representing our family. I was the thin 7 in the middle, with Lou and Will leaning over me. Even now – and they're both long dead, actually – I still sometimes think of Lou as 8 and Will as 9. 'Dear God, please take care of the immortal souls of 8 and 9,' I sometimes pray. And I feel them at my side, Will watching me, Lou with her profile turned.

A lot happened the following day. Mr Dowdswell gave me a Severe Reprimand, Knacky Mick was taken to hospital, and Uncle Pepino was arrested for illegal trading. Aunt If, who is something of a gypsy to look at, read catastrophe in the stars, pawned her sewing machine to raise Peppy's bail, and cried on Lou's shoulder. 'At least,' said Lou to her sister-in-law, 'you've still got your own house.' I left them and got a bus to the hospital. Our lottery ticket was stuck up on the mantelpiece behind a glass unicorn. Knacky Mick, when I found him, was Irish-blue under his stubble and dosed to his skull. 'Suppressing me, they are,' he muttered. In his locker were his match-boxes and his tins of shoeblack, piled up. 'Come to a party,' I said, 'I'd like to invite you to my eighteenth birthday party.'

'Very good,' he said.

I didn't mind the hospital. I sat by Knacky Mick for quite a while. A drip was hitched up to his vein. Other patients winked at me, the ones on their own without visitors. Knacky Mick slept a drugged sleep. The room was high and light and full of people whispering. It wouldn't be bad, I thought, working here. This was the first time I ever imagined having a job quite far away from Will and Lou. It gave me an odd feeling, as if I'd made myself an orphan.

Now, four things were coming: the Gardening Cup, my eighteenth birthday party, Pepino's trial and the housing lottery. No wonder Lou couldn't breathe. These things were like weights on her chest. My ideal future was one in which there was nothing to fear and nothing to hope for. I didn't mind if we got chocolate powder for my party or not. I didn't care if we went to live in a new flat with a refrigerator or not. 'The trouble with Dougie,' said my cousin Pat, dreaming still of her Louisiana clapboard house, 'is he's got no imagination.' Well, I didn't care if I had imagination or not either. The thing that was awful was that Lou had started to care so much about everything, she seemed deranged. And I cared about that. I wanted her to be like she'd been when she'd won the solitary egg – contented.

Our pre-fab garden looked neat on Cup Day. We'd stuck in the shearings from a conifer hedge in my park, to look like a new little conifer hedge. We took down our washing line. Mr Dowdswell let me borrow the edging shears to straighten up the grass. It wasn't bad. The adjudicator smiled at Lou's new home perm and said, 'Very nice. Congratulations.' Under the perm, her malaria was still raging away. 'It means a lot to us,' she said, in a choked voice. And the adjudicator took off his look of admiration and put on a look of pity and I knew we hadn't won.

'We haven't won, Louie,' I told her.

'You know nothing about anything, Douglas,' she told me back. Which, in a way, was true.

Wedderburn Wicklens gave me forty Senior Service cigarettes on the day of my birthday. I didn't smoke, so I gave them to Willou, who did. I thought how odd it was that Wed hadn't noticed I didn't smoke. But there were a lot of things Wed didn't notice, like for instance, he quite often called Patricia 'Candice'. 'If you call me Candice again, I'll kill you!' she once told him. But this threat of death didn't seem to do the trick. Half way through my eighteenth birthday meal, a huge belch rumbled up out of his stomach and he said quickly: 'didn't hear that, did you, Candy honey?' 'Who's Candy?' asked Willou simultaneously. Patricia slammed down her knife and fork and ran out into the hot night falling. Pepino stood up. Beside my gypsy Aunt If, he looked like a little yellow duck. '*You!*' he yelled. 'You mind! You Yanki-panki!' And then he sat down again and Wed got up and wandered lazily out to Patricia.

We were eating pork ribs, for which Pepino had paid four pairs of nylons. Our fingers and chins were mucky and red from Lou's sauce of boiled tomatoes. Wed told us we should call this meal *spare*ribs and Will guffawed with derision, 'Typical American!' he said, 'call everything superfluous!' We picked the last shreds of meat from the ribs and washed these pickings down with beer. Lou had got her chocolate powder and her egg powder and on the afternoon she was told the winner of the Queen Mary Gardening Cup lived in Camberwell, she cried away her hopes into an enormous cake. She wrote (she hadn't got a fantastic imagination either) D 18 on the top with angelica she'd bought before the war. It made me uneasy. I thought, I'm glad she couldn't tattoo it onto me.

Knacky Mick never came to my birthday party, he was too ill. I saved him some cake. I thought, I've only got one friend and that's Knacky Mick and he's going to snuff it. I felt a bit like crying, but Lou and Will had their eye on me. Full of beer, they said, 'This is a new start, Dougie. This is your chance to start again.' I started to say I was perfectly content as I was, but nobody was actually listening. Will and Lou and Peppy and If had turned away from me and were lighting up the Senior Service I'd given them and talking about their chances of being rehoused, in Peppy's case in Brixton jail and in Willou's case in William Petrie Buildings, the lotteried flats with fridges and radiators. I looked round to see what was happening to Pat and Wed and I saw them kissing by the conifer hedge. I unwrapped the bobble hat Lou had knitted for my birthday present and put it on. The thought that Lou's fingers had fashioned every one of the stitches that went round and round my head made me feel very warm and happy. 'Just look at him!' she said a while later, blowing smoke at Peppy. '*Honestly!*'

On the morning of the housing lottery, Lou couldn't face cooking barracouta, so we had bread and jam for breakfast. Will turned on the Home Service to calm his wife's beating heart. I left as early as I could to walk to my park and it was a beautiful morning, still and shiny and the smell of the park in summer was as fantastic to me as the smell of the Majestic cinema was to Lou. A consignment of bedding geraniums had arrived, and I started to dig over the bed where they'd go in. I tried not to think about 879, or about Lou waiting with thousands of other women to hear the numbers called out. There were fifty-one flats in William Petrie Buildings and at least twenty times that number of applicants. Mr Dowdswell came by to look at the geraniums. 'Good work, Douglas,' he said approvingly, and then tapped my bending back and said in his confidential stammer: 'No more bla . . . no more yer bloody barley next year, thank Ga . . . thank God!' 'Hooray, Sir,' I answered.

When I got home, Lou was resting and Will was mushing up the barracouta we hadn't eaten for breakfast. 'Don't disturb your mother,' said Will.

'We didn't get one, did we?' I said.

'No,' said Will.

I went to wash my hands at the sink. Outside, the stuck-in conifers were going brown.

'869 was lucky,' said Will, 'and 849 and 859, but not 879. Shame we had the 7.'

I stared at Will and then beyond him to the bedroom where Lou was lying in the aftermath of her malaria. *Willou.* 8 and 9. Without me, they would have got lucky. I was the 7 alright. I'd made them lose.

That August Knacky Mick died and I applied for a job at the hospital where I'd visited him and where I've been now all my life. I told Willou this was my new start, and they were proud of me. But my last day at the park was one of the saddest things I can remember. They'd harvested the barley. I sat in the sunshine, staring at all the litter left among the stubble and thinking about my country.

Solid Geometry

Ian McEwan

Ian McEwan was born in 1948 and spent much of his childhood around the world because of his father's military postings. He studied at Sussex and East Anglia. He has written two collections of short stories, FIRST LOVES, LAST RIGHTS (which won the Somerset Maugham Award) and IN BETWEEN THE SHEETS, and five novels, THE CEMENT GARDEN, THE COMFORT OF STRANGERS (shortlisted for the 1981 Booker Prize), THE CHILD IN TIME (winner of the 1987 Whitbread Novel of the Year Award), THE INNOCENT and BLACK DOGS (shortlisted for the 1992 Booker Prize). Most of his novels have been filmed. He has also written several television plays, including SOLID GEOMETRY and THE INITIATION GAME, and the libretto for Michael Berkley's oratorio OR SHALL WE DIE? His most recent book is THE DAYDREAMER. He lives in Oxford.

∫

Solid Geometry

In Melton Mowbray in 1875 at an auction of articles of 'curiosity and worth', my great-grandfather, in the company of M his friend, bid for the penis of Captain Nicholls who died in Horsemonger jail in 1873. It was bottled in a glass twelve inches long, and, noted my great-grandfather in his diary that night, 'in a beautiful state of preservation'. Also for auction was 'the unnamed portion of the late Lady Barrymore. It went to Sam Israels for fifty guineas.' My great-grandfather was keen on the idea of having the two items as a pair, and M dissuaded him. This illustrates perfectly their friendship. My great-grandfather the excitable theorist, M the man of action who knew when to bid at auctions. My great-grandfather lived for sixty-nine years. For forty-five of them, at the end of every day, he sat down before going to bed and wrote his thoughts in a diary. These diaries are on my table now, forty-five volumes bound in calf leather, and to the left sits Capt. Nicholls in the glass jar. My great-grandfather lived on the income derived from the patent of an invention of his father, a handy fastener used by corset-makers right up till the outbreak of the First World War. My great-grandfather liked gossip, numbers and theories. He also liked tobacco, good port, jugged hare and, very occasionally, opium. He liked to think of himself as a mathematician, though he never had a job, and never published a book. Nor did he ever travel or get his name in *The Times*, even when he died. In 1869 he married

Alice, only daughter of the Rev. Toby Shadwell, co-author of a not highly regarded book on English wild flowers. I believe my great-grandfather to have been a very fine diarist, and when I have finished editing the diaries and they are published I am certain he will receive the recognition due to him. When my work is over I will take a long holiday, travel somewhere cold and clean and treeless, Iceland or the Russian Steppes. I used to think that at the end of it all I would try, if it was possible, to divorce my wife Maisie, but now there is no need at all.

Often Maisie would shout in her sleep and I would have to wake her.

'Put your arm around me,' she would say. 'It was a horrible dream. I had it once before. I was in a plane flying over a desert. But it wasn't really a desert. I took the plane lower and I could see there were thousands of babies heaped up, stretching away into the horizon, all of them naked and climbing over each other. I was running out of fuel and I had to land the plane. I tried to find a space, I flew on and on looking for a space . . .'

'Go to sleep now,' I said through a yawn. 'It was only a dream.'

'No,' she cried. 'I mustn't go to sleep, not just yet.'

'Well, *I* have to sleep now,' I told her. 'I have to be up early in the morning.'

She shook my shoulder. 'Please don't go to sleep yet, don't leave me here.'

'I'm in the same bed,' I said. 'I won't leave you.'

'It makes no difference, don't leave me awake . . .' But my eyes were already closing.

Lately I have taken up my great-grandfather's habit. Before going to bed I sit down for half an hour and think over the day. I have no mathematical whimsies or sexual theories to note down. Mostly I write out what Maisie has said to me and what I have said to Maisie. Sometimes, for complete privacy, I lock myself in the bathroom, sit on the toilet seat and balance the writing-pad on my knees. Apart from me there is occasionally a spider or two in the bathroom. They climb up the waste pipe and crouch perfectly still on the glaring white enamel. They must wonder where they have come to. After hours of crouching they turn back, puzzled, or perhaps disappointed they could not learn more. As far as I can tell, my great-grandfather made only one reference to spiders. On May 8th, 1906, he wrote, 'Bismarck is a spider.'

In the afternoons Maisie used to bring me tea and tell me her nightmares. Usually I was going through old newspapers, compiling indexes, cataloguing items, putting down this volume, picking up another. Maisie said she was in a bad way. Recently she had been sitting around the house all day glancing at books on psychology and the occult, and almost every night she had bad dreams. Since the time we exchanged physical blows, lying in wait to hit each other with the same shoe outside the bathroom, I had had little sympathy for her. Part of her problem was jealousy. She was very jealous . . . of my great-grandfather's forty-five-volume diary, and of my purpose and energy in editing it. She was doing nothing. I was putting down one volume and picking up another when Maisie came in with the tea.

'Can I tell you my dream?' she asked. 'I was flying this plane over a kind of desert . . .'

'Tell me later, Maisie,' I said. 'I'm in the middle of something here.' After she had gone I stared at the wall in front of my desk and thought about M, who came to talk and dine with my great-grandfather regularly over a period of fifteen years up until his sudden and unexplained departure one evening in 1898. M, whoever he might have been, was something of an academic, as well as a man of action. For example, on the evening of August 9th, 1870, the two of them are talking about positions for lovemaking and M tells my great-grandfather that copulation *a posteriori* is the most natural way owing to the position of the clitoris and because other anthropoids favour this method. My great-grandfather, who copulated about half-a-dozen times in his entire life, and that with Alice during the first year of their marriage, wondered out loud what the Church's view was and straight away M is able to tell him that the seventh-century theologian Theodore considered copulation *a posteriori* a sin ranking with masturbation and therefore worthy of forty penances. Later in the same evening my great-grandfather produced mathematical evidence that the maximum number of positions cannot exceed the prime number seventeen. M scoffed at this and told him he had seen a collection of drawings by Romano, a pupil of Raphael's, in which twenty-four positions were shown. And, he said, he had heard of a Mr F. K. Forberg who had accounted for ninety. By the time I remembered the tea Maisie had left by my elbow it was cold.

An important stage in the deterioration of our marriage was reached as follows. I was sitting in the bathroom one evening writing out a conversation Maisie and I had had about the Tarot pack when suddenly she was outside, rapping on the door and rattling the door-handle.

'Open the door,' she called out. 'I want to come in.'

I said to her, 'You'll have to wait a few minutes more. I've almost finished.'

'Let me in now,' she shouted. 'You're not using the toilet.'

'Wait,' I replied, and wrote another line or two. Now Maisie was kicking the door.

'My period has started and I need to get something.' I ignored her yells and finished my piece, which I considered to be particularly important. If I left it till later certain details would be lost. There was no sound from Maisie now and I assumed she was in the bedroom. But when I opened the door she was standing right in my way with a shoe in her hand. She brought the heel of it sharply down on my head, and I only had time to move slightly to one side. The heel caught the top of my ear and cut it badly.

'There,' said Maisie, stepping round me to get to the bathroom, 'now we are both bleeding,' and she banged the door shut. I picked up the shoe and stood quietly and patiently outside the bathroom holding a handkerchief to my bleeding ear. Maisie was in the bathroom about ten minutes and as she came out I caught her neatly and squarely on the top of her head. I did not give her time to move. She stood perfectly still for a moment looking straight into my eyes.

'You worm,' she breathed, and went down to the kitchen to nurse her head out of my sight.

During supper yesterday Maisie claimed that a man locked in a cell with only the Tarot cards would have access to all knowledge. She had been doing a reading that afternoon and the cards were still spread about the floor.

'Could he work out the street plan of Valparaiso from the cards?' I asked.

'You're being stupid,' she replied.

'Could it tell him the best way to start a laundry business, the best way to make an omelette or a kidney machine?'

'Your mind is so narrow,' she complained. 'You're so narrow, so predictable.'

'Could he', I insisted, 'tell me who M is, or why . . .'

'Those things don't matter,' she cried. 'They're not necessary.'

'They are still knowledge. Could he find them out?'

She hesitated. 'Yes, he could.'

I smiled, and said nothing.

'What's so funny?' she said. I shrugged, and she began to get angry. She wanted to be disproved. 'Why did you ask all those pointless questions?'

I shrugged again. 'I just wanted to know if you really meant *everything*.'

Maisie banged the table and screamed, 'Damn you! Why are you always trying me out? Why don't you say something real?' And with that we both recognized we had reached the point where all our discussions led and we became bitterly silent.

Work on the diaries cannot proceed until I have cleared up the mystery surrounding M. After coming to dinner on and off for fifteen years and supplying my great-grandfather with a mass of material for his theories, M simply disappears from the pages of the diary. On Tuesday, December 6th, my great-grandfather invited M to dine on the following Saturday, and although M came, my great-grandfather in the entry for that day simply writes, 'M to dinner.' On any other day the conversation at these meals is recorded at great length. M had been to dinner on Monday, December 5th, and the conversation had been about geometry, and the entries for the rest of that week are entirely given over to the same subject. There is absolutely no hint of antagonism. Besides, my great-grandfather *needed* M. M provided his material, M knew what was going on, he was familiar with London and he had been on the Continent a number of times. He knew all about socialism and Darwin, he had an acquaintance in the free love movement, a friend of James Hinton. M was *in* the world in a way which my great-grandfather, who left Melton Mowbray only once in his lifetime, to visit Nottingham, was not. Even as a young man my great-grandfather preferred to theorize by the fireside; all he needed were the materials M supplied. For example, one evening in June 1884 M, who was just back from London, gave my great-grandfather an account of how the streets of the town were fouled and clogged by horse dung. Now in that same week my great-grandfather had been reading the essay by Malthus called 'On the Principle of Population'. That night he made an excited entry in the diary about a pamphlet he wanted to write and have published. It was to be called 'De Stercore Equorum'. The pamphlet was never published and probably never written, but there are detailed notes in the diary entries for the two weeks following that evening. In 'De Stercore Equorum' ('Concerning Horseshit') he assumes geometric growth in the horse population, and working from detailed street plans he predicted that the metropolis would be impassable by 1935. By impassable he took to mean an average thickness of one foot (compressed) in every major street. He described involved experiments outside his own stables to determine the compressibility of horse dung, which he managed to express mathematically. It was all pure theory, of course. His results rested on the assumption that no dung would be shovelled aside in the fifty years to come. Very likely it was M who talked my great-grandfather out of the project.

One morning, after a long dark night of Maisie's nightmares, we were lying side by side in bed and I said,

'What is it you really want? Why don't you go back to your job? These long walks, all this analysis, sitting around the house, lying in bed all morning, the Tarot pack, the nightmares . . . what is it you want?'

And she said, 'I want to get my head straight,' which she had said many times before.

I said, 'Your head, your mind, it's not like a hotel kitchen, you know, you can't throw stuff out like old tin cans. It's more like a river than a place, moving and changing all the time. You can't make rivers flow straight.'

'Don't go through all that again,' she said. 'I'm not trying to make rivers flow straight, I'm trying to get my head straight.'

'You've got to *do* something,' I told her. 'You can't do nothing. Why not go back to your job? You didn't have nightmares when you were working. You were never so unhappy when you were working.'

'I've got to stand back from all that,' she said. 'I'm not sure what any of it means.'

'Fashion,' I said, 'it's all fashion. Fashionable metaphors, fashionable reading, fashionable malaise. What do you care about Jung, for example? You've read twelve pages in a month.'

'Don't go on,' she pleaded, 'you know it leads nowhere.'

But I went on.

'You've never been anywhere,' I told her, 'you've never done anything. You're a nice girl without even the blessing of an unhappy childhood. Your sentimental Buddhism, this junk-shop mysticism, joss-stick therapy, magazine astrology . . . none of it is yours, you've worked none of it out for yourself. You fell into it, you fell into a swamp of respectable intuitions. You haven't the originality or passion to intuit anything yourself beyond your own unhappiness. Why are you filling your mind with other people's mystic banalities and giving yourself nightmares?' I got out of bed, opened the curtains and began to get dressed.

'You talk like this was a fiction seminar,' Maisie said. 'Why are you trying to make things worse for me?' Self-pity began to well up from inside her, but she fought it down. 'When you are talking,' she went on, 'I can feel myself, you know, being screwed up like a piece of paper.'

'Perhaps we *are* in a fiction seminar,' I said grimly. Maisie sat up in bed staring at her lap. Suddenly her tone changed. She patted the pillow beside her and said softly,

'Come over here. Come and sit here. I want to touch you, I want you to touch me . . .' But I was sighing, and already on my way to the kitchen.

In the kitchen I made myself some coffee and took it through to my study. It had occurred to me in my night of broken sleep that a possible clue to the disappearance of M might be found in the pages of geometry. I had always skipped through them before because mathematics does not interest me. On the Monday, December 5th, 1898, M and my great-grandfather discussed the *vescia piscis*, which apparently is the subject of Euclid's first proposition and a profound influence on the ground plans of many ancient religious buildings. I read through the account of the conversation carefully, trying to understand as best I could the geometry of it. Then, turning the page, I found a lengthy anecdote which M told my great-grandfather that same evening when the coffee had been brought in and the cigars were lit. Just as I was beginning to read Maisie came in.

'And what about you,' she said, as if there had not been an hour break in our exchange, 'all you have is books. Crawling over the past like a fly on a turd.'

I was angry, of course, but I smiled and said cheerfully, 'Crawling? Well, at least I'm moving.'

'You don't speak to me any more,' she said, 'you play me like a pinball machine, for points.'

'Good morning, Hamlet,' I replied, and sat in my chair waiting patiently for what she had to say next. But she did not speak, she left, closing the study door softly behind her.

'In September 1870,' M began to tell my great-grandfather,

I came into the possession of certain documents which not only invalidate everything fundamental to our science of solid geometry but also undermine the whole canon of our physical laws and force one to redefine one's place in Nature's scheme. These papers outweigh in importance the combined work of Marx and Darwin. They were entrusted to me by a young American mathematician, and they are the work of David Hunter, a mathematician too and a Scotsman. The American's name was Goodman. I had corresponded with his father over a number of years in connection with his work on the cyclical theory of menstruation which, incredibly enough, is still widely discredited in this country. I met the young Goodman in Vienna where, along with Hunter and mathematicians from a dozen countries, he had been attending an international conference on mathematics. Goodman was pale and greatly disturbed when I met him, and planned to return to America the following day even though the conference was not yet half complete. He gave the papers into my care with instructions that I was to deliver them to David Hunter if I was ever to learn of his whereabouts. And then, only after much persuasion and insistence on my part, he told me what he had witnessed on the third day of the conference. The conference met every morning at nine thirty when a paper was read and a general discussion ensued. At eleven o'clock refreshments were brought in and many of the mathematicians would get up from the long, highly polished table round which they were all gathered and stroll about the large, elegant room and engage in informal discussions with their colleagues. Now, the conference lasted two weeks, and by a long-standing arrangement the most eminent of the mathematicians read their papers first, followed by the slightly less eminent, and so on, in a descending hierarchy throughout the two weeks, which caused, as it is wont to do among highly intelligent men, occasional but intense jealousies. Hunter, though a brilliant mathematician, was young and virtually unknown outside his university, which was Edinburgh. He had applied to deliver what he described as a very important paper on solid geometry, and since he was of little account in this pantheon he was assigned to read to the conference on the last day but one, by which time many of the most important figures would have returned to their respective countries. And so on the third morning, as the servants were bringing in the refreshments, Hunter stood up suddenly and addressed his colleagues just as they were rising from their seats. He was a large, shaggy man and, though young, he had about him a certain presence which reduced the hum of conversation to a complete silence.

'Gentlemen,' said Hunter, 'I must ask you to forgive this improper form of address, but I have something to tell you of the utmost importance. I have discovered the plane without a surface.' Amid derisive smiles and gentle bemused laughter, Hunter picked up from the table a large white sheet of paper. With a pocket-knife he made an incision along its surface about three inches long and slightly to one side of its centre. Then he made some rapid, complicated folds and, holding the paper aloft so all could see, he appeared to draw one corner of it through the incision, and as he did so it disappeared.

'Behold, gentlemen,' said Hunter, holding out his empty hands towards the company, 'the plane without a surface.'

Maisie came into my room, washed now and smelling faintly of perfumed soap. She came and stood behind my chair and placed her hands on my shoulders.

'What are you reading?' she said.

'Just bits of the diary which I haven't looked at before.' She began to massage me gently at the base of my neck. I would have found it soothing if it had still been the first year of our marriage. But it was the sixth year and it generated a kind of tension which communicated itself the length of my spine. Maisie wanted something. To restrain her I placed my right hand on her left, and, mistaking this for affection, she leaned forward and kissed under my ear. Her breath smelled of toothpaste and toast. She tugged at my shoulder.

'Let's go in the bedroom,' she whispered. 'We haven't made love for nearly two weeks now.'

'I know,' I replied. 'You know how it is . . . with my work.' I felt no desire for Maisie or any other woman. All I wanted to do was turn the next page of my great-grandfather's diary. Maisie took her hands off my shoulders and stood by my side. There was such a sudden ferocity in her silence that I found myself tensing like a sprinter on the starting line. She stretched forward and picked up the sealed jar containing Capt. Nicholls. As she lifted it his penis drifted dreamily from one end of the glass to the other.

'You're SO COMPLACENT,' Maisie shrieked, just before she hurled the glass bottle at the wall in front of my table. Instinctively I covered my face with my hands to shield off the shattering glass. As I opened my eyes I heard myself saying,

'Why did you do that? That belonged to my great-grandfather.' Amid the broken glass and the rising stench of formaldehyde lay Capt. Nicholls, slouched across the leather covers of a volume of the diary, grey, limp and menacing, transformed from a treasured curiosity into a horrible obscenity.

'That was a terrible thing to do. Why did you do that?' I said again.

'I'm going for a walk,' Maisie replied, and slammed the door this time as she left the room.

I did not move from my chair for a long time. Maisie had destroyed an object of great value to me. It had stood in his study while he lived, and then it had stood in mine, linking my life with his. I picked a few splinters of glass from my lap and stared at the 160-year-old piece of another human on my table. I looked at it and thought of all the homunculi which had swarmed down its length. I thought of all the places it had been, Cape Town, Boston, Jerusalem, travelling in the dark, fetid inside of Capt. Nicholls's leather breeches, emerging occasionally into the dazzling sunlight to discharge urine in some jostling public place. I thought also of all the things it had touched, all the molecules, of Captain Nicholls's exploring hands on lonely unrequited nights at sea, the sweating walls of cunts of young girls and old whores, their molecules must still exist today, a fine dust blowing from Cheapside to Leicestershire. Who knows how long it might have lasted in its glass jar. I began to clear up the mess. I brought the rubbish bucket in from the kitchen. I swept and picked up all the glass I could find and swabbed up the formaldehyde. Then, holding him by just one end, I tried to ease Capt. Nicholls on to a sheet of newspaper. My stomach heaved as the foreskin began to come away in my fingers. Finally, with my eyes closed, I succeeded, and wrapping him carefully in the newspaper, I carried him into the garden and buried him under the geraniums. All this time I tried to prevent my resentment towards Maisie filling my mind. I wanted to continue with M's story. Back in my chair I dabbed at a few spots of formaldehyde which had blotted the ink, and read on.

For as long as a minute the room was frozen, and with each successive second it appeared to freeze harder. The first to speak was Dr Stanley Rose of Cambridge University, who had much to lose by Hunter's plane without a surface. His reputation, which was very considerable indeed, rested upon his 'Principles of Solid Geometry'.

'How dare you, sir. How dare you insult the dignity of this assembly with a worthless conjuror's trick.' And bolstered by the rising murmur of concurrence behind him, he added, 'You should be ashamed, young man, thoroughly ashamed.' With that, the room erupted like a volcano. With the exception of young Goodman, and of the servants who still stood by with the refreshments, the whole room turned on Hunter and directed at him a senseless babble of denunciation, invective and threat. Some thumped on the table in their fury, others waved their clenched fists. One very frail German gentlemen fell to the floor in an apoplexy and had to be helped to a chair. And there stood Hunter, firm and outwardly unmoved, his head inclined slightly to one side, his fingers resting lightly on the surface of the long polished table. That such an uproar should follow a worthless conjuror's trick clearly demonstrated the extent of the underlying unease, and Hunter surely appreciated this. Raising his hand, and the company falling suddenly silent once more, he said,

'Gentlemen, your concern is understandable and I will effect another proof, the ultimate proof.' This said, he sat down and removed his shoes, stood up and removed his jacket, and then called for a volunteer to assist him, at which Goodman came forward. Hunter strode through the crowd to a couch which stood along one of the walls, and while he settled himself upon it he told the mystified Goodman that when he returned to England he should take with him Hunter's papers and keep them there until he came to collect them. When the mathematicians had gathered round the couch Hunter rolled on to his stomach and clasped his hands behind his back in a strange posture to fashion a hoop with his arms. He asked Goodman to hold his arms in that position for him, and rolled on his side where he began a number of strenuous jerking movements which enabled him to pass one of his feet through the hoop. He asked his assistant to turn him on his other side, where he performed the same movements again and succeeded in passing his other foot between his arms, and at the same time bent his trunk in such a way that his head was able to pass through the hoop in the opposite direction to his feet. With the help of his assistant he began to pass his legs and head past each other through the hoop made by his arms. It was then that the distinguished assembly vented, as one man, a single yelp of utter incredulity. Hunter was beginning to disappear, and now, as his legs and head passed through his arms with greater facility, seemed even to be drawn through by some invisible power, he was almost gone. And now . . . he was gone, quite gone, and nothing remained.

M's story put my great-grandfather in a frenzy of excitement. In his diary that night he recorded how he tried 'to prevail upon my guest to send for the papers upon the instant' even though it was by now two o'clock in the morning. M, however, was more sceptical about the whole thing. 'Americans', he told my great-grandfather, 'often indulge in fantastic tales.' But he agreed to bring along the papers the following day. As it turned out M did not dine with my great-grandfather that night because of another engagement, but he called round in the late afternoon with the papers. Before he left he told my great-grandfather he had been through them a number of times and 'there was no sense to be had out of them'. He did not realize then how much he was underestimating my great-grandfather as an amateur mathematician. Over a glass of sherry in front of the drawing-room fire the two men arranged to dine together again at the end of the week, on Saturday. For the next three days my great-grandfather hardly paused from his reading of Hunter's theorems to eat or sleep. The diary is full of nothing else. The pages are covered with scribbles, diagrams and symbols. It seems that Hunter had to devise a new set of symbols, virtually a whole new language, to express his ideas. By the end of the second day my great-grandfather had made his first breakthrough. At the bottom of a page of mathematical scribble he wrote, 'Dimensionality is a function of consciousness'. Turning to the entry for the next day I read the words, 'It disappeared in my hands'. He had re-established the plane without a surface. And there, spread out in front of me, were step by step instructions on how to fold the piece of paper. Turning the next page I suddenly understood the mystery of M's disappearance. Undoubtedly encouraged by my great-grandfather, he had taken part that evening in a scientific experiment, probably in a spirit of great scepticism. For here my great-grandfather had drawn a series of small sketches illustrating what at first glance looked like yoga positions. Clearly they were the secret of Hunter's disappearing act.

My hands were trembling as I cleared a space on my desk. I selected a clean sheet of typing paper and laid it in front of me. I fetched a razor blade from the bathroom. I rummaged in a drawer and found an old pair of compasses, sharpened a pencil and fitted it in. I searched through the house till I found an accurate steel ruler I had once used for fitting window panes, and then I was ready. First I had to cut the paper to size. The piece that Hunter had so casually picked up from the table had obviously been carefully prepared beforehand. The length of the sides had to express a specific ratio. Using the compasses I found the centre of the paper and through this point I drew a line parallel to one of the sides and continued it right to the edge. Then I had to construct a rectangle whose measurements bore a particular relation to those of the sides of the paper. The centre of this rectangle occurred on the line in such a way as to dissect it by the Golden Mean. From the top of this rectangle I drew intersecting arcs, again of specified proportionate radii. This operation was repeated at the lower end of the rectangle, and when the two points of interesection were joined I had the line of incision. Then I started work on the folding lines. Each line seemed to express, in its length, angle of incline and point of intersection with other lines, some mysterious inner harmony of numbers. As I intersected arcs, drew lines and made folds, I felt I was blindly operating a system of the highest, most terrifying form of knowledge, the mathematics of the Absolute. By the time I had made the final fold the piece of paper was the shape of a geometric flower with three concentric rings arranged round the incision at the centre. There was something so tranquil and perfect about this design, something so remote and compelling, that as I stared into it I felt myself going into a light trance and my mind becoming clear and inactive. I shook my head and glanced away. It was time now to turn the flower in on itself and pull it through the incision. This was a delicate operation and now my hands were trembling again. Only by staring into the centre of the design could I calm myself. With my thumbs I began to push the sides of the paper flower towards the centre, and as I did so I felt a numbness settle over the back of my skull. I pushed a little further, the paper glowed whiter for an instant and then it *seemed* to disappear. I say 'seemed' because at first I could not be sure whether I could feel it still in my hands and not see it, or see it but not feel it, or whether I could sense it had disappeared while its external properties remained. The numbness had spread right across my head and shoulders. My senses seemed inadequate to grasp what was happening. 'Dimensionality is a function of consciousness,' I thought. I brought my hands together and there was nothing between them, but even when I opened them again and saw nothing I could not be sure the paper flower had completely gone. An impression remained, an after-image not on the retina but on the mind itself. Just then the door opened behind me, and Maisie said,

'What are you doing?'

I returned as if from a dream to the room and to the faint smell of formaldehyde. It was a long, long time ago now, the destruction of Capt. Nicholls, but the smell revived my resentment, which spread through me like the numbness. Maisie slouched in the doorway, muffled in a thick coat and woollen scarf. She seemed a long way off, and as I looked at her my resentment merged into a familiar weariness of our marriage. I thought, why did she break the glass? Because she wanted to make love? Because she wanted a penis? Because she was jealous of my work, and wanted to smash the connection it had with my great-grandfather's life?

'Why did you do it?' I said out loud, involuntarily. Maisie snorted. She had opened the door and found me hunched over my table staring at my hands.

'Have you been sitting there all afternoon,' she asked, 'thinking about *that*?' She giggled. 'What happened to it, anyway? Did you suck it off?'

'I buried it,' I said, 'under the geraniums.'

She came into the room a little way and said in a serious tone, 'I'm sorry about that, I really am. I just did it before I knew what was happening. Do you forgive me?' I hesitated, and then, because my weariness had blossomed into a sudden resolution, I said,

'Yes, of course I forgive you. It was only a prick in pickle,' and we both laughed. Maisie came over to me and kissed me, and I returned the kiss, prising open her lips with my tongue.

'Are you hungry?' she said, when we were done with kissing. 'Shall I make some supper?'

'Yes,' I said. 'I would love that.' Maisie kissed me on the top of my head and left the room, while I turned back to my studies, resolving to be as kind as I possibly could to Maisie that evening.

Later we sat in the kitchen eating the meal Maisie had cooked and getting mildly drunk on a bottle of wine. We smoked a joint, the first one we had had together in a very long time. Maisie told me how she was going to get a job with the Forestry Commission planting trees in Scotland next summer. And I told Maisie about the conversation M and my great-grandfather had had about *a posteriori*, and about my great-grandfather's theory that there could not be more than the prime number seventeen positions for making love. We both laughed, and Maisie squeezed my hand, and lovemaking hung in the air between us, in the warm fug of the kitchen. Then we put our coats on and went for a walk. It was almost a full moon. We walked along the main road which runs outside our house and then turned down a narrow street of tightly packed houses with immaculate and minute front gardens. We did not talk much, but our arms were linked and Maisie told me how very stoned and happy she was. We came to a small park which was locked and we stood outside the gates looking up at the moon through the almost leafless branches. When we came home Maisie took a leisurely hot bath while I browsed in my study, checking on a few details. Our bedroom is a warm, comfortable room, luxurious in its way. The bed is seven foot by eight, and I made it myself in the first year of our marriage. Maisie made the sheets, dyed them a deep, rich blue and embroidered the pillow cases. The only light in the room shone through a rough old goatskin lampshade Maisie bought from a man who came to the door. It was a long time since I had taken an interest in the bedroom. We lay side by side in the tangle of sheets and rugs, Maisie voluptuous and drowsy after her bath and stretched full out, and I propped up on my elbow. Maisie said sleepily,

'I was walking along the river this afternoon. The trees are beautiful now, the oaks, the elms ... there are two copper beeches about a mile past the footbridge, you should see them now ... ahh, that feels good.' I had eased her on to her belly and was caressing her back as she spoke. 'There are blackberries, the biggest ones I've ever seen, growing all along the path, and elderberries, too. I'm going to make some wine this autumn ...' I leaned over her and kissed the nape of her neck and brought her arms behind her back. She liked to be manipulated in this way and she submitted warmly. 'And the river is really still,' she was saying. 'You know, reflecting the trees, and the leaves are dropping into the river. Before the winter comes we should go there together, by the river, in the leaves. I found this little place. No one goes there . . .' Holding Maisie's arms in position with one hand, I worked her legs towards the 'hoop' with the other. '. . . I sat in this place for half an hour without moving, like a tree. I saw a water-rat running along the opposite bank, and different kinds of ducks landing on the river and taking off. I heard these plopping noises in the river but I didn't know what they were and I saw two orange butterflies, they almost came on my hand.' When I had her legs in place Maisie said, 'Position number eighteen,' and we both laughed softly. 'Let's go there tomorrow, to the river,' said Maisie as I carefully eased her head towards her arms. 'Careful, careful, that hurts,' she suddenly shouted, and tried to struggle. But it was too late now, her head and legs were in place in the hoop of her arms, and I was beginning to push them through, past each other. 'What's happening?' cried Maisie. Now the positioning of her limbs expressed the breathtaking beauty, the nobility of the human form, and, as in the paper flower, there was a fascinating power in its symmetry. I felt the trance coming on again and the numbness settling over the back of my head. As I drew her arms and legs through, Maisie appeared to turn in on herself like a sock. 'Oh God,' she sighed, 'what's happening?' and her voice sounded very far away. Then she was gone . . . and not gone. Her voice was quite tiny, 'What's happening?' and all that remained was the echo of her question above the deep-blue sheets.

A Moment of Happiness

Clive Sinclair

Clive Sinclair was born in London in 1948 and educated at the Universities of East Anglia and California at Santa Cruz. His first collection of stories, HEARTS OF GOLD, won the Somerset Maugham Award in 1981. He was also awarded a Bicentennial Arts Fellowship in 1980, allowing him to spend a year writing and teaching in America. His second collection of stories, BED BUGS, appeared in 1982. In 1983 his biographical-critical study of Isaac Bashevis Singer and Israel Joshua Singer, THE BROTH-ERS SINGER, was published and he was part of the 'Best of Young British Novelists' campaign. His other novels include BLOOD LIBELS, COSMETIC EFFECTS and AUGUSTUS REX. He lives in St Albans with his son Seth.

A Moment of Happiness

I live in fear. That's a state of mind, not my address.

Years ago I sat my exams at the Charles University. I had learned my work well and I was not nervous, until I saw the booklet that I was required to fill with my answers. I knew that in three hours it would be full, but I also foresaw the impossibility of my ever doing it; I felt that I was an insufficient motor to fulfil the inevitable. I tried to start the first question, but my hand was unable to control the pen. I could not form a single letter. Sweat began to roll along the lines on my hand and flow on to the page. I ran out of the hall. My sweat looked like teardrops on the page. All my professors were sympathetic, but they still failed me. Now no one will believe that I am an educated man.

It is six in the morning. Through my window I can see that the Vltava is turning gold with the rising of the sun. A beautiful sight, but I am immune to it; it fails to excite a single response in me. All it means is that it is time to move my bowels and to dress. Some days I am constipated, other days I have diarrhoea, less often I am regular. Every morning I examine the lavatory bowl, like an ancient sage, to see if I can divine what sort of day I have in store. This is fundamentally much more important than either the weather or the view. Today my movements have been very loose, which means I must pass the hours between now and bedtime in constant anticipation of further activity, presaging who knows what stomach complaint.

Once I discussed this morbid hypochondria with a doctor acquaintance and he, priding himself on his psychological insight, said that I did not trust my own body, would not believe that all those millions of interdependent functions could go on performing in harmony day after day without supervision. He accused me of introspective paranoia. Perhaps he is right. To me to get through a day is an achievement. As for the future, I have no faith in that at all. At best it is a process of gradual decomposition. I think only in the terms of the present and the past. I try to make the future as similar to the present as I can by sticking rigidly to an established dogma: I always get out of bed on the same side, I eat the same breakfast, I buy the same food in the same shops. My only desire in this life is to be a character in a photograph: smiling with remembered pleasure, eternally fixed in the present.

In many ways today is not normal. I have to work. *Rude Pravo* has a bold red headline: 'PLNÝ ZDAR XV SJEZDU STRANY!' It is, of course, the start of the XVth Party Congress. And my beloved Prague is full of flags; equal numbers of Czech flags and Russian flags. To mark the occasion our local shop is unusually well-stocked with imported fruit; grapefruit, oranges, bananas and pineapples. This glut, which lured me into over-indulgence, must explain this morning's diarrhoea (I have been a second time). My job, which is going to last the whole of this week, requires me to stand beside a stall piled high with miniature Czech and Russian flags. This is situated outside (of all places!) the Pan American office. I sell a few flags, but mostly people ignore me and look at the posters in the window which say, 'Come to the USA and help us celebrate our Bicentennial'. On the opposite side of the street a peasant woman in head-scarf and embroidered apron is hawking painted eggs for Easter. When someone buys one she nicks the top and bottom off the shell and pulls a ribbon through it. I do not have much appetite, but I eat a little lunch: garlic sausage, a pickled cucumber and some rye bread. Afterwards I have to go to the toilet again.

In the afternoon the sun goes behind a black cloud and I begin to feel chilly standing around in the street. I notice a couple walking towards me carrying the English edition of Ctibor Rybár's guide to Prague. I approach them waving a

Russian flag and ask, 'Do you wish to exchange money?' I can see that this has surprised them. They have been saying 'no' to money-changers all day, but I have got them off guard.

'I will give you forty crowns to the pound,' I say. This is twice the official rate.

There is a moment's hesitation, then they ask to change £10.

We complete the transaction in the Café Europa. I hate it there. It is supposed to look like a Parisian café but looks are nothing; nowadays it is full of riff-raff: gypsies and workmen from the new Metro. The waiters wear ill-fitting tuxedos and are rude to everyone. I do not understand how the authorities tolerate them; probably because they never enter the Café Europa. Very sensible. I was once served pork there that was off, and I ended up in bed for a week with terrible cramps. I assure the couple that it is an excellent place to dine. They order a glass of mineral water and a bottle of Coca-Cola. The girl tells me that a friend of theirs came to Prague, met a Jewess in the Staronova Synagogue, stayed with her nine days, and married her six months later. She shows me a clipping from the *New York Times*. It is an article the fellow has written about his trip to romantic Prague.

'For years Czech émigrés in New York and London had regaled me with memories of the beauty of Prague,' I read. 'The city itself claims the affection of the 1968 generation of emigrants who, often in the same breath, described the charms of its women and the bankruptcy of its politics.' The piece makes me want to vomit. I do not recognise the city he is writing about. It may as well be Xanadu.

'Robert couldn't get to the shul quickly enough,' says the girl. 'I think he was hoping to meet an exotic Jewish girl for himself.'

I look at this Robert more carefully and wonder how I did not see before that he is Jewish. I can tell by the sharp way his eyes are examining me. I do not like the Jews. They trust nobody but themselves. I can see that he is growing suspicious of me; he has noticed that my fingers are short and stubby. I have been told this is a sign that I am not a pleasant person. I sit on my hands. I smile at the girl and begin to explain that I was not always this insignificant.

'I once worked for Cedok,' I say, 'and I used to take tours all over Eastern Europe. But in 1969 they gave me an important tour to Italy. And this, I must tell you, was my downfall. You know why? It is very simple. I went out with twenty persons and I came back with four. On the last day, at Trieste, I am sitting in the coach waiting for my party and only these four turn up. The rest want political asylum! And you know what? The coach driver also vanished. They had to send me out a new driver. When we returned at last I was fired. Just like that. Is it my fault people want to leave this country? I tell you, it's got so bad now that no one trusts anyone anymore. Everything must be a big secret!'

The girl is sympathetic, but that Robert is weighing up in his mind whether he should believe me. Well, it is the truth! I happen to know that a Cedok guide was sacked for losing practically a whole group in the West.

The staring eyes of the Jew have made me afraid. I make an excuse and hastily leave the café. There's no real reason, I've told those stories many times before. But walking back to my rooms, without warning, my stomach turns to water. I feel dizzy. I know every stone in the street but I lose all confidence in my ability to get to the other end. I begin to run, to race my fears, imagining fearful phantoms lurking in the shadows, the secret policemen of my subconscious, trying to grab me. To arrest me for what? For being a fraud, a counterfeit man? A drunk full of Pilsner staggers towards me. He nods to me as if in recognition of a fellow sufferer. Madness! I do not suffer. But even as I turn the corner I know that the drunk has straightened up and is watching me.

Next day I meet the couple again. I would rather not talk to them, but they seem anxious to tell me how much they have seen of Prague.

'This morning we saw the tomb of Rabbi Low,' says the girl, 'and we left a note with our names on it.'

'Have you heard all about Rabbi Low and his famous Golem?' I ask. Surely they are not interested in that superstitious rubbish! Then I recall that Robert is a Jew. I consider telling him why the Nazis did not destroy the Prague ghetto. Because they wanted to preserve it as a museum of a vanished race. Now there are hardly any Jews left in Prague and the synagogues are maintained by the goverment as museums. And the chief sightseers are our wonderful East German comrades. Such ironies give me much pleasure.

The girl is still talking.

Ah, now what has Mr Robert got to say?

'One thing I miss, not being able to speak the language,' he says, 'is the fun of eavesdropping. When we get back we will be asked, "What were the people like? Happy?" And all I will be able to say is that they looked like people: some looked pleased, others looked miserable. How am I supposed to tell what they are thinking?'

I am thinking: what if I were to accuse this Jewboy of being a Zionist and then rape his girlfriend? I nod sympathetically.

The girl pulls something out of her handbag and says, 'Look what we bought with the money we changed yesterday.'

It is an ancient coin, tiny and silver. What would anyone want with that?

'It's supposed to be a dinar of Vratislav II,' says Robert.

Supposed! The suspicious kike. If he got it at Starozitnost's it *is* a dinar of Vratislav II.

'I'll tell you two something,' I say confidentially, 'on my mother's side my ancestors go right back to this Vratislas II. He was the first real king of the Czechs, you know. Founded that monastery right up there on top of the castle. Strahov. Yes, I was once a person of high rank. I had money. When I was seventeen I inherited our family estates. They were worth something in the order of half a million. In those days, you can imagine! Well, I made a fantastic success of it. Implemented so many reforms in forestry that I was awarded an honorary degree in agriculture from Charles University. Then came the war. And you can guess what happened after. The communists have it all now.'

A person approaches me to buy a Russian flag. I think it's a fellow. I look more carefully and see he's got a huge chest, like a hunchback turned round. Daft! They're tits. I look at the person's face again and see that it is a very ugly girl. I think: what sort of life can she lead?

Robert wants to know about some book. He says he has been asked to get it for a friend. He reads me the title from a notebook. *Vabank* by Alexej Pludek. Why should anyone he knows outside of Czechoslovakia want such trash? Perhaps he mixes with dissidents. In his notebook I glimpse the address of someone in Prague. Perhaps if he is taking out something he also brought in something. Something like illegal manuscripts. I memorize the address; tonight I will telephone it to the police.

'Ah, you want to buy *Vabank*,' I say. 'You know it has just been awarded our National Book Prize? It's all about Zionism. About the plot, begun in 1967 with the Six-Day War, continued in Czechoslovakia in 1968, and so on, for Jews to seize the governments of all the major world powers. A novel way of looking at the events of 1968, don't you agree? Oh! I believe I have just made a pun.'

I am beginning to enjoy myself. But both of my friends are looking uncomfortable. They do not know if I am serious or not.

'I am not against the State of Israel, you understand,' I say, 'far from it. But I think it should only be a homeland for Hebrews. Not Khazars. You see, most people who call themselves Jews are really Khazars, descendants of a Black Sea tribe who converted to Judaism for political reasons and then dispersed through Europe. These are the people of the diaspora, not the Hebrews.'

What can they reply to that?

'I'll tell you something else,' I say, 'about the Dead Sea. We're all led to believe that it's dead because it's full of salt. Yes! But no one says that there are ten different mineral salts in it. I'll tell you something. Those salts are worth more than America's entire annual gross national product. How do I know? Well, I spent years working on the Dead Sea. But I was forced to suppress my findings. Because what I knew would have started a Holy War! *Jihad*, the Arabs call it. On the strength of rumours of my work I was offered the directorship of Amman University. It is all documented. I have the letters at home somewhere.'

It is apparent that Robert does not believe a word I am saying. He is not attempting to argue or contradict, he just wants to get away from me as quickly as possible. But I am enjoying myself too much. Did I not sense it was going to be a good day when I laid that near-perfect shit this morning?

'My brother, you know, is looked on by the Arabs as a Prince,' I inform the pair, 'a fake one, of course, like Lawrence of Arabia. He entered Cairo as a sergeant in the Aussie army sometime in forty-four – oh, yes, he got out of Czechoslovakia in late thirty-eight – and right away met this little Arab boy. Hamil. And Hamil asks, "What's your name, sergeant? You look more like one of us than an Aussie." And my brother says, "Saladin." You see, it's the first Arab name that comes into his head. Hamil looks at him, and runs off. About an hour later there's two thousand Arabs knocking on his quarters crying, "Saladin!" And Hamil says to my brother, "I've brought all your relatives to see you." I have to tell you that on a certain day of each year all the members of the Saladin family meet in Cairo. The very day that my brother showed up. There had been rumours. Stories that the head of the family had escaped the great massacre and fled to Australia. And here he was, returned. The next day there were newspaper headlines this high saying: "Prince Saladin is Back!" After that my brother stayed on in Cairo. He became an agent. He got behind German lines. Smuggled hashish and secrets. When the war was over he became the leader of twenty thousand students. I'll tell you, if it wasn't for my brother the whole of Cairo would have burned down in fifty-two. You've heard of the Fires of Cairo? But my brother held his men under control. Nevertheless, Nasser had him tortured and thrown out. He was afraid of him.'

All dictators fear men who are popular. They must watch over the State like I monitor my body. They must counter any abnormality with severe repression; anti-communists must be met with antibodies. Secret policemen are the penicillin of the nation. Like mould growing on the corpse of a leaf, there's a thought. When the body is purged the machine will run efficiently. I have heard that if ants cannot function properly they are taken away from the nest by three fellow workers and destroyed: one holds down its legs, another flattens its abdomen, and the third injects it with poison. I am no insect, but I am frightened. Not of Germans or renegades, but of invisible germs; of a revolution within. The State does its best to ensure control of the future, but there is no guarantee. The best it can do is rearrange the past to suit itself, and to stabilize the present in such a way that it becomes, simultaneously, a reflection of both past and future, thus liable to strict checks.

Six long black Russian limousines are edging down the road; the first flies the Hammer & Sickle. They are full of delegates to the Party Congress. Chubby men in grey homburgs with beige scarves in V's around their necks and black overcoats buttoned right up; chaperoned and chauffeured by secret-service men; immunized against the world. They give me reassurance, but what a joy it would be to assassinate one of them. Suddenly I understood how the germs that I destroy daily must feel.

The two English tourists are too intrigued by this procession of the powerful to bother much over my latest monologue.

'We must go now,' says the girl in response to a look from Robert.

'Wait!' I say. 'I have one last thing to tell you.'

That's got them! No confessions from me, though. I have something else in mind.

'My brother lives in London now,' I say. 'I hear from him very often. He tells me that there is an excellent Czech restaurant in London. You must visit it. They serve magnificent knedliky. And schnitzels like you've never tasted. Not made with veal, but with pork that's been beaten flat till it's as thin as a pancake. Oooh, my mouth is watering. It is situated in Hampstead, West Hampstead. The Czech National House. You know of it? Our airmen who flew with the RAF founded it after the war was over. There is a photograph of the Queen on the wall encrusted with diamonds. How do I know this? My brother tells me. He also writes that all the Jews in Golders Green come and eat there every night, because they are smart, and they know when they are on to a good thing. You will go there? Undoubtedly you will see my brother. He looks just like me. Can you do me one favour? I see that you have a camera around your neck. Will you take a photograph of me for my brother?'

Robert opens his camera case. He fiddles with the exposure meter, sets the speed and the correct aperture. He places the camera to his eye and twists the lens until he has me in sharp focus. I smile. The shutter clicks. And so on a small piece of celluloid is a picture of me. Preserving me for that single 1/60th of a second in my life when I am not afraid.

A Family Supper

Kazuo Ishiguro

A Family Supper

Fugu is a fish caught off the Pacific shores of Japan. The fish has held a special significance for me ever since my mother died through eating one. The poison resides in the sexual glands of the fish, inside two fragile bags. When preparing the fish, these bags must be removed with caution, for any clumsiness will result in the poison leaking into the veins. Regrettably, it is not easy to tell whether or not this operation has been carried out successfully. The proof is, as it were, in the eating.

Fugu poisoning is hideously painful and almost always fatal. If the fish has been eaten during the evening, the victim is usually overtaken by pain during his sleep. He rolls about in agony for a few hours and is dead by morning. The fish became extremely popular in Japan after the war. Until stricter regulations were imposed, it was all the rage to perform the hazardous gutting operation in one's own kitchen, then to invite neighbours and friends round for the feast.

At the time of my mother's death, I was living in California. My relationship with my parents had become somewhat strained around that period, and consequently I did not learn of the circumstances surrounding her death until I returned to Tokyo two years later. Apparently, my mother had always refused to eat fugu, but on this particular occasion she had made an exception, having been invited by an old schoolfriend whom she was anxious not to offend. It was my father who supplied me with the details as we drove from the airport to his house in the Kamakura district. When we finally arrived, it was nearing the end of a sunny autumn day.

'Did you eat on the plane?' my father asked. We were sitting on the tatami floor of his tea-room.

'They gave me a light snack.'

'You must be hungry. We'll eat as soon as Kikuko arrives.'

My father was a formidable-looking man with a large stony jaw and furious black eyebrows. I think now in retrospect that he much resembled Chou En-lai, although he would not have cherished such a comparison, being particularly proud of the pure samurai blood that ran in the family. His general presence was not one which encouraged relaxed conversation; neither were things helped much by his odd way of stating each remark as if it were the concluding one. In fact, as I sat opposite him that afternoon, a boyhood memory came back to me of the time he had struck me several times around the head for 'chattering like an old woman'. Inevitably, our conversation since my arrival at the airport had been punctuated by long pauses.

'I'm sorry to hear about the firm,' I said when neither of us had spoken for some time. He nodded gravely.

'In fact the story didn't end there,' he said. 'After the firm's collapse, Watanabe killed himself. He didn't wish to live with the disgrace.'

'I see.'

'We were partners for seventeen years. A man of principle and honour. I respected him very much.'

'Will you go into business again?' I asked.

'I am – in retirement. I'm too old to involve myself in new ventures now. Business these days has become so different. Dealing with foreigners. Doing things their way. I don't understand how we've come to this. Neither did Watanabe.' He sighed. 'A fine man. A man of principle.'

The tea-room looked out over the garden. From where I sat I could make out the ancient well which as a child I had believed haunted. It was just visible now through the thick foliage. The sun had sunk low and much of the garden had fallen into shadow.

'I'm glad in any case that you've decided to come back,' my father said. 'More than a short visit, I hope.'

'I'm not sure what my plans will be.'

'I for one am prepared to forget the past. Your mother too was always ready to welcome you back – upset as she was by your behaviour.'

'I appreciate your sympathy. As I say, I'm not sure what my plans are.'

'I've come to believe now that there were no evil intentions in your mind,' my father continued. 'You were swayed by certain – influences. Like so many others.'

'Perhaps we should forget it, as you suggest.'

'As you will. More tea?'

Just then a girl's voice came echoing through the house.

'At last.' My father rose to his feet. 'Kikuko has arrived.'

Despite our difference in years, my sister and I had always been close. Seeing me again seemed to make her excessively excited and for a while she did nothing but giggle nervously. But she calmed down somewhat when my father started to question her about Osaka and her university. She answered him with short formal replies. She in turn asked me a few questions, but she seemed inhibited by the fear that her questions might lead to awkward topics. After a while, the conversation had become even sparser than prior to Kikuko's arrival. Then my father stood up, saying: 'I must attend to the supper. Please excuse me for being burdened down by such matters. Kikuko will look after you.'

My sister relaxed quite visibly once he had left the room. Within a few minutes, she was chatting freely about her friends in Osaka and about her classes at university. Then quite suddenly she decided we should walk in the garden and went striding out onto the veranda. We put on some straw sandals that had been left along the veranda rail and stepped out into the garden. The daylight had almost gone.

'I've been dying for a smoke for the last half-hour,' she said, lighting a cigarette.

'Then why didn't you smoke?'

She made a furtive gesture back towards the house, then grinned mischievously.

'Oh I see,' I said.

'Guess what? I've got a boyfriend now.'

'Oh yes?'

'Except I'm wondering what to do. I haven't made up my mind yet.'

'Quite understandable.'

'You see, he's making plans to go to America. He wants me to go with him as soon as I finish studying.'

'I see. And you want to go to America?'

'If we go, we're going to hitch-hike.' Kikuko waved a thumb in front of my face. 'People say it's dangerous, but I've done it in Osaka and it's fine.'

'I see. So what is it you're unsure about?'

We were following a narrow path that wound through the shrubs and finished by the old well. As we walked, Kikuko persisted in taking unnecessarily theatrical puffs on her cigarette.

'Well. I've got lots of friends now in Osaka. I like it there. I'm not sure I want to leave them all behind just yet. And Suichi – I like him, but I'm not sure I want to spend so much time with him. Do you understand?'

'Oh perfectly.'

She grinned again, then skipped on ahead of me until she had reached the well. 'Do you remember,' she said, as I came walking up to her, 'how you used to say this well was haunted?'

'Yes, I remember.'

We both peered over the side.

'Mother always told me it was the old woman from the vegetable store you'd seen that night,' she said. 'But I never believed her and never came out here alone.'

'Mother used to tell me that too. She even told me once the old woman had confessed to being the ghost. Apparently she'd been taking a short cut through our garden. I imagine she had some trouble clambering over these walls.'

Kikuko gave a giggle. She then turned her back to the well, casting her gaze about the garden.

'Mother never really blamed you, you know,' she said, in a new voice. I remained silent. 'She always used to say to me how it was their fault, hers and Father's, for not bringing you up correctly. She used to tell me how much more careful they'd been with me, and that's why I was so good.' She looked up and the mischievous grin had returned to her face. 'Poor Mother,' she said.

'Yes. Poor Mother.'

'Are you going back to California?'

'I don't know. I'll have to see.'

'What happened to – to her? To Vicki?'

'That's all finished with,' I said. 'There's nothing much left for me now in California.'

'Do you think I ought to go there?'

'Why not? I don't know. You'll probably like it.' I glanced towards the house. 'Perhaps we'd better go in soon. Father might need a hand with the supper.'

But my sister was once more peering down into the well. 'I can't see any ghosts,' she said. Her voice echoed a little.

'Is Father very upset about his firm collapsing?'

'Don't know. You can never tell with Father.' Then suddenly she straightened up and turned to me. 'Did he tell you about old Watanabe? What he did?'

'I heard he committed suicide.'

'Well, that wasn't all. He took his whole family with him. His wife and his two little girls.'

'Oh yes?'

'Those two beautiful little girls. He turned on the gas while they were all asleep. Then he cut his stomach with a meat knife.'

'Yes, Father was just telling me how Watanabe was a man of principle.'

'Sick.' My sister turned back to the well.

'Careful. You'll fall right in.'

'I can't see any ghost,' she said. 'You were lying to me all that time.'

'But I never said it lived down the well.'

'Where is it, then?'

We both looked around at the trees and shrubs. The light in the garden had grown very dim. Eventually I pointed to a small clearing some ten yards away.

'Just there I saw it. Just there.'

We stared at the spot.

'What did it look like?'

'I couldn't see very well. It was dark.'

'But you must have seen something.'

'It was an old woman. She was just standing there, watching me.'

We kept staring at the spot as if mesmerized.

'She was wearing a white kimono,' I said. 'Some of her hair had come undone. It was blowing around a little.'

Kikuko pushed her elbow against my arm. 'Oh be quiet. You're trying to frighten me all over again.' She trod on the remains of her cigarette, then for a brief moment stood regarding it with a perplexed expression. She kicked some pine needles over it, then once more displayed her grin. 'Let's see if supper's ready,' she said.

We found my father in the kitchen. He gave us a quick glance, then carried on with what he was doing.

'Father's become quite a chef since he's had to manage on his own,' Kikuko said with a laugh. He turned and looked at my sister coldly.

'Hardly a skill I'm proud of,' he said. 'Kikuko, come here and help.'

For some moments my sister did not move. Then she stepped forward and took an apron hanging from a drawer.

'Just these vegetables need cooking now,' he said to her. 'The rest just needs watching.' Then he looked up and regarded me strangely for some seconds. 'I expect you want to look around the house,' he said eventually. He put down the chopsticks he had been holding. 'It's a long time since you've seen it.'

As we left the kitchen I glanced back towards Kikuko, but her back was turned.

'She's a good girl,' my father said quietly.

I followed my father from room to room. I had forgotten how large the house was. A panel would slide open and another room would appear. But the rooms were all startlingly empty. In one of the rooms the lights did not come on, and we stared at the stark walls and tatami in the pale light that came from the windows.

'This house is too large for a man to live in alone,' my father said. 'I don't have much use for most of these rooms now.'

But eventually my father opened the door to a room packed

full of books and papers. There were flowers in vases and pictures on the walls. Then I noticed something on a low table in the corner of the room. I came nearer and saw it was a plastic model of a battleship, the kind constructed by children. It had been placed on some newspaper; scattered around it were assorted pieces of grey plastic.

My father gave a laugh. He came up to the table and picked up the model.

'Since the firm folded,' he said, 'I have a little more time on my hands.' He laughed again, rather strangely. For a moment his face looked almost gentle. 'A little more time.'

'That seems odd,' I said. 'You were always so busy.'

'Too busy perhaps.' He looked at me with a small smile. 'Perhaps I should have been a more attentive father.'

I laughed. He went on contemplating his battleship. Then he looked up. 'I hadn't meant to tell you this, but perhaps it's best that I do. It's my belief that your mother's death was no accident. She had many worries. And some disappointments.'

We both gazed at the plastic battleship.

'Surely,' I said eventually, 'my mother didn't expect me to live here for ever.'

'Obviously you don't see. You don't see how it is for some parents. Not only must they lose their children, they must lose them to things they don't understand.' He spun the battleship in his fingers. 'These little gunboats here could have been better glued, don't you think?'

'Perhaps. I think it looks fine.'

'During the war I spent some time on a ship rather like this. But my ambition was always the air force. I figured it like this. If your ship was struck by the enemy, all you could do was struggle in the water hoping for a lifeline. But in an aeroplane – well – there was always the final weapon.' He put the model back onto the table. 'I don't suppose you believe in war.'

'Not particularly.'

He cast an eye around the room. 'Supper should be ready by now,' he said. 'You must be hungry.'

Supper was waiting in a dimly lit room next to the kitchen. The only source of light was a big lantern that hung over the table, casting the rest of the room into shadow. We bowed to each other before starting the meal.

There was little conversation. When I made some polite comment about the food, Kikuko giggled a little. Her earlier nervousness seemed to have returned to her. My father did not speak for several minutes. Finally he said:

'It must feel strange for you, being back in Japan.'

'Yes, it is a little strange.'

'Already, perhaps, you regret leaving America.'

'A little. Not so much. I didn't leave behind much. Just some empty rooms.'

'I see.'

I glanced across the table. My father's face looked stony and forbidding in the half-light. We ate on in silence.

Then my eye caught something at the back of the room. At first I continued eating, then my hands became still. The others noticed and looked at me. I went on gazing into the darkness past my father's shoulder.

'Who is that? In that photograph there?'

'Which photograph?' My father turned slightly, trying to follow my gaze.

'The lowest one. The old woman in the white kimono.'

My father put down his chopsticks. He looked first at the photograph, then at me.

'Your mother.' His voice had become very hard. 'Can't you recognize your own mother?'

'My mother. You see, it's dark. I can't see it very well.'

No one spoke for a few seconds, then Kikuko rose to her feet. She took the photograph down from the wall, came back to the table and gave it to me.

'She looks a lot older,' I said.

'It was taken shortly before her death,' said my father.

'It was the dark. I couldn't see very well.'

I looked up and noticed my father holding out a hand. I gave him the photograph. He looked at it intently, then held it towards Kikuko. Obediently, my sister rose to her feet once more and returned the picture to the wall.

There was a large pot left unopened at the centre of the table. When Kikuko had seated herself again, my father reached forward and lifted the lid. A cloud of steam rose up and curled towards the lantern. He pushed the pot a little towards me.

'You must be hungry,' he said. One side of his face had fallen into shadow.

'Thank you.' I reached forward with my chopsticks. The steam was almost scalding. 'What is it?'

'Fish.'

'It smells very good.'

In amidst soup were strips of fish that had curled almost into balls. I picked one out and brought it to my bowl.

'Help yourself. There's plenty.'

'Thank you.' I took a little more, then pushed the pot towards my father. I watched him take several pieces to his bowl. Then we both watched as Kikuko served herself.

My father bowed slightly. 'You must be hungry,' he said again. He took some fish to his mouth and started to eat. Then I too chose a piece and put it in my mouth. It felt soft, quite fleshy against my tongue.

'Very good,' I said. 'What is it?'

'Just fish.'

'It's very good.'

The three of us ate on in silence. Several minutes went by.

'Some more?'

'Is there enough?'

'There's plenty for all of us.' My father lifted the lid and once more steam rose up. We all reached forward and helped ourselves.

'Here,' I said to my father, 'you have this last piece.'

'Thank you.'

When we had finished the meal, my father stretched out his arms and yawned with an air of satisfaction. 'Kikuko,' he said. 'Prepare a pot of tea, please.'

My sister looked at him, then left the room without comment. My father stood up.

'Let's retire to the other room. It's rather warm in here.'

I got to my feet and followed him into the tea-room. The large sliding windows had been left open, bringing in a breeze from the garden. For a while we sat in silence.

'Father,' I said, finally.

'Yes?'

'Kikuko tells me Watanabe-San took his whole family with him.'

My father lowered his eyes and nodded. For some moments he seemed deep in thought. 'Watanabe was very devoted to his work,' he said at last. 'The collapse of the firm was a great blow to him. I fear it must have weakened his judgment.'

'You think what he did – it was a mistake?'

'Why, of course. Do you see it otherwise?'

'No, no. Of course not.'

'There are other things besides work.'

'Yes.'

We fell silent again. The sound of locusts came in from the garden. I looked out into the darkness. The well was no longer visible.

'What do you think you will do now?' my father asked. 'Will you stay in Japan for a while?'

'To be honest, I hadn't thought that far ahead.'

'If you wish to stay here, I mean here in this house, you would be very welcome. That is, if you don't mind living with an old man.'

'Thank you. I'll have to think about it.'

I gazed out once more into the darkness.

'But of course,' said my father, 'this house is so dreary now. You'll no doubt return to America before long.'

'Perhaps. I don't know yet.'

'No doubt you will.'

For some time my father seemed to be studying the back of his hands. Then he looked up and sighed.

'Kikuko is due to complete her studies next spring,' he said. 'Perhaps she will want to come home then. She's a good girl.'

'Perhaps she will.'

'Things will improve then.'

'Yes, I'm sure they will.'

We fell silent once more, waiting for Kikuko to bring the tea.

Iguana Hunting

Hernán Lara Zavala

Translated by the author in collaboration with Andrew Jefford

Hernán Lara Zavala was born in Mexico City in 1946. He teaches literature at the University of Mexico and is co-ordinator of a narrative workshop in Cuernevaca. His works include two collections of stories, DE ZITILCHEN and EL MISCO, and a novel, CHARRAS. 'Iguana Hunting' was one of the first stories he wrote, and, he has said, 'in a sense it was dictated to me by the muses, or rather from the unconsciousness of childhood which included the Mayan myths, the awakening of sexual life, and the power words have in the minds of young people to evoke sensations yet to be known. The idea came without much effort, but also without my having clearly in mind just where the twisting point would emerge in the account of childhood experience. The final story turned out to be quite different from the original project.'

After three years studying at the University of East Anglia, Andrew Jefford has worked in publishing and in journalism. He currently writes for the *Evening Standard* and a variety of other publications, as well as writing books about wine. His poetry has been published in *The Spectator*.

Iguana Hunting

In those days we went into the wild to hunt. I had come from the city to stay with my grandparents in Zitilchen for my holidays, and I'd already made some friends. From the low hill that rises south of town, Chidra, the half-breed Mayan, would first go to call for Crispin. When he reached the house, he gave a long whistle and out Crispin came: short, nervous, cunning. Then they came to fetch me. On their way they collected the stones we were to use. They were special stones, almost round, and they rattled in our pockets as we journeyed on.

When they got to our farm Chidra whistled again, and my grandfather would come to the door to let them in. Chidra lived in the wild, and had eaten no food. Not so Crispin. He lived a few streets away and I knew he had had a good breakfast. Both, however, accepted the hot chocolate and rolls my grandmother offered them. While we ate, my grandfather, tall but stooping, joked gravely with us, as was his manner. With Crispin particularly: the old man was very fond of Crispin. He used to call him 'don Crispin' and every now and then he'd suggest jobs for him inspired by his diminutive stature and resilient character. He asked him once: 'How would you like to join the army when you grow up? Your height would be greatly in your favor.' Crispin responded with a dutiful chuckle, revealing the dough between his teeth. In the meantime, Chidra, his mind elsewhere, ate voraciously. My grandfather seldom addressed him. I recall, however, one of his few observations about Chidra. He was talking to Crispin about Padre Garcia's extravagantly mystical sermons: 'No,' he said, 'you're qualified for all sorts of jobs but not that of a priest. You're too much of this world. I would have to think of somebody else for that . . . Chidra, for instance.' I don't remember Chidra's reaction.

Although we actually proposed iguana hunting, our expeditions were likely to involve anything. In our forays we spent our time looking for V-shaped branches to make catapults with, or stealing wedges of honeycomb from the hives left out in the fields. Often, as we were walking out of town, we would climb the wall of some orchard to steal oranges or to take a swim in the reservoir. On such occasions I arrived home for dinner clutching my damp underpants in my hand. As soon as my grandmother saw me she'd say: 'Have you been swimming in Tomás's reservoir again? The day he finds out you'll be in big trouble and it'll be no use coming to me.'

Many were the times we went out to hunt, but it has to be admitted that iguanas were not easy prey. We'd occasionally catch one – and then we'd sell it to a well-known iguana-eater in town – but their natural colors served them all too well. We hunted turtle-doves, lizards, and, on one occasion, even an armadillo that Chidra grabbed by the tail. As soon as we were on our own, shooting here and there at the slightest movement in the bushes, Chidra, who in the presence of adults was invariably silent and reserved, could restrain himself no longer. He would tell us the strange occurrences that, according to him, he experienced in his daily walk back home. These tales always provoked Crispin's anger and contempt. Chidra spoke, for instance, about the afternoon when, returning home from town, he had seen a herd of elephants.

'I yelled out for help but nobody came . . .'

'That was when you took coffee for the first time in your bloody life. I don't know how many coffees you had, but it drove you crazy,' said Crispin, annoyed.

Chidra, however, would not be swayed. He told us that sometimes when he was on his way home toward midnight he could hear somebody hissing insistently: 'pssst . . . pssst . . .'

But he never dared turn around to see who it was because he was sure the noises were produced by Xtabay, the evil woman from Mayan mythology. He explained to us that those who turned to see her could not resist her summons since, apart from her feet, her beauty was irresistible. She hid behind the trunk of a ceybo tree and those who responded to her charms woke up next morning with their bodies covered with thorns.

We knew the legend of course. But when Chidra talked about it, he was charged with such conviction that almost every boy in town – Crispin excepted – listened to him enthralled. He told us about a cave in the heart of the wild that led directly to hell. He told us about a wandering Indian, known as Tzintzinito, who was condemned to roam endlessly through the wild.

On one of those mornings Chidra told us that while returning from the camp where his father worked collecting gum, he had seen a naked woman with beautiful long hair bathing in a deep pool. Half joking, half serious, Crispin said:

'Of course you'll tell us she was Xtabay.'

'I don't know,' answered Chidra. 'The woman I saw in the pool had the whitest feet I ever saw. She had long golden hair.'

'He's a liar.'

'No, I'm not,' said Chidra, crossing himself and kissing his thumb.

'When was this?' I asked.

'Yesterday afternoon.'

'That's hardly the time Xtabay would come out.'

'We'll get him now,' said Crispin. 'Prove it.'

'If you want. But I'd better tell you it's a long way.'

'He's afraid,' said Crispin.

'Let's go,' answered Chidra. 'If you're willing, let's go.'

Chidra knew the area well. Not only because he lived in the wild but because of his father's work. Chidra was responsible for bringing him food and other necessities every so often. Once in the wild he was the official guide. We left town. We passed the orchards, we passed the hives, we penetrated the wild. We struggled through the undergrowth, parting bushes and trampling weeds. Chidra, confident of his capabilities, moved his head restlessly like a wild animal on a fresh scent.

There was something uncanny about the whole affair. In Zitilchen, days are usually hot and cloudless. That day, however, was humid and gray. When we were in the thickest and most tangled part of the wild we suddenly came across some ancient ruins. Crispin and I were stunned. It was a small abandoned Mayan village but so well kept that it seemed inhabited. We were silent, looking around in awe. After a while Chidra said, 'This way. We're nearly there now.' Crispin stared at me. I could sense that, like myself, he was afraid as well as fascinated.

Chidra moved forward again, parting the scrub that stood in our way. Nobody thought about the iguanas. Our sole concern was finding out the truth about Chidra's tale. Finally we came to the edge of a large pool. It was a transparent green and its waters were unusually quiet and still. There was nobody around. We found a clearing and hid behind some mangrove trees while we tried to agree what to do. Perhaps there never had been anyone around, except in Chidra's imagination. Crispin wanted to go back to town and repeated constantly that Chidra was a liar. A bloody liar. They had a long argument and were about to come to blows when I saw somebody moving on the other side of the pool. We quickly fell silent, curious to see who it was. A bearded man appeared. We could see him clearly: he was dressed for the bush. He wore glasses and was smoking a pipe. He had a saucepan and as he came to the edge of the pool, he put some soil in the pot and sank it in the water, emptying it some moments later. He was about to leave when a woman, dressed just like him, appeared, bringing a few more utensils to be washed. We couldn't hear what they were saying.

'There she is,' said Chidra slowly.

And it was true, she was just as Chidra had described her: a tall, blonde woman. We saw them for just a few minutes; as soon as they finished their washing they left the pool. We stayed on, still waiting, when Crispin broke our silence. He stood up and said, 'Shit! I've got a dreadful itching. What the hell is it?' He lifted up his shirt to show us his back.

'Ticks,' said Chidra.

'Blast!' said Crispin as he took off his shirt.

'We must be covered in them too,' Chidra said to me, looking at his ankles, scratching himself and standing up to take off his own shirt. I did the same. We undressed ourselves in order to shake off the ticks from our clothes. Chidra even had ticks in his armpits, entangled in the wispy hair. We were covered in them. We were still naked when Chidra began to talk about the woman we had briefly seen, full of the fact that this proved he was no liar. He told us again how, the day before, as he was wandering around the mangroves, he had seen a tall, blonde, white woman bathing in the pool. He described her meticulously. He had seen her in her entirety: feminine, naked, almost divine. He was enraptured. Carried away by Chidra's description, I noticed, at first with alarm and then with relief, that all three of us were experiencing the very same sensation.

Our bodies full of ticks, very tired, we got back to Zitilchen well after dark. We reached my grandfather's farm. I waved good-bye to Crispin and Chidra. My eyelids were heavy. My friends walked down the street. I thought about the blonde woman. I felt the ticks all over my body. Thorns. I was exhausted yet Chidra had a long way to go. Once in the house I went straight to my grandmother.

'I'm covered in ticks,' I said. 'Help me get rid of them.'

'What's a few ticks,' she answered. 'They're not black widows. Come on then, off with your clothes and lie down in bed while I warm up some wax.'

Feeling her press me all over with the hot wax, I heard her ask:

'For heaven's sake, there's thousands of them! Where on earth have you been?'

'Today we met Xtabay,' I answered, satisfied.

An Afternoon in America

Jonathan Holland

Jonathan Holland was born in Macclesfield, Cheshire, in 1961 and educated at university in London. His work has appeared in FIRST FICTIONS: INTRODUCTION 11, BEST SHORT STORIES 93, NEW WRITING 3 and *Stand* magazine. His first novel, THE ESCAPE ARTIST, was published in 1994. He lives in Madrid.

An Afternoon in America

McBride wandered into the building society the other day, thin, pointy-faced McBride, downtrodden and hunched up and wearing sunglasses in February. It was like they were all that was left of the old McBride.

'McBride,' I said through the grille. 'Thought you'd be in California by now.' This I meant kindly.

'Aah,' he said. 'Fuck off.' Still a bit of twang to his voice, too.

I hadn't spoken to the bloke for five years. I wasn't going to ask how he'd been keeping, not after that. He looked as if he'd been locked up, and if he hadn't, then he looked as if he ought to be. The worst thing was that, despite the swearing, I don't think he recognized me.

'Funny,' I said. 'School. Seemed bad at the time. I feel quite fond about it now.'

McBride took the ten pound note I'd given him and held it up to the light. Squinted up and through it. Didn't speak, though. It was slightly sad not to hear him speak.

He just hurried away. Well, it wasn't clever, what I'd said.

It was after the Easter holidays. The academic lives of about a hundred sixteen-year-olds were drawing to a close. Our English teacher was a pony-tailed admirer of Michael Foot and a strong contrast to the pig-eyed spite engines that made up most of the staff. 'Hi,' Mike Curry would say at the start of lessons, rubbing his hands together, hopping from one foot to the other.

'OK,' he said. 'Your stories. You kick off today, McBride.'

I was right behind McBride, dreading my turn. I had spent three hours the previous evening in Bollington Library, copying out a story by Henry Somebody which I hoped Mike Curry had never come across. I didn't concentrate on McBride, merely made some last-minute adjustments to *The Real Thing*. As I tinkered, I realized that the coughing and shuffling which formed the natural background to lessons had ceased.

I looked up at Slash Hyde. Even Slash Hyde was all ears.

'From New York,' McBride read out, 'we headed on up to Buffalo. We worked our way round the Great Lakes and crossed the border into Canada for a rendezvous with Janine's cousin Taco Paco, a Mexican smuggler gone north to turn over a new life. Spent a little time at Thunder Bay, crashed out under the arcing, starlike glimpses of a new future. Going, we were moving. Then it was down through Duluth to Minneapolis and due south through Des Moines to Kansas City, bright nightwind in our hair, the smell of burning oil, burning rubber, our feet jammed hardflat down on the running boards, rushing fearless into the oncoming lights. Me and Janine.

'We hugged the Gulf of Mexico as far as Houston, Texas, and lifted the jewels off the neck of the faceless daughter of a dollar billionaire. Diamonds in the dust of America, falling, a cascade of release in the shadows and sweat and sun of America: Charlie Parker on the radio.

'In California we held hands, Me and Janine. Filled with the charge and the burning we lay in the hot sand and we sang and we sang, and then we leaped overtumblingover, devilsdice, into the bluedeep Pacific, and when we came up, we looked at each other and laughed without control and our noses were dripping and O her lips and in our faces we saw all the Whys we'd never known, and we kissed while the beaten white sun lowered its shy face behind the Californian mountains, kissed for love and for fear, victims of our love, Me and Janine for ever.'

McBride stopped.

Silence. There'd been nothing like it since Slash Hyde let off a stink-bomb in Divinity.

'Mmm,' said Mike Curry. 'Really good, McBride. Really atmospheric. Any American blood in your family, as a matter of interest?'

'No, sir.'

'Well, just one tiny thing, then. It sounds rather as though the punctuation could do with brushing up.'

Slash Hyde stood.

'Excuse me, sir,' he said, a small miracle in itself. 'I don't think it matters, like, the punctuation.'

'Well, Hyde, it does, you know. If McBride really wants to communicate—'

Greatorex stood up to interrupt. The class idiot, an albino.

'That were a great story,' he declared. 'Nothing wrong with that story, sir.'

Two or three others murmured their approval, and then somebody at the back, probably Nuts O'Brien, started to bang his desk lid. In ten seconds, chaos: shouting, clapping hands, whistling. McBride stood and looked about him, wiping his hands on his trousers and blinking, a silly grin on his face.

Mike Curry was grinning, too.

'OK,' he said loudly. 'That's enough. Good one, McBride.'

When it had died down, he pointed at me.

'Sir. When the porter's wife,' I started up, 'who used to answer the house-bell, announced, "A gentleman and a lady, sir," I had, as I often had in those days – the wish being father to the thought—'

'Oh, shut it, Pownall,' shouted Slash Hyde. 'That's crap.'

'Not only that,' said Mike Curry. 'It's stolen crap.'

But there was chaos again, and nobody else heard him.

The Central School was small and news-hungry enough for the reputation of McBride to become legend in a short time. He breathed the air of triumph for three days, and it brought with it a change in his bearing. Previously silent and forgettable, McBride took to acknowledging the people who greeted him with a nod, a wink and the word 'hi', not unlike Mike Curry. He was seen with Debbie Hough herself in Water Street, waiting for the last bus to Congleton and, Tone Willis reported, 'wearing a bloody bootlace tie'. In lessons, McBride took to stretching himself out, his fingers crossed behind his head, with the serenity and aloofness of one bathing in hard-won applause. But the school's public memory was shorter than McBride believed. There was too much else, in the way of events, vying for space.

In the changing rooms after football, I caught him standing and chewing gum in front of a mirror, backcombing his hair and murmuring to someone under the gurgling cisterns. I concealed myself behind a pillar. A glance round the side showed that the someone was himself.

'You know something?' McBride said to his reflection, his eyebrows high on his forehead as slowly he nodded. 'You're a fucking cool guy. Don't you worry 'bout a thing.' McBride winked at himself and smiled. 'Hey,' he said. 'Shit.'

'McBride!' I called out. I had to break this. 'Give us some of your gum.'

McBride wheeled about.

'I've not got any.'

'What you're chewing. Well, not that actual gum.'

'No,' he said, and opened his mouth. I wasn't about to start exploring McBride's mouth, but it did look as though there was nothing there.

'What you up to, McBride?' I asked, keeping my distance.

'What?'

'Talking to yourself. You want to watch it.'

Suddenly, McBride altered. His face twisted itself into a sneering smile and his jaw grew busy again as he looked at me sideways.

'Hey,' he said. He drew the sound right out. 'Shit.'

I couldn't handle that. I turned and went.

McBride's condition became steadily worse. He was obliged to continue wearing the school uniform, but sticking out from beneath his trousers there was now a pair of white, spurred boots. From being twitchy and agitated like the rest of us, McBride fostered a languidness which brought him into lessons long after the bell, with the excuse, for example, that he'd had a little business to attend to back there. To accompany this, there was an accent which at first sounded merely outlandish but which soon became identifiable as that of a youthful John

Wayne. Rumours circulated, unconnected with McBride's new Americanness but made plausible by its oddity. McBride was a poofter. McBride had sex with his mother.

Any affection Slash Hyde might have felt for McBride quickly evaporated. Slash Hyde came to believe that McBride needed the shit hammering out of him, and so it was that McBride found himself being cornered after school one day, behind the changing-hut down by the running track. I went along with Slash Hyde and Nuts O'Brien to see what would happen.

'Get that fuckin' cigar out your mouth,' was Slash Hyde's first request. 'And take those sunspecs off. Listen, McBride. You're nobody's friend. You fuck your mum.'

McBride stood up. He was chewing gum again and today had gel in his hair. He pushed the sunglasses up with his forefinger and smiled. Chuckling and nodding as if he knew precisely where Slash Hyde was coming from and envisaged no problems in dealing with Slash Hyde, he took the cigar from his mouth and studied it.

'Hey,' he drawled. 'Slash. It's OK, man.'

'What's *Oah Kie*, McBride?'

'Hey, Slash,' repeated McBride. 'The *shit*. The *shit's* OK. Say, I got a little something here might interest you guys.'

He lowered his sunglasses. His hand moved to his pocket.

'He's got a fuckin' gun, Slash,' muttered Nuts O'Brien, which could easily have been true.

Instead, McBride drew from his blazer pocket something which looked like a massive cigarette. Not taking his eyes off Slash Hyde's, McBride placed the massive cigarette between his lips. He took a light from his cigar, which he then tossed over his shoulder into the long-jump pit.

I don't recall much of the next two hours apart from their excitement. It was like Mike Curry's lesson again, except that this time it lasted longer and we were in the sun and free to really laugh and swear. We sat or squatted in the long-jump pit and brought our attention to bear on McBride, who every so often drew out another massive cigarette. The effect of these made McBride expansive and us reflective.

'Look around you,' McBride invited us. We saw an old man

struggling to get his lawnmower started. We saw a mongrel cocking its leg against the fence.

'Small lives, in a small town, in a small country,' breathed McBride, smoke jetting thickly from his nostrils. 'There has to be more to life than this.' He juxtaposed local and American place names to make his point. Matlock and Mississippi, Pott's Pool and Thunder Bay, Littleworth and Los Angeles.

'Here, he's right,' croaked Slash Hyde, now on his back. 'He's fuckin' right. I know what he's on about.'

'That story I read,' said McBride, 'that story was my life in exactly three years from now.' He explained to us a thing called the American Dream, which he had got from books. I wondered at the courage of McBride in mentioning books to Slash Hyde, but Slash was just spread out there in the sand with his mouth open, laughing occasionally, sometimes when nothing funny had been said. The American Dream, McBride told us, was just a fabulous thing. Who, he asked, had ever heard of the English Dream?

'Not me,' said Nuts O'Brien. 'Fucking *hell*.'

'It's the land of youth and of possibility,' McBride told us earnestly. 'Now listen. Dickens, Smollett, Milton. OK? Now. Hemingway. Kerouac. Capote.' We listened to the sounds of these words and muttered our agreement that there was something more exciting about the second group, although we couldn't put our fingers on it.

'"Michael McBride",' said McBride. 'Who wants to be called "Michael McBride"? I'm "Dean Columbus".' That was true, too. Who wanted to be called 'Brian Pownall'? I didn't even have a nickname. McBride was coming out with all this stuff.

'Why "Columbus"?' asked Slash Hyde.

'You could do worse than read a little history, Slash,' said McBride, and didn't get hit.

'Here, read your story again,' said Nuts O'Brien. 'OK, Slash?'

McBride read and we all lay on our stomachs in the long-jump pit. Before too long the long-jump pit had turned into Long Beach. The lawnmower likewise became a Harley Davison: the dog ceased to figure. The story of McBride and Janine was the story of a journey across America. The journey, McBride explained, was more important than the arrival. In our minds, we tasted the dust and sweat of America. We drank bourbon in its roadside bars and rode at a hundred-and-twenty miles per hour down its desert highways. We met prostitutes in motels (I think McBride must have left this part out with Mike Curry) and we listened to lonely saxophones in tenement blocks. Finally we plunged into the blue Pacific, all of us there with McBride and his Janine, with whom I found I too was slightly in love.

I felt shattered when McBride had finished reading, and thought I was going to be sick.

'You been out there, McBride?' asked Nuts O'Brien with nonchalance.

'Only in here,' McBride said, tapping his temple with his forefinger. 'But I'm getting out, guys. Soonest.'

'Ow,' said Slash Hyde. 'I feel fuckin' terrible. What was that stuff, McBride?'

'Mary Warner,' said McBride.

'Ow.' Slash Hyde pulled himself to his feet. 'Fucking hell. You trying to poison me, McBride?'

'Hey, Slash.'

'Make me feel better, McBride. Go on. Ow, my fucking *head*.' He plucked the sunglasses from McBride's nose and sort of folded them in half.

'Cool it, Slash.'

But Slash was not to be cooled. 'You cunt,' he said. He took a fistful of McBride's hair and pulled McBride's head down on to his knee, which he simultaneously jerked upwards. 'You bastard,' he said. Twice he stamped on McBride's groin as McBride lay there, his mouth half full of sand, trying to sing something.

'Sweet American dreams, McBride,' said Slash Hyde as he staggered away through the lengthening shadows.

Nuts O'Brien followed. I felt I should stay to help McBride to his feet. But I didn't want the hassle of being linked to McBride. It was safer being linked to Slash.

McBride's chance to 'get out' came sooner than he thought. The following day Mrs Hyde rang the headmaster and McBride was expelled that afternoon. Slash Hyde, Nuts O'Brien and myself were put on report for the term. I heard later of legal proceedings, but never got the details.

'Off he goes,' Nuts O'Brien said, at the school gates at the end of McBride's last day. 'Riding off into the fuckin' sunset.'

Slash Hyde's vow was that he'd wrap McBride's head round a lamp-post if he ever saw him again, but privately I disagreed. Life at school was dull, after all, and it was only someone with a Slash Hyde mentality who could fail to see that our afternoon in America with McBride was something to be cherished and perhaps even worth being punished for. I went back to the library and found out that Hemingway was a writer and not, in fact, a place, and that he wrote little stories about big men which didn't taken long to read and weren't hard to understand. My own vow was that I would never again copy out a story for Mike Curry, but would try to write my own.

An odd vow, really, I realized later. Because McBride's story was as far from being his own as a story can be.

His absence led to the growth of a new interest in him on my part and raised questions which you didn't normally ask about your schoolmates. Did he have sex with his mother? Where did he live?

I found out and called round at his house.

'Hey,' he said. 'Good to see you.'

The surprise must have showed on my face, because McBride then told me that getting out of that school was the best goddamn thing that ever happened to him and that in two weeks he was leaving the country.

McBride's bedroom was a different world. It was badly lit, and since McBride wore a new pair of sunglasses, I was surprised he could make out anything at all. The room was covered, ceiling included, with posters of American film stars of the 1950s, and smelt strongly of the stuff we had smoked in the long-jump pit. No Snoopy posters for McBride. No *Star Wars*. His shelves contained about ten books, not one of which was connected to his formal education – not even an atlas, which was how I'd guessed he'd written his story. McBride put on some music which he told me was called 'bebop' and took from his wardrobe a bottle of Jack Daniels.

'Hey, Ma,' he called down the stairs. 'Two glasses and some ice for my friend here and I promise not to break anything.'

'I've got an interview,' I told him. 'At the Halifax.'

McBride smiled in such a way as to equate the prestige of a job in a building society with that of piles. 'Must be very nice for you,' he said.

His mother came in with two glasses, a meagre, tired woman who didn't return my greeting. I knew then, seeing her in the flesh, that I'd never be able to ask if she had had sex with her son. As for asking McBride, I wouldn't have trusted his answer anyway.

'What you going to do in America?' I asked him.

'Well,' said McBride. 'There's the chance of a little script-writing.'

The term was unfamiliar to me.

'You know,' said McBride. 'Hollywood.' He raised his glass, squinted up and through it. 'To Hollywood,' he said.

'To Hollywood,' I heard myself saying.

'Then a bit of travelling,' mused McBride. 'Me and Janine. Janine's an ex-whore from the Southside. Waiting on me in New York.'

'Sure.' I'd never said 'sure' in my life, and it was somehow fun.

'Yeah, best thing I ever did,' said McBride, 'getting out of that goddamn school. Try these.'

He handed me the sunglasses.

'See how good it all is?' McBride said. 'How dark?'

Oh, he was mad. His way of looking at the world was all his own. But it was fun, in an odd way, there in his room. I had McBride under my skin. I couldn't forget how right I thought he'd been.

The next thing, six weeks later, was when the end of school was days away.

JOYRIDE GOES HAYWIRE

Dean Columbus, sixteen, of Paradise Street, last week crashed a 1956 Ford Mustang stolen from the house of Mr Norman Allan, second-hand car dealer of Lake Drive, Prestbury. The alcohol in Columbus's blood was found to be more than twice the legal limit. In addition, police found five grammes of cannabis. Columbus, a former student of the Central School, was treated for minor injuries before being taken into police custody.

My first thought was an odd one – that they had arrested the wrong person, that they were faced with the problem of charging Dean Columbus but releasing McBride.

I sat in our front room and imagined McBride careering squealing-tyred through the Lancashire countryside, making up the words to go along with Charlie Parker, his fingers round the neck of a bottle of Jack Daniels, his arm round the shoulders of his imaginary Janine: seeing Los Angeles for Littleworth, dusty highways for winding lanes, tenement blocks for oak trees – seeing a big, dark mysterious world for a small, too-clear one. I imagined him feeling really, really good, laughing and singing away, and not giving a damn if the feeling didn't last. It made me feel slightly envious, that feeling.

I thought it would all make a good idea for a story. I wrote the story in the style of Hemingway and was all set to put it in for Mike Curry's end-of-term competition. But I got nervous about it and tore it up. I mean, people would only have laughed.

The Holiday's Over in Old Alexandria

Anthony Sattin

Anthony Sattin divides his time between writing and travelling. The author of SHOOTING THE BREEZE, a novel, and LIFTING THE VEIL, a history of travellers and tourists in Egypt, 1768–1956, his journalism has appeared in a range of publications, including *The Sunday Times*, *The Daily Telegraph* and *TLS*. He is currently working on a novel set in Cairo and London.

∫

The Holiday's Over in Old Alexandria

'This city will always pursue you.
You'll walk the same streets, grow old
in the same neighbourhoods, turn grey in these same houses.
You'll always end up in this city. Don't hope for things
elsewhere:
there's no ship for you, there's no road . . .'

from *The City* by C.P. Cavafy (1910)

Here is Spiros Spironodos in the centre of a large room that was once the Restaurant Union. He is short, stout of figure, once the very image of a *maître d'*, now sitting alone somewhat slumped and abandoned at the restaurant's only remaining table, his head laid upon the thick volume of Mme E. Saint-Ange's *Livre de Cuisine*. Beyond the sound of cats licking out their bowls, all is silence.

Outside the room the Rue Ancienne Bourse is empty, as it has been since the old stock exchange building was demolished. But other streets are busy again as life flows back into Alexandria after the *Eid el Kebir*, the religious holiday to commemorate Abraham's sacrifice of a lamb in the place of his son Isaac. In Mecca, where thousands of Egyptians took part in the annual pilgrimage, there was an obligation to kill in imitation of the patriarch. There was no such obligation in Alexandria, but sacrifice seems to have become part of the city's tradition and where a couple of days ago there were flocks of sheep grazing in public places and being herded through city-centre traffic, now there are only bones chewed by dogs, skins left to dry on rooftops. The streets are slippery in places with blood and discarded guts.

As in biblical times, when the animals' throats were cut their blood was left to run out and then gory hand prints were daubed on cars and city buses and the door posts of homes and offices, and children dipped in their hands and painted each other's faces. All this to ward off the evil eye and satisfy the blood-lust of the angel of death. And yet the door that leads to Spiros Spironodos, his head on Mme Saint-Ange's great work, received no such protection.

The Restaurant Union, like the demolished Bourse, the Sporting Club, the San Stefano Casino and the neo-classical synagogue, belongs to old Alexandria. Not the original Greek city, for nothing has survived of the view that enflamed the passions of Antony and Cleopatra. Spiros Spironodos' door opens onto colonial Alexandria, the twin of Marseilles or Naples rather than Cairo or Aswan, the voices of its inhabitants echoing ever more softly from the poems of Constantine Cavafy and Lawrence Durrell's quartet of novels, their sound reduced to a whisper. Can you hear them? The chorus passing with exquisite music? And pass they must – without degrading themselves, without empty hopes – for what place is there for them in a modern city of exploding population, forgetfulness and factories?

Spiros Spironodos prefers not to consider this question, just as he chose not to see the paper kites and plastic bags that were floating above him on the corniche skyline as he walked from his apartment to the restaurant this morning, just as he also managed not to see the hundreds of children crowded like swallows beneath palm trees and playing around the blackened statue of the nationalist leader, Saad Zaghloul.

The morning is passing but the children are still there, the bright colours of their holiday clothes already fading beneath the sun and dust, while their parents, brothers, sisters, aunts, uncles, cousins and neighbours cover the available sand of the beach. Elsewhere, the spirited girls for whom the city is famous, watched by their mothers in head scarves and men with appetite, ride the clanking trams over subsiding tracks. All across the city Alexandrians are going back to their offices, quays and factories, are driving taxis, selling fish in the street markets, smuggling cigarettes, shining shoes, frequenting the club, seizing whatever opportunities the city offers to get them through the morning with smiles on their faces, with easy conscience, or with a wad of bank notes in their pockets. For them Alexandria is a place of passions, of impossible loves and terrible longings, of irrevocable decisions. As it was for Cavafy and Cleopatra. As it has been for Spiros Spironodos, which is why his head of grey hair is lying, peaceful at last, on the one thousand, three hundred and seventy-five pages of Mme Saint-Ange's book.

Beside the entrance to the Ancienne Bourse, a discreet plaque offers the information that the Restaurant Union was 'fondé en 1919'. Spiros Spironodos wasn't born until a few years after that and he had already served a long apprenticeship by the time he reached the Union's back door. First there was Il Ritrovo, an elegant restaurant started by Italians and sold to Greeks, where he had waited on cotton traders and commodity brokers from the Stock Exchange. They sat beneath a huge painting of 'Diana Returning from Hunting' and he can still remember the tunes with which the two violinists serenaded guests at lunchtime. Then there was the revolution of 1952, the madness four years later when a British army invaded Egypt, the closure of restaurants in Alexandria and the realization, painful, inescapable, that for people like him the good times were over.

He had wanted to leave the city and had thought about taking a ship, finding a road, going to Greece. He still had family there and the only girl who ever showed him any serious intent had already gone. But something had kept him and he had found work on the sea front at the tea-rooms of Delices. He never made it to Greece, never got married, but there were other things and before long he was moving from Delices to the patisserie and restaurant Pastroudis, from waiter to *maître*. Then, in 1964, his big break came: the Union opened its doors and welcomed him in.

Spiros Spironodos arrived at the Union intending to stay. He took to running the place, preparing new menus, searching through recipe books for inspiration that he could share with the chefs, and through books of etiquette for information he could impart to the rest of the staff. He checked early each morning that only the best ingredients had come from the markets, that the tables were precisely laid, the sauces bubbling, the wine chilled, the *eau gazeuse de menthe* still fizzing. It had taken so much work to get the place running the way he wanted it, but in spite of all his efforts the restaurant never again deserved the accolades it had received before the revolution, when the locally-published Schinder's Guide had praised its 'select atmosphere and quiet locality', its 'high-class French cuisine'. Even Schinder's could see that the Union still had 'one of the best kitchens in Egypt', but the best wasn't as good as it had been. The *maître* blamed it on the clientele because although there was still a chance that he'd have a film star or foreign politician at the window tables, elsewhere he was increasingly likely to find a local businessman, a Russian agronomist or European tourist.

Spiros Spironodos had made his efforts to keep the stars. There had been many stories told at the Union, and they said that Montgomery had conducted certain engagements of the north African campaign from a table over near the window. That was before his time. It was Rita Hayworth, after she married the Aga Khan, who belonged to him. When their secretary telephoned to reserve a table, Spiros Spironodos had chickens flown over from France because he knew they were her favourite. That took some organization, but nothing was impossible and accommodating stars was as much a part of his role as being at his station in time to adjust his jacket and tilt his head at the young man whose task it was to pull down the awnings, with *Restaurant Union* printed across them in bold, which kept out the Mediterranean sun and brought in customers.

He is still there a generation later, when most of his friends have left Alexandria or been buried with her past, still there at midday, the hour when the first customers used to wander in off the hot street and demand drinks before they would even look at a menu. He is there and it is still hot outside, but the windows are boarded over and the shutter only half raised. Dim light, dust and cats enter, and the noise of the modern city, far off. No one will come today, which is just as well because he has nothing to offer them if they do.

Five years ago – or maybe more than that already – when the Restaurant Union was still serving its customers, when Spiros Spironodos was as vigilant as he had always been, the old pasha who owned the place died and left the restaurant, like the bulk of his estate, to his three sons. The pasha gave no explicit instructions concerning the restaurant, but each of the sons, who seldom appear in the city, had his own ideas about what should be done. One wanted to sell, another wanted to leave it as it was while the third thought it deserved some investment, a refurbishment, an adjustment to attract the attention of the new Alexandrians whose tastes, like their politics, are now dictated from the Nile valley not from Europe. Spiros Spironodos knew what he would like to do with the sons, but he was a practical man and he expressed enthusiasm for the plan to refurbish the place. 'It will make all the difference,' he assured them. He would even clear out the area at the back, which had been a bar in the days when such a thing was still respectable in Alexandria, and install a grill for food to be taken away, for fast food, for hamburgers. Even women in veils would be able to come there.

But the sons still haven't agreed to spend the money and meanwhile matters have been made more complicated by an inspector of taxes finding irregularities in the accounts. The tax collectors have argued, investigated and then demanded money and the sons have replied by stalling. And each morning for the five years that this has been going on – excluding Muslim holidays, when he stays at home, and Christian holidays when he celebrates by going to church – Spiros Spironodos has crossed the city to the Restaurant Union to feed the cats that keep out the rats, to ensure that everything is in order and to read the work of Mme E. Saint-Ange and other culinary masters. While the tax inspectors investigate and the sons stall, Spiros Spironodos has been keeping alive something of the spirit of the Union.

But five years is a long time, too long for old Alexandria. Piece by piece, person by person, it has slipped away from him until he too has wanted to slip away. He caught himself saying it once, the other day. 'I wish I could go.' The words ricocheted around the room, recently emptied in an overnight raid, and have now come back to haunt him. He knows he is not the sort of person to do away with himself. He knows just as well that this old Alexandria is leaving him. More than that he does not know.

Spiros Spironodos raises his head from the cover of the thick book and looks across to where the brightness of the street slips under the shutter. The sun has failed to cross the dusty parquet to reach his table, so he gets up and switches on an electric light overhead. He sighs. Even the lights appear to have changed voltage. He rubs his eyes a little, pushes his glasses up his nose. His black suit looks as if he has slept more than just a morning in it, but then time no longer has any meaning for him. His cuffs are frayed and dirty too, and his trouser fly is open, but he does nothing about it.

He is desperate. There has been another burglary over the Eid and now the restaurant's cutlery has been stolen. The chairs have already gone, those sturdy wooden Czech-made chairs which had supported the Union's customers since 1919. A few things are still piled in one corner, all that is left of the old fixtures and fittings apart from the lone table at which the old *maître* is sitting, and the *maître* himself.

Perhaps he should go now. There have been offers. One, in particular, for him to manage the restaurant of a new hotel on the Red Sea. For a while he has enjoyed thinking about going there. Yes, he will go. He smoothes his grey hair with the palm of his right hand. The problem is that you can't have a deluxe hotel at the Red Sea. They don't have the facilities for it. His smile, benign, understanding without being condescending, makes it clear that he has seen it all before. So it will be a medium hotel, which means that the food will also have to be medium, like – he clears his throat apologetically – like Egyptian food. And that's no good. He shakes his head vehemently, left arm over the chair back, right hand on the table top. There isn't a *cuisine Egyptienne*. It all comes from Lebanon or Turkey or elsewhere. Egyptians? Pfha. They kill their food with spices, burn their onions, do terrible things. It is all bad . . . bad for the digestion. Even kebab and kofta, felafel . . . these are not Egyptian. If proof is needed, then just look at the way Egyptians prepare them. You should see it. Terrible. Just look at what it does to their bodies.

Cuisine *in* Egypt. Now that can be more successful. He remembers, as though it was only yesterday, the time when Alfred was with him. He smiles again, this time as if he is watching the Swiss chef for the first time. Alfred? He was an artist. Take, for example, the day a pasha came in with eight important Frenchmen. This pasha wanted to offer his guests the local food – only natural, no? But he also wanted to impress them. How to do this? Alfred, he was equal to the challenge and prepared them kebabs and kofta on swords, flaming and dramatic. But it was the salad that was Alfred's *chef d'oeuvre*. He presented it like a map of Egypt, lettuce for the desert, tomatoes for the Nile, the Mediterranean in onions, while Spiros Spironodos had made the dressing, chanting the rhyme Alfred had composed to guide him in his task. 'One miser for the vinegar, and one wise man to put in the salt, a gallant to pour the oil, and a fool to come and mix it all up.'

Spiros Spironodos recites this rhyme out loud in his thick Greek accent, and laughs, the sound filling the dark spaces of the restaurant while his hands are again busy with long-finished tasks. 'Alfred? He was all of those things.'

They served the Frenchmen wine from the vineyards planted outside Alexandria by Nestor Giannaclis. Giannaclis was a Greek tobacco trader who had been invited by one Prince Muhammad Ali to come and make cigarettes in the city. That was at the beginning of the century and at that time if you put in a large order, say for a thousand cigarettes, you could have your name put on them for free. Spiros Spironodos remembers this because his father smoked Giannaclis cigarettes. But Giannaclis' ambitions didn't stop at cigarettes. He knew that the best gift ancient Egyptians ever gave to the Greeks was wine. So he found the right place, the ancient land – it had become desert – and he imported vines from France and Italy, employed Greeks to grow them and Germans to make the wine. The result was good, very good.

Giannaclis had no son, only a daughter – and what a girl she was. Married a Greek called Pierre Akos. That Pierre was a gambler and a friend of King Farouk, so when the revolution came and the King went, Pierre knew that he should be going too. He went to Libya to grow vines there, and made many expenses, and then came Gaddafy . . . Even Pierre has died. And the Giannaclis wine? You can't drink it. You wouldn't want to, even if there was a glass of it left in the restaurant. It's like water. It is worse.

For a moment it seemed as if the room was busy, but he sees that it is only occupied by his memories and his heavy Greek accent. Once again time separates itself out into now and then and Spiros Spironodos experiences a moment of dizziness as he falls from one to the other. He looks up and offers his empty palms to the heavens.

It is now lunch time. Another morning passed without news. He doesn't want to think about that so he stirs from his table and returns Mme Saint-Ange to her place above the kitchen that serves as his office, still busy with papers. From the desk he picks up the *menu du jour* for Sunday, 7th August 1966:

Crème de Volaille
Crevettes à la Russe
Tournedos au Madère
Pommes Fondantes
Salade
Pudding

Alfred, quoting some nineteenth-century master, had said that in order to learn the art of cooking you had to learn French, and who speaks French in Alexandria now? Some, yes. But even before the old pasha died, less and less people had been coming through the Union's doors, their numbers reducing like some over-refined sauce. So for whom will he now practise the art of cooking? Who is there to appreciate the work?

His thoughts are disturbed by the entrance of two men carrying a wooden sideboard. One of them, in jeans and short-sleeved shirt, comes over to ask if it will be possible to store the sideboard in the empty restaurant as the place where they are supposed to store it has still not opened after the Eid. The *maître* waves them towards the back as if they are boys bringing fresh herbs from the country, watching closely as they haul the piece over to the corner reserved for the new bar.

They leave as abruptly as they entered, laughing amongst themselves. Spiros Spironodos ambles after them, towards the door, muttering, too far back to be heard. He doesn't know how things have turned out this way, that he sits in an empty restaurant while the man with the sideboard has six shops in the area selling shirts. All with the same shirts. By now he must be a millionaire and he drives the new model Mercedes. The old pasha was rich, but he never drove a new model Mercedes like that ... In Spiros Spironodos' school they were taught things like book-keeping, typing and short-hand, not how to become millionaires. Spiros Spironodos taught himself French and learned his other skills on the job at Il Ritrovo, Delices, Pastroudis and then at the Union. But what he knows from them and the likes of Mme Saint-Ange belongs to an Alexandria inhabited by Greeks and Italians, British and French as well as Egyptians. You can read all that on the Union's menu, with its eleven different ways with crevettes, its dishes from France, Italy and Greece. Well, the pasha's sons have objected to the menu and maybe Mme Saint-Ange doesn't have all the answers any more. He knows they are living in a time of change and suspects that he will have to learn how to prepare hamburgers the American way, as they have tried to do in Cairo and even across the city in the main square. Hamburgers. Hmmm ... *Steak haché* is what Mme Saint-Ange would have called it. He'll have to serve the local Stella beer, very cold, with that sort of cuisine.

He pulls down the shutter and bolts the Union's front door from the inside. As he has done each lunch time for five years, or a little more by now, Spiros Spironodos makes sure the cats have water, switches off the dull electric light and lets himself out of the Union's side entrance, the old bar door, into the alley. It is filled with rubble and stinks of urine and although he has tried to train himself not to notice these details, he can't help but see that a sacrifice has been made during the Eid and various parts of animal have been thrown there. The alley needs to be cleared out, now the holiday is over, but that can wait. There is another reason for him to scrape away some bone and skin with the walked-down heel of his shoe: to reveal the tiled area which used to be the Union's 'Garden Bar', protected from the unwanted attention of passers-by with a wall of boxed bushes. He looks up and down the alley. As he has nothing to do with

Alexandria's tradition of sacrifice, he believes that the pasha's sons will be interested in his plan to tear down that side wall, cut off a little from the back of the restaurant and open a take-away grill, to be reached along the alley. This is his compromise, his offering to the new Alexandria. He can see it now, so stands and looks at it for a few minutes before turning away.

The alley leads him out onto the Rue Ancienne Bourse, which had been in the centre of Alexandria until even the shape of the city had changed. The street is still empty apart from the red and green bunting, left over from a long-past procession or holiday, fluttering from the lamp posts. Spiros Spironodos is hungry. He has been thinking about the menu from the 7th of August 1966 and although he can't remember that Sunday in particular, he remembers the soup, the crevettes, and the tournedos which Mme Saint-Ange so accurately describes as being 'popular in good restaurants, because of the speed with which it can be served, as well as the ease with which it can be prepared in a hundred different ways.' He would relish eating one there and then, and considers going over to Pastroudis, but . . . well, without being too blunt . . . how can he say it? Pastroudis isn't as it used to be. There's still the Italian restaurant, Santa Lucia, owned by a Greek now. They have their three stars. He shakes his head. Never mind the stars: they don't have the personnel to make it what it was, no one like Spiros Spironodos to go into the kitchen and make sure everything is being done properly.

He won't find what he wants at Santa Lucia and, not knowing where to go, he wanders out towards what he calls Place Muhammad Ali, what is now known as Liberation Square, its old palaces carved up into little offices, its elegant pavements busy with street sellers, its spaces filled with the gallabiyas and skirts, the jeans, the head scarves and tight-arsed trousers of office workers, market traders and dockers, all back at work now the holiday is over, all thinking of beans and burgers, of chick peas and whatever else it is that they eat for lunch. A lively girl pushes through the crowd and turns her head for a moment. A tram rattles over the old tracks and makes the pavement tremble. Vapours rise from vats of stewing beans, from greasy frying pans, from tobacco burning in the bowls of waterpipes and from cars crawling around the statue of another old pasha. The short, stout figure of Spiros Spironodos, his crumpled black suit still open at the fly, ambles out into the square in search of lunch and is swallowed by the crowd.

Terminus

Andrew Cowan

Andrew Cowan was born in Corby in 1960 and lives in Norwich with the writer Lynne Bryan and their daughter Rose. His first novel, PIG, won a Betty Trask Award, the Ruth Hadden Memorial Prize and the Authors' Club First Novel Award, and was shortlisted for the John Steinbeck Award. He also received the Sunday Times Young Writer of the Year Award. His second novel, COMMON GROUND, will be published in 1996.

∫

Terminus

Before they saw the man die they were sitting alone on a bench at the terminus, sharing a portion of chips and watching the tourists. The man's name was John Cheery although they weren't to know this until the ambulance came. Then a voice in Billy's head would remark *Not so cheery now, John,* and afterwards repeat it until he began to feel guilty. Later he'd include the voice in his anecdote of the death as a kind of confession, unsure if it revealed his maturity or childishness.

Half an hour before he died John Cheery was saying goodbye to his friends in a pub by the harbour. He found them there every September. They were local men with stony faces and they betrayed no surprise when he appeared at the bar. As he drained his last glass he told them, 'I got one the other night anyway, first for years. Felt rotten afterwards. The wife came and sat on me, in my dream, up there in the digs. She undid me. I always dream about her when I come here.'

And the barman said, 'You'd think she'd just leave you be.'

A stream of buses also departed from the terminus that lunchtime, and as their engines ticked over Melanie drummed her fingertips on her belly, which made Billy feel squeamish, and nervous. 'There were all these other women there too,' she said, 'and they just stared into space like moon cows, huge great moon cows.' She spoke rapidly, in a voice that was almost a whisper, as if willing her words to escape unnoticed. 'They were older than me, and the woman on reception was foul, so patronizing, she kept calling me *girlie*.' She picked another chip from the nest in his hand. 'Girlie,' she sighed.

Their bench was bolted to a shelter of perspex and steel, half a mile from the crush of the people in town. At their backs the land fell away to the shore, which is where they had wanted to be; and where they usually went, though not often in daylight. One evening in May they'd met and parted before the last bus had arrived from the depot. The sea had swelled in the darkness, tolling the bells of the buoys, creaking the boats on their moorings. A ferry had shimmered as it rounded the headland, lights had winked from the masts of the yachts. That had been their first time, and later they'd descended to the bed of sand in the rocks as if to their own private place. But today the rocks were unstable and the steps had been closed. A web of yellow tape barred their way.

Across the bus-bays in the sunshine stood the Tourist Information Office and the new public toilets. A queue of taxis stretched away to the train station, itself the end of line, beyond which the town rose steeply, a clutter of churches and trees and flinty grey cottages. Most of the houses now traded as shops and holiday lets. The local folk lived further out in streets not marked on the sightseeing guides and everywhere else was cars and caravans and coaches. Within a week the car park next to the terminus would be empty, a wide concrete nothing, and Melanie and Billy would be amongst those who remained. Melanie took another chip, and whispered, 'These are disgusting.'

'So don't eat them,' said Billy.
'If I don't eat I feel sick,' she whispered, and Billy felt the air cool, become darker.

For eighteen weeks Melanie had eaten and wept, and when the tears came it wasn't from worry or fear or simple unhappiness or pain; she wept because this was her condition. She loathed it and quietly cursed as she sobbed, but she could not prevent it. And always beside her Billy hunched his shoulders and waited. He was sensitive to tears, like a sailor to breezes; he felt their approach like a change in the weather. As Melanie's sobs now subsided she told him, 'I couldn't sleep, I was all hot, I thought I was going to lose it. I had these terrible pains. I kept going to the toilet to see if there was any blood.' Then taking another chip she whispered, 'You should've come to the clinic with me.'

'I never know what to do,' he murmured. 'You never say what I should do.'

On the night his first child arrived John Cheery had gone to bed drunk. In old age he would still remember the price of his beer that evening, and he could recite the date of every penny increase until it reached a round shilling. But he never spoke of his daughter. The labour was early and unexpected and his wife, who was seventeen years old, sent him out through the backs in his pyjamas to find a midwife. But his mind was still clouded and a fog had descended. The air smelled thickly of fermentation and the local brewery stables. In the murk he took a wrong turning, three times hammered the wrong door. And when finally the nurse appeared, holding a candle before her, the baby had already been born. Her birth was the last act of her life. John Cheery buried her in a grocery crate two days later.

In the cool ceramic quiet of the new public toilets Melanie smoothed the front of her dress and faced her reflection. She was wearing dark glasses that hid the smear of black round her eyes and when she removed them she noticed another thing that was new, a flush of red that spread back from her cheeks to her neck. For months there had been nothing, no visible sign, but now her appearance was changing, shifting, surprising her from mirrors. In the striped canvas sack that hung from her shoulder she found a tube of lipstick and drew it over her mouth, painted herself older. There was a smell of chip fat on her fingers. She held her breath.

Billy bundled the wrapper into a ball and tossed it from the shelter. On the pavement outside the Tourist Information Office a man in shorts was making a film of his wife. She was sitting on a wall and shuffling some leaflets, a bank of shrubbery behind her. The other tourists steered around them but the man still lowered his camera, watched impatiently until they had gone. There was a stack of postcards in his waistband, flecks of grey in his beard and hair. His wife seemed to be talking to the camera, or at least

Billy imagined she must be, because there was nothing in her surroundings that was remotely worth filming.

On this stretch of coast there was no pier or fun-fair or penny-arcade. The only slot-machines sold cigarettes and condoms. But in the centre of the town, at the rear of the civic building, there was a cinema where Melanie worked as usherette. She had not been trained in courtesy. To the tourists, as she ripped their stubs in two, she presented the same distracted half-smile as she did to those faces which knew her. They watched her pale sandalled heels as she led the way up the stairs in the dark, sought her eyes when her torch found their seats. She always looked away to the screen; and later, when the film reached its end, she hurried ahead of them to the exit and down the road to the harbour. Billy sold whelks and cockles and mussels from a trailer parked on the quayside. When he saw her descending he placed a carton of whelks on the counter, laid two wooden forks beside it.

'Lipstick's a bit heavy,' he told her. He raised the brim of his sunhat and narrowed his eyes, but Melanie ignored him. She fixed her gaze on the man with the camera until Billy began to feel foolish. Finally he sighed and re-shaded his eyes.

'Help me, Billy, look,' she said then.

Later they would have no memory of John Cheery standing, taking the air, walking towards them. This was the first and all they knew of him: an old man slumped on Melanie's shoulder, neither upright nor horizontal, already dying, uncontrollably trembling. When Melanie slipped out from beneath him he didn't topple but continued to shake, and Billy said, 'Is he having a fit? I don't know what to do.' Then to the man, 'Can I help you up? Are you having a fit?' John Cheery's face was red, but not from the sun.

In the carpeted hush of the Tourist Information Office Melanie took her place in the queue and waited until the woman at the counter had transacted a sale. Looking down she saw she was standing on the join between a blue and red carpet tile, and stepped backwards for luck, both her sandals on red. Then on tiptoe she called, 'Excuse me, but there's a man having a heart attack,' and felt herself flushing. The other heads were turning to see, but the woman ignored her, clasped her hands on the desktop. She smiled to the first in line. 'He's across there,' Melanie added, 'in the bus shelter.' The woman hesitated then, smoothing the front of her sweater. She glanced to a pale wooden door marked PRIVATE.

'You go on,' she sighed, 'I'll phone for an ambulance.'

Billy bent to help the man upright, but he was too heavy to move; not unless he embraced him, which he could not do. The old man was slobbering now. The tremor in his chest had carried to his jaw and it was making his teeth clack, but his gaze was direct and unblinking. Billy searched the man's eyes for annoyance, aware that he was young and failing, not wanting his to be the last face the man saw. But there was nothing, no accusation, not even pain or alarm, and Billy heard himself asking, 'What shall I do?' He touched the man's trembling arm, as if this could prevent him from falling. He wondered if he should leave him.

The image fixed in John Cheery's mind as he died was of a woman and two girls. A wind whipped across them as they stepped from their house and the woman hugged her dressing-gown closer. She was small and barefoot and wouldn't dress until evening. Her face was worn, without make-up, and in her short pale fingers she held a freshly-lit cigarette. She used it to point with, a prod towards the neighbouring house. Her girls hurried from their gate and ran up the next garden. They laughed as they hammered the front door. They were half-sisters and called John Cheery *Grandad* though they bore no relation. As they shouted through his letterbox the woman waded into the long grass and peered over her fence. She shook her head. She thought she had heard him returning, but the house was still empty.

An old lady was watching from the corner of the bus shelter. Her face was interested and smiling. When Billy saw her she came closer, as if invited, and placed a hand on his back. She was holding a new brush, the head wrapped in blue plastic. It matched the colour of her frock. 'Perhaps he should be lying down,' she said. 'He doesn't look very comfortable to me.' So Billy crouched at John Cheery's feet and hugged the old man's legs to his side, cradled them as he might a child, awkwardly, self-consciously. The woman propped her broom against the rear of the shelter. She curled a gentle hand behind John Cheery's neck and spoke into his ear. 'Can you talk to me?' she asked. 'Can you say something?' Then to Billy she said, 'I think you should take his arms.'

Billy bore the weight of John Cheery's body but the old man slumped in the middle. His eyes seemed to roll upwards; his face darkened. 'He's very heavy,' Billy said as he lowered him.

'He's had a long life,' the old lady replied.

In the pub by the harbour John Cheery had said to his friends, 'She's never been near the sea, I asked her to come but she wouldn't have it. No one to look after the girls. She couldn't leave them. She was married at seventeen first time, but he left her. He reckoned the girls weren't his so he left her. The oldest's eleven, red hair. The other's five and she's dark. Then there's a third on the way.' He winked. 'All different fathers.' When the cab had arrived to collect him she'd come from her house in her dressing-gown and John Cheery had sat in the passenger seat, his door open, whilst she shivered in the damp air. She had given him a bag for the train, some rolls and biscuits, a girlie magazine. Then she'd kissed him on the lips and called the girls to come forward. John Cheery pressed fifty pence pieces into their hands. Before closing the cab door the woman had said, 'Send us a postcard.' And he'd nodded to her fag, her belly, and replied, 'Look after the little 'un.' The driver had coughed as he started his engine.

The old lady felt in John Cheery's mouth for his dentures. She removed his cap too, and his spectacles, and placed them on the bench at her side. As she wiped her hands on her frock Melanie whispered beside her, 'It's a heart attack. You can tell because of his face. We learned it at work. I've forgotten everything else.' And they looked to the blue-uniformed woman hurrying across from Tourist Information. Her head was down and she was watching her footing, her heels clacking across the bright concrete. With a catch of breathlessness she said, 'I've told my girls where I am,' and gingerly knelt beside the old man. The motif on her sweater said *We'll show you where, we'll get you there*. She tugged it over her head, quickly checked the buttons on her blouse. 'Right,' she said then, smiling to Melanie. 'Recovery position.'

Later Billy would say the man was probably dead from the start, that even if he'd recovered he would have been paralysed on one side, probably brain damaged. He would say they should have allowed John Cheery to die where he sat, still wearing his cap and glasses, still with his teeth in. Another day he would read a book of first aid and satisfy himself that all their efforts had been futile. And finally he would attend classes and become an expert in practical first aid, but he would never find another opportunity to use it.

Before she took hold of his wrist and searched for a pulse, the uniformed woman arranged John Cheery's limbs in the posture of a climber on a rock face. A rivulet of piss ran along the gap in the paving slabs and she laughed as she said, 'There's something here somewhere.' Then she asked Melanie, 'Can you find it?' and repositioned her knees on the concrete.

'I think he should be on his back,' Melanie whispered.

In the pub they were interested in John Cheery's neighbour and asked questions as they accepted his drinks. His face now coppery with whisky, he told them, 'She moved in the year after my wife died. She looked after me. I looked after her. I paid her TV licence first off. The van came round, so I paid it. There was no food for this weekend, or that weekend, so I helped her. I gave her the money. Because she was crying. Always crying.' Her electricity was about to be cut off, and he gave her £140 for that. Her gas bill was £90. The telephone was more. 'She ever pay you back?' they asked him. 'No, nothing. Never will,' he said.

The woman from Tourist Information laid a neat square of white handkerchief over John Cheery's mouth, left an imprint of lipstick as she blew through it. Billy was surprised to see the old man's stomach inflate. He scratched his scalp through his sunhat, concentrated his gaze on Melanie as she depressed the man's chest. Her action was gentle and rolling and she made the barest impression. There ought to be more give, Billy thought, but he kept his distance, felt the first onlookers gathering behind him. The old lady bent towards Melanie. 'Keep it going,' she encouraged her, 'you're doing fine, just fine.' Then to the woman, 'I think you should hold his nose. Hold it closed.' Billy watched the swell of Melanie's breasts as she pumped, the smooth contour of the bulge in her dress. Her arms were straight and thin, locked at the elbow, a faint down of fair hair tracing their outline. Sometimes they had pressed down on him like that.

With the end of season they would make their first home in the old town. Like the trailer on which Billy worked, the cottage belonged to Melanie's parents, a holiday conversion tucked away from the sun. Shells and sea urchins hung above the kitchenette in a fishing net. Through a porthole window at the rear it was possible to catch a glimmer of ocean. On Saturday mornings for three summers Melanie had gone there to tidy after the visitors, and always began in the bedroom, expectant and hopeful, like the tourists who combed the shoreline every evening at low tide, gathering leavings she would later discard. In the autumn it would be Billy who cleaned out the rooms. And whilst he painted the ceilings and doors, pinned pictures to the walls, disinfected the worktops and corners, Melanie would be lying upstairs in their bedroom, practising her breathing. Outside the fog would smell of the sea, and when her labour began, early and unexpected, Billy would run down the hill in his slippers, clutching a handful of coins for the telephone.

There were many noises which might have been the ambulance – horns sounding on the busy seafront road, the reversing beep of buses, the rush of the waves – and each time he heard something Billy felt as if waking from sleep, a brief moment's alertness before he sank again into numbness. Behind him a voice murmured, 'It only has to come down the road. It would've been quicker on the bus.' And looking round he noticed the bearded man with his camera, not filming now but watching intently, absorbing every detail. Beyond the crowd there was sunshine. The mini-buses continued to arrive and depart, depositing the last tourists from the fishing villages, collecting mothers and children for the housing estates. A few rucksacks and shopping bags had been left unguarded at the bus-bays, and as the onlookers slowly multiplied the interior of the bus-shelter became darker and quieter. Billy wondered about the man's name, if he had any family, any children, but he watched Melanie and said nothing, felt the distance slowly widening between them.

'Swap?' said the woman from Tourist Information, and Melanie released herself from John Cheery's chest, slumped back on her haunches. She closed her eyes and dropped her shoulders, felt the sweat on her forehead, the dampness in her dress at her sides. Her heart pulsed in her ears, she could hear the sea and the old lady speaking beside her. 'Deep breaths now, deep breaths, you're almost there.' Wearily Melanie bent to add her own lipstick to the square of white handkerchief. She had not been aware of the gathering strangers, the dimming light and the absence of air. But as she lifted her face now she began to feel her confinement. She tried to inhale. The old man was dead, she was sure. And she hadn't enough breath to share. She glanced around for Billy and saw him standing amongst strangers. His sunhat was lopsided. She felt herself tilting also and reached a pale hand towards him.

'I'm here,' he said then, and she was weeping, falling against him.

When the crowd thinned, stepped backwards, there was a smell of salt air and diesel, and Billy heard a voice say, 'She's a lovely looking girl.' He pressed his nose to the back of Melanie's head, and whispered, 'Well done,' so quiet she would not hear him. The bearded man stepped forward and held John Cheery's wrist. His wife stood outside, tracing a finger on the timetable. The faces of the spectators were dark against the blue sky, and some shook their heads when the uniformed woman fished inside the old man's jacket. She said, 'I suppose he has a name,' and carefully pulled out his wallet. Then Billy glimpsed the approaching ambulance. It was descending the hill from the town, appearing and disappearing through the stacked green of the trees. 'Here it comes now,' he mumbled. And louder, 'This is the ambulance now. It's coming!' But it was heading in the wrong direction, following a slip road to the rail station. He got to his feet and started to run, heard Melanie's voice shouting behind him. Outside in the car park a breeze lifted his hat from his head, and for a moment he faltered, but didn't return to retrieve it.

'Does she do anything for you?' the men had asked in the pub, and John Cheery told them, 'I used to play with her.' His teeth clicked and he rubbed at the side of his chin, watching their faces. 'She let me,' he said. 'She let me play with her. Not straight off. It was the girls, she needed the cash. She used to fetch my shopping – I gave her my wallet and sent her out to the shops. But that cost me, the change was never right, so I stopped it. She took my washing instead. Still does. I paid her to do it, pocket money, and I said she could do the ironing, but she burnt my shirts. No good.' He shook his head, spoke quietly. 'This was early on, after the wife died. I was bad then, poorly, but she helped me.' The men nodded, and he said, 'Later she came round nights and she let me touch her. But I couldn't stay hard. He'd go all soft on me. I got close to it once, but I couldn't satisfy her – old man like me. She needed a younger man. I asked her to marry me once, I told her she'd make a good wife if she tried. But she laughed.' He grinned, raised his last glass to his lips. 'She laughed,' he said.

The first paramedic loosened the valve on an oxygen cylinder. 'So what do we know about him?' he asked. And the woman from Tourist Information said, 'His name is John Cheery.'

The large-handled electrodes sent a pulse through John Cheery's body that caused him to jerk from the ground. The sound was a hollow thwack like a slap, and the paramedics repeated this at intervals, the old lady standing over them, patiently waiting. In one hand she held her new broom, in the other John Cheery's cap as if it were a bowl, his teeth and spectacles and wallet inside. Billy and Melanie watched from the sea wall. The yellow plastic tape whirred on the sea breeze behind them. Melanie's dress flapped at her knees. Billy moved close against her, his chest to her back, and cupped his hands under her belly. 'Shall we go down to the rocks?' he whispered, and she shook her head. She pressed against him, guided his hands upwards, and then they felt the first kick, a tiny pulse under his palms. Melanie smiled. She looked to the ambulance, and saw the sheet being pulled across the dead man's face, heard the tide pulling away from the shore. Billy gazed out past the harbour. A ferry glinted in the sunshine. It was rounding the headland, growing out of the distance towards them.

Killing a Pig

Deirdre Madden

∫

Killing a Pig

One morning in January, a little convoy left S. Giorgio for the mountains. Franca packed her mother-in-law and Davide into the car, together with four bottles of *spumante* and some cakes and chocolates she had taken from the shop, including a four-kilo cake, wrapped in gold foil and tied with a red ribbon, that looked like a gift-wrapped bomb. Lucia and Ted came in my car, and shortly after a quarter to eight, we all set off.

Almost as soon as we left the village, by the high back road, instead of the route I usually took to the lower village and the plain, we were into territory where tourists rarely ventured. It was a strange phenomenon, for every year thousands of people visited S. Giorgio, but invariably went back down the hill afterwards, as if there were a line on the road at the back of the town, beyond which they were forbidden to go. The real reason that they didn't go there was because the guidebooks didn't tell them to. Perhaps in any case they wouldn't have liked the scenery, for there was a harshness up in the mountains which there was not in the softer, lower hills, with their olives and vines and ploughed fields, with the gentle open contours of the land. Here, the valleys were high and closed, the roads steep and twisted. We passed outcrops of friable white rock, from which grew stunted trees and bushes. Sometimes the land had fallen away, and the whole root system of the tree could be seen. For all its harshness, I thought it had a real beauty of its own, unlike the soft, easy loveliness of the lower land, with its muted colours. Not least of the mountain's attractions was the view it afforded. Looking back, we could see S. Giorgio now far below us. From that angle you couldn't see the new town, just the back of the village, neatly walled, and pale in the clear light of the morning. It looked as it must have done so long ago, at the time when town planning was an innate skill, when people still lived on a human scale, and did not build sprawling, malfunctioning towns. There was a light mist on the floor of the valley, so we could see only faintly the sprawling glitter of the towns down on the plain, but off in the distance was clearly visible the chain of blue mountains that stretched away to the south.

I had been up here many times before, but it was Ted's first visit, and he was enthusiastic, much to Lucia's amusement, who thought it the dullest place in the world, and couldn't imagine what anybody could see in it. We drove through a tiny village, completely closed and shuttered up. 'Nobody stirring there today,' Ted said. 'That's because there is nobody there,' Lucia said. 'Very few people live up here now. When Mama was growing up there were lots of villages and isolated farms, but now there's hardly anybody. They got smart,' she laughed, 'and moved down the hill, the way Mama did when she got married.' I had heard before that the population hadn't grown much for twenty years, but had simply relocated, with people moving down the hill to work in shops and factories and offices. Now the hills were empty, but for a few remaining farmers, such as Franca's brother, whom we were on our way to visit, and a sprinkling of foreigners, who bought old farmhouses and restored them, grew lavender and kept bees and did not mix with the locals.

'I think this is great,' Ted said. 'I think I'd like to live here. Maybe I'll buy a house and fix it up. What do you say, Lucia? What about that one there – that would be nice, wouldn't it?' She almost fell off her seat laughing. He was pointing at a place that was almost a complete ruin. 'He's crazy, your boyfriend, Aisling.'

I didn't join in the laughter. Lucia had obviously developed a real adolescent crush on Ted, which was normal, if you think about it, as she was an adolescent. I couldn't reason that way at the time, and I was irritated by the way she was flirting and giggling with him, and how he was teasing her. I had looked forward so much to this day out, but already I was aware of a black mood closing in around me. The silent huff I sank into was a waste of energy, for neither Ted nor Lucia took any notice of it, and went on talking.

'You think I'm kidding?' Ted said, trying to keep a straight face. 'I think it would be great. Wouldn't you like to marry a farmer and live up here, have kids, keep hens, stuff like that?'

'You really are crazy,' Lucia said. 'Me? Marry a *contadino*? Nowadays, nobody wants to marry them, don't you know that? They have a marriage bureau in Perugia, and almost all of the men on their books are farmers. Women come up from the south, from Calabria and Sicily and marry them. Nobody here wants them.'

'So it's the bright lights for you then. I suppose you'll be off to Rome as soon as you're eighteen.'

'I didn't say that,' Lucia interjected quickly, suddenly serious. '*Sto bene qui*. I like it here. I like it at home with Mama and Papa. They do that in other countries, go away, but I don't want to do it. When Aisling's not here, I'll get married and move upstairs. If you're happy and you have everything you want in a place, why would you ever go away?'

'Why indeed,' I thought grimly. 'Why bother to live your life when you can let not just your parents, but the whole of society live it for you?'

After a time, the mountains closed in, so that we could no longer see down to the plain. We arrived at the farm almost an hour after we left S. Giorgio. Franca and Davide had arrived just moments before, and were unloading the car. The door of the farmhouse was open, and we all went in. The kitchen was almost empty. Patrizia, Franca's sister-in-law, was making pasta, the wooden board before her already piled with yellow ribbons of tagliatelli. Franca's mother, an old woman in black, was sitting on a low stool beside a blazing wood fire. When we greeted her, she looked as blankly at Davide, her son-in-law, as she did at Ted, a complete stranger. Patrizia was delighted to see everybody again.

'Where are the others?' Franca asked, as Davide carried in the wine and cakes. 'Michele's on the hill, with the second pig,' Patrizia replied. 'The others are down in the barn with the pig that was killed yesterday.'

'We'll go see Michele first.' We went out of the house with Franca, and followed her along a narrow path which wound behind a gentle rise. As we got nearer we could hear a light clink-clink-clink, clear in the air, like a bell being struck. And when we went round the corner and saw what was there, suddenly I felt dizzy, sick to my stomach, and then I felt foolish, for what, after all, had I expected to see on such a visit?

A little huddle of people were standing around a dead pig, which was hanging by its back legs from chains attached to a strong wooden post. The pig had been half split open, and the people gathered around were in the process of cutting it completely in two. The clink-clink noise was the sound of a hammer and chisel against the bones of the pig's spine. The animal's ears were flopped over its eyes, as if it couldn't bear to look at what was happening. The warm open cavity of the body smoked in the cold air. I was glad that we hadn't got there any earlier. The ground was splashed with blood, and a trio of hefty cats sat under an old broken cart a short distance away, impassively waiting to be fed. Michele and the others were delighted to see us, and the pig was ignored for a few moments while a full round of greetings and introductions took place. Michele offered his wrist to be shaken, because his hands were covered with blood. He looked at me very intently, and I felt uncomfortable. Franca slapped the side of the pig admiringly, and it swung lugubriously on its chains. Michele got back to work with his chisel, and Ted took some photos of the pig, which confirmed Lucia's belief that he was crazy.

'The others are down in the barn, you can go and see them if you want,' Michele said, but Grazia, one of the women who had been holding the pig steady, interjected. 'Don't go just yet. Let's see if the wedding has started.' Grazia was huddled up in heavy clothes and boots. Her crude apron was covered in blood. She led us to the edge of the rise, and looking down, in a lower valley far below us, we could see a church with a group of people standing outside. 'I've been watching them all morning,' Grazia said. 'Look, here they are now.' A car pulled up and a figure in white got out.

'It's Paola Calzolari, do you remember her, Franca? She went to live in Frascati and married a man there, but it didn't work out. They had a little daughter, and got divorced three years ago. Now she's living with another man, and she's pregnant again, and this time she wants to do it in church. I suppose she hopes it'll be the last time. Her little girl's to be an attendant. Here she is.'

The figure in white was followed by a child in pink. Some people who had been waiting gathered around them, and they stood for a short while talking. Then they all disappeared into the church, and from where we were, it was as neat and as swift as a clockwork toy. 'Good luck to them, anyway,' Grazia said. She wiped her hands on her apron.

Franca said, 'I always tell Lucia, when the time comes for you to get married, don't settle for a civil service. Go to church, because you're going to need all the help you can get.' They all laughed, and as we turned away, she added, 'Anyway, whatever gets you through your life, grab at it, that's what I always say.'

We turned back to where the pig was hanging. It was so solid, so dead, the cold dead fact of the pig's body hanging there was a shock to me, and it remained in my mind throughout the day.

We left the hill, and the steady clink-clink of metal and bone followed us, as we went down to a shed at the side of the house. When Franca opened the door there was a mixed confusion of voices, noise and light, of greeting and introduction, but above all, the two things that struck me were, first, the coldness of the shed, and second, the stench of blood which had been evident up on the hill, but was much stronger here. I recognized some of the people, and I was introduced to the butcher who had been hired for the day, and was there to oversee the correct preparation of the meat. With a long slender knife he was shaping the fat at the edge of a pig's leg into the familiar shape of a ham, which would then be salted and hung to dry in a cold place. The protruding knob of bone was glossy and white.

Ted and I spent the morning in the shed. After the hams were completed, piles of chops were cut, some set aside for lunch that day, some wrapped for the freezer. Meat was prepared to make salami and sausages. They put a lot of pepper in some of the salami, and then tied a red ribbon to the string around it, so that they could tell it from other salami, the ones that were not *piccante*. For the sausages, the butcher clamped a mincer to the table, and produced a jar of damp grey intestines, which looked like overwashed elastic. A long length of intestine was fitted over the end of the mincer, and by a combination of gently pressing on the meat in the hopper and coaxing along the rapidly filling intestine, a long meaty cord appeared, which the butcher deftly twisted into links. Ted took a turn with the mincer, but he wasn't very good at it, and almost minced his fingers, so he let the butcher take over again.

Around noon, Lucia and I went up to the kitchen, taking with us a pile of sausages and chops to be cooked for lunch. Patrizia and Lucia started to set the table for fifteen people. Franca's mother was still on the little stool, huddled over the fire. She had the saddest face I've ever seen. 'I'm cold,' she said to me. 'I'm always cold. I sit by the fire all day, and no matter what I do, I can never get warm. See,' and she drew her hands away from the blaze and touched my face. She was as cold as marble. It was all I could do not to let her see how repulsed I felt. It was like talking to and being touched by a person who was already dead, and whom the family had simply neglected to bury.

Franca came over and started to poke vigorously at the fire, stoking it up at the back, and raking out the burning embers at the front, where the meat was to be cooked. She opened a wooden chest where the firewood was stored, and took out a huge log. The fire sparked and crackled when she put it on, and flames licked quickly up the side of it. Franca beamed with delight. 'Nothing like a good fire, is there? It's company. I could sit and look at a blaze like that from morning to night. Do you know the old saying, Aisling – "A hearth without a log is like a man without a prick."'

Franca's mother looked confused. 'What's the proper name for it, Franca? I don't remember. The Italian name for the man's thing.'

'Penis.'

'And the woman's thing?'

'Vagina.'

Franca smiled. 'Poor Mama. She only remembers the dialect

words for them. They've got a million names in dialect. Probably never needed the Italian words. Not that words matter that much, I suppose.' She lifted a grid-iron down from a hook above the fire, opened it, and began to neatly arrange pork chops on it as she went on talking. 'Things aren't the way they were in Mama's time. They aren't even the way they were in my time, and thank God or whoever for it, that's what I say. All that stuff they told us when I was growing up, to frighten the hell out of us, and it did, too. Sometimes it still puts me off. Sometimes I still feel guilty, even now. Can you believe that? It won't be like that for Lucia. I'd rather she got into the odd scrape, so long as she enjoys herself, so long as she's happy.'

Franca closed the grid-iron, and set it carefully over the raked-out glowing wood embers. Then she took down another grid-iron, and began to prepare the sausages in the same way.

We went on getting ready for lunch – setting out glasses, fetching wine from the cellar, dressing salad, slicing up bread. At about ten to one, Patrizia put the pasta on to cook, and Lucia was sent to call in the workers.

What with the early start, the cold weather and the hard work, everybody was hungry, and more than did justice to the meal, which was a huge affair. One thing that annoyed me was that I didn't get to sit beside Ted. Michele slipped in beside me and throughout the meal kept plying me with more food than I could possibly eat. He also topped up my glass constantly, so that I couldn't keep track of how much I was drinking. I didn't like it that he was so attentive to me, and I kept trying to catch Ted's eye. For a long time he didn't notice me, because he was so busy laughing and eating and talking, and when at last he did look my way he was so delighted with the lunch and life in general that he didn't seem to notice that anything was amiss. I was vexed and angry.

The meal went on and on, as if lunch itself was reluctant to end, trailing off almost two hours later into grace-notes of ice-cream, *spumante*, cheese, chocolates, coffee and liqueurs.

Afterwards, most of the people went back out to work, while Lucia and I helped clear up after the meal. When that was done, Franca called me into the parlour to look at some photographs on the wall. She showed me a picture of her grandmother, her mother's mother, a voluptuous woman with soft eyes. 'Nonna was so big,' Franca said fondly. 'I remember when I was little and she hugged me, I'd almost disappear into her. She had the biggest chest I've ever seen on a woman: each one was like a head.'

When I went back to the shed, Grazia was standing by a bucket which contained the ears and snout of the pig. She lifted them out in turn, and casually scorched the bristles from them with a small blow torch, before throwing them back in the bucket again. Michele was cleaning the table. He poured a glass of white wine over it, which was rubbed well into the grain of the wood before they began to prepare the lard, kneading it and mixing it, and putting it in glass jars to be stored.

By late afternoon, the job was done. All the meat had been butchered, the last links twisted into sausages, all the ribs, the cheeks, the ears: everything had been dealt with. Everyone was satisfied, not least the cats, who had been given the fatty scraps from the lunch. The butcher said that he would be back the following day, to deal with the second pig.

When dusk had fallen, Michele and Patrizia took Ted and me on a tour of the farm. Ted had been in Italy for years, but it was the first time he had been on an Italian farm, and I suspected it was a long time since he had been on a farm anywhere. When Patrizia opened the byre door, and we went in, the warm fug of the animals was strong and comforting after the cold air outside. The six pale cattle who were generating this heat staggered nervously to their feet and stared at us. Back outside again we saw pens full of geese, rabbits, ducks and chickens, and a flock of long-legged Biblical sheep. The sounds and smells of the farmyard reminded me, not always pleasantly, of growing up on my father's farm in Ireland.

We went into another outhouse, where some of the pork from the day's work was already in store. Apart from the hams and salamis suspended from the beams there were odd-looking pieces of offal, hanging from hooks. I didn't know which bits they were, and I didn't ask. There were buckets full of blood, and the same solid sweet stench which there had been all morning in the shed where the butchering had taken place. Michele reached up to the rafters and lifted down a bunch of grapes which had been hung there months earlier to dry. He offered them to us to taste, and beyond the initial sharpness there was a memory of sweetness locked in the heart of them, as though the sun of the past summer was still contained in these winter grapes.

Then Michele wanted to show us the house too, and so we trooped from one dim, tiny room to another. I felt increasingly nervous. Michele kept standing too close to me, and was staring at me intently all the time. As at lunch, I couldn't understand why Ted and Patrizia didn't notice this. We saw a gun hanging over a wide bed in a room that smelt of sweat. I longed to get back to the warm brightness of the big kitchen, away from these claustrophobic rooms that looked somehow familiar to me, as if I had seen them in a dream. I turned around and saw with horror that Ted and Patrizia weren't there. I could hear them talking and laughing in the hallway, where they had lingered to look at a picture. I was alone with Michele. I turned back. His face was inches from mine.

I don't remember what happened next, which is probably just as well. They must have carried me out of the house, for I remember coming to on the front step. I cried and clung to Ted, and I'll never forget how embarrassed everyone was, particularly me, as the initial shock began to wear off. Everyone was keen to explain it away, I was tired, I was *nervosa*, I was so sensitive that all that blood and offal had been more than I could take.

A second meal had been prepared in the kitchen, not as large as the first, but still more than enough. This time Michele sat beside Patrizia, and I was left in peace to pick at a bit of cold meat and some salad. The evening trailed on, because in Italy people find it hard to say goodbye, and so they extend the day for as long as is possible. After dinner, somebody pulled out a pack of cards. I sat by the fire with Franca while Ted tried to learn the rules of some complicated four-hand game, but even the cards, with their suits of sticks and cups, were strange to him. He partnered Lucia, and she pretended to be furious as he lost trick after trick on them, until they eventually lost the game.

When the time did come for us to leave, it was a slow parting because there were so many of us, and everybody had to be said goodbye to individually. They told us to come again, to come back at Easter when the hams we had seen being prepared that day would be ready to eat. Ted wanted to drive my car back but I insisted that it would be no problem for me, and a sleepy Lucia directed us down the twists and bends of the road, back to S. Giorgio.

A Regular Thing

Lynne Bryan

Lynne Bryan was born in Leicester in 1961 and now lives with her partner and daughter in Norwich. Her writing has already appeared in various anthologies and her collection of short stories, ENVY AT THE CHEESE HANDOUT, was published by Faber and Faber in 1995. She is now at work on her first novel.

A Regular Thing

I'm confused. For years I hoped Emily would stop charging me. Now she has I find I don't want it. I feel the bottom has dropped out of my life. I feel threatened, insecure.

I'm thirty-six. I first met Emily when I was twenty-nine. At Astley Central Library.

I started work in the library at sixteen. A natural step: I've always been fond of books and during school days was nicknamed SS (Studious Steven). But I'm not intellectual. Most books are beyond me. Like the books Emily reads on advanced economics.

I'm just comforted by books. Well-thumbed books with cheesy pages and broken spines. Like the paperbacks in the Romance section. At sixteen I kept away from Romance, thought it sissy. Now I'm Section Head.

I met Emily two months into my promotion. I was rummaging behind the Loans Counter for the most recent edition of the *Romance Writers' Quarterly* when I heard coughing. The coughing was accompanied by a voice. Such a voice, husky but efficient. 'Excuse me,' it said. 'But I'm in a rush. Can you stamp my books now?'

Used to disappointments I expected the voice to belong to an elderly spinster with a smoker's larynx. So I was abrupt. 'Sorry,' I said. 'I don't work the Loans Counter. I'll get Miss Pedi to deal with you. MISS PEDI!'

Then I saw Emily. My eyes worked upwards from her girlie breasts to her face with its cold eyes, its bob of oily hair. My heart somersaulted and my penis began to stiffen. I rubbed it casually against the Loans Counter.

'Hello,' said Emily. 'I'm called Emily.'

'Steven,' I replied.

'Steven,' she said. 'Nice name. Before Miss Pedi comes can I ask a question?'

I nodded, flushed. Something told me the question wouldn't be about books.

I'm not usually daring. I tend to stand back, watch others walk into the Lions' Den. But Emily bewitched me. She has tremendous power. She knows how to make a coward brave.

When we met at the fountain she looked like a lonely man's dream: tight black jumper, skirt, and those little lace-up booties with pointy heels made from shiny plastic. I felt ill-equipped. 'I haven't much money,' I said. I clutched my thin wallet; even as Section Head I earn less than my father who sweeps for Astley Precision Tools. 'I can stretch to a Chinese and a couple of beers.'

Emily smiled, an amazing smile, lips curling back to show their fleshy pink underside. 'What do we want with a Chinese?' she said. 'Let's make our own entertainment.'

Emily took me to her home, a flat above a babywear shop. A small flat with one main room painted white. Two archways led from this room. Through one archway was a kitchen; through the other, the bathroom. Swinging bead curtains hung from each archway. They were identical, depicting a cinema usherette wearing a skimpy pink bunny outfit. Around the usherette's neck hung a tray. The tray rested on her large breasts. She smiled a big smile, and a bubble led from the smile. 'Peanuts, Sir?' she asked.

I didn't know what to make of the flat. It was so sparse. The bead curtains provided the only real decoration and they seemed deliberately over the top. Like they'd been chosen as a statement. But I couldn't work out the statement. They hung there, shimmering, threatening. And instead of asking Emily about them, I turned to her bookcase.

The bookcase ran between the curtains. It was huge. Filled with books. For a while, I examined the books. They were all on finance. 'What's wrong, Steven?' asked Emily. She slid a thin arm round my shoulders.

'There's not a novel in sight,' I said.

'Or a book about women's troubles,' she laughed. 'I'm a practical girl. I'm into what makes the world go round.'

'Money,' I said.

'And sex.' She took my hand and led me to the only other piece of furniture in the room – her bed.

I'd dated before Emily. Mostly nice girls with soft bodies and big eyes. Willing girls. But unadventurous. No costumes. No games. No dirty talk. No slapping, kicking, punching, or spitting. Emily sat astride me, bending her arms behind her back, making her small breasts point forward like individual jellies, and showed me what I'd been missing. She made me feel like a king, a conqueror. 'Emily,' I said. 'That was wonderful.'

Afterwards, I thought we'd have a drink, swap stories, relax with each other, feel our way. But no. She started talking business. 'That one was for free,' she said. 'Charging first time is counter-productive. You'll not come back for more. Not unless you're desperate. And I don't want you if you're desperate.'

I don't consider myself an idiot. But perhaps I am. Perhaps Emily saw me coming. Sometimes I check myself in the mirror, to see if it's written over my face. But there are no clues. Only my spectacles, my thin mouth, my blondish hair, my bad skin stare back.

'But Emily,' I protested. She placed a finger on my lips and hushed me.

'Don't knock it,' she said. 'It's a good deal.'

My body was hungry for Emily so I began to see her on a regular basis, once a week, twenty pounds a time. But I wasn't swept along. Mentally I kept distant, tried to sort out the situation. I took to spying on her.

Early mornings, library lunch times, dinner times and most evenings I waited outside her flat to catch her at it. But no men in dirty rainmacs, no young boys anxious to lose their virginity, only a small woman dressed in a suit and carrying a briefcase.

'So Emily, you're not a prostitute?' I asked, casually as I could.

She lay on her bed, looking wonderful: her top half naked, her legs covered with a wrap of black silk.

'No,' she said in her husky voice. 'I'm your lover.'

'But then why do you charge me?'

Emily explained. She said men had treated her badly. They had taken her love and used it against her. So now she charged. Because charging meant she was in control, charging meant she was safe. She spoke matter of factly, like she was reading a shopping list. But I believed her. It made sense to me.

The confidence strengthened our relationship. We began to see more of each other, took the test, and stopped using condoms, and though Emily continued to ask for money I felt encouraged, hopeful. I imagined a day when we'd be like any normal couple, exchanging our love freely.

After a year we bought a flat together and I took Emily to meet my parents. They hated her. On sight. They wouldn't admit to it. They were polite. They asked her about her job, gave her ham and salad sandwiches, iced fancies and a cup of weak tea. But you could see it in their eyes. My mother looked Emily up and down. As she took in Emily's thigh boots, hot pants, and lycra top, her face was blank, her pupils marked with distaste. She actually said, 'A word in your ear, Steven. Is this the right kind of girl for you? Isn't she a bit unclean?'

I replied, 'I love her, Mother. We get on well together.'

Then I began to feel less positive. There were days when I'd look at our relationship and see nothing. Emily and I would meet after work, go out for a meal or to the pictures, return home, and yet still seem separate. I knew it wasn't my fault. I offered myself; told her my history, my likes and dislikes, my longings. But Emily was so closed, only gave out at night when we touched. And she spoilt that by charging.

At one point I nearly cracked. Her charges rose above the rate of inflation. They began to cripple me. And I had to take an extra job, collecting pools monies from Astley's nastiest estate – Craigheath. It wasn't a pleasant job. I had a couple of dangerous customers who once got me in a back alley. They beat me. They took off my glasses, stood me against a wall, and pushed ring-covered hands into my face. 'Poor poor Steven,' cooed Emily when I returned home.

'You could stop it, you know,' I said to her as she dabbed a cotton wool ball over my cheeks, nose, ears. The ball was soaked in Dettol. It stung. To take my mind off the pain I concentrated on Emily's breasts which moved across my chest, tickling.

'How can I stop it?' she asked, innocent. 'Should I take up karate, go out for revenge?'

I squeezed her hand. The Dettol trickled brown down her skinny wrist. 'Getting ready to thump me now, are you?' she said. Her eyes were strangely bright.

I went to the doctor. I told Emily it was because my wounds were infected. It wasn't a total untruth. Blue-green pus lined a cut which ran across my cheek.

I chose a locum. I didn't want to confess to my regular, who'd seen me grow, who'd watched my testicles drop. The locum traced her gentle finger along the cut, then asked me what I'd really come for. 'Sexual problems?' she asked.

'Sort of,' I confided.

The locum listened carefully. She nodded her head, made notes. 'I think you should approach the mother,' she advised. 'You shouldn't blame the mother, mothers get blamed for too many things. But I think you should have a chat. Mothers can be very helpful.'

Emily's mother dresses like a man. She favours double breasted suits made from merino. Beneath which she wears a white shirt, and a yellow or black tie. She sports cufflinks, Argyle socks, and brogues. Her hair is cut to the scalp; her face free of make-up.

Emily introduced us at the flat-warming. I recognized her immediately. 'You used to visit Emily at her old place,' I said. 'Tuesdays and Thursdays. I saw you.'

'Yes,' said Emily's mother. 'I know all about your spying.'

I hated her then. Now not at all. She speaks her mind, and, beneath the macho stuff, has a heart. Emily loves her too. The flat seems to lighten when she's around. There's more laughter, and Emily opens up, tells stories I've never heard before.

It took me a while to confide in Emily's mother. I was reticent because I thought she didn't like men. I imagined her as a woman's woman. Of course I couldn't ignore the evidence. But somehow I thought of Emily as a one-night stand: Emily's mother lying back and taking it because she wanted a child. But no.

Emily's mother is hetero through and through. 'She's a real fire-cracker,' my boss, Mr Brudly, disclosed. 'A rare and dangerous woman. Our affair lasted five months.'

'Yes,' said Emily's mother when I faced her. 'It ended badly. I told him it was over whilst waiting my turn at the Outpatients.'

Then I learnt that Emily's mother knew about her daughter. About how she charged me. 'Emily has told me all,' she said. 'But there's little I can do. My daughter's headstrong, opinionated. She'll always approach life her own way. You could try to make her jealous. But that's a crude device. I suggest if you love her, then just persevere.'

'But,' I said, lifting my head from her fly-buttoned lap. 'But I don't even know if she cares for me. She's so controlled.'

Six months ago, Emily made the spare room into an office. She left her job as financial adviser for Dryson, Dryson and Sons to go it alone. I was worried. For a while I thought it'd cost me more for sex. Extra revenue to cover loss of earnings, or to fund the computer, desk, headed notepaper, filing cabinets, photocopier, and electronic pencil sharpener. But she didn't seem to need it. Emily poached clients from her old firm. She ran an advertising campaign which promised personal service; a promise headlined beneath a profile shot of Emily looking her best. Soon her desk diary was full and she was having to turn away clients.

She now has a host of regulars. Mostly men, though some are women. The women power-dress and carry briefcases. They snub me. The men wink.

I was jealous of the men. I took a fortnight off work to check Emily was giving them financial advice and nothing else. One evening she came to me and said, 'This business is kosher, Steven. I only want to sleep with you.'

That night Emily and I had our first real row. From opposite sides of the bedroom we slung insults, grievances. Emily said I was a typical chauvinist. I told her she was a typical whore. We made our demands: Emily wanting to be loved for herself, me wanting free sex.

That argument may have been behind Emily's change of mind. That and my decision to become celibate. Though I still desired her, I turned my back on her.

Eventually she confronted me, complained that her incomings from our sex were at an all time low. 'Why, Steven?' she asked.

She looked confused when I explained. 'This isn't normal, Emily,' I said. 'My paying you has to stop. It puts a barrier between us. I've lived with you for years and still don't know what you're thinking. Since meeting you I've been on an emotional roller-coaster. I'm tired out.'

She watched me closely. Her cold blue eyes unsympathetic, searching. I began to cry. I lifted my hand to my face, and that was when she changed. The eyes stayed the same cold blue, but her chin, her cheeks, her mouth lost their hard edge. She wasn't my Emily.

A week later she handed me a letter to read on my way to work. I slid it in my jacket pocket, fearful of the white envelope, the bold 'STEVEN' on the front.

I entered Elder Park, found a bench by the pond. The sun shone, gardeners raked stray twigs and Coke cans from the murky water, the boat-keeper untied the paddle boats. I listened to the sound of rope dragging across wood. Then I opened the letter.

At first I couldn't read the writing. It seemed to blur, and inside I felt sick, imagined Emily was saying goodbye. When I could focus I was surprised to see her words stretched across the page, gigantic, urgent, saying something very different. *'Dear Steven, I've decided to stop charging you. It doesn't make sense. We've been together for so long. Let's start afresh. Emily.'*

I read the letter three times. Each time I felt more elated, felt my future advancing – hopeful, warm, blessed.

Now I'm not so sure.

Emily hasn't charged me for a while. In the early days it was glorious. Real pleasure. I found my wallet growing fat. I treated myself to new clothes, bought Emily finance books and sexy underwear. We made love whenever and wherever. The foreplay was exploratory. Our caresses not governed by how much I could afford. And after sex we would open up, reveal our fears, desires. Emily had some terrible tales to tell. A man had once tried to set fire to her, threw a lighted box of matches at her hair. Another man had kept her locked in his room, chained to his bed. I would hug her as she spoke of these things. And she was generous. When I spoke of my past, and my petty difficulties with girls who'd behaved too nicely, she never condemned, never claimed her experiences as more important, more painful. Then she flipped.

I should've seen it coming. Emily is a professional. If she chooses to do something she does it right. She does not cut corners. She began to borrow books from my section of the library. She would devour the slim pink volumes, jot down endless notes on Romance. She would take these notes everywhere with her, consult them when washing, eating.

She wears rose print dresses now. Puts a large silk ribbon in her hair to soften it. She's talking of selling her business. She wants me to be the breadwinner, while she stays at home. She wants to get married. She wants to have children. She's become submissive, her conversation punctuated with phrases like 'Whatever you think, darling', her love-making conventional. She's lost her cold cold gaze.

Last night, I telephoned her mother. 'Please do something,' I begged. 'I can't stand this. It's torture.'

Emily's mother laughed. 'I've told you before, Steven, I have no control over my daughter. She's stubborn. Besides why are you complaining? Isn't she giving you what you've always wanted?'

I was silent.

'Well, isn't she?' pushed Emily's mother.

'I suppose,' I replied. 'I really don't know.'

This morning I wake, raise myself on an elbow, watch Emily as she sleeps. She is very beautiful. Despite the little girl ribbon. Despite the flannelette nightie. I touch her upon the shoulder, brush a hair from her mouth.

I am so confused. I wonder whether I should've let things be, not forced her to change. I have no answer. I feel like the floor has been taken from under me. That I have nothing solid to stand on. I feel desperate.

Flag Day

Glenn Patterson

∫

Flag Day

In a courtyard, watched over by solidly complacent walls, a man is lying stretched out on a rectangle of grass. The sun shines as one might expect it to on a June afternoon and the man, with his eyes closed and his head resting on his lightly locked hands, appears to be asleep. A breeze, desirable given the heat, rolls and ricochets in the confines of the yard and in time causes a shadow to pass across the man's chest and face. This does not seem to penetrate his repose, nor yet when the breeze at length subsides and the shadow falls once more across him does he show any sign of recognition. But an afternoon in June, or July, is long and the consciousness of a man in sleep rises and wanes like the breezes, which themselves may cool and return ever more insistently, becoming, perhaps, winds. And so it is on this afternoon. The shadow passes and repasses with a random regularity that is eventually difficult to ignore. The man opens his eyes; eyes in the shroud of a shadow. He tilts his head back further in his hands, gazing to the top of the confidently historic building behind him, and sees that the shadow is the shadow of a flag. He allows his head to sink forward again, but does not relax. He lies watching the shadow of the flag as it plays across his body and remembers . . .

. . . A boy, a long time ago, about the age the man would have been then; but maybe not so much like him as he might at first have thought. It is summer there too, June or July, the man cannot be quite sure and the boy perhaps is as yet too young to know. He is old enough, though, to know the smells of the street where he stands; the smell of pasties and soggy, overfried onions; the smell like old underpants of fish in the sun; the smell of potatoes, bad and thrown away, and cabbage leaves, mashed and tramped by the feet that too smell. He catches his breath as he looks about for his mummy. He looks for her, but cannot see her; he sees only the unknown bodies pushing and shoving and stepping aside so as not to stand on him; sees the rotten wooden carts and the cars stacked rickety with cartons, the faces red-wet from screaming and huffing boxes. He strains on tiptoe to see beyond the bobbing hats and scarves and oily slicked hair and there he sees a man on a white horse, staring at him.

The horse, one foot raised, its head down and steaming, is big, big, bigger than any horse he has ever seen. The boy rocks on his heels, trying hard to swallow the lump growing in his throat. The man on the grass stares back through the years at him, stares back through the tears at him; the man on the giant white horse, his sword held pointy and high, just stares at him. The boy, eyes wide with fear, rolls on the balls of his feet, from side to side and round and round, his mouth filling with hot spit as he sways; round and round and from side to side . . . And then he is sicking, there in the street, with the cabbage leaves tramped and mashed and the potatoes bad and thrown away, among the feet that too smell and that now jump back and turn towards him.

'What the . . . Is there nobody minding this wean? Watch where you're standing . . . Missus, hey, missus, is that your wee fella?'

No longer sicking, only coughing and retching, dribbling bitter bile down his chin. And crying now; now that the soft clean hands hold him and the soft clean voice speaks to him.

'Sammy, Sammy, my wee darling, what is it, love? There, let mummy wipe your mouth for you. Did you think I was lost? Did you not know mummy was just behind you getting vegetables, hm?'

Peach powdered peachy down against his face, jerked by gulps; yeralrights crooned in his hot ears as the market people gather round, well-meaning.

'Poor kid's scared stiff.'

'Stop your crying now. What's the matter, sweetheart?'

The boy has no words for it. The man on the grass has, but he is too far away in time and cannot help. The boy has no words, but will try.

'There's a . . . There's a . . .' No words; points. 'There.'

The grown-up heads turn, unsure, eyes that don't yet understand blankly scanning the stalls and trucks, following the direction of the trembling little finger, until as one they light on a nearby gable wall. They look from one to the other, to the boy and back again; from boy to mother, from one to the other, to the gable wall. A low rumbling sound begins to well; it is the murmur of knowing. Faces crease into lopsided smiles, gums show pinky-red as the murmur breaks into gently affectionate, well-meaning, grown-up laughter.

The boy is nonplussed, but his mummy is smiling with the rest and the fear and panic that had gripped him have started to die away. A big man, with a happy lined face, who laughed first and heartiest, steps forward from his barrow, hands outstretched. Feeling safer, the boy allows himself to be swept up in his big man's arms. From years yet to come there is a despairing cry: NO! But the man on the carefully calculated rectangle of grass that isn't his own has lost control and above the hubbub no one can hear; no one takes a blind bit of notice. The strong trader's arms bear the boy aloft, carry him shoulder-high, kind mummy nicely smiling by his side, towards the gable wall.

'See now, d'you see? There's nothing to be afraid of. Sure, it's just a picture. Isn't that right, mummy? Sure, isn't it only a picture?'

'That's all it is, Sammy. It's a lovely one, isn't it?'

Maybe it's because he's not very old, or maybe it's because he's old enough, but the boy does not take this as a question. It *is* a beautiful picture. His mummy tells him; she is smiling; the other people are nodding and smiling. It is a beautiful picture. The boy believes and he smiles too.

'Three cheers for good King Billy,' the people shout. King Billy holds his sword aloft. 'Three cheers for wee Sammy.' They don't shout that, but it feels to the boy as if they do. Another man is reaching something up to him.

'Here, sonny, have yourself a flag to wave.'

The boy takes the tiny Sammysize Union Jack and he waves it and waves it and they all call three more cheers for good King Billy and Remember 1690 and the boy is passed from smiling face to smiling face until he reaches back to the nicely smiling face of his mummy. He is tired from first the sicking and the crying and then the laughing, cheering and waving; he falls asleep in her arms. King Billy stares; Remember 1690. The man on the grass stares at the shadow as it plays across his body; remembers . . .

. . . Sammy's mummy clearing the dinner things off the table. His sister and brothers have been excused to go out and play, but Sammy's not leaving that table until he's finished what's in front of him, or he'll get rickets and never grow up right. Slowly he chews the going-cold food, gazing past the chair where his daddy waits on the tea drawing, into the backyard at the swarms of midges flying in crazy, lost squiggles above the thick, overgrown privet. He chases a last pea around his plate with a chip on the end of his fork, 'Nnnyeeow!' Daddy says the tea's drawn and mummy sits down while he pours it. They hold hands and look at Sammy, who catches up with the pea and squashes it with the chip on the end of his fork. He glances at his mummy and daddy, holding hands as they drink their tea and look at him. Sammy can't figure out their look. He pulls his hands quickly away from his plate and dives them under the tablecloth. He pushes his chest right against the table, sticks his neck forward, closes his eyes as tight as he possibly can and smiles hard, clenching his teeth together where he has teeth and gums where he has only gums. His daddy says something very low under his breath which Sammy doesn't know:

'Inthenamagoocrise.'

'Ssshh, Sam,' his mummy says hurriedly.

'Well,' his daddy goes on anyway, 'I don't know, Maureen, sometimes he's bloody strange.'

'Sa-am! The child.'

'Ach, it doesn't matter half the time what you say. He's away off in a dream world. I'm sure it's not normal.'

Sammy's mummy's voice sounds somehow sad when she speaks again.

'He's just a bit different from the others. Maybe he's bright for his age,' she says, but it's hard to tell whether or not she believes it.

They stop talking and Sammy lets himself go loose, blinking. He has been wondering why he does that, close his eyes and smile so hard it hurts, but now that he has stopped he does not wonder anymore. His mummy and daddy are still watching him; his daddy shakes his head.

'Imagine, making himself sick in front of all those people.'

'But I told you, Sam, the wee fella was scared, he'd never seen a painting like that before. You must admit, that King Billy's a quer size.'

'Three chairs for good King Billy,' says Sammy, in the voice he heard in town.

Daddy stares at him a moment longer; mummy squeezes his hand lightly, her eyes soft and round as she looks into his. Then daddy smiles. He shakes his head again, but this time making a laughing snort sound down his nose. Mummy's eyes are brighter and she squeezes his hand more tightly.

'Three chairs for good King Billy,' Sammy says, laughing. The voice is the borrowed one, but the laugh is his own and it is true.

'That's right, son, you tell 'em,' mummy jokes, her finger tracing a circle in the air. 'Honestly, Sam, if you'd seen his wee face when your man handed him the Union Jack. He waved it and jiggled it for all he was worth.'

Still smiling, daddy, his thighs big and very strong, gets up and comes over to Sammy. He places one hand on the back of his chair and the other on the corner of the table. The skin on his arms is thickly speckled with dirt from his work; shave and brush-up time isn't until later and he only gets to wash his hands before dinner. With his hands so white like that it looks to Sammy as if he's wearing a hairy black undershirt. He thinks maybe one day he will go to work like his daddy in the shipyard and have a hairy black undershirt . . .

'Hey, big fella,' his daddy's voice breaks in, 'd'you not hear me? I'm talking to you.'

Sammy remembers and looks up into his daddy's dust-freckled face.

'What?'

'The word, son, is "pardon".' Sammy corrects himself and his daddy starts again. 'I said, are you going to be your da's wee Orangeman?'

Sammy's mummy says 'Sa-am', but not the way she did earlier. They are happy, Sammy too, though he has a funny picture in his head.

'Daddy,' he asks, 'what's an orangeman?'

His daddy straightens, hitching his trousers and breathing in at the same time, so that he seems to be pulling his tummy up to his chest.

'An Orangeman? Why that's somebody that's in the Orange Order, in a lodge. Mind when I go out on a Thursday night with your grandpa and your Uncle Davie? Well, that's the lodge we go to then. Aye, and you and your brothers can all join when you're older. Won't that be good?'

Sammy forgets to answer, he is thinking.

'And are you an orangeman, mummy?'

'Away you go, you wee daftie. I'm a lady. You have to be a man to be one. That's why they're called OrangeMEN.'

'But what are they for?' he asks her, resting his head sideways on his hand.

Mummy shrugs and laughs.

'No good asking me that, you'll have to ask your daddy there.'

His daddy has his back to him as he returns to his mug of tea. Sammy's eyes follow him until he reaches his chair and is finally facing him once more. His expression is odd; Sammy thinks at first he is angry, but it is not that. Maybe he's hurt Sammy asked his mummy instead of him.

'What are they for, daddy?' he asks again, wanting to know and not wanting his daddy to feel left out.

He still does not seem angry, but he scowls into his tea just the same. He shifts slightly in his chair as he replies:

'Well, it's all different nowadays . . .' He pauses and shifts again in his chair before going on. 'You see . . . well, long ago they were like soldiers' – he does not sound so unsure now ' – they were like soldiers and they helped King Billy fight the Rebels at the Battle of the Boyne and the Siege of Derry. Right?'

Daddy slurps his tea in a that's that way and they sit for a time in silence. But Sammy still has his head to one side.

'Daddy,' he asks, frowning, 'what's "seach"?'

His daddy slaps the table so that Sammy's plate rattles and tea slops out of the teacups onto the tablecloth.

'That's it,' he shouts, angry now.

Mummy jumps to her feet and busies about clearing the last of the dinner things, saying to Sammy isn't it time he was away from the table and gave his mummy and daddy a bit of peace and quiet to finish drinking their tea. Sammy is glad to get down from his seat.

'What do you say?' asks his mummy.

''Scuse me from the table please, that was very nice thank you,' he recites as he walks quickly to the kitchen door, not wanting to look round.

'That's a good boy. Now, take yourself out and play for a wee while before bed.'

Sammy trails his flagstick down the gravel path to the gatehole at the front of his house and looks across the playing fields. The trees at the far side, tall and close, like a fence around the estate, are orangey-red in the sun that is still bright enough to make him squint. He can't see anything clearly, but on the last pitch before the trees he makes out shapes he knows to be those of his brothers and the other big lads playing football. Eusmie's calling:

'Use me, use me, use me, use me, use me . . . Ach, why didn't you use me?'

Beside Sammy, girls laugh, taking off Eusmie's voice.

'Usemeusemeusemeuseme,' they grunt.

The girls are playing skipping, double-enders, with a lamppost, painted red, white and blue every summer, for one of the enders. Sometimes Sammy joins in, but Nessa, his big sister, is there tonight and she doesn't always let him. He leans against the wall beside the gatehole flicking off fuzzy green moss with one end of his flagstick and boring into the wall's cracked and crumbling cement with the other. He stands there, flicking and boring, hoping the girls will see him; but they take no notice. Tired of waiting, he puts his shoulder to the wall and scrapes along it towards them, scuffing his shoes through the chunks of cement that he gouges out as he goes.

'Nessa, Nessa,' his sister's friend Mary shouts, so suddenly even Sammy looks up. 'Nessa, there's your Sammy and you want to see what he's doing.'

Sammy snatches the flagstick away from the wall, but Nessa has spotted him already and is flying towards him, her pigtails swinging, her skirt tucked into the legs of her knickers from skipping.

'Sammy, stop it, will you, or I'll call my da,' she shouts, loud enough, you'd think, to call everybody's da. 'D'you wanna pull that whole flipping wall down on top of you?'

Sammy stands before his sister, arms behind him, back to the wall.

'Anyway, who said you could come out at this time?' she asks, narrowing her eyes.

'My mummy and my daddy. They told me to get outside and play.'

'Well play then and stop hanging around here. Away over to our Billy and Eddie.'

'Not allowed across the fields,' he says, squinting into the blood-orange sun, 'you know that.'

'Tough,' she says, tossing the word over her shoulder with her pigtails as she turns deliberately and swans back to her friends.

'Ach, Nessa, go on,' Maisie appeals on Sammy's behalf.

Nessa grits her teeth and says firmly, 'No, he's too wee.'

But Maisie is one of the few who will answer Nessa back and she does not give in.

'Sure,' she insists, 'we need another ender anyway. And look at him, he's miserable, so he is.'

Sammy isn't miserable, though. He's leaning against the wall, thinking about what was said at dinnertime, barely aware that he is swishing his flag in the little pile of rubble he has made. He doesn't see Nessa shrug her shoulders, nor, at first, does he hear her calling to him.

'Hey, Buck Alec,' she shouts a second time, 'do you wanna play or not? Stop your moping and get over here quick if you do.'

He hears this and shuffles over, shy. The end of the rope is untied from the lamppost and handed to him. Each girl has a spell at the opposite end, but Sammy never moves; Nessa is doing the bossing and she sees to that.

'Right, right, let's have "In-Spin",' she orders when it is her go at ender. She tugs the rope towards her, making Sammy stumble sideways and bump into the red, white and blue lamppost. Nessa pretends not to have noticed and as Sammy is getting himself straight again she begins to turn the rope in time to the song that the skippers have not yet begun to sing. Sammy has to think very hard and use both hands to turn the rope properly at the best of times, and now he's not even sure of the tune. His sister doesn't help him, the way some of the other girls do, going slowly at first and gradually getting faster; but Nessa is a good ender, she holds the rope firm and turns it so strong that soon Sammy can feel what she's hearing, even though he can't hear it himself. He grips the rope and finds it starting to turn at the pace set by Nessa. Maisie steps up, hopping and swaying slightly from side to side as the rope slaps the tarmac to the rhythm of her chant.

'In – spin –'s I – go – in –' call – my – frie – end – Sa – lly – in.'
'In – spin –'s I – go – in –' call – my – frie – end – Ma – ry – in.'

Sammy listens to the slap, slap, slap of the rope; he listens to the words and hears them at the same time as the rope slaps the tarmac:

'In – spin –'s I – go – in . . .'

He watches the girls come and go and come back again, until he forgets to look to see which is which. The rope swirls round and round and round, looping and falling, looping and falling, seeming in the end to turn of its own free will. From across the playing fields the football match sounds out of tune.

'Use me, use me, use me, use me . . .'

'SAMMY!'

Nessa is bawling at him. He remembers the game; he had not forgotten it totally, just forgotten to think about it hard enough; now he remembers. He looks down at his hands; they are still making little circles, but there is nothing in them. Nessa holds her end, but the rest of the rope lies limp on the road. Mary is crumpled beside it, clutching her knee and snuffling.

'What're you trying to do, wee lad, break Mary's neck?' Nessa is flaming, she hates anything to go wrong when she's at the rope. 'See what you've done, you've skinned her whole knee.'

'I'm sorry Nessa, sorry Mary, I didn't mean it, honest I didn't,' Sammy says, scrambling on the road for the rope. He tries to turn it, but it's no use, the song has got confused in his head and anyway, Nessa won't join in. Mary is still snuffling; his sister points her finger at him.

'I knew it,' she tells Sammy as much as Maisie and the others, 'I knew this is what would happen if we let him play.' Then she's shouting at Sammy alone. 'You wee spastic, you let your flipping end drop. Give us back the rope, we were better off with it tied to the lamppost. Why don't you go and play with someone your own age? There's the Kellys at their gate, away and bother them, they're about your level.'

Sammy lets go of the rope, sulking; he is ashamed and hurt.

'Well I never meant it,' he says again as he walks the couple of steps to the wall to pick up his flag from where he dropped it. The skipping has started again already, the rope is tied back onto the lamppost, Nessa is turning it smoothly and with ease.

Sammy looks down the street to the Kellys' house. The two of them are at the gate, watching him. When they see his eyes on them, they back off a bit up the pathway. The Kellys hardly ever come out to play. Eddie, Sammy's oldest brother, says they're fenians; his mummy says they're twins. Fenians is why they have red hair and twins is how come they always wear the same sort of clothes. One of them has his hair over to the left side and that's Emmet, the other's hair is combed to the right and that's Iam. They watch Sammy and Sammy watches them back. He tilts his head to one side and pulls a face; the Kellys laugh. He pulls another and they laugh again; Iam sticks his tongue out. All this time Sammy is walking slowly towards them, wondering why they never play in the street. He thinks it must be to do with them being fenians and twins and both having red hair and always wearing the same sort of clothes. But he doesn't know why it's to do with that. By the time he reaches their gateway he has decided it doesn't matter anyway.

'D'youse two wanna come out and play with me?'

The constant flick, flick, flick of the shadow of the flag begins to irritate the man as he lies on the neat rectangle of grass in the yard that is not his home. It distracts him, intruding upon his memory, or whatever it is he calls what is going on in his mind, so that he can picture more about the skipping than he can about that game. Why does it not stand out more? He searches and searches, eyes shut tight, jaws clamped together in a grimace, but for the life of him he can find nothing more than Cowboys and Indians. But there is something different; isn't there? There has got to be, but oh, the details, the details. He thinks. Something, something, is different, something more than just the words. Flick, flick, flick. He relaxes with a defeated puff of air. Only the words are different; the words and the knot of kids sniggering as Mrs Kelly, unconcerned by her straggly half-curlered hair, apron and slippers, runs from her house towards Sammy, tears already beginning to trickle down her cheeks.

She doesn't drag Sammy, in fact he has to trot to keep up with her, but by the time they reach his front door he too is crying. He doesn't know why; maybe it's because he feels he is supposed to have done wrong; maybe it's just seeing Mrs Kelly, a lady like his mummy, with her face streaked with dirt from where she's tried to wipe away the tears. As she bangs on the door, Mrs Kelly's chin and lips are trembling; she is breathing noisily and her apron, dusty with flour, heaves up and down. Sammy feels funny, calling at his own front door, and when his mummy answers he cries all the harder. The moment she sees him she drops to her knees beside him.

'What is it?' she asks, sounding scared. 'What's happened to you?' Sammy doesn't know either and can't tell her anything. She looks round, worried, at Mrs Kelly. 'Has he hurt himself, Sadie? Did he fall or something?'

The girls have stopped their skipping and have come to the wall at the bottom of the garden; someone has run across the playing fields and told the big lads, who have picked up their ball and their jumpers and are hurrying back towards the houses. The apron, dusty with flour, heaves up and down, up and down.

'Good God, Sadie, what is it?'

Gradually, Mrs Kelly's breathing becomes slower, deeper.

'I'll wait 'til your man's here,' she manages to say at length.

Sammy's mummy, looking more frightened then ever, rises, using the wall of the porch for support.

'Sam, Sam,' she calls into the house, her voice loud but thin. 'Come here quick.'

It is shave and brush-up time and Sammy's daddy bounds down the stairs wearing no shirt, only a vest. He is rubbing shaving cream off his face with a hand towel, but blobs of it cling to the hairs of his ears and nostrils, making his face, already pinky-red with hot purple blotches from the water and the rubbing, look all the more raw. A smear of blood, wiped from a cut on his chin across his cheek to the side of his nose, makes Sammy think of the dirt streaks on Mrs Kelly's face. His daddy seems to take everything in in one glance and speak at the same time.

'Okay, what's the carry on?'

'You may ask her that,' Sammy's mummy says, pointing at Mrs Kelly. 'She came running up here, hammering on the door, trailing our wee fella with her.'

'Ask me?' says Mrs Kelly, her chin starting to tremble like it did before. 'Ask this pack of vultures gathered here staring at me. I'm a laughing stock; me, my two weans and our whole bloody family.'

'For pity's sake, Sadie, catch yourself on . . .' Sammy's daddy begins, but Mrs Kelly cuts him off:

'Don't you dare tell me to catch myself on, Sam Craig. Youse have none of youse in this street the face to come out and say what youse actually think of us. No, instead youse take it out on two wee kids that can't answer back for themselves. Well, I hope youse're bloody proud.' She turns as she says this and faces the crowd, grown-ups now as well as children, milling about in the street. 'I hope youse are bloody proud the lot of youse.'

Mrs Kelly's face crumples into a cry, but the sobs, when they come again, make no noise; she lifts her apron to her eyes, pressing on them with her thumbs. Some of the neighbours start to walk away, muttering, others stay on, watching closely. Sammy's daddy shrugs his shoulders at them and pantomimes his confusion. A bubble of blood swells from the cut on his chin.

'I don't suppose you can tell me what's going on?' he asks Sammy, trying to make a joke. Mrs Kelly lets go her apron and shoots him a glance that says she's glad he finds it all so funny.

'Of course he can, isn't that what I'm saying. I caught this one of yours playing with my twins: King Billy and the Rebels at the Siege of Derry, if you please. And ther's no prizes for guessing who were the Rebels.'

'Ach, Sadie,' says Sammy's mummy in a nervous half-laugh, 'the wee lad's only four. How's he supposed to know different? He can't have meant any harm by it.'

'No harm? No harm with half the street looking on and sneering?' Mrs Kelly's voice is more sad than angry now. 'Listen Maureen, I know the kids round here don't play with my ones; and I know why. But I'd far rather nobody ever bothered with them again in their lives than made fools of them like that. Okay, so your Sammy's only small, but it makes no difference; I'm damned if I'm going to stand idly by while this sort of thing . . . I mean right outside my own front door . . .'

Her voice has been getting quieter and quieter and now it seems just to go away altogether. She shifts her weight from one foot to the other, her eyes darting about as if she's put something down and can't remember where. Sammy's daddy dabs his bloody chin with the hand towel.

'Sadie, I don't know who put him up to it, but I can tell you here and now, he never got it from this house. Ask Maureen.'

He jerks his thumb towards Sammy's mummy. She doesn't really appear to hear these words, but she moves her head in a mixture of a nod and a shake all the same. Mrs Kelly smiles a strange twitch smile, wiping her palms on her apron, dusty with flour, and starts back down the path. As she reaches the gatehole Sammy's mummy calls her name, raising her hand like she wants to say something. But when Mrs Kelly turns briefly she can manage nothing and in the end lowers her hand slowly.

'All right, now, that's it,' Sammy's daddy shouts to the people in the street. 'Are youse going to stand there all night gawking?'

'When Sam Craig speaks . . .' as he is so fond of saying. The remaining onlookers drift away and Sammy is left on the doorstep with his parents.

'You,' daddy tells him. 'Inside.'

Sammy sits on the middle cushion of the big dark red settee, waiting quietly. His mummy and daddy come in from the kitchen where they have been talking since Mrs Kelly went away. They look at him like they did at dinnertime. Now, though, Sammy doesn't give them his smile, he simply sits on the edge of the cushion, his hands limp between his legs. His daddy is still in his vest, but he has cleaned his face properly. As he walks to the armchair opposite the settee he rubs his hand backwards and forwards on his cheek, so that you'd think someone had slapped him. He sighs when he sits, making slow, broad sweeps with his head as he speaks.

'Ah, Sammy, Sammy, Sammy' – he begins quietly, but his voice becomes gradually louder and harder – 'Sammy, Sammy, SAMMY. In front of all them people.' He leans forward suddenly. 'Have you no sense whatsoever?'

Sammy's mummy shushes his daddy and crosses the room to her son. She puts her arm around his shoulder and squeezes it gently. His daddy shakes his head again and falls back into his chair.

'For God's sake, I didn't think when I explained to him about King Billy tonight he'd go straight out and call the only Catholic children in the street Rebels.'

'Stop it Sam,' mummy says. 'I thought we'd agreed in there it wasn't the wee lad's fault. He couldn't have known.'

'What do you mean he couldn't have known? You're the one that's always on about how bright he is. Do you mean to tell me, at four years old, he's the only person in these parts doesn't know the Kellys are Catholics? How could he not know? Sadie Kelly was right – nobody does play with her kids. And, sure, she's never done herself dragging them off to that chapel, practically telling their beads as they walk along.'

'Well perhaps he just didn't realize that Rebels were Catholics.' His mummy's fingers dig into the fleshy part of his upper arm. She asks him another of her notquestions. 'Was that what it was, son?'

'Now that's being plain stupid,' his daddy says in the voice he uses for making fun of someone. 'And stop putting words into his mouth. Listen, he's my son too, don't forget, and it pains me as much to have to say it as it does you to have to accept it, but admit it for once, Maureen, there are times when the wee fella is flipping odd.'

Sammy has not moved since all of this began, except when his mummy's arm around his shoulder pulls him closer to her.

'Take a look at him now,' his daddy goes on. 'It's like I said earlier, he's in a world of his own. I'm serious, I think we should get him seen to.'

'God forgive you, Sam Craig, that's a dreadful thing to say.' Sammy's mummy hugs him to her chest, shaking. She rubs her face in his hair, kissing his head and talking all at the same time. 'There's nothing at all the matter with him. Nothing.'

'Well maybe you're right there; maybe there *is* nothing wrong with him a good hiding wouldn't fix. And by God, Maureen, the way he's headed, one of these days he's going to get a hiding he won't forget in a hurry.'

Mummy lifts him down onto the floor.

'Come on, son, up you get. Bed for you.'

'What about my supper?' Sammy asks her.

'Just you go and get yourself ready and mummy'll bring you up a glass of milk and a biscuit shortly.'

She hugs him again but he does not say goodnight to her, he will see her in a minute. Uneasy, he walks to the chair where his daddy sits, shielding his eyes with his hand like a cap. Sammy touches his arm.

'Daddy, I'm going to bed now.'

He stands for a moment, but his daddy's hand doesn't budge. He turns to his mummy who is staring straight ahead, tightlipped. She waves a hand towards the door without really looking at him. As he goes out into the hall, Sammy says a last 'I'm away', but neither his daddy nor his mummy seem to hear him now and they don't reply.

At the top of the stairs he stops and listens. He hears them shouting and knows the argument has started in good and earnest. He tries to make out the words, but all he can catch is his name. In his room he does not get ready for bed, instead he sits down by the pillow and waits for his supper. The argument goes on. Outside his bedroom window, the sky is dark purple with streaks of red like smeared blood. The other children have started their games again and he hears their voices as if from far away.

'In – spin –'s I – go – in –' call – my – frie – end . . . Use me, use me, use me, use me . . .'

He sits on his bed by the pillow and waits, dangling a stick between his legs, a stick with a tatty bit of cloth on the end of it, dusty with cement. He lets it flick backwards and forwards on his bedroom floor. He sits on his bed and waits, flicking the

cloth backwards and forwards, forwards and backwards on his
bedroom floor . . .

. . . The shadow passes and repasses with a random regularity that
is eventually difficult to ignore. The man opens his eyes; eyes in
the shroud of a shadow. The shadow of a flag. He lies watching
it as it plays across his body. Then he rolls over, rolls out of the
shadow of the flag so that he is lying with his face to the grass;
the warm-smelling grass.

Flick, flick, flick. The boy sits by the pillow waiting for his supper,
flicking the flag, squeezing it harder with every flick, until at
last the stick snaps and it falls to the floor. He stares at it a
moment, then his gaze drifts to the bedroom window and the
sky beyond, dark purple with streaks like smeared blood. The
stairs creak under the weight of footsteps that are too heavy to
be his mother's. Sitting on the bed, waiting.

Felix

Anne Enright

Anne Enright lives in Dublin where she was born in 1962. Her short story, FELIX, was included in FIRST FICTIONS 10, Faber and Faber's introduction to new writers. She went on to write a book of short stories, THE PORTABLE VIRGIN, 1991, and a novel, THE WIG MY FATHER WORE, 1995.

∫

Felix

Felix, my secret, my angel boy, my dark felicity. Felix: the sibilant hiss of the final x a teasing breath on the tip of the tongue. He was the elixir of my middle years, he was the sharp helix spiralling through my body, the fixer, the healer, the one who feels. But when he was in my arms he was simply breath, an exhalation.

Did he have a precursor? He did, to be sure. There might have been no Felix at all had I not loved, one summer, a certain boy-child in my Tir na nÓg by the sea. Felix was as young as I was that year, the year I first fell asleep, and when he whispered me awake, my life became fierce and terrible. (Look at that tangle of thorns.)

Believe me, I write for no one but myself. Mine is not the kind of crime to be spoken out loud. This, then, is the last, or the penultimate, motion of these fingers that burned alive on the cool desert of his skin. You can always count on a suicide for a clichéd prose style.

I was born in 1935 in Killogue, a small town in the west of Ireland. My father was a small, introverted man of uncertain stock, who ran the pub that faced out on to the town square. My mother died of creeping paralysis in my seventh year, and nothing remains of her in my mind save the image of a woman sitting in the parlour in a perpetual Sunday dress, her throat caught in a stained circle of ancient diamanté and a charm bracelet at her wrist. When they laid her out, again in the same room, with the glass-fronted china cabinet pushed precariously against the back wall, I noticed that her 'jewels' had been removed. This sensible, pious figure seemed to have nothing to do with the woman I remembered, and I was suddenly aware that she must have undressed like that every night, unless she wore the diamanté to bed.

My father grew more nervous after my mother's death, his silences grew longer and were punctuated by sudden rushes of speech, always about the harvest or the Inland Revenue, the goings on 'beyant'. He began to sleep over the bar at night, bringing a small iron bed into what had once been a storeroom, and leaving the bedroom that they had shared intact. He became a crusader for the gombeen class, claiming that there was no such thing as good staff to be found. The days were spent in a silent frenzy of suspicion, watching every boy who was brought in to serve behind the bar, until the explosion burst loose and the boy was sacked – for not charging his friends, or shortchanging the regulars, or simply for sloppy work, licking the knife that was used to cut the sandwiches. Meanwhile, I sat outside, squatting on the kerb that faced the square, where I could see over the brow of the hill to the sea beyond. The strand was hidden by a dip in the road, and it looked as though the water came right up to the crest of the hill and joined it in one clean blue line. I ran towards it like a plane taking off, hoping to dive straight in, always disappointed to discover the street below, the untidy line of houses, the sea wall, and then the beach with its load of mothers wrapped up against the cold, children playing in the sand, and the breakers rolling in beyond.

I was nominally attached to a good woman who lived in a run-down house between the hill and the strand; who washed my clothes, fed me and let me go – perhaps because of some old debt she owed my father, perhaps for a small fee. As far as I can remember, I was a brave child. (It is not the loss of innocence that I regret, but the loss of that courage.) I swam in the deep, underwater world of childhood, my limbs playing in the shattered light of the sea. I loved the cold shock, diving off the cliffs, my body growing numb as I prised free the starfish that hid in the crevices, or teased the nervous mouths of translucent sea anemones. I chatted easily and dangerously with the visitors to the town, with a friendliness that came as second nature to the daughter of a publican. Old men with whiskey breath would lift me on to the bar counter, tip the wink to my father for a bag of crisps and call me 'princess'.

It was the summer of my eleventh year. I was grown wild – more reckless in the sea, more brash with the locals and coy with the tourists, who filled the town with their white, bared flesh. My father picked on a young boy called Diarmuid to help behind the bar, some distant relative from Galway with (I can't continue this for much longer) . . . with the black hair and fine, blunt cheekbones of a Connemara man. Daddy gave over the storeroom to house the boy and slept again in his old room, treading carefully and with a sense of unfamiliarity over the wooden boards. His presence there was light, but unsettling. He brought back the ghost of my mother with him.

I must stop. 'Ghost', 'flesh', 'fine, blunt cheekbones', these words are all strangers to me. I am trying to construct a childhood, so I can pick my way through it for clues. 'Felix came *because*' . . . because in the summer of my eleventh year, my father hired a boy called Diarmuid. Any other boy would have done, any other childhood. The secret must be in the style. If I must choose some way of lying to myself, I thought, this might be the most appropriate. Take on the cadences of an old roué in a velvet smoking jacket, cashmere socks, and a degree of barefaced and thoughtful dignity that is not permitted to the rest of mankind. But look at me. I am a woman of fifty-one years of age, in a suburb of Dublin; not exactly sitting with rollers in my hair, but certainly subject to the daily humiliation of coffee-morning conversation and the grocer's indifference. I buy winter coats in Clery's sale. I have a husband. Every year we drive to the same guesthouse in Miltown Malbay. There has been no tragedy in my life, you might say, apart from the ordinary tragedies of life and death that Ireland absorbs, respects and buries, without altering its stride. In my clean, semi-detached house there are only a few sordid clues; my daughter's empty bedroom, a doll without a head, one broken arrow from a boy's bow, that sits like so much junk at the back of the coal house. Where is the poetry in that?

I have always been struck by the incongruous picture of an old woman with a pen in her hand. Is it not slightly obscene, Ms Lessing, to show your life around like that? Of course your neighbours are rich, they respect you, they are proud to have you living nearby. They don't watch you in the street and say, 'Why write about orgasms, when you look like that?'

Middle-aged women write notes to the milkman, not suicide notes. When they die, they do so quietly, out of consideration for their relatives and friends. And then there is the subject of perversion. Old women are never perverts. They may be 'dotty' or 'strange', poor things, they may, and often do, 'suffer from depression', but they emphatically do not feel up boys in public parks. Their lust is a form of maimed vanity, if it exists at all. It is not the great sweeping torment of the poet. It is not love. The only thing we suffer from is the menopause ('Let me tell you something, Iris dear, the change of life is a blessing . . . when he stops . . . you know, wanting things in the middle of the night.' I want I want I want). I want I want I want. I am not an hysteric. I am a woman of ten and a half stone with a very superior brain. I do not know what the word 'maternal' was ever supposed to mean.

So it is back to the smoking jacket and the man with refined hands who translates Baudelaire for a hobby; the man with a bubble of hot poison in his loins and a super-voluptuous flame permanently aglow in his subtle spine, poor fella, may he rest in peace, God bless him. It is back to the summer I fell asleep (in fact a bout of glandular fever) and Diarmuid, who is no lamia, but a man I met in the street the other day, short, fat, his 'Connemara bones' laced with a filigree of hot purple veins. Incidentally, I too have read my Poe and Proust, my Thomas Mann and Mallarmé, none of whom cares? None of them chased things that were real. My boy-child *was* real. Does that mean that I am not a poet? Oh, but I am. I am a poet not quite in curlers, because I make the poets' claim that '*Form . . . ja wesentlich bestrebt ist, das Moralische unter ihr stolzes und unumschranktes Szepter zu beugen*.' You see. In a woman who dresses from Clery's sale, such tactics can only be childish.

The summer when I was eleven was hot, salty and golden. I would come out of the sharp light of the street and into the pub, lean my cheek against the worn dark wood of the bar, and watch Diarmuid. The wood was soaked with the smell of every old hand that had worn it smooth, and Diarmuid smelt of old men too, his clothes saturated with smoke and spilt porter. But under the clothes he smelt alive. My father did not object to my proximity to the boy – he was too busy scrutinizing him for signs of another kind of fall and with it, the excuse to put him back on the train, back to the rocky fields and sour crop of the family farm. But Diarmuid kept his small hands clean. He spoke like an old man to the customers, neither overly familiar nor reserved. He wiped the counter constantly in wide, smooth circles and he rinsed the cloth out every hour. His small body was steady and sure, with the singular grace of a young boy whose limbs have not yet betrayed him into awkwardness. But he knew that he was being watched, and when my father turned away from him, disgusted by his virtue, I would catch the flicking eye and the wild incomprehension of a horse at the start. We never spoke.

It seems to me now, with plenty of adult, if somewhat perfunctory sex behind me, that I did not know what I was feeling then, or even that I was feeling at all. I now know what it is to ache, and how to free that ache by some mechanical means – I am speaking, I suppose, of my husband, of whom it must be said, I became very fond. And you will excuse my tone, I remain prissy about mere sex, though I would go from the coffee-morning euphemism that was conjugation with my husband, straight to the mordant touch and cool, shy eyes of Felix, who recreates in me, and refines beyond endurance, that first passion. Perhaps passion is the wrong word. The sight of Diarmuid made my limbs feel large, as though I were sick. My whole body emptied itself out of my eyes when I looked at him. Objects became strange, and made me clumsy. At night the sheets felt as though they were touching me, and not the other way around.

So one afternoon, with the place deserted, I slid under the flap that guarded the space behind the counter, and I pressed my hot, flat body wordlessly against his. It was a matter of instinct only.

The brittle, swollen feeling in my skin broke and melted away. It was several days before we learned how to kiss.

I took some tins from the shelf, poured a can full of new milk into a bottle that had once contained stout, and corked it firmly. I took my blue cotton frock and the red Sunday dress, wrapped the food in them and secured the bundle with my father's best funeral tie. We found our separate ways in the dark to the flat rock that lies fallen at the end of the headland to the north of Killogue. The feelings of the week before seemed very strange as we stood and watched each other. I laid my cardigan in the shelter of the slab of rock and lay down on it. After a silence that went on forever Diarmuid lay down with me.

What do you want? 'The sceptre of his passion'? 'My deep, throbbing heart'? Descriptions of the sexual act always pain me. I am reminded of a book published by a vanity press in the United States, where the hero puts – no, *slides* his hand into 'the cleft of readiness' and finds 'the nub of responsiveness'. And, in fact, that description will do as well as any other. We fooled around, like children. There was no technical consummation, though some pain. We didn't have a clue, you could say. That was all.

Why bother? We all have had our small, fumbling initiations on dirty sofas or canal walks. Why bother to remember, when it is our business to look for the better things in life, and our duty to forget. ('A bunch of baby carrots please, and a pound of potatoes, isn't it a nice day, thank God,' the last words spoken by this atheist, pervert and hopeless cook.) Sentiment is all very well (wedding cake), even large emotions – so long as they are mature (sound of baby's first cry, the look of love in paralysed husband's grateful eyes). But what about passion? Passion *is* the wrong word. I am speaking of the feeling that hits like a blow to the belly in ordinary places. See that woman in a headscarf stop dead on the footpath, her mouth shaping to form a word. But before she remembers what it is, the image is tucked away, the shopping bag is changed from one hand to the other, and she walks on. What kind of images collect in an old woman's head?

My moment of passion was a cold one. I woke up just before the dawn, a white light spreading over the bay turning the sea to a frosted blue, and a shivering in my body that scarcely left me intact. Every organ was outlined with a damp pain and I could sense every muscle and bone. I couldn't feel the ground, or the clothes on my back. I was floating inside my numb skin like the jelly of an oyster, and my shell seemed to have sprouted some extra limbs. They were Diarmuid's. He lay in my arms asleep, and a perfect, empty, blue freedom was all around. The sun had not yet risen. I was already feverish.

School settled over me like a blanket when you are sick. Up at seven, silence till eight, Mass, breakfast, class. I didn't want to speak and there was no room for friends. Instead, I showed off to the nuns as though they were the old men in my father's bar; my hand was permanently up in the air, my poems were read out at assembly.

I was allowed special access to books, and my religion essays were scattered with references to St John of the Cross, Julian of Norwich, even Kierkegaard. You may not think that it is possible, but yes, it is possible to be so clever at sixteen, and then to ignore it. And I was the cleverest of them all. The other girls whispered about escape into town, while I read under the sheets. I thought about Diarmuid, but not for long, there was no relief in it. I decided to become a nun, decided to become a writer, decided finally, to become nothing at all. I lost my faith, in the best male tradition, but did not consider its loss significant. There was something about the nuns that made individual lives seem inconsequential, and I admired them for it. What I wrote, I burned and forgot.

Daddy died the summer I left school – he had only held out for the sake of the fees – and so I was free to turn down my university scholarship, despite Sr Polycarpe's pleading, and three novenas from my English, biology and maths teachers respectively. I took a flat on the Pembroke Road and a secretarial job. I also took a boy from the office home with me one night and woke up to find that he had fallen in love. We got over the embarrassment with a small wedding, me in a blue suit and pill-box hat, a light veil of netting at the front. When we went to France on our honeymoon, I pretended not to speak French. This is why, I suppose, I am plagued with travel sickness and we spend our holidays now on the Irish coast.

My husband is a good man, and I love him, though not in the usual way. By this I mean that he is kindly, not that he is dull – I have learned to find interest in the expected. I should write about my daughter too, I suppose, except that this confessional mode agitates and bores me. Something, somewhere, marked my life out like this. I make up childhoods to try and explain. Nevertheless, I do not change. I gave birth to a daughter and I did not change.

One morning (a writer's lie this, like all other 'realizations'), one morning, it could be said, I looked in the mirror and found that I was middle aged.

Do you understand? I looked in the mirror and found that I was middle aged. The relief was overwhelming. My anonymity was crystallized, my life since Diarmuid was staring me in the face, tepid and blank. Everything had dropped away – *I could do anything now*. What interests me, I thought, is not life, the incidents that fill it, not images or moments, but this central greyness. I saw that I was ready. It was into this greyness that Felix would drop, like a hard little apple into the ripe ground.

Felix was only a small boy that I loved. Will you believe that I did not harm him, that I made him happy? And not only with sweeties. I knew his mother, a proud, vulgar woman, and had shared my pregnancy with her, putting to rest her useless fears about breech births and extra chromosomes. I even (the irony of it!) placed my hand on her tight belly in the seventh month, a gesture that in our semi-detached world belongs to the husband alone. There was the little nugget of Felix, wrapped up in the silt of her body. I sometimes wonder whether I corrupted him then with that touch, whether my voluptas was sent through his transparent limbs, turning them into the clean, radiant flesh that was to possess me before he was fully grown.

In the meantime, I was the woman up the road and my daughter was his friend. They played doctors and nurses on the front porch, I suppose. Recently I dug over their dolls' graveyard. I took some pleasure in their growing, though grazed knees and the simple, sloppy cruelty of children hold little charm for me. Felix was quiet – even then, you could not tell his arrogance, his animal calm, from the shyness of other small boys. In retrospect, he was probably beautiful, and I kissed him often, as children need to be kissed. (Was I a bad mother? Oh no.) When I regret all those wasted caresses, I comfort myself with the fact that I could not have known. Looking at myself as I was, I can only see what those two children saw, a solid, transparent shape that wasn't quite flesh, but 'mother' – the creature that was wrapped about them like certainty.

When gradually things began to change between them, I did not notice that either, and would have found it tedious if I had. My daughter started slamming doors and stealing lipsticks. One afternoon she came home crying and hid up in her bedroom. I was attacking the hall with the vacuum cleaner, hoping that the noise would disturb the concentration her self-pity seemed to require, when the knock came at the door. There was Felix on the doorstep, a grown boy, with an indifferently guilty look on his face, and his overlarge hands thrust into his pockets. Little Miss Madam opened her bedroom door and shouted down the stairs, 'You've spoilt everything!'

What a charming scene! I looked at Felix (he smelt of gutting rats and climbing trees) and he looked back at me and laughed with an innocent, evil sense of complicity. That same cold dawn broke over my body and I had to shut the door.

Please believe me, I waited for months. I did not touch him, but carried instead a deep, hard pain in the bowl of my pelvis. I became clumsy again, everything I reached for fell to the floor and the kitchen was a mess of fragments. All that I saw opened up the ache, and I wanted the whole world inside me, with Felix at its centre, like a small, hard pip. His sharp, grey eyes became blank again. Perhaps he was waiting too, though it seemed that when he looked at me, he saw nothing at all. I only had to touch him to become real.

He came to the house one day when she was out. I sat him in the kitchen on the promise of her return. I made a cup of tea and the impudent child held the silence and looked bored, while one knee knocked and rubbed against the table leg. I set down the mug of tea and the Eden-red apple on the table before him and then . . . I leaned over and touched him, in a way that he found surprising.

Small, dirty, strange. Felix's eyes focused on me and it was like falling down a tunnel. He put his hand on my arm, to stop me, or to urge me on, and the pain I carried inside me like a dead child dropped quietly, burning as it went.

Our subterfuges became increasingly intricate, snatching an hour here or there while I pushed my daughter out to hockey practice, piano lessons, even horse riding. Lucky girl. Meanwhile Felix and I pressed out the sour honey of the deepest ecstasy that man or beast has ever known. And while she bounced along on rattle-backed, expensive old nags, while my husband fretted over mislaid returns and his secretary's odour, I wrapped Felix, insensate with pleasure, in the fleshy pulp of my body where he ripened, the hard, sweet gall inside the cactus plant.

Then, of course, she found the letter:

> Dear auntie Iris,
> Mammy is sick and I can't come today.
> > Love
> > Felix.
> PS Larry Dunne was talking about sex again today enough to make you puke. He says he has been putting it into Lucy down the road but I just had to laugh because he obviously hasn't seen any of that and was just blowing. I nearly said about you but I didn't. Don't worry.

I never throw hysterics. So how could I have reared such an hysterical child? She gave up the riding lessons, the hockey, the piano, and became a large, uncultured lout. She corrupted my boy. She lived at my throat and by the time she left, he had turned into a large, normal young man. He went to discos, he wanted to get into the bank. His mother boasted of his many girlfriends, and complained that they never lasted long. I can imagine why.

I could have killed myself then. I allowed myself to fantasize cancers and car accidents. I should have killed myself even before Felix, but I didn't have a life before, so it was ridiculous to think of throwing it away. Felix made everything possible, including dying, and it is for this that I am grateful, more than for anything else. I lived, of course. For a while I thought of finding a replacement, combing housing estates like a queen bee, waiting for the look of recognition. There was one supporting lead in a school play, but that blank gleam in his eye was only stage fright.

Recently I discovered their dolls' graveyard; decapitated plastic, split by my spade. There was clay in the artificial hair.

So. Adieu Adieu Adieu. Self-indulgent, I know, but what do you want me to become? My husband's nurse? (Oh, the grateful look in his paralysed eyes.) And then one of the army of widows, with headscarf and shopping bag, who stop in the middle of the street, shake their heads and say 'Someone must have walked over my grave.' Felix.

Felix sitting on my headstone, with an apple in his fist, like he sat at the bottom of the bed, laughing, puzzled, amazed at every inch of me. Felix at that particular point of refinement where wonder, cruelty and hair-trigger skin make even the imaginary and the ridiculous real. He could look at offal, at grass, at the streaks his fingers made on my thigh with the same indifferent glee.

It is easier to die when you have seen your own flesh, for the first time at forty-seven – because dying is a very corporeal act. I don't want to drift away. I want to splatter.

I met him in the local shop one day at the height of it all.

'How's your mamma, Felix, and haven't you grown?' and he turned to his friends.

'Stupid old bat,' he said. Making up was very sweet, and his tears tasted hot as needles.

A Whore's Vengeance

Louise Doughty

Louise Doughty is a novelist, playwright and critic. In 1990 she won an Ian St James Award for 'A Whore's Vengeance' and a *Radio Times* Drama Award for her first play, *Maybe*, later broadcast on BBC Radio Three. Her second play, *The Koala Bear Joke*, was broadcast on BBC Radio Four in 1994. Her first novel, CRAZY PAVING, was published in 1995, and she is currently working on her second.

A Whore's Vengeance

'There is a promise made in any bed.
Spoke or silent, a promise is surely made.'
The Crucible ARTHUR MILLER.

My mother and father used to fight and he would end up beating her. Then he would sob his heart out as she lay on the floor. 'Why do you make me do it?' he would cry at her. Then, looking up at the ceiling, he would give a great shout, '*Why*?'

They died in 1680, when I was five. The Indians came in the night. Later, I used to tell the other kids I had seen the braves smash their heads against the farmhouse wall. It wasn't true. I was nowhere near at the time. I only made it up to scare them. My mother had been due to give birth again and was ill with it so I had been sent to stay with my aunt and uncle in Salem, until her time came. When I first heard the phrase 'big with child', I thought it meant that grown-ups looked tall when they stood next to children. I used to think all adults were big with child.

I hated living with my aunt and uncle. They had to keep me, of course, after my parents were killed. They stuck a mop in my hands the minute I was big enough to hold it. They treated me like a skivvy. Wash this, scrub that, clean over there and don't speak till you're spoken to – oh, and while you're at it, take that sullen look off your face. Sullen? I was furious. How dare my parents dump me here? For every sweeping movement of that brush, I imagined I was prodding a pin into my aunt's face or my uncle's pious arse. He was a reverend, my uncle. *The* reverend, to be precise. Reverend Paris of Salem, and I, his niece, valued about as much as his black slave, Tituba. They made me sick.

As soon as I grew old enough, I was farmed out, to be a slave in other people's houses and earn my keep. That was how I ended up there, at the Proctors'. They had a small farm, some way out of Salem. I begged my uncle to send me to a family who lived in town. I couldn't stand the thought of being stuck out there with some fat old wife and husband and screaming, red-faced farmhouse brats. I sulked from the moment they told me I was going till the moment I arrived. My uncle drove me over in the cart. He said he was doing it to curb my wild nature. Ha.

As I climbed down, clutching my small bag, Goody Proctor came forward to meet me. She smiled, the way those good women can when they know they are being nicer to you than you probably deserve. 'Welcome to our home, Abigail', she said, magnanimously. I smiled back with my mouth. My uncle came inside with us but didn't stay. More important things to do. He kissed the top of my head, bidding me farewell, but I said nothing. I wasn't going to let him off the hook. Goody Proctor walked back outside with him and I heard their voices murmuring. He was telling her to beat me, no doubt, if I gave her any trouble. When she came back in, she looked a little nervous, as if I was a stray she had been landed with unexpectedly. This one's a pushover, I thought.

She took me upstairs to my room, the usual poky little cupboard, clean and unforgiving, designed to make you look forward to leaping out of bed in the mornings and scrubbing the floors before sunrise. 'I'll leave you alone for a while. Come down when you're ready,' she said. After the door shut behind her, I burst into tears. To be stuck here, out here, miles from anywhere, until my hands were raw with housework and my face cracked by peering into dusty corners. I couldn't stand it. Damn my uncle, damn my aunt, damn the Proctors, damn them all. I'd run away. I'd run away to Boston.

After I had finished, I straightened my apron and my bonnet and went downstairs. I knew as soon as I looked at Goody Proctor that she had heard me crying. She came forward and put her hands on my shoulders, giving me a look of such agonizing pity it made me want to stick something up her nose. 'It must be very difficult for you, a young girl like you,' she said. I decided to play on her sympathies and sniffed. 'Leaving your family. You must miss them very much.' Miss my uncle? It was the only good thing about being sent out to this hole. I nodded. 'Well I'm sure you'll do fine here,' she continued. 'I'll not lie to you, the work is hard, but we have a fair farm, my husband and I. The land is good.' She took her hands from my shoulders and wandered over to the window, gazing out across the fields. 'It is a good land,' she repeated, 'good, and beautiful, a great gift.'

That's all I need, I thought, some half-wit sentimental rubbish about how great this mother earth is. It's farming that does it, and the loneliness. Turns their wits. The men are just as bad. She showed me round the building and the outhouses and then we went inside and started on a small supper. 'It'll be just the two of us tonight,' she said, stirring a pot with some brown muck in it. 'My husband has taken our boys out round the farm. They'll not be back till late.'

Perhaps it was just hindsight. I don't know. But I'll swear I had some sort of premonition when she said it. My *husband*. She spoke of him delicately, as if she was discussing a mole on her face or some ailment it wasn't quite polite to mention. They don't get on these two, I thought. They don't get on at all.

Later she bundled me upstairs, muttering something about how tired I must be. Not too tired, all the same, to be given a list of duties to be started in the morning. There was a basin and a jug of water by my bed, cold of course. I couldn't bear to wash. At least at my uncle's we had Tituba to heat some water for us. The blankets were coarse and the straw in the mattress packed so tight it might as well have been a slab of stone. I lay awake for a long time. After a while, there was the sound of doors opening and shutting downstairs and the murmur of voices.

In the morning, I splashed my face and dressed myself quickly. The room was so cold. It had just grown light. I went and looked out of the small square window. Goody Proctor was standing in the yard, filling a bucket at the pump. I saw her look towards the house and speak to someone I couldn't see. Then she came forward and disappeared from view. I went to my bedroom door and opened it a crack. From downstairs, I could hear voices.

'I am sorry, John, but we need wood.'

'I have a day's farming ahead of me, Elizabeth.'

'I didn't notice how low we were until after dark.'

A door slammed.

I went back to the window and looked out into the yard. From the house emerged John Proctor, striding, axe in hand. He marched over to a log pile by the fence and took a large log from it. He stood it on one end and then lifted the axe, high, high up above his head. For a moment, he was poised there, his arms uplifted and his face taut. His shirt had ridden up above his belt and a flat, brown stomach was revealed. His legs were wide apart, his feet planted solidly on the solid brown earth. The axe glinted, and fell.

There was a light tap at my door. I turned quickly and began smoothing the blanket on my bed.

'Good morning, Abigail. Did you sleep well?'

'Yes, very well, Goody Proctor.'

Downstairs, we laid the table together and I was introduced to the boys, one thin and sensitive looking and the other, the younger, tearing round from wall to wall and jumping and talking about farming. Goody Proctor smiled indulgently. 'Matthew takes after his father.' She laid out five bowls on the table. 'We all eat together as a family here, Abigail.' Well that's something, I thought. She told me to sit down while she ladled porridge into the bowls. I was starving. It was all I could do not to seize my spoon and wolf it down there and then. I noticed she put very little in her own bowl, even less than in the children's. She saw me watching her and smiled nervously. 'I do not eat well in the mornings.' Then she went to the door and called her husband.

John Proctor was not as tall as I had expected. He came in standing straight, his shoulders square. Brownish hair curled against his forehead and thick eyebrows hung over a lowering gaze. He was wearing a tough cotton shirt and dark breeches. He was glaring. Sweat from his exertions stood out on his forehead despite the morning chill. He had the axe in one hand, holding it half way down the shaft, and a bundle of wood cuttings cradled in the other arm. His hands were rough and heavy. Our eyes met.

'Thank you, John.' His wife came forward and took the axe from his hand and hung it up on the wall behind him. He walked over to a large wicker basket to the left of the fire and let the wood cuttings drop into it. Then he came and took his seat at the table. Goody Proctor chivvied the boys to sit down before sitting herself and saying a short grace. We all muttered amen, and began to eat. For a minute or so, the only sounds were the spoons scraping against the wooden bowls.

The first thing John ever said to me was, 'Well now, Abigail, do you miss the great goings-on in the town?'

I looked down at my bowl, then back up at him. 'Well, Mr Proctor, I don't know really.'

'Abigail is bound to be a little homesick to begin with,' said Goody Proctor.

'Well then,' replied her husband, 'we must do all we can to make sure she feels at home.'

We were lovers within a month.

I wasn't the first housemaid to be dismissed by Goody Proctor. They had had quite a turnover, that household. Rumour in the town said she was a slave-driver and dismissed so many because none satisfied her in their work. I remember Mercy Lewis telling me about Sarah Hall, the clerk's daughter, who got sent back after two weeks. A month later, she left Salem altogether to go and live with an aunt in Andover, for her health, her family said.

My uncle beat me senseless for getting the sack. I'll never forget it, as long as I live. Afterwards, I lay face down on my bed sobbing, digging my nails into the pillow. All the same, every one of them, all the same. Always. From my room, I had overheard John confess his wickedness. I knew what was coming. Goody Proctor's feet pounded up the stairs. She dragged me down by my hair and pushed me out of the door. She was strong, for such a virtuous woman. She flung my things out after me calling, 'Harlot! whore!' All the usual stuff. I landed on my knees in the yard, grazing my hands. My bonnet was hanging from my neck and my hair was loose. John was standing in the doorway watching, completely helpless. His cheeks were damp with tears. Just like my father. Exactly like my father. These men. What good would it have done if I had begged for her forgiveness? None. Somebody has to be the bad one. Besides which, I wasn't sorry and I wasn't going to pretend I was. She pushed him back inside and slammed the door. I picked myself up, and my things, and brushed the dirt off my apron. Then I began the walk back to Salem, five miles in the dark.

I knew what would happen when I got back. I knew I would be beaten. All the same, trudging along the road, all I could think about was John. John. I couldn't believe that he had confessed to her out of shame and guilt. I couldn't believe that he was just like all the others, my uncle, my father. He couldn't be. Not my John. He had held my face when we made love, in the shed, on the ground. He held my face so tightly, gazing at me with eyes that burnt holes in mine, looking, looking. As if he would die if he didn't look. Elizabeth and he hadn't made love since their youngest was born and he said even before that, when they did, she would never look at him. She would look at the ceiling, at the walls, never at him. He bruised me sometimes. I couldn't believe he had gone back to her, not after all the things he'd said and done to me. It must be part of a plan, I thought, as I trudged along. He must have told her deliberately, so that he can be with me. He's worked it all out somehow. He'll come after me on his horse.

After a while I had to stop. She had thrown me out in my slippers. My boots were still in their kitchen corner. I kept stumbling in the dark and catching my toes. It was freezing cold but I was completely numb. I sat down and rubbed my feet and listened for the sound of horse's hoofs tumbling along the dirt track. It was impossible that he would not come after me. Quite impossible. There was a strong wind blowing. I strained my ears to listen. So many sounds. It's amazing how many noises can sound like the far-off clatter of hoofs. I knew he would come after me. He had to come. It was all part of his plan. We would go to Boston. Nobody would be able to find us there. We would have our own house and make love in a bed and fall asleep and wake up together. Putting my slippers back on, I began to cry, but I didn't stop believing he would come after me. I didn't stop believing it until I was on my uncle's doorstep, banging on the door to wake up Tituba. It was a stupid thing to do, in retrospect. I should have hidden in the barn or in the church till daybreak and then tidied myself up first. I had lost my senses by then. I was dirty and tired and freezing cold. The grazes on my hands and knees were stinging and my feet were bleeding. My head ached where she had pulled my hair. I wanted to be bathed by Tituba and put to bed, the way she would when I was little, scrubbing my back until it tingled and glowed, humming a negro song.

It wasn't her who answered the door. It was my uncle, in his nightshirt, peering out into the darkness and calling fearfully, 'Who's there?'

'It's me, uncle.' My voice was quite steady. I had stopped crying and was steeling myself for what was about to come. I stepped into the light. 'Abigail.'

'Abigail?'

Well of course the whole house had to be raised to hear of my wickedness. I didn't tell him why she'd thrown me out but I had to tell him I'd been dismissed. He only would have found out later and then I would have been beaten for lying as well. He must have known it was something bad, to be hurled out in the middle of the night. He started raging about how he had brought me up, put clothes on my back, educated me, and so on and so on. I stood in front of him, swaying from exhaustion, while my aunt clucked around like a hen and Tituba stood shaking in the corner. I think she half expected to be beaten as well. She often was when my uncle was in one of his tempers. Get on with it, I thought, looking up at him while he shouted and quoted scriptures about ingratitude. We all know what you're going to do. Get on with it.

Later, Tituba came to me in my room with a mug of hot milk, mumbling soothing noises. I was in pain and could only be cross with her for not getting to the door before my uncle did, not that it would have made much difference in the end. Whilst she dabbed at my back with a damp cloth, she told me about what had been going on while I had been away. Apparently, there was some move to oust my uncle from his position. There had even been a meeting when he had been called to explain some irregularities in the parish accounts. She had listened outside the door and heard a lot of shouting. Good, I thought, not really considering that if my uncle was replaced we would all have to leave this house. Things were bad all round, she said. One of the farmers was bringing another suit against a neighbour in the country court and there was talk that if he succeeded he would be bringing them against others, including my uncle. 'These bad times, Miss Abigail,' she said, curling her bottom lip and rocking back and forth, 'bad times, bad times.'

Funny how right she turned out to be, stupid old Tituba. Everyone in that town hated each other. They had done for years. Everyone thought they were being persecuted. They all had axes to grind. They were just waiting, waiting, waiting for it all to explode. My uncle once said in church, 'Remember, when you point a finger at someone . . .' (raising a hand, making the gesture) 'there are always three of your own fingers pointing back at you.' It was one of the few intelligent things I ever heard him say. Shame no one listened really.

I didn't start it, you know, all that witchcraft stuff. They started it, my uncle and the others. I just joined in at the appropriate moment. Even then I only did it because they were pointing their fingers at me. It didn't occur to me to get my own back on John until well after it had all begun. 'A whore's vengeance,' he said in court – which is one way of looking at it I suppose.

We had to run away when things got out of hand. I took Mercy Lewis with me. She had been as much involved as me and, anyway, I needed her help to get to Boston. I wasn't sure we would make it. They probably set up blockades on the roads behind us but we had a day's advantage over them and managed to slip through. I knew we would be all right once we made it to the city. Anyone can disappear in Boston. Especially a whore. I didn't have any illusions about how we would have to earn a living. We had to go somewhere where there would be no questions asked. It was either that or thieving, and I preferred to earn an honest living.

At first, we were turned away. We were filthy. Skinny, seventeen and desperate. We hadn't eaten for over two days. Mercy was coming out in red blotches all over her face and I had a sore growing on my neck. Then, at the fourth place we tried, just as we were moving on, the madam called us back.

'Come here a minute,' she said, 'you.' She was looking at me. Mercy was near collapse, clinging to my arm. I tried to make her stand up straight. The madam took my chin in her hands. A wave of violet scent hit me and I nearly fell over. I had never smelt it before. She looked at me closely. I couldn't tell whether she was being hostile or just curious.

'You . . .' she said. 'Two girls. I've heard about two girls on the run from up-country, all that hullabaloo up there.' Mercy panicked. 'It isn't us, it isn't us,' she babbled, and began to cry. The madam dropped my chin and sighed theatrically, 'Oh for God's sake get her in here, off the street.' I pushed Mercy forward and followed.

Madam led us through into the kitchen where she made a sullen-looking girl in petticoats serve us soup from a huge dark stove. Back in Salem, they were still cooking soup over fires. I stared at the stove while we ate. A real stove. The girl in petticoats flounced out, pulling a face. I suppose we smell, I thought. 'Don't mind Mary,' Madam said, 'she's always a bit uppity when it's her turn to cook.' I stared at her. She laughed. 'Oh yes, missie, you cook as well in here. We take it in turns. We have a woman in for the evening meal but we all muck in together for the rest of it. Fair's fair.' Mercy had fallen asleep with her head on the table. Madam came and sat next to me on the bench and covered my hand with hers. 'Now look here, missie, whatever you want to call yourself. You're all right underneath that mud, you'll clean up and I can tell you know what goes on and you'll be good. But I'm not sure about your friend here.' I looked at Mercy and then back up at her. She had very round blue eyes and huge powdered cheeks. She reminded me of a poppet doll I sewed once back in Salem. I gave it dimples with a cross-stitch either side of its mouth. 'Abigail,' I said, 'my name's Abigail. And you take me and Mercy or neither of us.' A broad grin spread across her face. 'I knew it. I knew it.' She gave out a laugh and slapped her thigh. 'I knew it was you I'd heard about. I could tell by your eyes. You showed that Salem lot, my girl, by God you showed them. Pious fools. You showed them.' I couldn't help smiling as well. She made it seem like an enormous joke. For the first time, it all seemed like one enormous, breathtaking joke. 'All right, you're in.'

'And Mercy?' Madam looked at her, then back at me, sighing, 'Well, well, Mercy too, then. See she pulls her weight, mind. And if you go, she goes with you.' Then she went over to a cupboard and pulled out a pewter jug and two large mugs. 'Cider!' she declared with relish. 'Cider to celebrate! I hope you don't mind only cider but I never drink anything too strong at this hour.' Only the men were allowed to drink in Salem. We clunked our mugs together and drained them. Madam turned and went to the door and shouted out, 'Mary, go and see if that back room at the top is fit.'

She told me later that she turned back to see that my head was on the table next to Mercy's.

That was three years since. I've stayed with Madam. I could have moved on, even set up a place of my own, but I like it here. It wasn't easy at first. I hadn't really thought about what it would be like, lying back for some grunting animal, knowing he would pray for forgiveness on Sunday, turning and smiling at his wife and worshipping her for her ignorance. My first customer turned out to be called John. That helped in a way. As he lay there, panting and groaning like a stuck pig, all I could think was, my God, if only you could see how stupid you look. If only you could see. 'Oh my darling,' I whispered in his ear, 'Oh my love.' Madam gets good reports of me from the regulars. 'It's the way you lie to them, Abby,' she said to me the other day, 'nobody lies to them like you. It's those eyes, the way you look at them.' It was John that taught me that. He was the first man who ever touched me. He taught me how to look and look and *see* – how to lie with glances and finger-tips.

I'm Madam's favourite now. She's grooming me to take over the business when she gets too old, although that won't be for years yet. It caused some jealousy when I first got here but everything is fine now. At dawn, we all get together in the parlour to swap stories and relax. The customers are thrown out into a Massachusetts sunrise, massaging their eyes and consciences. Madam locks the door and breaks open a bottle. We have a bit of a party. I like entertaining the others with my stories of the bad old days. They're always asking me. 'Then of course there was that day in the courtroom, when John finally decides to discredit me as a witness by telling the judge him and me had done the business. I deny it, of course, so the judge summons his wife to give evidence. She doesn't know that John has come clean already and says her covenanted husband is as pure as a new born baby. I am vindicated – and he is branded a liar as well as a devil-worshipper.' Madam loves that bit of my story. She slaps her thigh and roars with laughter, that deep rich belly laugh she has. 'The best thing about Christians,' she says, spluttering cider, 'is you can always rely on them to pretend they're better than the rest of us. Leaves them wide open. Never fails.' Before I came, apparently, some of the good townspeople tried to close Madam down. She went to see a few judges with whom she was *very* well acquainted and begged for their assistance in continuing a service to wayward men with less self-control than their good selves. She promised to make a donation to the church and put a Bible in each room. We stayed open.

'Tell us about how your uncle used to watch you in the bath,' says Ann. 'Well, when I was little . . .' I begin. They've all heard it before but they listen eagerly, waiting for the punchline. When it comes they throw themselves backwards and scream with mirth. Even Mary and Elizabeth smile, lying on the sofa, wrapped in one another's arms. Mercy crouches next to me, rubbing her latest bruise. She always gets them. I never do. It's odd really. I don't know why she should attract those types but she does. For the first six months or so, she kept having nightmares. She used to cry out in her sleep. Once she even said we should go back. We would only be whipped, she said. 'Don't be stupid, Mercy,' I told her, 'people died because of what we said. They'd hang us soon as see us.' She knew I was right. Virtuous people have long memories. Most of the girls here are on the run from something. Occasionally we get visits from a constable but no one tells him anything. We all stick together here. If he gets too nosy, Madam gets on to one of his superiors. Apparently, I have achieved some degree of infamy. Rumours of my whereabouts are rife.

After a couple of hours of chat, it's someone's turn to go out and buy fresh bread and cheeses, or make soup. We eat until we're stuffed, then slope off to sleep until early evening. Only Madam stays up. She must catch a few hours somewhere but she never seems to rest. She's never tired either. She is always there, beaming through her powder. Not that she's soft. Last month, she threw out a girl called Beth who made herself ugly and stupid with drink. She'd get rid of Mercy if it wasn't for me. If I ever do get my own place, I'll take Mercy off the game and let her do all the cooking and cleaning. You need a full-time housekeeper in a place like this. I don't know how Madam does it sometimes, running somewhere this size on her own. I couldn't do it. She can't delegate, that's her problem. She'll have a job handing over to me when the time comes. I ought to get my own house really, but it's difficult when you start up. You have to build up the customers' trust. You have to nurture them. It would be much easier to take over Madam's clients.

I think about it upstairs, lying awake in the room I share with Mercy. It always takes me a while to get off. White beams slip through the wooden slats of the shutters, into the darkened space around me. Traders are shouting in the street outside. Mercy whimpers in her sleep. Downstairs, Madam will be sitting at the table going through the books. What I'd really like is the biggest place in the country, open twenty-four hours a day, with the girls working in shifts. Mind you it would mean employing a lot of other people apart from the girls, to keep it running. I might have to employ some men. My mind is churning it over as I grow drowsy. Keep it small to start off with. Several small houses. I don't dream of Salem, well, not like Mercy anyway. I dream of John sometimes, out in the yard, when I first saw him. He is standing there, the axe raised up in his two fists, his face taut and haunted. A bolt of sunlight hits him as the axe falls down and down and down and I, underneath, watch it hurtling slowly towards me. I wept no tears when they hanged him. He could have saved himself. If he had confessed, it would have bought him enough time. They released the people still in prison after I ran away. By then they had realized the whole thing was a dreadful mistake. Still they never prosecuted the other accusers. Everybody had accused everybody else by then and it would have meant prosecuting the whole town. When they looked around for someone to blame, I was handy. They conveniently forgot it wasn't me who started it. Ah, well. Enough of that. It brought down a few learned men, reverends and judges. John would move back and forth inside me, so slowly, looking at me, gazing, holding my face so steady. My eyes would stare back, wide open. Boston is growing every day. New immigrants flood in. 'Look at me,' he would say, moving back and forth and holding my face, *'look at me.'* There's no shortage of customers, and the new silks are coming in from Europe. His eyes promised such volumes. Vengeance means nothing next to survival, but it's helpful when the two coincide.

An Ugly Night

David Rose

David Rose is fifty-four, a Scot who now lives in the south of England. He has been a reporter for newspapers, magazines, radio and television, working for Independent Television News for over twenty years covering assignments around the world. His story, 'An Ugly Night', won the first Ian St James Award for new writers.

An Ugly Night

At the Border with the North, they made the kid get into the boot of the Mercedes among all the boxes because he hadn't got his passport.

'For fuck's sake, keep quiet or we'll all get nicked,' Tillie said, looking down at the kid's pale face. Then he closed the boot.

It was pitch black in there and the edges of the metal cases were sharp. After a while the kid could feel the car stop and he could hear voices but he couldn't hear what they were saying. They seemed to go on for a long time. Then he couldn't hear anything.

Suddenly the lid of the boot opened. The kid put his hands over his eyes. Three big hands reached in towards his face. All the hands held guns.

'No, please, no,' he said. He took his hands away from his eyes and stuck them straight out of the boot. Three men in dark uniforms were looking down at him. Their faces were in shadow. 'Please,' he said.

'Get out the car slowly,' the man nearest his head said in a thick accent. 'Keep your hands up at all times or you're a dead man.'

The kid climbed out awkwardly. He had trouble getting over the rim of the boot without using his hands. He fell on his knees in the road. The policeman with stripes on his sleeve pointed and the other two picked the kid up below his arms and shoved him flat against the side of the car.

'Keep still now while we search you,' the Sergeant's voice said.

The big hands felt his body all over, even between his legs. They took everything out of his pockets. Then something cold and hard pressed into the back of his neck.

'We're going to take a wee walk over to the Station,' the Sergeant said. 'Don't even think of making a run for it.'

'I won't, I promise,' the kid said.

The pressure on the back of his neck steered him away from the car. He started to walk slowly towards a low, concrete building with barred windows. From the corner of his eye, he saw the crew. They were filming him, Charles' face half hidden by the camera, Tillie holding out the mic in its fat windshield. Then they started to move towards him, still filming.

The kid thought, Mum's going to see this on the news tonight; she'll die.

The crew moved directly in front of him. They walked backwards; he could see his reflection on the lens. Then the camera started to shake and they stopped walking and he almost bumped into them. Tillie took his arm and turned him round. John M., the reporter, was holding an empty Coke bottle up near his face. The kid felt the back of his neck where the cold circle had pressed. He looked back towards the car. The three policemen were leaning against it. One pointed at him, then he took off his hat and beat his thighs. When the kid turned round, Tillie was laughing so much he'd had to sit in the road.

Charles and Tillie had been giving the kid a hard time ever since they'd arrived in Dublin two days before. It was his first trip away from London. Maybe someone had given them a rough time on their first trips.

Now they were all on their way to Derry to relieve the crew there. After the Border, Tillie took over the driving from Charles. The kid sat in the back of the Merc with John M. There wasn't much room with the gear filling the boot. He had Tillie's box of tapes on his lap and Charles' overnight bag under his knees. Tillie asked for *Rumours*, and the kid passed it forward. Tillie turned Fleetwood Mac up loud and wound the car up to eighty-five. Outside sheets of rain were hitting the motorway from a dark grey sky. Tillie got his tin of Old Holborn out and started rolling a cigarette, steering with his knees.

The kid was scared. He wanted to talk about what it'd be like in Derry. But Charles had reclined his seat and was lying back smoking. John M. was reading newspaper cuttings and making notes. Tillie snapped the car lighter in and then held it to his roll-up. The kid pressed the rocker switch in his door so the window opened a little.

'Close it, Lassie,' Tillie said. He'd started calling the kid that after dinner the night before. He said the kid's long hair and big nose reminded him of a sheepdog. The kid's real name was Lance and he didn't like the nickname but there didn't seem to be a lot he could do about it. Tillie gave everybody names so maybe it meant they were starting to accept him.

The kid pressed the other side of the switch. 'Might things've quietened down in Derry?' he said.

'I bloody well hope not,' John M. said, putting away the cuttings into a transparent envelope. 'After we've been dragged up. Anyway they've got to keep the temperature up to show Maggie she can't starve three of their guys to death.'

'Fucking mad Micks,' Charles said without opening his eyes. 'I hope another three've died today.'

'What happened to the other crew?' the kid said.

'I don't know exactly,' John M. said. 'Apparently they just want out. Must've been something heavy for Andy to want to leave. News Desk said they'd lost their car, but that can't be it.'

'How could they lose their car?'

'It was stolen. Nasty men took it away from them. Luckily they had the gear out at the time . . .'

Tillie turned Fleetwood Mac down slightly. 'I bet the back was full of Nigel's empties,' he said. 'IRA probably want a reporter who's not totally brahmsed, so they marked his card.'

'If you hadn't fucked his wife, he probably wouldn't be in such a state,' Charles said.

'If he hadn't been smashed all the time, she wouldn't have wanted it so much,' Tillie said and he laughed. 'Anyway that's not supposed to be general knowledge.'

'He used to be a good reporter,' John M. said. 'They shouldn't have sent him over. Considering what's been happening, he's had bloody little on . . .'

'You'd have done better with a Royal Wedding coming up?' Charles said.

'Maybe.' John M. settled back against the seat. 'We'll see tonight if you can keep the camera from shaking too much.'

The kid heard a heavy throbbing over the noise of the car and the tape. He leaned across to look between the two front seats. A khaki helicopter was hovering over the motorway half a mile ahead. They rushed below it. The kid turned to look out of the back window. The chopper was still hanging there, red lights winking below its belly.

'Been thinking,' he said. 'Like it's better to ask now than mess it up when we're working.' In the front Tillie's tobacco tin clicked open. 'Can I put the lights on when there's a riot or shooting? I mean, is it OK?'

'Lassie,' Charles said. 'Do as I tell you. That's all you have to do.'

'There's only one thing you'll need to remember tonight, Lassie,' Tillie said, licking the cigarette paper.

'Yeah,' the kid said.

'Before we go out tonight,' Tillie said. He held the lighter to his cigarette. 'Before we leave the hotel, right? Go to your room, take your strides off and stick a pair of rubber pants on.'

The kid lay back and tried to make himself comfortable, but he couldn't close his eyes. His forehead felt sticky and his stomach was moving around. It was probably the heat and smoke in the car. Then he remembered that he'd had lobster the night before in Dublin. Charles had ordered it for them all but he didn't really like shellfish; he'd wanted a fillet steak.

They took the ring road round Belfast, beside the Lough, with the lights of the city starting to come on to their left. The rain was turning to drizzle as they picked up the M2. Dark clouds lay low over the hills, making it seem later in the evening. They were seventy miles from Derry, though, as the man said, if they hurried they might do it in sixty.

When they got to Derry, John M. made Tillie drive up into the Creggan for a look round before they checked into the hotel. The kid thought the big estate didn't look anything special. Earlier in the year, just after he'd got his full spark's ticket, he'd been wiring similar houses in Mitcham. They saw a row of burnt-out cars across a side street but they could have been there for months.

'At least it's stopped raining,' he said.

'Yeah, they'll be out to play tonight.' John M. rubbed his hands together briskly. 'Right, let's hit the hotel.'

They found the other crew round a table in the corner of the Cocktail Bar. They all looked exhausted, even Andy.

'Hey,' John M. said. 'What the hell's that you're drinking?'

'Green Deadlies,' Ricky, the sound-recordist, said. His white sweater was unbuttoned. Several thin gold chains lay around his neck.

'You wankers,' Tillie said. 'We drive all the way up from Dublin because you're all too pissed to go out. Fuck me.'

'You're a cunt, Tillie,' Andy said. 'Except a cunt's a useful thing.' His big jaw was flecked with stubble.

'Who you calling cunt, you cunt?' Tillie said, laughing.

'Sit down and have a drink, dogsbreath,' Brian, the lighting man, said.

The kid saw the people at the bar were looking at them, but the others didn't seem to notice.

'Three Green Deadlies,' John M. said. 'Whatever they are . . .'

'Joe knows,' Ricky said.

'What are you having, Nigel?'

Nigel got to his feet without looking at any of them. 'I'm taking the crew out tonight,' he said. 'It's my patch, my story.' He gathered up a pile of papers and his drink. 'We'll leave at ten.'

'Sod that,' John M. said, watching Nigel trying to get the door open.

'Go and get the drinks, for fuck's sake,' Andy said.

The kid lifted over a chair and put it beside Brian's. He'd met Brian in the Lighting Room in London. Brian had a lot of silver hair but his face was quite young. He was staring at the kid as if he'd never seen him before.

'OK, so it's your story,' Charles said to Andy. 'I could do with an early night.'

'Fuck you, Winfield,' Andy said. 'Nigel can do what he likes. We've been pulled off the story.'

They all sat waiting for John M. to bring back the drinks, but a black-haired woman at the bar wanted his autograph. Then she asked him what Martyn Lewis was like.

When he came back with a tray, they all had to shuffle sideways to give him room to pull a chair in. He gave the kid a pint of lager. 'I thought Nigel wanted out,' he said.

'He's had a bad time,' Andy said, taking out a Marlboro. 'Yesterday and the night before and the night before that. But yesterday, when they nicked the car, they took Nigel away for over an hour.'

'Did he say what happened? Did they knock him about?'

'He didn't say.' Andy blew smoke across the table. 'But while we were waiting for him, a couple of the lads said they were pissed off we weren't getting more on about the riots. We said it was London that was dropping the stories. It wasn't Nigel's fault . . .'

'Maybe,' John M. said.

'He did say they had all the gen on his family, his London address, phone number, his kid's names and ages, his wife's phone number . . .'

'I could've given them that,' Tillie said.

'Honest, Tillie, you'd fuck a barber's floor if it had hair on it,' Andy said.

'Then why the hell's he suddenly talking about going out tonight?' John M. said.

'He's been drinking brandy and Benedictines since twelve.'

Ricky picked up an empty glass and chinked it against the top of another glass. 'What's that sound like?' he said.

'Nigel Buxton reading the papers in the back of the car,' Tillie said. 'First thing in the morning.'

'Right,' Ricky said. 'He's been totally out of his turret since we arrived, hasn't he, Andy?'

The cameraman shrugged his heavy shoulders and looked away. The black-haired woman waved at him to join her.

'They shouldn't have sent him,' John M. said.

Then Tillie told them about the kid getting into the boot at the Border. After they had another couple of drinks, John M. suggested they'd better have something to eat before they went out.

'Tell you what,' Tillie said. 'Let's have an Ugly Night when we get back.'

'Jesus,' Andy said.

'What's an Ugly Night?' the kid asked.

'You'll find out, Lassie,' Tillie grinned. 'You could do pretty well, sniffing them out with that pea-shooter of yours.'

The kid hung up his good trousers and sweater in the built-in wardrobe in his room. He felt like having a shower but he couldn't be bothered. He lay on the bed. His Mum'd be expecting him to phone, but she'd worry if she knew he was in the North. She'd also know something was wrong if he rang and didn't tell her. He decided to ring the next day when everything was OK.

He went down for dinner even though he didn't feel hungry.

Tillie said there was no room for both Nigel and the kid in the Merc. The kid had to take Brian's Astra and give Nigel a lift. He felt they could've all squeezed up.

'This your first time in Derry?' Nigel said thickly.

'Yes,' the kid said. He hoped the reporter wouldn't tell him about his wife. He was having to drive as fast as he could to keep the Merc in sight. They were on a steep climb between old houses. There were no street lights. The car's headlights showed all the houses were boarded up. Most of the boards had huge slogans or flags painted on them. There were no people about.

The kid was leaning forward so as not to lose the other car. He hoped all the people had decided to stay at home. Then they could go back to the hotel and Tillie would tell jokes and maybe he'd try to tell one too. He'd like to sit beside Andy.

When they reached the top of the hill, the road levelled out. Nigel sat up. 'Welcome to the Creggan,' he said. The road bent left in a long curve, hiding the Mercedes. The kid wished Tillie would slow down.

Suddenly there were bright lights ahead. A long fire, dark figures moving around it and standing in the road ahead. The kid braked but the car arrived quickly. To the right, blocking a side-street, was a burning barricade, a couple of cars on their roofs, old furniture, boxes. The car's windscreen was filled with people, waving the car to stop, then their faces, masked and unmasked, bending to peer in.

'Drive on,' Nigel shouted. 'Don't stop.' The kid's foot moved from the brake to the accelerator and pushed it down carefully in case he hit anyone. The figures ahead divided gracefully to let them through. There were shouts and a couple of loud bangs against the side of the car.

'Faster,' Nigel screamed. 'Drive!'

The kid flinched and pressed the accelerator all the way in.

They found the Merc parked half way down the long hill of boarded-up houses. Charles and Tillie were getting their gear out of the back. As the kid parked in front, Nigel raised his arm and took a couple of swallows. The kid locked the car.

'Get a move on, Lassie,' Tillie's voice called. 'Get your light and give us a shine.'

The kid slung the battery light over his shoulder. Charles gave him the heavy spare battery for the camera to carry, then he closed the Merc's boot. The car light went out. Two tiny red glows showed where Tillie and Charles were. He switched on the hand-basher. They covered their eyes.

'Put it on the road, for fuck's sake,' Tillie said. 'You go ahead and show us where we're walking.'

They were stopped twice before they reached the barricade. Once by some police or Army who they never saw, but whose voices warned them not to go any further. The next time it was half a dozen men or youths who circled them like stray dogs, flashing torches in their faces and on their gear. One, called Francie, was told to go with them. On the way he tapped a cigarette off Charles. When he lit it, the kid saw he was wearing a knitted balaclava helmet like the one his Mum used to make him put on when it was freezing. He'd hated it. The man had pulled down the wool over his chin to get the fag into his mouth.

Two police Land Rovers drove up fast, as if thinking of charging the barricade. Then they stopped and the front one started to reverse but the second one hadn't got the message and was blocking the way. There were wire grilles over the windscreens and side-windows. The kid couldn't see anyone inside. Two black barrels stuck out at the side of each, moving like antennae, back and forth.

Suddenly the road was full of figures, blacker than the night, screaming and shouting, throwing rocks hard, against the steel.

The kid was shocked at their ferocity. He felt glad he was English and just there to do a job. He felt sorry for the hidden policemen who were just trying to do a job too.

A petrol bomb hit the windscreen of the first Land Rover; burning petrol covered the grille and bonnet. There were screams and cheers. The kid imagined the policemen inside, seeing the faces with their open screaming mouths, lit by the flames trying to reach them. The first Land Rover reversed anyway, crashing into the one behind. It wheeled back in a tight arc, freeing the first one. They both sped off down the road.

In the flickering light of the barricade, the figures danced triumphantly, hands above their heads.

Charles took the camera off his shoulder and put it on the ground.

'Did youse get that?' a voice said. It might have been Francie who'd brought them up the road.

'I expect so,' Charles said, putting his cigarettes away. The crew sat on a low wall. John M. was beside the barricade talking to an older man.

'Shine your light over here, mister,' a young voice said.

In the garden, below the wall, there were twenty or thirty bottles, each with a rag stuffed in the neck. Most were milk bottles, but the kid recognized one red label: Tizer, the Appetizer. He used to buy that on the way back from school. Two young lads were loading a dozen bottles into a plastic milk crate. Then one got it onto his shoulder and went off between two houses.

'What the fuck do you think you're playing at, Lassie,' Charles said. 'Come on.'

As they crossed the road, Tillie said, 'What's the difference between an Irishman peeing in the sink and a nigger peeing in the sink?'

'I don't know,' the kid said. He was glad Tillie was telling him a joke, but he hoped no one else was close enough to hear.

'The nigger takes the dishes out first.'

There was a tall hedge on the other side of the road. 'Get ready to get behind that the next time they come,' Charles said, putting the camera down in the pathway to a house.

'They won't shoot at us,' the kid said to show he knew they were winding him up.

A couple of wild shouts came from down the road. The kid could see a crowd shifting against the flames of the barricade. Behind the hedge, to the kid's right, there was the clink of bottles. Someone rasped a match and then swore.

The two Land Rovers came back slowly as if they were unsure. Their headlights lit four men staggering, two at each end of a telegraph pole. They dropped it on the road, blocking the Land Rovers' escape. The dark figures rushed at the vehicles, threw and then ran back to the sides of the road for more ammunition. Beside him three ran out of the garden with blazing bottles. Two hit, the front wheel and near the driver's window; one sailed over the top. The flames of the barricade and the petrol bombs seemed to the kid to freeze the attackers' movements for an instant, like strobe lighting at a disco.

There were four bangs from the Land Rovers. Two of the attackers ran back, laughing and shouting. The third tried to dive over the hedge but hit the top of it. The kid could hear him cursing and the others laughing at him. The kid couldn't see the crew. He thought he would stay where he was to show he wasn't afraid. Even he knew they were just firing plastic bullets.

The first Land Rover crunched over the barrier then the second seemed to get stuck; its back wheels were off the ground, spinning. In front of it, dancers turned and twisted in the headlights. The two barrels sticking out of the side drew level with the kid, then they came together like a man's eyes squinting. Two petrol bombers ran out of the garden. The kid held up his unlit light above his head to show who he was. The bottles burst flaming against the Land Rover. One of the barrels looked directly at the kid then it jerked. The hedge splintered and a window broke in a house behind. The back wheels found a grip and climbed slowly over the log and away. In the street, silhouetted against the flames, the dancers were leaping and shouting.

Someone ran over the kid's legs and yelled at him. He found he was lying on the pavement. He couldn't remember deciding to get down. He got to his hands and knees. Glass fell, tinkling, from the hand-basher's reflector. A woman began screaming behind him.

Charles and Tillie and John M. walked out of the garden. 'Come on,' John M. said. 'We need the light to do an interview. There's a woman who says the glass hit her baby.'

'Lying cow,' Charles said.

'I dunno,' Tillie said. 'Free plastic surgery and they're still complaining.'

When the kid showed them the broken light, John M. said he'd better go back to the car to get a bulb. The reporter said they could interview the woman in her front room beside the broken window. She could hold the baby if it wasn't screaming too much. Then he told the kid to get a move on.

Once the hill had hidden the barricade, the road was very dark. He pointed the light at his feet and tried to switch it on. Then he remembered it was broken: that was why he was going back. It seemed a long way. He was just wondering if he could've walked past the cars, when he found he was beside the Merc. He touched it and felt his way round to the front. He held the chrome Mercedes circle and reached forward into the darkness. He felt nothing, then he took a step forward and touched the back window of the Astra.

He felt round the rim of the boot till he got the handle. He couldn't remember whether the lock was in the handle or just above or below it. He should've borrowed Tillie's lighter. Just when he was about to give up, the key slipped in. He lifted the boot and the interior light came on.

The kid rested the hand-basher on the metal case containing the telescopic stands. The bulb was broken but the reflector itself seemed OK though the rim was bent. He found the box of spare bubbles and put one in, but it still didn't work. He wanted to close the boot and get in the car and wait till the crew came back. There wasn't much point in going back if he didn't have a light. Then he saw Brian had a spare battery light, tucked to the side of the boxes, behind the driver's seat. He pulled it out. The bright white light startled him. He put two spare bulbs in his pocket. At least he'd be able to see walking back. He put the strap over his shoulder.

He'd just pulled the lid down and was locking it when a voice said, 'We're taking your car.'

The kid turned, holding the light. Three young men, two with only their eyes showing through balaclavas, were very close. Behind him someone knocked his arm down so the light pointed at the road.

'It's not mine,' the kid said.

'Give us the keys,' the voice in front said.

He pulled the keys out of the boot and a hand took them from him. The light on the road showed two pairs of black lace-up boots, one pair of dirty tennis shoes. The driver's door opened and the tennis shoes jumped into the car. By the car's interior light he saw the man without a mask searching for the ignition. The engine started, revved and the car jerked away down the hill, the driver's door swinging.

A voice from the darkness shouted and an arm hooked the door in. After about fifty yards the lights came on and the kid watched them till they disappeared.

'Oh God,' he said. 'It's got my bag in it.' The soft black leather holdall his Mum had given him last Christmas. His Walkman, his diary, his camera. He wondered if whoever had knocked his arm down was still behind him.

'When you see them again, can you get something out for me?' he said. 'Please.' But there didn't seem to be anyone there. After a few minutes, he started to walk back up the hill.

The crew stood in a doorway at the top of the street. To their right the barricade was burning. To their left, down the hill, a line of dark shields blocked the road. The kid could see helmets moving behind the shields. Behind the helmets were a row of lorries and Land Rovers. He pulled back into the doorway and lent against the door. A thin lad about his own height but maybe a couple of years younger crouched by the crew staring down at the police line.

'Would you mind if we put the light on you for a few seconds?' Charles said, wiping the camera's lens carefully.

'Would that get me on the news, d'you think?' The boy was jumping from one foot to the other.

'Bloody sure it would,' Tillie said.

'Would you get me shouting about it being for Bobby, Bobby Sands?' the boy said. He pulled at his finger joints so they cracked.

'We can't guarantee that,' John M. said. 'It depends how space is, but I promise we'll say somewhere the riots are a protest at the hunger strikers' deaths . . .'

'Fuck it, you're on,' the boy said.

'Get your light on,' Charles said, lifting the camera to his shoulder. 'Keep it over me and follow exactly where I'm shooting.'

The boy picked up each of the bottles then he selected one with a red Tizer label. He pulled a little more of the rag out of the top then he twisted it together. Charles slid down the wall so the lens was level with the boy's face. The boy flicked a Zippo and cupped his hands. Then he stood up and peeked round the corner. John M. tapped him on the shoulder. He held out both hands opposite the camera to remind the boy where he should throw.

The boy ran back along the edge of the houses, and the crew lost sight of him.

'He won't do it,' John M. said.

'Bet you he will,' Tillie said. 'He's got the brains of a rocking horse.'

The kid hoped John M. was right and the boy had changed his mind and gone round the barricade and away into the darkness.

Then they saw him, running like an Olympic javelin thrower, his left arm straight forward, his head back, and his right arm cocked. Then his whole upper body spun, his left arm, balancing, swung behind him, while his right flew forward and upwards and the bottle rose in a long arc, flaming in the sky and then fell, bursting, beyond the shields. Charles moved slightly out of the doorway and pulled focus on the policeman who jumped out of the line slapping at the flames which covered his head and shoulders.

Charles held the man till he fell on the ground, hidden by helmeted figures. Then he panned quickly to his right. The kid swung his reflector above the camera and the light hit the boy as he stood with his clenched fist held high. He glanced at the crew then he raised his other hand and shimmied his hips and swayed both arms as if he was holding a football scarf above his head.

'Murdering pigs,' he shouted. 'That's for Bobby Sands and Francie Hughes and Raymond . . .'

From seven feet away, the kid heard the plastic bullet break his jaw. The boy spun away from the crew holding his face and fell in the road.

The kid's arm fell.

'Keep the fucking light steady,' Charles hissed. The boy's legs were moving as if he was dreaming of running. From the other side of the road, nearer the barricade, three dark figures ran out and pulled at the body.

'Put the light out,' one shouted.

'Keep it on,' Charles said. There were no more shots from the police line.

'Jesus,' John M. said beside the kid. 'Did you get that OK?'

'No,' Charles said, lowering the camera. 'I didn't bother switching on.'

'I've never seen pictures of anyone actually getting hit with one,' John M. said. 'I'm sure that's the first ever . . .'

'Is he dead?' the kid said.

'If he ain't,' Tillie said, 'he won't be giving the police any more rabbit for a while.'

The crew walked backwards up the road, keeping close to the houses. There were only two plastic shields left at the bottom and the Land Rovers were reversing out of the line. The barricade had almost burnt out and there were only a few small boys playing behind it.

They crossed a bit of rough ground, stumbling in the dark. No one suggested the kid put his light on. Then a torch was shone in their faces.

'Was it you put the light on the boy?' someone said.

'Look,' John M. said. 'He asked us to put it on him so he could get on the news. He asked us to.'

'Would you do anything these kids asked you to?' someone else said.

'How is he?' John M. asked.

'He's on his way to the hospital now,' the first voice said. The torch was switched off and the crew walked along a street and then down the hill to the Mercedes. Somewhere along the way Nigel joined them. The kid could hear his shoes tripping and catching.

'Someone's going to have to walk,' Tillie said as he stowed the gear away. But Nigel just got into the front passenger's seat and Charles got behind the wheel and the rest of them squeezed up in the back.

'I bet they've used your wheels to take him to the hospital,' Tillie said. 'That's if they haven't gone straight to the Bjorn Borg.'

The kid thought of the boy lying on the back seat of the Astra, his legs moving as if he was dreaming of dancing or running. His head was lying on a soft black leather bag. His face went light then dark as the car rushed past street lights. Blood was flowing from his mouth.

'Honestly,' John M. said. 'I've never seen a picture of someone getting hit like that, right in front of the camera.'

'It's my story,' Nigel said slowly. 'I'm going to voice it. No one's going to drop this one.'

John M. made Charles stop the car and the two reporters got out and stood arguing in the middle of the street. In the end they tossed a coin. Nigel lost.

It was past midnight when they got to the hotel. At Reception Nigel just walked away from them. The other crew were still in the Cocktail Bar though the lights were off behind the bar and the grille was down.

'Go and get the night porter to take our drinks, Lassie,' Tillie said. The kid went back into Reception and found a tiny man in a crimson uniform.

When the drinks came, Tillie told the man to put them on John M.'s room.

'What the hell,' the reporter said.

'So who's for an Ugly Night?' Tillie said.

'There's not enough time,' Charles said, sniffing his Remy Martin.

'Yes there fucking is.' Tillie laughed. 'We'll take these drinks down. Deadline a quarter to two at the bar. Twenty quid each. You in, Andy?'

The big cameraman took a bite out of the side of his glass. The kid could heard the crunching. 'Why not?' he said. Then he went on chewing the glass.

They all put their twenty pounds onto the table except John

M. and the kid. The reporter said he had to ring the hospital and he wanted to start editing early in the morning in case Nigel forgot they'd tossed.

The kid got his wallet out, then he said, 'What the hell's an Ugly Night?'

'Shit', Tillie said. 'I forgot you know fuck-all about anything, Lassie. Right, pin back your ears and listen. You go down to the Disco and try to pick up the ugliest tart you can find, chat her up, dance, do whatever you have to because at quarter to two you've got to bring her to the bar and kiss her . . .'

'Bloody hell,' the kid said. He could hear the glass cracking in Andy's mouth.

'And the winner is the bloke with the ugliest.' Tillie was counting the money. 'Give us your twenty then.'

'What do you do when you've kissed them?' the kid said. He hadn't used any of the two hundred he'd drawn in London.

'Just keep the old minces on me,' Tillie said. 'I'll show you.' He reached over and took two tens from the kid's hands. 'There we are, a hundred and twenty quid. Ready steady go.'

Ricky and Brian raced each other to the door. Charles said, 'It's so pointless. They're all repulsive.' He sat twirling the Remy round his glass.

Tillie folded the money and got to his feet. He stuffed the notes in the back pocket of his jeans. 'One of the three of us will win it,' he said. 'It's our lucky night, like being there when the boy was shot. We'll get an award for that, bet you any money. We're also going to win now. Charles because he hates them all or me because I need the money to support all the ugly tarts I used to be married to or Lassie here because he'll have beginner's luck.'

Two trickles of blood ran down Andy's unshaven chin. 'Bullshit,' he said. 'You won't win nothing.'

The kid watched the dancers flickering in the coloured lights. Tillie was dancing very close to a tiny, pretty girl. The kid wondered if he was being set up again. Then he saw Ricky dancing with a woman who was well over six feet tall. She looked puzzled behind her round spectacles. The kid thought she wasn't often asked to dance and certainly not by someone good-looking like Ricky, wearing white shoes and all the gear.

Ignoring the disco music, Charles steered his partner gracefully through as if she was a queen. She had a heavy square face and her mouth was surrounded by livid boils. She stared deep into Charles' eyes as they posed, still for a second, at one end of the floor, then he swept her off again.

Brian had found someone's mother, probably just as she was leaving because she had a coat and hat on. He was unbuttoning her coat, but shouting into her ear so she didn't notice.

The kid went to the bar where Andy was leaning. He was going to have a pint but when Andy asked him he said he'd have a brandy. Andy made it a large one. On the way down to the Disco, Tillie'd said Andy's technique was to wait until the deadline and then grab the ugliest girl in reach.

'The trouble is I fancy them all,' the kid said, smiling. Andy was taking a long time to get the cigarette packet out of his shirt pocket.

Ricky brought his girl to the bar. She was as tall as Andy or Ricky. The kid thought she must be as heavy as Andy. Ricky kept his arm round her waist.

'This is Patricia,' he said seriously. 'And this is Andy and this is Lassie.'

'Lance,' the kid said.

Ricky said something to Patricia, bringing his mouth right up to her ear then he kissed the side of her neck. She closed her eyes behind the round spectacles.

Ricky bought two drinks. 'You two had better get a move on if you're going to find a beauty like this one,' he said. 'You gorgeous little thing.' He lent forward and kissed her big man's face. 'Yummy, yummy, yummy, I've got love in my tummy,' he sang.

The kid walked away from the bar. He found himself having a slash in the Gents on the main Reception floor. He could just go to bed, but the boys would say he'd chickened out. He could just go back and drink with Andy and grab the nearest girl. There was nearly an hour left. But she might object. It would be awful not to find anyone, to be the only one of the boys alone. He didn't mind if he didn't win. He could never ask a girl as ugly as Ricky's to dance; she'd know he was taking the piss. He'd just go out and get someone to dance.

He washed his hands and ran them through his hair, lifting

it up from his forehead and trying to put the waves back in. He wasn't bad-looking, despite what Tillie said. He could get someone to dance. He'd tell her his name was Lance. He'd take her to the bar and buy a drink back for Andy but he wouldn't mock her like Ricky. Shit, he'd been looking at the wrong place, at the dancers. He should've been looking at the girls who weren't dancing, who no one had asked to dance.

Two local boys came in laughing. He stopped arranging his hair. They were both about his age.

'You're right on with her,' one said. 'Jesus, shouldn't I know?' he demanded looking down at the urinal.

The kid passes a row of dark backs, silhouetted against the flames of candles stuck in wine bottles. If he goes inside to look at the faces, they can all look at him. As he ponders, one head turns close to him. He sees a pile of curly, blonde hair above a wide face. She smiles at him. He bends over her. She nods and rises and keeps on rising, a big girl, no, not big, the same height as him, but fat. She rises until she stands there, still smiling despite being so helplessly exposed.

She doesn't look bad to the kid who's swaying slightly as he waits for her to edge her way out, people lifting their legs and sniggering as the great bulk of her leaves its safe mooring and slips out, unstoppable once under way, towards the small tug which surely cannot, but yes, she casts an arm through his and he steers her out to the perilous dance floor.

On the way the kid takes in the fact that she's far from skinny, but his mum is fat and so's his dad. Anyway he is entranced by the kindness of her smile and he also likes the way she's holding his arm. The girl's sheer bulk could be a problem on the crowded floor except she dances lightly and gracefully. At first they dance apart, either because of the fast music or because they do not yet know each other. They don't speak either: he is satisfied to be dancing and is aware that he is not sober. She, she seems simply happy to be dancing.

Then, at first between dances, in the tiny gaps between the records, they start to speak. Her name is Mary, Mary Hamilton. She lives just outside what she calls Londonderry. She is an international switchboard operator for British Telecom.

Soon, though they are still dancing apart, one or other is bobbing forward to speak in the other's ear, placing a steadying hand on a shoulder. Then the music slows and he stops strutting and shaking in front of her and stands, serious with possibilities, and she takes his hands and pulls him close and adjusts his slim body to her satisfaction. Soon his eyes are closed above her shoulder. Her arms are holding him; her body seems all around him. It seems to him he is safe for the first time that day.

Without opening his eyes, he tells her about coming across the Border, making a joke of it. But she doesn't laugh; in fact she stops smiling and frowns slightly.

'Why should they be so cruel to you?' she says.

'Actually I was dead scared,' he says.

While they dance, his mouth moving in the perfumed hair above her right ear, he tells her what great guys they are really, how maybe being shot at around the world has made them tough, how they don't mean any harm, it's just their way of getting through another day, how, after a few more days, they'll just accept him. He tells her how much he wants that, to be accepted as one of the boys, to be treated as an equal.

'They'll get fed up with teasing you soon,' she promises. 'People always do.' She looks sad for a moment, but he doesn't see.

'To tell the truth,' he says, 'I don't know if I can handle the job. We did a riot tonight, up at the Creggan and I hated it. I was so scared. I really was. The others enjoyed it. They were laughing all the time. Maybe I'm too much of a coward.'

Once he's started he can't stop. He tells her about the petrol bombers and the trapped Land Rovers and the window being broken behind him, about the car being stolen and how he didn't argue but was so frightened he forgot his bag, about the hill with the fire at the top and the row of shields at the bottom, about having to put his light on the boy dancing in front of the flames, and the shot which hit him and how everyone seemed to be pleased and how he thought he was going to be sick, how he felt he had been shot himself.

And the music has stopped twice and started up again and the last two tunes are fast and they are the only couple who're hardly moving. Except when Ricky and the large woman drop in behind them and imitate them until Ricky gets fed up with not being noticed.

'Poor Lance,' she says, and it seems to him she opens up her body so he fits more deeply, more sweetly.

'But don't you see?' he insists. 'I put my light on him. I lit him up so they could shoot him . . .'

She says nothing at first, swaying gently, rocking him in her arms. 'Did he ask you not to?' she whispers. 'Did he not want to be filmed?'

'No, he wanted to be on the News. He said we should put the light on.'

'There you are then. He took the responsibility.'

It sounds as if it could be true. The kid hadn't made the boy throw petrol bombs and dance in front of the police. The kid opens his eyes again. Brian has his woman's back turned. She's still got her coat on. He winks hugely. The kid frowns and pulls away slightly.

'What's wrong?' she says.

'Nothing. You've made me feel better.'

He sinks back into her but he turns his wrist behind her neck so he can see his watch. It is nearly twenty to two. The floor isn't so crowded. Ricky and Brian are still dancing. The kid manoeuvres the girl round. So is Charles. But where's Tillie?

'They don't mean any harm,' he whispers.

'You're getting tense again,' she says kneading his shoulders. The kid relaxes against her again. Of course, he'll kiss her, but while the others will be making fun of theirs, he won't be. The other girls are much uglier than Mary so there's no chance he'll win. He can just kiss her and lead her back to the dance floor and sink into her again. Someone taps his shoulder. Ricky. He points to the bar.

'Let's go and have a drink,' the kid says. The other boys are standing out of the crush for last drinks, to the left of the bar. Ricky's huge woman is still dancing against him while he smiles lovingly. Charles' punkish girl is scowling and he is kissing her hand. Brian's mother is having difficulty standing so he is hugging her.

All the men are checking their watches. The clock above the

bar says it's past five to two but bar clocks are always fast. The kid's watch says there's less then a minute to go.

'Why are we standing here, darling?' Mary says because he's not buying a drink.

'These are the other lads,' the kid says. 'We said we'd meet here . . .'

Somebody is shouting outside. The two swing doors to the stairs crash open. Andy strides in. He is carrying someone. A huge black boot hangs over one of his arms. A shiny steel frame encloses the tiny leg above the boot.

Andy makes for them, then veers off behind a pillar in the direction of the dance floor. He reappears still spinning. The girl's mouth is open in a scream of pleasure or panic. Andy puts his own big red mouth over hers.

A door opens in the corner where they are all standing. The door is marked Private. The bar staff have been coming and going through it. But it is Tillie who emerges. He surveys them one by one, grinning, and then very slowly, graciously, like a conjuror, he pulls from the door a small old woman, wrapped in a patched dressing gown, her hair in curlers. Tillie stands as proudly as Nureyev. He pulls her in, across his body and passes her to his other hand. He looks at her with pride.

The old woman looks at them all shyly. 'I was asleep,' she says.

'Mrs Enwright,' Tillie says. 'This is love. This is the real thing.'

With great tenderness, he cradles her head on his left arm, touches her cheek with his right and bends his face to hers. The kid is watching, mouth open, as Tillie, mouth clearly open too, passionately kisses the old woman.

Then the kid sees that he is the only one not kissing. Mary is looking at the floor. It may be that she hasn't seen the old woman or that she is too kind to watch.

'I love you, Mary,' he says.

'Lance,' she says, smiling, and he moves back between her big arms into that soft expanse of breasts and stomach and thighs. Her lips are warm and they slip delightfully over his. He has the smell of her hair again and her fingers are stroking the back of his neck.

Then someone shouts and the kid, surprised, looks up and sees the old woman stagger and nearly fall as, laughing and shouting, Tillie suddenly withdraws her support. Andy puts the crippled girl down carefully on a chair and runs towards the swing doors. Brian and Charles and Ricky are running too, shouting and laughing, slapping each other on the back.

The kid finds they are slapping him on the back too and laughing with him and he's laughing and shouting, all the way up to Tillie's room where they fling themselves on the beds and ring room service for drinks.

And, after a while when they ask his opinion about the winner, he stops thinking about the circle of girls standing downstairs and the flickering coloured lights playing on each of their faces in turn.

The Day The House Fell Down

Mark Illis

Mark Illis was born in London in 1963. He has had three novels published by Bloomsbury: A CHINESE SUMMER, THE ALCHEMIST and THE FEATHER REPORT. His short stories have been published in a variety of magazines and anthologies. He is currently living in West Yorkshire, working as a Centre Director for the Arvon Foundation.

The Day The House Fell Down

Various theories were advanced, but the exact cause of the explosion was never ascertained. Litigation, once started, quickly gathered momentum: sides were taken, accusations were made and argued, retracted and repeated, but the only consensus eventually reached was that a long established structural defect was probably at fault. A combination of unusual circumstances had brought crucial pressure to bear.

They were sun-bathing in the garden. It was late August. That enervated, end of the summer feeling. Mona had a book open in front of her and was occasionally reading, and Warren was dozing, when the grumbling, then thundering crash roused them both. Mona remembered afterwards that she had been studying Warren's face, interested in the way its wrinkles and creases were erased in sleep, leaving it smooth and still, pink and boyish. A flying fragment of glass, dart-like, narrowly missed impaling itself in his cheek.

What they saw, when they looked, was that four walls of their bungalow had been reduced almost to rubble, while the roof lay in pieces, mainly in the garden. Mona's first thought was that a bomb had fallen, perhaps the bomb. Warren thought he was dreaming. Something in the quality of the early afternoon air told them both that they were wrong: birds, briefly alarmed, were already singing again, the sun was still hot and unfiltered by any kind of cloud, the pages of Mona's book still turned in the gentlest of breezes. Over the ruin, the dust shook and swirled and, in its own sweet time, settled.

Later they agreed that their marriage nearly collapsed on the same day as their home. When Mona had fully taken in what had happened, and had edged her way through fallen bricks and slates to examine the damage, she laughed. She did it properly, a belly laugh without a trace of hysteria, her bony brown shoulders rising and falling ever so slightly tickled by the fringe of her curly hair. With one finger she pushed a window frame, standing empty and unbolstered at waist height, and it toppled into what used to be the kitchen. She studied the scene in front of her. A table had survived the accident, and the remains of lunch – plates and crumbs of quiche – were still in place, waiting to be cleared and washed. An unbroken glass lay on its side and a puddle of water dripped on to the floor, each distinct drip framing silence.

'This . . .' said Mona, and paused, trying to find the right expression. Her single word hung in the air, suspended, almost adequate in itself. Hands on hips, topless and grinning, she turned to Warren. 'This is phenomenal.'

Warren was standing too, his out of condition stomach slightly over-hanging his brief black trunks. He could feel the sun burning his neck and shoulders and the backs of his legs. His mouth was open half an inch, not enough to look foolish, just enough to convey anger as well as surprise.

'This is funny to you?'

'To be honest,' said Mona, 'I can't pretend to be unhappy.' Still smiling, ignoring his temper, she spoke with an airiness that for a moment made Warren wonder if she had somehow engineered the catastrophe. 'I mean it's a clean slate isn't it?' She failed to suppress another laugh. 'You could call it that, I think?'

Distress, welling up like a blush, gradually overwhelmed Warren's other emotions. 'This was our hiding-place,' he said, 'our priest's hole.'

She came towards him and rested a hand on his upper arm, then moved it quickly, as if scalded. 'Hot,' she said, miming surprise. He didn't react. 'Sweetheart,' she tried again, '*accept*. It was on the cards. It might as well have been, let's face it, a house of cards.' She smiled at her phrase. She was definitely in a smiling mood. She felt like someone whose argument has just been proved, and is trying hard not to say 'I told you so'.

He pulled away from her. 'What do you mean, "it was on the cards"? What are you saying?'

She took his hand and pulled him forwards again. 'Let's both have a closer look.'

They went through the wrecked front door – 'I suppose it's safe,' she said – and they began to explore. Warren was in the sitting-room, trying to get at the stereo that would never play records again, wanting to unplug it, when he heard a shout from Mona. He gave up trying to climb the shifting pile of rubble in front of him, and he followed the sound of his wife's voice. He found her in the bedroom, standing next to a remarkably clean bed. 'I took off the duvet and some masonry,' she said, 'and it was good as new. Look at it.'

The sheet was pristine, uncreased and bright white in the sun gushing into the decapitated room. Mona stood next to the bed, sweaty, a little dusty, her chest rising and falling after her exertion. He saw moisture glistening in her cleavage. Now a different feeling welled uncontrollably through Warren. While his eyes and the downward curl of his mouth showed that his distress was essentially undiminished, he shook himself and climbed over the fallen wardrobe towards her.

She opened her arms to him, laid her palms on his warm skin. 'We're like a couple of randy phoenixes.'

Wriggling, she pulled down his trunks, while he slid her bikini bottoms over her hips and let them drop down her legs to her ankles. Each took a step out of their briefs, thigh sliding smoothly over thigh. On the bed he felt the sun falling freshly on to his cool buttocks, and as they rolled over on the firm, bouncy mattress he caught glimpses of the sky, exposed, like a vast pool above them. Her face filled his view, her weight upon him, soft and pressing.

The waist-high walls, and the scattered bricks and glass and splinters of wood, the dust and the broken furnishings and the dangerously dangling wires, even the direct burning warmth of the sun and the still rich blue of the sky, only very gradually impinged themselves again on the awareness of the couple on the bed. For Warren it was like slowly, progressively remembering a bad dream. Another change in the balance of his emotions: a diminishing of satisfaction and composure, a sense of something torn apart, a sense of bereavement, and the stirring of anger again as he turned his head and saw Mona eyeing the ruin of their bedroom with placid equanimity. He understood. To her, this was the conclusion of the argument that had continued off and on since shortly after their honeymoon. She was already thinking about where they were going to move: she had in mind a large flat not too far from the centre of town, near a pub and within reach of a park by preference. Neighbours who dropped in now and then. Dinner parties.

'Isn't this . . .' said Mona, '. . . nice?'

Not his idea of home comforts. His idea of an ideal home was a bungalow, because who needs a second storey when there's only two of you, and the only view you want is of your beautiful garden? It was, or used to be, a fully detached bungalow, set back from the quiet road, near a few shops and only just within commutable distance of town, and the anonymous office where he worked.

In a characteristic pose, lying on her back with one hand behind her head, holding a fistful of curls, Mona seemed to be thinking aloud. 'We'll stay with Muriel, and we can start house-hunting on Tuesday. I'll take the day off work. We better ring the insurance today,' – now she turned to Warren – 'that's your department. I wonder if we can sue. Do you think we can sue?'

For a moment he had the illusion that the depthless sky was below him, receding now, and he was in danger of plunging downwards into it. His fingers clutched the sheet. A feeling of width, and risk. A lasting change had occurred, as unexpected as the sudden revelation of a spreading disease. There could be no more privacy. Society, which he had always felt was laying siege to him personally in railway carriages, in the street and in the office, seemed to have succeeded in shattering his last place of retreat.

Mona shook him gently by the shoulder. 'Where are you? I said, "Do you think we can sue?"'

'Yes,' he said, 'I don't know. It depends. Why did you say it was on the cards? What do you mean it was a house of cards? What are you saying?'

She laughed. 'Well, look at it!' Then, seeing his irritation, she sat up, and knelt on the mattress. 'Honey, just accept it, it's happened. It has happened, hasn't it? You *know* I've been wanting to move, I *said* I can't pretend to be sorry. Why should I pretend?' Arms extended, palms outward: the essence of reasonableness.

There was another shift in Warren's feelings, this time a jolting one: he was suddenly, unexpectedly, furious.

He sat up and brushed aside the hands that moved towards him. 'This was our *home*. Didn't it feel that way to you? It felt that way to me. It was safe, we were *safe* here. You don't understand what I'm saying, there's a communication gap, I'm not getting through, am I? Look at these walls.' He put a hand to her cheek and moved her face, like a slow motion slap. '*Look* at these walls. This was no house of cards.'

He looked round with her, and caught sight of himself in a broken dressing table mirror, splintered images of himself, naked, red and indignant, spluttering, against the background of the remains of the bedroom. Conscious of the absurdity of the image, he bounced off the mattress and made his way to a lopsided but largely undamaged chest of drawers. Mona watched the jerky movements of his thighs, buttocks and back as he found some clothes. He needed some cream really, the sun had already caught him. She said nothing for a while, hoping that his irritable snatching at the drawers would release some of his anger, or that the familiar routine of dressing might calm him a little. She saw him dwindling gradually, into a disconsolate sulk. It didn't happen. He was nursing his mood, feeding it with silent provocations and responses. As he pulled on a pair of shorts, she got off the bed and spoke.

'Of course it was our home,' she said. 'It was always that.' He bent over to fasten his sandals and she was unable to see his face. A persuasive tone: 'It wasn't a *for*tress. I know your attitude, but perhaps you'll have to adapt. Have you thought of that? Look at it, it's useless now.'

Still silent, he left the room, clambering over the wardrobe in front of the door with as much dignity as he could manage. Mona's voice rose in exasperation behind him. 'What is it you want from a marriage anyway? Is this all you want?'

He was already out of the room, but she picked up a brick from the floor anyway, and waved it.

Although he could have climbed, or in places even stepped over the outside wall, Warren left the house by the front door, pausing only to grab an overcoat from a sagging hook in the hall. He walked out on to the road and, by habit, turned towards the shops and the station, unsure of where he was heading, following the route most familiar to him.

She'll learn, he was thinking. Devil-may-care attitude. She'll *have* to learn, you can't go through life like that, it's just not on, you have to learn the rules. It's dangerous to be so casual, nothing less than dangerous.

Lost in his speculations, Warren had begun muttering aloud to himself, and people stared at him as he passed. He made an odd figure, his hair unruly, his round face red, his thin shins bare and brisk beneath his unsuitable overcoat. As he approached the village the pavement around him was becoming crowded. There was only a small cluster of buildings around the station, a restaurant, an estate agent, a funeral parlour and some shops, but an unusually large crowd was moving along in the same direction as Warren, a Saturday afternoon rush-hour.

'Breaking the rules,' he was saying, 'big mistake.' His pace was increasing, and he cannoned off someone in front of him, barely noticing, not hearing an irritated 'Watch yourself.' Someone behind him just missed stepping on his heel, and walked into his shoulder instead. Warren still didn't notice, simply speeded up, dodging people, bumping into them, unaware of their angry looks and complaints, bouncing back and forth among them as if hopelessly unco-ordinated.

As he left the village, however, Warren realized that he had already passed the station and had crossed the short, picturesque bridge over the river. Like a driver automatically stopping and starting in a traffic jam, he only gradually became conscious of his mode of motion. He was moving through a growing mass of people like a fouling footballer dribbling through a clumsy opposition, and he was approaching . . . he was approaching a fairground. Bank Holiday weekend. He had been hearing the music for some minutes. At the top of the hill leading down to the common he stopped and gazed at the huge, maze-like, multi-coloured fair. He was immediately pushed forward again with a curse as someone collided with him from behind. He moved slightly to one side and hit someone else. The crowd was gathering momentum as it went down the slope, and there were no side-roads in sight. The road itself offered no obvious relief, because it was jammed with cars as the pavement was with people. If he squeezed over to the other side, or walked up the white line . . . Warren surrendered himself to the cohesive pull of the crowd. It occurred to him that he might kill half an hour at the fair as easily as anywhere else. With an inward, fatalistic shrug, he acknowledged that it was easiest in fact to be anonymous in the crowd. He adjusted his pace to that of those around him, became inconspicuous, descending the hill without any more collisions, and he entered the fairground through a colourful, unbroken corridor of stalls manned by yelling, scary-looking adults and children and infested, in almost every case, by a mutant menagerie of garish cuddly toys.

Dodgems, Ghost Train, Gravity Mover, Octopus, Catwalk, Caterpillar, Haunted House, House of Fun, Hall of Mirrors – Warren moved through the maze, around its roundabouts, over matted, dirty grass, through the swarm of children, youths and parents. His mood of fatalism was waning as he became, to his surprise, increasingly engaged by the atmosphere: sights and smells and shouts and the groan and whine of heavy machinery. Portions of oily black moving parts showed beneath glaring painted and lacquered wooden panels. The undertone of squalor was candid. A snarl in the wolfish grin of the man offering him the darts.

'Fifty pee come on only fifty pee have a go have a go what do you say have a go what do you say?'

He took the darts and had a go, scored under twenty-one on the pitted board five feet away, and won a moulting pink elephant drawn from a selection which included lime green leopards and neon orange snakes.

'Well done well done take it home to the kiddies. Who's next to win a prize who's next to win who's next?'

Warren squeezed the elephant into one of his large overcoat pockets and moved on, surveying the scene with an amiable sense of aloofness. The virtual razing of his home had returned almost to the status of a dream, and the ease with which he moved among these people, so many people, reassured him profoundly. No one is looking at me, he thought, no one cares about me or has time for me. I am invisible. Conformity is the passport, no one questions it.

He was approaching the queue for the Helter Skelter. It was less a queue, he realized, than an impatient gathering, an intimate knot of people round the stumpy, striped tower. Warren savoured his sensations. It smelt here of . . . wood shavings and sugar. He warily examined the people waiting for their turn. Children mostly, shepherded by fathers. He saw one man who was alone, and felt an interest in him for that reason. He wore a loose anorak as unsuitable for the weather as Warren's overcoat. Did he too have an air of wariness? Warren felt he could almost have been watching himself. No, he was with someone, that thuggish looking T-shirted man he was brushing up against . . . no, he was alone, it was just a movement of the queue. But then why . . . ? The man in the anorak left the queue, giving up his chance of a ride, and walked towards the shadows of an amusement arcade, dropping on his way a wallet into the bag of another man who was buying candy floss. It was a slick and unobtrusive manoeuvre which Warren only noticed because of his cautious observation of the people around him. He turned back now to the pickpocket's victim, and their eyes met as the man's hand went to his pocket, looking for the money for his son's ride. Warren watched his face change, watched his hand move to another pocket, and another, and then, fascinated, watched himself become focused in the man's eyes, watched a thought appearing, traced in the man's spreading frown, which seemed to make his face smaller.

Warren felt an impulse, and acted on its prompting immediately: he turned and walked away, retreating towards the Ghost Train in the corner, where a grinning spook leant over the doors to the dark tunnel, seeming to beckon. Perhaps it would be wise . . .

A hand on his shoulder pulled him round.

'Ten seconds.'

'What?'

'That's how long you've got. Where is it?'

The man from the queue, much bigger at close range, much more real now Warren could read the word MUSCLE on his T-shirt, and see the spot quivering slightly at the side of his mouth, and see the yellow teeth, speckled with toffee apple. A boxer's nose: fat, flat and flared.

'My dad will hit you if you don't tell.'

The son, in jeans and a sleeveless T-shirt that also said MUS-CLE, was a miniature copy of the father. Warren believed him.

'I haven't got it, I saw the man who took it, he's in the amusement arcade, I mean that's where he went, only he hasn't got it either because he gave it to someone, I don't know where he went.'

Warren accompanied this not very convincing speech by pointing his hands this way and that, in an unintentional parody of concern. The man's face clenched. Warren had thought it was clenched before but he realized he must have been wrong because it definitely clenched now. Even the man's temples, flat and hard beneath his cropped hair, were menacing, like the sides of a battleship. Warren thought he saw a bicep twitch.

'You're not talking your way out of this. You were the smart bastard pushing people around coming down that hill, yes I saw you, how many wallets did you lift then, eh? I nearly did you then, but I'm going to do you now' – ('He's going to do you,' said his son excitedly) – 'unless you empty the pockets of your fucking overcoat, fucking overcoat in this weather, right now. Let's start with that one,' he revealed his speckled teeth again as he pointed at Warren's bulging side pocket, 'shall we? Have I hit the jackpot already? Have I? What's in that pocket right there, why don't you just tell me, eh?'

'An elephant,' said Warren, anxious to appease, without thinking, 'a pink elephant.'

Quite suddenly, a very large fist seemed to explode against his nose and right eye. He staggered back, but before he had even realized what had happened he was jerked forward again on to another fist pistoning into his stomach. He sat down and shut his eyes for several seconds, choking. Noises reached him from above. As Warren opened his eyes he saw the man's booted foot approaching at speed. He twisted just in time to save himself a broken rib, and got a badly bruised arm instead. As he curled his head into his elbow he glimpsed the appalled face of the man's son, wide-eyed and open-mouthed, staring at his father in terror.

'What it was, quite simple, he asked for it, that's what it was.'

'That type is a parasite, that type is simply a parasite.'

'Fair enough, I heard it all, fair enough.'

'Asked for it he did, stood there and asked for a kicking.'

Warren, partly deafened by his own breathing, wasn't sure if people were really saying everything twice or if his ears were full of echoes.

'That's enough. Would someone kindly tell me what exactly is going on? You sir, would you kindly tell me what exactly is going on?'

It was this touch of bored, authoritative politeness that persuaded Warren to lift his head and open his eyes. What he saw, however, made him close them again at once, as he might have if he had been on one of the more frightening rides he had seen earlier. A circle of faces was peering down at him, hateful faces displaying curiosity and hostility, great round moon-like faces hovering over him, their true feelings out in the open at last, judging and unpitying. Warren felt that a vast conspiracy against him had finally chosen to reveal itself.

'He's awake,' said the boy, 'he's awake now.' He touched Warren's shoulder. 'Are you awake?'

'Give the man some air now, stand back please.'

Warren re-opened his eyes, but only a little, at the sound of the policeman's voice. One of them in any case didn't want to open at all. He dimly saw his controversial pink elephant dangling in front of his face.

'Is this yours, sir? I'll be needing a statement.'

With his limited vision Warren followed the elephant to a hand, to an arm, and to a face beneath a black helmet. It was a relatively unhostile face, a face reserving its judgment. A statement. If he could find a clear, concise statement, it might begin to make sense of the situation.

'Someone hit me?' he said.

This turned out to be a mistake. The chorus of voices started up again, different pitches of accusation and insult competing with each other. The policeman, helping Warren to his feet, was about to intervene again, when a new voice over-rode the rest.

'I can help here, I have seen this man before.'

Warren, on his feet now, though stooping and clutching his stomach, looked at the newcomer. In his confused state, he didn't take much in. A silver-haired man with a large nose. His head was tilted back so that he seemed to be using the nose to line up Warren in his sights. He was faintly familiar . . . was he a neighbour? Warren didn't know any neighbours well enough to expect them to step in like this to vouch for him.

'He was in the thick of a crowd earlier,' said the man, lowering his nose very slightly as if the weight was proving too much for him, and turning it towards the policeman. 'He was in the thick of the crowd, and he was bumping into everyone, including myself.' A pause for effect. 'And now I too find that my wallet has disappeared. This man has taken my wallet, there's no question about that. I have no doubt that he's a professional. I have no doubt at all that he's passed it on by now to an accomplice.' The nose was redeployed towards Warren. 'That is the procedure, I believe?' Warren was speechless. 'Well, what do you have to say for yourself? Surely you have something to say?' He turned back to the policeman with the air of a man who has proved his point. 'My name is Douglas Stride, officer, and I will make a full statement.'

The first man nodded. 'And me. I'll make a statement too. What more do you want? He's got nothing to say. Nick him.'

The policeman removed his fingers from the bridge of his nose, which he had been nursing like a man with a headache. 'You'd better come with me, sir. You'd better all three come with me. It's probably all on video anyway.' He nodded to one side and Warren saw, tucked in beside the Ghost Train, a chequered van with long dark windows and a big birthday cake attachment on the roof, topped by a perspex nodule.

'Bloody hell,' said the MUSCLE man, impressed, 'there's always someone watching, isn't there?'

Warren had been in the room for an hour when the drunk had staggered in to join him and had chosen, perversely, to sit on the bench beside him. He had introduced himself as 'Parker, Jake Parker.' Now he was sleeping, his head resting on Warren's shoulder, and he was belching softly in his sleep. Warren felt that soon one of them would throw up. On the whole, he hoped it would be himself.

He had answered questions and filled in forms. He had asked at an early stage whether he should call his solicitor. 'No need for that,' they had told him, 'unless you did it of course. We'll just have a glance at this video, and see what we're doing. Or what *you're* doing really. In fact you could go home for now, if you like. It would be more *helpful* if you stayed. Won't take a jiffy.' Warren had stayed.

He was in a bland, well-lighted room, like a doctor's waiting room. A variety of stale human odours blanketed a faint scent of disinfectant. There was a table, two upright seats, and a bench like a pew along the wall. Warren reassured himself: it could be a doctor's waiting room. His gloomy thoughts began to gain their own momentum. Soon, he decided, a young uniformed receptionist with an expensive hairstyle will put her head around the door to announce: 'They're ready for you now.' Only she'll lead me, not to the doctor, but to the judge, and she'll sit at a desk and take notes while my accusers have their say.

Warren ran a hand over his scalp, and when he brought it down again he saw hairs between his fingers. He shook his head – a brisk, irritated shake without much movement. 'No, no, no,' he said.

There was a stirring at this from Jake, a waking grunt, and Warren stiffened. He felt that it was safest not to move, although assessing other people, he admitted to himself, was not one of his strong points. Nor was being so close to them. Nor was talking to them. Why was he speechless when the silver-haired man, Stride, was pontificating? No one will defend you, Warren told himself, unless you defend yourself.

Craning his neck, he gazed out of the window above him, comparing this pinched portion of the sky unfavourably with the view he had seen, but not enjoyed, earlier that day. A loud belch from Jake reminded him that the standard of company had also declined. A question occurred to Warren so vividly that he wasn't sure for a moment if he spoke it or not: Did I really leave my naked wife in the sunshine on the bed to embrace this stinking, belching drunk? As he had earlier in the day, Warren noticed his own absurdity. It was embarrassing. His emotions experienced a tidal change, his timidness swamped by mutually dependent self-pity and self-disgust. Uncontrollably, he felt a sudden shivering aversion for the man next to him, for the people who had accused him, for the careless policemen he could hear outside the door. He seemed to pulse with a hatred he could not express. He tried to breathe slowly but could not. Stress, he said to himself, ulcers, heart disease. This helplessness was something he had always been expecting to overtake him sooner or later. Slowly, and quite gently, Warren began to bang his head against the wall he was leaning on.

Jake suddenly came to life. 'No, no, don't hurt yourself! No, *don't*! Don't hurt yourself, don't do that.'

Warren obediently stopped. He was impressionable at the best of times, and his nature would not allow him to sustain violent emotions.

When he had thought about prison in the past, it had been a variation on his dream of an ideal home. He had imagined a south-facing cell of his own, with a bed and some books on a makeshift shelf, a tin mug with his toothbrush in it, and a shaft of light coming through the barred window, falling on his pillow. Dust dancing in the beam. Warders who respected his space. It had all seemed attractive. What he had forgotten, he now realized, was overcrowding.

Pleased with his success, Jake raised his head and tried a new gambit: 'Afternoons you know, you know afternoons? They go on and on don't they?' He smiled companionably, his eyes unfocused, like his words. Spittle emerged now and then from the corner of his mouth, and he licked it away. A sing-song lilt entered his voice. 'On anon anon anon . . .' He interrupted himself with another, more violent belch. He swallowed and licked his lips. 'Do 'pologize,' he said complacently.

Warren had decided that his dream might still be attainable, but he would have to do something really despicable, in order to get into solitary confinement. He was considering this problem. He knew himself well enough to realize that it was unlikely that he would do anything *really* despicable. Something mildly contemptible, possibly. Something selfish, something he would repent at leisure, certainly. Something stupid, something rash, something in bad taste, even something unnecessarily violent though probably with mitigating circumstances. That was it though, as far as he could tell, those were the limits within which he operated.

By now Jake was pretty sure he was an accomplished raconteur. He sat up a little straighter, put a brotherly arm around Warren's shoulders, and spoke again, with careful lucidity. Only now and then would his eagerness to communicate garble his words.

'Lissen, what you have to do, I know what you have to do . . . you . . . havetohave *rules*.'

Warren paused in removing the arm from his shoulders. 'Roles?'

'*Rules*.'

'Oh, rules.'

'*Have*tohave rules.'

Now Warren had deciphered the words, it seemed to him that Jake had been mind-reading. 'What rules? What are your rules?'

A belch. 'I tole you, don't *hurt* yourself is a rule. You muss lissen or you won't learn.' He said it impatiently, as if reminding a child. Repelled by his tone as well as his breath, Warren stood up and looked at him for the first time. Jake was a small man, with a small, slim face dominated by thick wet lips and a livid black eye. He looked ridiculous. He was creased over on the bench as if perforated along the waist. But Warren was abruptly aware that he too had a black eye, and that his clothes were much less respectable that Jake's. He looked down at himself. He looked like a flasher. But to be patronized by Jake, in his gin-soaked breath. Warren sat down at the table and began to play with a tin ash-tray, rolling it on its edge, tapping it on the table surface.

'I'm sure you have other rules?'

The answer came easily: 'Never ever lose a frenn. Easy to lose, frenns, hard to find them again.' A damp sniff. Jake's eyes were wet. 'It's verr, verr sad to lose a frenn.' He shook his head. 'No, don't lose them.' He looked at where Warren had been, seeming to notice for the first time that he had moved. Mouth hanging open, he moved his head around until he found him again. He stood up unsteadily. 'Are you my frenn?'

Warren tried to think, but found that his faculties were not fully in order. It was impossible to read Jake's attitude: he was maudlin, but was he belligerent?

'No,' he said, 'I'm not your friend.' He was immensely pleased with himself.

Jake walked over to him, placed his hand on his shoulder again and looked at him carefully. 'Thass all ri',' he slurred generously, his diction deteriorating further. 'Doan worry, thass fine. Doan make *enmies*!' he declared. 'Rule number . . . number . . .' Through the hand gripping his shoulder Warren felt the paroxysm that accompanied a terrific, shuddering belch. Jake threw up into his lap. A colourful flood of vomit fell over and between his bare legs, down his shins and on to his sandalled feet.

'Warren Winter?' An officer had opened the door. Warren rose and marched purposefully towards him, leaving wet footprints on the way, determined at last to assert himself. Before he could speak the officer, with a dubious wrinkle of his nose, said, 'Would you like a wash before you go, sir?'

On his instructions, the police car dropped Warren on the bridge, half a mile from home. He thanked the Constable at the wheel, who nodded and said 'Be good.'

Warren closed the door, restoring the red line that ran along the side of the white car. He took a deep breath of the fresh air, and the smile on his face broadened as he stretched indulgently. The sun was low now, glaring into his eyes and throwing long shadows on to the river. Over the hill behind him the fair was already lit up, turning the light grey, sounding from the bridge like a distant party. A few people were passing, and some stared curiously at Warren. He ignored them. After two hours in the bare room, some of it spent in despair, he had felt only exhilaration at his release, and now he was well satisfied with himself, almost smug about surviving his ordeal and emerging 'Beaten,' he murmured, 'but unbowed.' This self-satisfaction was mingled with the glow of a self-consciously generous man. He had declined to press charges of assault on his supposed victim, or charges of libel (suggested by the policeman) on Mr Stride, who had written a largely fanciful statement and then disappeared in a hurry after seeing the exonerating video.

Warren had achieved a sense of peace. Things, he felt, were falling into place. He had asked to be dropped off at the bridge so that the view might enhance this sense. The river was conducive to calm, and the trees bowed over it, staid and shaggy. Houses unrolled their tidy gardens down the banks. There was an immaculate, infectious tranquillity about the scene. The long summer evening was beginning.

He found himself unimpressed. It is a small step from peace to acquiescence, but he felt unable to make it. Ex-con and survivor of an exploded house, he felt out of place, and subtly trammelled. The balance of his feelings was upset again, his emotions seemed to travel tangibly inside him, like impulsive movements of the blood. The day had awakened something in Warren that made him uncomfortable with this pleasant view. He thought briefly of his garden, and the sense of contentment it encouraged, and then he looked away, down to the dark water, moving sluggishly below. When he finally moved on, heading for home, he limped slightly, as if he had just remembered some nagging, disabling pain.

Warren hadn't called Mona from the police station. Now he imagined her worrying about him, trying to cope with the authorities and wondering whether she should leave to see her sister Muriel before he returned. He had acted thoughtlessly to leave her in such – he chose his word – in such an *unusual* situation. 'Unusual' was a good word, it suggested no over-reaction.

The cul-de-sac was almost blocked by the big van, the cars and the fire engine. When he walked into the garden Warren saw immediately that Mona, in bikini briefs again and a T-shirt, was holding her own competently. In fact she was competently holding a glass of wine, a sandwich and a conversation with a fireman. About thirty other people were milling around the garden.

'Here he is at last,' cried Mona, raising her glass as she caught sight of him. 'Better late than never my love.'

'What?' The one quiet word was all he could manage.

'Where have you been?' Mona met him as she approached, opening her arms awkwardly, seeming to offer him the wine and the sandwich. Friends and strangers watched them, and saw Mona stop herself as she was about to embrace him. 'What happened to you? Your poor face?' Her attempt to disregard his absence was washed away by her concern. She raised her hand towards his eye at the same time that Warren did, and the wine was knocked away from her. The glass fell on a jagged piece of slate, shattering loudly.

'My face?' Warren was becoming aware of the eyes on him, they were beginning to penetrate his capable mood and strain his composure.

'Your eye, my love. Don't you know that you have a black eye?' Tenderly she touched the swollen, discoloured skin, thinking of the smoothness of his sleeping face that morning.

Warren flinched. 'Yes,' he said. 'No. I'll tell you later.' He looked around. 'All these people.'

'Well, yes,' said Mona. Her hand went reassuringly around his waist, under his overcoat. 'They're here to help.'

The men from the council, the firemen, the policemen, the gas men, the neighbours and their children, the sister-in-law and her husband, the . . . was that the milkman?

Warren looked at them all, and they all looked away, continued interrupted conversations, became interested in note-books or fragments of piping, as if overcome by sudden waves of tact.

Warren was maintaining appearances, but his new-found bravado was leaking away. The concept of wide horizons received a qualified welcome, and he was prepared to accept the idea of surviving challenges, but all these *people*. It was a mass invasion of his territory, an occupation following a bombardment. Still, he was maintaining appearances. He met the eyes suddenly of the silver-haired man from the fairground. Stride. That was why he had recognized him, he had seen him in the street and at the station, he was a neighbour, as Warren had guessed. Stride looked pompous, even aggressive, but he looked away when Warren's stare did not waver.

Warren disengaged himself from his wife and walked through the groups of people, jostling them carelessly, towards the remains of his house. He was aware now that his peaceful mood was as fragile as the house had been. Meditatively, he picked up a fallen brick and placed it on a low wall.

An officious voice intervened: 'Now then sir, no touching if you please.'

Warren whirled round, and his composure shattered. 'This is my *home*.'

The owner of the voice, one of the firemen, scratched an ear and raised a sceptical eyebrow.

'We can rebuild it,' said Warren, his voice rising in pitch and volume. Faces turned again. As a policeman offered her another drink, Mona watched anxiously. Arms raised like an Old Testament prophet, Warren addressed all the faces turned towards him. 'Why not? We can, we *can* rebuild it.' There was a general movement in his direction, as if his audience was settling in for a speech. Even Stride, comfortable in the crowd, advanced. Warren backed away and, finding himself on his threshold, he broke the flimsy yellow tape barring his way and marched through his front door.

He was in the hall. The walls on either side of him rose above his head but in front, where three more walls should have been blocking his view, he could see a tree and one of the taller bushes in the garden. He hung up his overcoat on the sagging hook and it fell to the ground, leaving behind it a powdery white niche. He watched the plaster float like dandruff on to his coat. To escape the eyes he knew were on his back, he moved on to the sitting room. His fingers ran absently over ridged and torn wallpaper. The exterior wall in the sitting room had collapsed in an inverted arch, so that in the middle it could be stepped over with ease. As he moved around the mound of rubble in the centre of the floor, people watched. There were spectators outside the kitchen too, where Warren straightened the cutlery on the table. More people outside the bedroom, people looking in, exchanging whispers and nods. Warren's watched face was impassive, while his fingers continued to stray over bricks and battered possessions in different rooms.

Back in the hall he saw that most of the people were still gathered outside the front door. He turned away and, cursing the dust, put a finger to his eye, and found a tear. He sniffed loudly, then jumped as a hand rested on his shoulder. The officious fireman? He turned to see Mona, and felt a surge of pleasure that it was her face, and no one else's, that he saw.

She looked askance. 'I don't know why you're getting sentimental. I've hired a van. We can take everything we want. There's no problem.'

He shook his head. 'The dust.' He tugged at a hanging strip of wallpaper, which came away in his hand. 'This is no problem.' He dropped the paper. 'House of cards, this. It's not really the point any more, is it?'

'Are you going to tell me about your face? And why you're limping? You're a sight you know, I think your body's given up in sympathy with the house. Where have you been?'

'I've been to the fair,' he said. 'Up and down and all around. There's a lot I want to tell you.'

'Are you all right, then?' Mona was watching him carefully.

He seemed not to hear. 'There's more at stake here,' he said, 'than all this. There's an idiom to be learnt.' All day people had been asking him to speak to them, give them answers, explanations and statements. 'And there are as many different images as you'd find in a Hall of Mirrors. I don't know.' He thought of his neighbour in the garden, ashamed to meet his eye, but eager not to miss any of the action. How many brash or competent personalities are built on such suspect grounds? It was a consoling thought. He was trying as he spoke to achieve some control over his fluctuating feelings. For a beginning, through an effort of quelling, of inward dialogue and pep-talk, he was aiming for some confidence in himself. Some kind of foundation at least. 'I don't know.' He became aware of his wife's gaze, and tried a smile. A twisted smile in a sun-burnt face, bright red around the large, purplish black eye.

'We'll start loading that van,' he said, 'before the place gets looted. There's villains everywhere, you know.'

She shook her head. 'First I'm going to put some cream on you. It'll be a start anyway.'

'In the bathroom?'

'Yes.'

'Have you noticed about the bathroom?'

'What about it?'

'It's the only room not visible from outside. And it still has a lock.'

'Yes.'

'Yes, and I was considering . . .'

'Yes.'

'I was thinking that we could . . .'

'I said yes.'

Some people outside got bored and left, but most stayed. Most were still eager to hear what Warren had to say for himself, believing themselves competent to judge his words.

Woodsmoke

Kathy Page

Kathy Page's short stories are collected in AS IN MUSIC (Methuen) and widely anthologized; she is working on a new collection. She was awarded an Arts Council bursary in 1994. As well as writing for radio and television she has published four novels, the most recent being FRANKIE STYNE and THE SILVER MAN (Methuen).

ʃ

Woodsmoke

The thin man came into the cafe, late, four days in a row. Each time he drank only a small coffee, a glass of water. But that particular day he ordered a lemon cake as well and ate it quickly without using the fork, leaning over the table and pressing his finger on the plate to pick up crumbs. His skin seemed sallow against the white of his shirt; a foreigner, I thought, though I couldn't tell what kind, and not a tourist. From the way he spoke, in a careful, educated way, I knew that it must be a long time since he came from wherever it was he belonged to: a dry country, I guessed, mountainous, where people lived scattered thinly among their sheep and goats, were careful and burned fires all year long. Where the single city was full of the sound of bells; the streets lined with country people selling fruit and bolts of cloth. An old, quiet place, with cars only for the important people – not sunny, not bright with chrome and neon like here. I was very young then and I liked only new things.

The first time he had appeared I was angry. Summer was over; people went home early: often not a single customer pushed through the glass doors after eight o'clock, so that I could eat, sweep, and still have thirty minutes to sit on a stool with my shoes off and my books open. But as it turned out, the foreigner was never a nuisance: he did not put on the juke box and he did not expect to talk to me the way most men do. He simply sat with his back to the mirrored wall and looked out of the window towards the sea, or read a newspaper. When I turned off the lights behind the bar, he would shift slightly in his chair. When I went to pick up the chairs and stack them upside down on the tables, he took his own cup to the counter, before wishing me goodnight and leaving me with five minutes still to sweep the floor. So I had grown used to him and that evening, when I looked up from my book and saw him sitting there still as one of the stones on the beach, I asked:

'Have you been here long?' As if he had been waiting for me to speak, his answer: 'eight years' overlapped the question. He rose quickly to his feet and brought over his cup, plate and glass, although there were still fifteen minutes to nine.

'I am working at the hospital,' he continued, 'just started. Paediatrics. It took me six years to re-qualify, although I was fully trained in my own country and head of a department, in fact.'

'I am studying too,' I told him as I put my books away. 'Languages. But I can't do it full time. It will probably take me sixty years to get my degree, so don't complain.'

'You're from the country,' he said.

'Maybe,' I told him, because I didn't like it that it showed still; I had felt ever since school began that I didn't belong there, with the perpetual dust and the lame cattle and the bent old women, the men with no teeth, but in the places they taught us of. The foreign man smiled in a quick, shy way that I liked: so different from the slow grins of the local men. I surprised myself by saying:

'Would you like to come home with me?'

'Yes, please, I would,' the man said.

We walked quickly through the streets and up the stairs to where my two rooms were: the small kitchen with its Calor stove and stone sink, the other with my books, table and folding bed. The shower was on the floor below. I poured some wine. We sat side by side on the cream lace spread that Grandmother had given me before I left. I unbuttoned his shirt. His skin was a pale, woody brown, not honey coloured like mine nor rich chocolate like that of the man before him. I pressed my face into its warmth, breathed him in. He smelled like something burning, like woodsmoke, part bitter, part mystery. And his nipples, when I found them with my lips, were also bitter. But it was a kind of bitterness that was almost sweet in the way that it made me want to taste more of it: I leaned into him, slipped one hand around to his back, running my fingers down the side of his spine. I pushed against him, wanting him to lie down so that I could sit astride him and look down into his face. I was sure in my bones that this foreigner would be a good lover, sensual, considerate. But he resisted me and sat there quite straight on my bed.

'You see, I had to leave my own country,' he said suddenly. I could feel his voice vibrating in his chest. I wanted him to touch me now, not to talk. 'I went in a hurry, because of the regime,' he continued, and I knew that I ought to ask him where it was, and what regime, and what they had against him; I knew that at the very least I ought to want to know what language it was that he spoke there. But it was a long time since I had brought a man back to my room. I eased his shirt away from his shoulders, breathing in the smoky smell of him.

'I had a wife,' he said, 'who died.' Then, I had to stop. I straightened myself and looked into his face. He looked down.

'I am sorry,' I said and I told myself that this wife was in the past tense and had he not, after all, come home with me?

'You do want to make love?' I asked, and there was a long pause. The man looked over my shoulders into the corners of the room.

'After all, I don't think so,' he said. My body felt cheated, yet he relaxed and smiled, as if something good had happened. He reached behind him for his jacket and took out a photograph. 'That's her,' he said, 'those – are children.' I looked. The slender woman and the two children, one girl, one boy about three and four, were wearing ordinary western clothes and sat, smiling, in front of an intricate geometric pattern painted onto a plastered wall.

'I'm sorry,' I said again. But I did not ask him their names, nor where the children were, although I felt that this was what he wanted. He put the photograph back into a leather wallet tooled with patterns like those on the wall in the photograph and in silence we finished the wine. Then he put on his crisp white shirt and buttoned it up. I watched while he rinsed the glasses out under the tap in my kitchen.

'I'm sorry I haven't been more help,' I said at the bottom of the stairs.

'Really, it's nothing,' he said and suddenly he hugged me very tight so that I could smell the smokiness of him again, even through his clothes. Then he was off, walking rapidly down the narrow street which smelled of other people's evening meals. I went back upstairs to my books.

Much later that night, as I lay on the narrow bed looking at the street lamp opposite, it came to me that for certain I was the middle one of three. The stranger would have made love with the woman before me, sensually and with consideration, several times, and in the morning, over their hurried coffee on the way to work, he would have told her about leaving his country, but not about his wife and children. When he never returned, that first woman would have felt angry and far more cheated than I myself had, just a few hours ago.

The one after me, he might meet in one month's time or in ten years' time. They would not go home to his place or to hers, but sit quietly in a calm room or a bench in the flower gardens in the city park, or even opposite each other at a quiet time in an ordinary, smartish cafe like the Oasis. He would tell her that he had left his country in a hurry, because of the regime. He had to pay four months' salary for papers. How he had crossed the mountains on foot in winter; two of the others had died. He had spent six months in a transit camp. He would explain how he had received one letter from his wife, bravely telling him not to worry and that it was for the best, she understood. But he did worry, of course, as the months passed with nothing more from her and each new arrival telling how much worse things were at home. Then someone came who had witnessed it: a sharp winter's day with dogs barking and the quiet street suddenly full of soldiers and noise. She told him the number of his house and the colour of his wife's hair. And what about the children? You asked, and so I must tell you, the witness said. Them too.

You could never know for sure what would have happened if he had stayed. He might have survived: if he had, in hiding perhaps, for how long would he have been able to save his family? Might not his presence have made things worse for them? Perhaps his wife would have suffered more if she had known he was in prison? Maybe he, a married man, should never have challenged the regime? Shouldn't he have thought of the consequences, bided his time?

It was impossible to judge. But also it was impossible to deny that he had left them behind; that they had met their deaths without him. With this the third woman the stranger would weep, and she would too; perhaps they would make love, perhaps just once, but in any case they would be friends for many years.

I remember lying there on my bed, with my hands behind my head, somehow knowing all this and thinking at the same time with another part of my brain how I would graduate, competent in Spanish, German and Russian, fluent in English which is still what everyone wants. Then I would stop working at places like the Oasis Cafe and see the modern world with my own eyes. I aimed to eventually specialize in simultaneous translation for conferences and so on, so even after I had finished my degree there would be more to learn: I had already looked into it: one year in London, if they accepted me. Oh, I badly wanted to ride in aeroplanes and stay in hotels on expenses.

And all of it has come true. I am sitting in a hotel now, with a fridge of drinks and twenty channels to choose from. It's the last evening and there have been no complaints about the interpretation, which amounts to praise. I sit here in my dressing gown, smelling of Chanel and consider myself: I have always sent money to my younger sister, who looked after Grandmother until she died (also, I send glossy postcards of every new country I visit) but in thirteen years I have never returned to see them in the village, and I even missed the funeral. There seemed to be so little time, I was afraid that if I returned I would never escape again.

Laughter comes from the bar below and they are not so bad, these engineers, not really. I could go down if I chose, but I do not. Instead I sit here and think of the place I find myself calling home, and of my incredible luck – for if all of us smell of smoke, I think, only some of us can go back, and I am one of those. And the red dust path, winding like a lazy S, is still there, and the well, and the branch house under the tree, and in it my sister though she will be older, and angry at first. I think of the smell splitting sticks for the fire. I sit here and think of woodsmoke, of the stranger: how different I would be with him, now.

Eight Published Works By Donald Cousins

D.L. Flusfeder

D.L. Flusfeder was born in 1960. His first novel, MAN KILLS WOMAN, was published in 1993. He is currently completing his second, LIKE PLASTIC. He has also worked as a cinema projectionist, a television critic and – assisted by his memories of the UEA course – as a teacher of Creative Writing in Pentonville Prison.

Eight Published Works
By Donald Cousins

Pleasure and Pain & other poems by I.L. Lemeer, reviewed by Donald Cousins

It was with some trepidation that I turned to this first collection of verse from I.L. Lemeer. The young poet has already gathered to himself quite a reputation, based on the fury and fervour he is said to display in his public readings. Having lamented at some length as to our present dearth of poetic talent, this reviewer was particularly anxious to see if Mr Lemeer's work would do justice to the creativity of his press agents.

Alas! he does not deserve the laurels heaped upon him, indeed, how could he? What we are offered is a skilfully rendered presentation of some rather hackneyed themes. I find no fault with the technical facility of Mr Lemeer's work; he is a most competent versifier. And true, he displays a certain virtuosity that is remarkable in one so young. His description of the libertine's torture chamber in 'Send No Flowers' will continue to send shivers down my spine for some time to come!

Where I do find greatest fault is in the poet's lack of any authentic voice. Of course, the vocabularies of sin and degradation provide excellent metaphors for the poetic appetite, but: I would say the name Charles Baudelaire to see how Mr Lemeer reacts. If one chooses to appropriate another poet's idiom, one might at least do so with a gesture of homage or perhaps a tone of irony. Mr Lemeer has taken Baudelaire's diction and concerns and attempted, unsuccessfully, to transplant them to our own age. It does not work. He essays the *flâneur*, he becomes a *poseur*.

At times I began to feel an inkling of that fervour which Mr Lemeer is said to bring to his public readings. There is at least an underlying anger to several of the poems in this collection. The short piece, 'Some Of My Best Friends', comes immediately to mind. This piece rings true with a modicum of fiery conviction. But anger, what of it? Ever since the kitchen sink era of the 1950s we have grown used to outpourings of anger from our younger *littérateurs*. Indeed, we have grown almost wearily ready to expect it.

However, despite these cavils, one must praise Mr Lemeer's facility with verse. One can only hope that he eventually finds an idiom and a manner more suitable to his precocious talents.

New Writings by I.L. Lemeer, reviewed by Donald Cousins

This is Mr Lemeer's second collection and I wish that I could say he has come of age. We do not have enough good poets to ignore the efforts of those struggling to join their ranks. Unfortunately, he is still the young prodigy, interesting for his precocity if not for his achievements. One is reminded of Dr Johnson's famous remark concerning the dog that walked like a man. The marvel lies not in the quality of what he is doing but in the fact that he is doing it at all.

This new collection contains both prose and poetry, the stories being often pathetic in tone, the poems mostly bathetic in effect. Granted, there is a certain superficial power to some of the pieces. I was shaken by the murderous twist at the end of 'Absolute Zero' and thrilled by the cruelly flat tone of 'First Confession'. There is no denying the surface appeal of Mr Lemeer's talent. But when one looks beneath the surface, there is little to be found that is genuinely 'new'. Occasionally he strikes a chord of novelty but that is all. Mr Lemeer is no literary pioneer expanding the boundaries of contemporary letters. Pathfinding will have to be the task of more serious, more lofty talents.

There is little between the covers of *New Writings* to justify the hysterical praise that Mr Lemeer has attracted. I believe we are witnessing what the Americans term the 'flavour of the month' syndrome. One seriously doubts whether I.L. Lemeer will ever achieve any kind of significant status.

Prison Notebooks by I.L. Lemeer, reviewed by Donald Cousins

The chequered career of I.L. Lemeer continues apace. After his recent troubles with the authorities, Lemeer spent six months in gaol, mostly at Wormwood Scrubs. There has been such extensive media coverage that this reviewer feels sanguine about ignoring the sensationalist details of the case, preferring rather to concentrate on the literary merits of the work at hand. Suffice it to say that Lemeer's recent bout with publicity has done little to harm the sales of his books.

The present work is a slim one and, despite what some of its more fanatical admirers might claim, does not hold its place in the pantheon of great prison literature. This is no *House of the Dead* or *Thief's Journal* or even an *On the Yard*. In fact, this work hardly qualifies as literature. It might more accurately be described as 'agit-prop' (*id est* 'agitation-propaganda' for those of you unfamiliar with fashionable jargon). What Lemeer has done is to compose vignettes of prison life, which might or might not be rooted in genuine experience (he claims they are, but we have no way of knowing), then using these vignettes as the points of origin for a more general discussion of how the system may best be reformed.

Now, this is no doubt worthy stuff. I do not wish to carp with anyone who wants to make this world of ours a better place, but I do have issues to raise with anyone who attempts to cloak a discussion of social reform in the guise of literature. Literature is created from conflict, not polemic. Lemeer would have been well served by the introduction of another narrative voice (perhaps he might have included the opinions of the prison governor?). It is not my business to tell authors what to write. However, I feel duty-bound to indicate what I consider to be the flaws in the work of a writer who has been hailed as such an authentic voice of his generation.

Certain portions of the *Notebooks* are, nevertheless, compelling. Lemeer has employed his talent for observation to great effect in his account of the prison black market system. His description of 'Barrow Boy' Beauchamp is especially grisly and riveting. Other episodes are not quite so successful. I am particularly concerned about the chapter entitled 'Revenge of the Screws'. I do think that Lemeer might have used his position as opinion-maker a little more responsibly.

A Grand Adventure by I.L. Lemeer, reviewed by Donald Cousins

Another work by Mr Lemeer is released into the market place, destined, no doubt, for the number one position on the best sellers' list for some time to come. Would that the list were synonymous with literary merit! What discerning bibliophile would consider *That Dang Orang-Utang* or *The Captains of Industry Cookbook* (the works that are currently occupying the top two positions in that self-same list) necessary acquisitions for his library? No, the true extent of Mr Lemeer's achievement will have to be decided at the court of a sterner judge.

A Grand Adventure is a picaresque novel set in the sixteenth century. It follows the adventures of a motley crew of rogues and buffoons, led by the philosopher-brigand Anselm, as they wend their brutish way across Europe, looting in the wake of the bubonic plague. Such is the somewhat callous premise. As a series of antic romps, the novel is acceptable. Anselm's battle with the blind priest is quite a minor miracle of sustained comic writing and is, I am sure, destined for the anthologies. There is even a theological discussion that is quite remarkable for its giddy verbal flights of fancy.

However, one harks back to the author's early books, remembering the daring risks he was taking in both poetry and prose, and one grows a little sad. This reviewer is particularly disappointed, having been a champion of Mr Lemeer's from the early days. It is a shame when one of the brighter stars of our literary firmament falls. When artistic excellence and vaulting ambition give way to mediocrity and even, dare I say it?, vacuousness. Suffice it to say that this most recent work of

I.L. Lemeer's is his least demanding and most formulaic to date.

The Pleasure Party by I.L. Lemeer, reviewed by Donald Cousins

After a long time at one journal, there is the tendency to atrophy, for the closing-in of horizons. An insidious parochialism sets in. There is the need for change, to see different faces, to sit at a different desk, to learn new ways. I am grateful to this newspaper's editor for giving me this forum as literary correspondent. And, as to thoughts of Another Major Newspaper, I have no regrets, no resentments, only pleasant memories and some good friends.

It is perhaps fitting that I should begin my tenure with a review of the latest work from this country's most hailed *littérateur*. It has been my lot to have followed the career of Mr Lemeer from its infancy. I was present at what I believe to have been the first public reading of his poetry. I do not wish to 'blow my own trumpet' but I believe Mr Lemeer's meteoric rise to success was at least partially due to my personal patronage in the form of (justifiably) laudatory reviews of his early published verse and fiction. That, however, is all ancient history, a topic to be left to the literary historians of a future age. Let us turn to the work under discussion.

Mr Lemeer has been touted as a suitable candidate for the honour of Nobel Prize laureate. He has already 'cleaned up' the shelves of our own domestic prize cabinet and it is probably too much to ask that the Swedish Academy of Arts and Letters should not get caught up in the rather hysterical fervour that surrounds Mr Lemeer's life and art. If he does claim that laurel wreath, one can only hope he does so with a work more deserving of the tag 'great' than this present one. Mr Lemeer is without doubt a gifted writer. It would be a genuine shame were he to squander his undeniable talents at the fickle roulette wheel of public acclaim. Ever since he achieved his early successes, he has allowed his talent to dissipate and dwindle. There is still some left. One can only hope that he is able to muster enough of it to justify the hysteria that attends him.

The Pleasure Party is a glibly written work taking the world of TV soap opera as its locale. It is engaging in the most trivial way and boasts a certain fashionable nihilism. However, one does not feel confident that its author will ever produce the type of work that he is possibly still capable of so long as he remains more interested in cultivating the affections of a certain well-known model and actress instead of devoting his energies to the craft that has been so generous to him.

Sir,

The work of I.L. Lemeer has been rewarded with the Nobel Prize for literature. I would like to raise a small dissenting voice to the clamour of acclaim that has babbled ceaselessly on ever since the Swedish Academy made its announcement. Writing as one formerly employed as literary editor of two major newspapers before being hounded into premature retirement, and a published poet, I feel myself not unqualified to make pronouncements concerning the award.

Mr Lemeer is a not ungifted writer who, if he ever chose to devote himself to his craft, could prove his early achievements to be not mere 'flashes in the pan'. As it stands, his *oeuvre* can perhaps best be described as slight. No, if one wishes to discover the towering giants of our literary age, one would have to look in directions other than Mr Lemeer.

Yours etc.
D. Cousins
(address supplied)

Sir,

I would like to make a brief comment on the most recent work from I.L. Lemeer. Speaking as the critic who gave Lemeer his 'big break', I think my voice has a right to be heard. Suffice it to say that, as a work of art, *Mambo Sun* ranks with the second league of the Saturday morning cartoons I used to watch as a boy at the old Barking Gaumont (no longer with us, alas: I believe the site now serves as Greater London's largest carpark). Yours etc.

D. Cousins
(address supplied)

Sir,

In the recent January 10 issue I was surprised by an error, unusual in your normally authoritative publication. There was a confusion of identity between Jerry Lewis the comedian and Jerry Lee Lewis the singer. The sentence, 'Jerry Lewis has lived half his life in the grip of Satan and the other half in the lap of God', should of course have read Jerry *Lee* Lewis. Otherwise, it was a most informative article.

Yours etc.
D. Cousins
(address supplied)

Sisters

Suzannah Dunn

Suzannah Dunn was born in 1963 and lives in Brighton. She has had short stories published in magazines, and is the author of a novella and short stories published together under the title DARKER DAYS THAN USUAL. She has subsequently had three novels published: QUITE CONTRARY, BLOOD SUGAR and PAST CARING.

∫

Sisters

The Snow Queen had returned. Mum says I shouldn't call her that because it isn't nice and because she's my sister. But it's so apt that I can't resist it; and, anyway, she's not my sister, not really. She's mum's daughter. I went along when mum drove into town to fetch her from the station. The streets were quieter than usual, emptier. It was mid-afternoon, the sun jabbing between the leaves of the trees and slapping onto the bodywork of the cars in front. I sat straight, trying to level my eyes with the sunstrip on our windscreen but I didn't have much luck and ended up squinting as usual. If it hadn't been August, if it hadn't been school holiday time then the kids would have been coming out of the primary school. But the afternoon was empty. Nobody hurried along to the wine bar for a sandwich or nipped into the Co-op for a tin of beans or a loaf of sliced white. Those who went out to work were still there, behind plate glass, watching the clock. Those at home groped behind net curtains to open their windows wider. Everyone was waiting but the evening was still hours away. The cars weren't yet queueing to leave the station car park; it wasn't yet time for the News or the evening meal, nor time to bath the kiddies, nor frying time, nor opening time.

We drove along the High Street past the school. The gates were closed and padlocked, a bolt driven into the asphalt. There were no children trailing cardigans in the dust or playing chase or clinging to pushchairs. There were no young mums to salvage mucky cardigans and stuff them into shopping bags or over pushchair handles; no parked cars with stickers warning you about deaf children or asking you to support the teachers; no satchels, discarded, hanging on railings, bulging with plimsolls and today's letter home thanking and reminding and adding a note of caution. Even the lollipop lady had deserted her post. No doubt she was at home, quite unrecognizable. But down some streets I saw children riding bikes and tricycles, racing to the post box and back, bumping over the cracks in the pavement and steering past trees planted by the Council in squares of crusty brown root-infested soil.

I wanted to stay sitting in the car at the station forecourt but mum wouldn't let me. So we went together to the platform. There are notices on the inside of train doors: *Do not alight until the train has stopped*. And that is just what the Snow Queen did when the train stopped – she *alighted*. A blue suitcase in each hand, a bag slung over one shoulder, she negotiated the steps without looking down. A man held the door open for her. No doubt she had practised deportment when she was younger, gliding up and down the stairs with a book on her head. Mum rushed forward to help her. I joined them and took one of the suitcases. A tupperware box lay at the top of her open bag: the Snow Queen had had a packed lunch. The teaspoon with which she had eaten her yoghurt was wrapped in a plastic bag to prevent it making a mess.

Why had she come to stay?

Mum wanted to know why I had asked: *She's free to stay if she wants, isn't she, she has been to stay before, hasn't she?* But now the Snow Queen was married, and I thought everything had changed. She has visited us three years beforehand, and the age gap of seven years had made all the difference; but now I was fourteen and somehow the gap between fourteen and twenty-one was not so great. Mum had decided that the Snow Queen could have my sister Lydia's room while Lydia was away. Lydie, I knew, would not be pleased. She feels similarly to me about the Snow Queen. You could never find anyone more different from the Snow Queen than Lydie. When we were small Lydie and I would fight and she would dig her nails into me and draw blood. Louise, the Snow Queen, had no scars upon her; and each of her nails was perfectly shaped. When she stepped down from the train I saw that her blonde bob had recently been trimmed. It has been highlighted again too; and if highlighted much more, her ends would need attention. It made her look as if she was going grey. It suited her.

I noticed her legs, too, as she walked ahead of me to the car. She had what grandma terms a well-turned ankle, nothing but bone. Lydia has square calves, thick ankles, the sort of legs that accompany flat sandals. Lydia and I are not alike in that respect: I exercise my ankles every evening as I watch telly, making arcs and circles. When she was young the Snow Queen had had a party frock. I know what mum says, I know that the Snow Queen had only a father, and that fathers don't know much about that sort of thing, but all the same I'm sure that I would have refused any party frocks. If she had been born a Victorian, the Snow Queen would have been one of those women with an eighteen-inch waist and a pained expression. I know that she's had a sad life and all that, but she's never made an effort to help herself.

The Snow Queen was not suited to the summer. In the car as we drove back along the High Street she was paler than ever. We drove past the arcade of shops that have been there for as long as I can remember. The pharmacy is crammed with Max Factor and Rimmel and Outdoor Girl, with cans of glittery hairspray which never sell, with meal replacement muesli bars, and jars of ginseng, and instamatic cameras and special-offer photo albums, comb cases and key-rings and packets of barley sugar. Next to the pharmacy is the hosiery shop, its window display never varying: tea-bag coloured tights alongside reduced price blue winceyette pyjamas, short sleeved winter vests (fawn, size 16), tapestry cushion cover kits (ideal as gifts), and a peg bag. We drove past the greengrocers and the pram shop. At the end of the High Street there is the Italian Restaurant, *Il Giardino*. The lunchtime menu was as usual chalked up outside: *Today, ravioli*. The Snow Queen suffered from travel sickness on hot days. Her eyes swam in a colourless face. She was pale and moist like a lump of sweaty cheese.

But ladies glow. The Snow Queen glowed with lines traceable

like lines of down, traceable in trickles: a line above her top lip and a trickle across her forehead. She held a handful of tissues soggy with cologne. I remembered that she had been on holiday with us to Majorca six or seven years previously. Mum had persuaded Lydia and me to go without our tops as we played at the poolside, to let the air get to us. The Snow Queen sat every day in her C&A bikini on a lilo, under a shade, reading a paperback and muddying slightly the edges of each page with the suntan oil that clung to her fingers. The sun had burned white rings around her pale blue irises. It lit them like the haloes which drift around the moon before rain. She stared at us through her albino lashes like a crazed moth, luminous and about to dive-bomb a lamp bulb. Later she took to wearing black reflective glasses. Lydia and I were convinced that she shaved her legs. No one could be as hairless as she was. Now, of course, I realise that she would never have shaved. She would have used some caustic lemon-scented lotion to melt it all away.

She was having a shower. She had had a cup of tea and then she had said she would like to freshen up. I had gone into the garden to catch the last of the sun. Everything was in shade except the rockery. I sat on a flat stone, facing the house. Mum was in the kitchen, at the window, drying the tea cups and replacing them in the cupboard. I could see her as she turned in the darkness between the sink and the shelves; the tea towel flickering, a broad strip of white linen. She bowed her head and wiped the inside of each cup with a sharp twist of her wrist. I could hear the shower. Water rose as thick hot steam through an open window, and splashed from drainpipe to drain near the back door. A ball of froth collected in the grid like a snowball. Why had Lydie left me to the Snow Queen? She had gone away for a week to stay with a friend. Perhaps that was why the Snow Queen had decided to visit. But, then, I doubt whether she had known; and I doubt whether she had cared. She might not have liked Lydia but she couldn't have liked me much more and I was still around. I had planned to have the weekend to myself; me and mum on our own around the house, taking the radio into the garden, dragging the sun lounger from the shed, and making plates of cottage cheese salad for lunch.

She is mum's daughter, not dad's. Mum had been married before and when she left her husband and went home to grandma the little Ice Maiden stayed behind with her father. They stayed up north somewhere. I suppose it was her home. We had visited them for the Snow Queen's wedding. She had been saving up, working in a bank. All girls who work in banks are engaged – solitaire diamond on the third finger, left hand – and have cheap mortgages. At her wedding the Snow Queen was dressed in white. She had enlisted the help of a local dressmaker to sew her in, tuck her up and hand-finish her in good time: the individual touch. She had booked a choir too. Lydia almost laughed herself sick at the reception because I said it was a shame that the Snow Queen had removed her veil for the photos. Mum overheard us and then avoided us all afternoon, being polite instead to ancestors and handing around plates of those stubby sausages speared with sticks. The Snow Queen's husband, Mike, was nothing special. At the reception he spent the first hour or so cavorting around the tableclothed trestle table with his Rugby Club chums, lobbing pineapple cubes and clenching carnations between his teeth. Later he looked flushed, his starched shirt stretched at the seams. He adopted a manner like that of a schoolboy at his father's funeral, humbly accepting responsibility and bursting with pride. Towards the end of the afternoon he lurched alone between tables cleared of everything but the currants and crumbs of icing dropped from the cake.

I sat in the garden and wondered how much longer the Snow Queen would stay in the bathroom. At the start of each visit she would line her potions along the window sill: conditioner with real silk; squeezy tubes and screw-top jars and a clear plastic toothbrush; unperfumed baby soap in a dish in a washbag. The little things annoyed me – why did she have to bring her own handcream? Why not use ours, kept in the cabinet? But she brought her own, *pour peau sec*; but no Dead Sea Mud face pack, and no hair gel. She had a modest array of trial samples and Boots own, all pine-leaf lotion green-coloured. I sat in the garden and listened to the tinkling of a distant piano: next door Mrs Trayherne was at her evening practice.

When the sun had disappeared from the rockery I went upstairs to my bedroom. I lay on my bed thinking how I'd like a bath, a cool clear bath: to lie in the water and trace the pattern in the tiles, the white wisps in the blue; and there was the shower curtain sweeping to the floor, thick flaccid plastic printed with grasses and butterflies; and mum's shower cap hanging frilly on a plastic hook. Before going to the bathroom the Snow Queen had spoken on the phone to her husband. We had been sitting downstairs at the kitchen table when the phone had rung. The Snow Queen had sipped tea, her legs crossed, her feet slipped into neat new olive-green Marks and Spencer shoes. I had gone into the hall to answer the phone because I had expected it to be for me. But it wasn't.

'It's Michael,' I called.

I had waited and dropped the receiver into her hand when she arrived. She had inclined her head, hair swinging, and placed the receiver to her ear.

'Hello?'

I waited a long time in my bedroom; how was I to have known that she was still in the bathroom? There are no locks on any of the doors in this house – we sing – so I had pushed open the bathroom door, and there she was: fully clothed, sitting on the edge of the bath, bent double; her feet in green shoes spread across the tiles; her hands clenched bloodless over the enamel rim; her eyes burning with tears.

Downstairs mum stood at a work surface in her apron, dicing a carrot, cutting into the chopping board. I sat on a stool, picking up the *TV Times* and flicking through the pages.

'What's wrong with Louise?' I asked her.

'Nothing that need concern you,' she replied.

She finished slicing and I reached over and took a piece. She swept the rest into her hand and dropped them into a colander.

'I'll be upstairs,' I said, 'in my room.'

I bit into the carrot and got down from the stool. I crossed the room and stopped at the door for a second.

'I'll be listening to records,' I said. 'I'll be down in time for tea.'

The Crispens

Denise Neuhaus

Denise Neuhaus is British and American. She has degrees in Economics, French and Creative Writing. She has written two novels, THE LOVE OF WOMEN (1993) and THE CHRISTENING (1995), both published by Faber and Faber. She lives in London.

The Crispens

'The number to the theatre is by the telephone,' said Mother, glancing at me in the mirror. I was lying on my stomach on the bed, feet in the air. She put on more lipstick, her mouth spread wide. Then she pressed her lips onto a folded Kleenex, leaving behind a dark pink kiss. I knew this was the way to put on lipstick. I had read about it in *Seventeen* Magazine. *Learning to put on lipstick takes patience and practice.*

My young womanhood with its endless evenings of practice loomed far away. I was only twelve; I could not wear lipstick. I jiggled my feet. What did people think about my mother when they saw her dressed up? Was she charming and cultivated? Did men admire her? Did they think that my father had a lovely wife? Maybe they could tell that she usually didn't wear make-up, that she went around in faded green cotton slacks and thong sandals. Maybe they thought, *Just somebody's wife. Somebody's old housewife. Somebody's old worn-out housewife trying to dress up and look good*.

My mother had once been young and beautiful; I had seen photographs of her, with a full skirt and three-quarter length gloves and a hat like a plate. Her hair was golden brown. That was before she married my father and had us.

She had told my sister and me, in the casual and significant tone she used for such announcements, 'The Crispens have invited me to the theatre next Saturday,' and I knew she did not mean the movies. When she went out with the Crispens, it was always somewhere out of the ordinary. She was sitting on our orange vinyl sofa, crocheting. She crocheted endlessly, blankets which she called 'Afghans' and pillow covers, of ugly colors, all of which quickly turned dingy and stretched out of shape.

Her usual tone was threatening. *I am going to play bridge at Mrs Ashland's this Saturday and if you kids smoke in this house or do ANYTHING I swear to God*.

She had never talked about the theatre before, but I knew that I was supposed to pretend that this was something she did all the time. I always tried to fulfil these silent demands. I could not bear to see her diminished, to suffer her haughty stare, her determined nonchalance, her raised eyebrows that meant, *And what is so remarkable about my going to the theatre?* Her affectations embarrassed me; I wanted to protect her from the poverty of her life.

I said, 'Oh,' trying to sound slightly bored, but my sister was only six and as usual didn't pick up the hint. 'You mean to see a movie?'

I snorted contemptuously. 'Dummy. The *theatre*. Not the movies. *God*, Lesley.' She immediately started to sulk. Mother didn't look up from her crocheting and I pressed my advantage. 'God,' I said, disgusted by her hopeless ignorance, 'don't you know *anything*?'

'Now, now,' said Mother softly, as if appealing to my mature self who was compassionate toward the handicapped, the deficient, the backward of this world. She glanced at me conspiratorially: she and I knew what the theatre was; Lesley was just an ignorant kid. I shouldn't tease Lesley; she was just a stupid, ignorant kid.

Lesley began automatically to whine. Poor Lesley. She would always be literal-minded, obtuse, arrested in childhood. She would never learn the pretensions of adults. She would never learn to drink coffee or alcohol or eat with her knife in her left hand or drop names without appearing to. She would never grow out of saying 'brung' instead of 'brought'. She would stay happily in the phases others outgrew, keeping her toy animals into high school, only to replace them with a collection of turtles, a tank of guppies, stray kittens. Her twenties she would spend working in a pet shop, cleaning animal cages. She would be offered promotions to the front part of the shop, and she would always refuse; she would be happy only when spared from having to talk to human beings.

She was still whining in the way we knew meant, *Tell me what I didn't understand. How am I supposed to know what you're talking about*? Mother interrupted her. She was going to have to rely on us kids to behave ourselves, she said. With our father overseas, and the theatre downtown, she would need to know that we could handle anything that came up. *Anything that came up*. What could possibly come up? Once Lesley had swallowed a penny. My mother called the doctor, but he said she didn't have to go to the hospital. In the summer, I sometimes stepped on a rusty nail or pulled an arm hastily through the barbed wire fence behind our house, and would run home, squeezing the split flesh until the beads of blood swelled and broke. I would have to get a tetanus shot at the doctor's.

These things could not happen so late at night. Lesley would go to bed, my brother and I would watch TV. Of course there were other, unspecified, possibilities: a fire, an obscene phone call, knocks on the door, burglars, *accidents*. These weren't, however, what she meant.

'I'm counting on you kids,' she said. This was her generic warning, but I knew she was talking to me. I was always the one in trouble, and paradoxically, the one she assumed would be responsible if something happened. Already she had given up on my brother, who was too passive to get in trouble, except with me, or to do anything about it when it arose.

Lesley was still mad, her eyes small and hard, her breathing rapid and tense, her mouth opening and closing. She clenched her fists, ready to throw a tantrum. She hated being the baby, being the stupid one, the one who never understood. She always would, too. At sixteen, at twenty-five, at thirty, Lesley was still the same. During my visits home, we – Mother and I – would shake our heads and roll our eyes over Lesley's howlers and it would drive her mad. *God, Lesley!*

It was only much later that I felt ashamed and angry thinking of this, the damage my collaboration wrought.

We lived in the very last suburb. Behind our fence was a creek and then barbed wire, and a field larger than our entire neighborhood with hundreds of cows grazing on it. Down the highway, past the houses, there were woods, and a lake, and the kids in the suburb built tree-forts there to hang out in and drink beer and smoke pot after school. We lived about an hour's drive from downtown and I had been there maybe three or four times in my entire life.

I spent the week trying to imagine what the theatre would be like. I had been to the ballet once, in elementary school, on a field trip. We went downtown in a school bus. The boys wore clip-on bow ties and the girls lace socks and patent leather shoes. On the end of each row sat a teacher or somebody's mother to chaperon us. They wouldn't let us get up at intermission. The stage was far away. One girl had a little pair of binoculars and showed off so much that everybody was whispering and trying to ask her for a turn and the teacher took them away.

I thought that the theatre would be small, chairs crowded intimately around the stage. Everything would be black. The set would be sparse. The play would be intellectual – something about ideas – with allusions to books that only cultured people would understand. My theatre was a sort of garret out of *La Bohème*, which my mother had seen with the Crispens, combined with the dark mystery of a night club. Because I thought of the Crispens as European, I elevated them from being merely rich and sophisticated; I made them bohemian.

Mrs Crispen was not European but I would forget that. Getting married to Mr Crispen had transformed her. I knew I was not supposed to mention anything about Mrs Crispen's former life, and this was not difficult. She was a new being.

Mrs Crispen's name used to be Mrs Jackson; she had been our neighbor and she had had three children. She was divorced and a secretary, the only working woman anybody knew. All the neighbors talked about her and her children, who were never called in at dark, and were allowed to eat anything they wanted and stay up as late as they liked. She wore gold sandals and velour jumpsuits when she was at home. She both fascinated and frightened me. The word *divorcee* suggested a series of men, excessive drinking, parties; things as far from my mother's life as could be imagined.

Yet, my mother liked Mrs Crispen and defended her to anyone who gossiped about her. When she married Mr Crispen, Mrs Crispen quit her job and sent her children to live with their father in Arizona.

Later, Mother would tell me that the children were sent to boarding school. This made me wildly envious; I imagined boarding school to be where girls learn to speak French and waltz and arrange flowers and give dinner parties. But Mother said it wasn't like that; it was a school for 'problem' children.

Mother only went out with the Crispens when my father was away. This seemed perfectly natural. My mother's other, stifled self belonged to the Crispens. Their charmed life was the one Mother would have led had she not married my father. I pictured her with some other man, who remained dim but generally resembled Mr Crispen, driving around in the Crispens' Jaguar, to one art gallery after another, from a French restaurant to the opera.

Nobody drove foreign cars then, and I thought it daring. Foreign cars were considered slightly eccentric, almost effeminate, like soccer, imported beer, a man carrying a bag.

Why did I assume that my mother's true life was this? As she put perfume behind her ears and on her wrist, I rolled over on my back and read the instructions on the package of ultra-sheer stockings she had bought. They were supposed to be rolled on, not pulled.

She came over and held out her hand for the package. She was wearing a new bra with no straps and her old beige slip. Under the slip she had a girdle on. Even though she was as skinny as a rail, her stomach stuck out like a shelf from having children.

She sat down next to me and I watched her roll a stocking up each leg. As the stockings unrolled, the millions of tiny holes on her calves became invisible and her knees, which were really bony like mine, were pressed into smoothness. I knew her legs by heart: the needle-thin varicose veins behind one knee, which she got when she was pregnant, her faint birth mark, the pale mole on the back of her right thigh. She had dry skin and let me put lotion on her sometimes after her bath. I particularly liked to slather it all over the cracks in her heels, and watch it soak in like dry, cracked ground filling with sudden rain.

She stepped into her dress and let me zip her. Then she picked up the black beaded bag she had had ever since I could remember and an embroidered shawl she had borrowed for the evening. She looked into the mirror a last time. She pulled on the curled tendrils of hair in front of each ear and patted the teased-up part on top.

I had watched her make her dress. I came home from school the day after she told us she was going to the theatre, and on the bed was a Vogue Original Design pattern and a folded square of black crêpe de Chine. I flung the material open, wrapped it around me and examined the pattern. I thought I would die if I did not someday have that dress. I was already taller than Mother, and larger boned, but just as thin and I knew it would make me look perfect.

It had no shoulders, but fell from the neck by a strip of rhinestones. It wrapped and twisted and had a slit in the back. It was a mini-dress and had cost $7.50 instead of the usual $1.95 because it was an original design.

I stared at the pattern envelope. I couldn't bring myself to open it and look at the instructions. I couldn't believe that dress could be cut out and sewn like a regular dress on my mother's Singer. It was a dress from a Paris boutique. English words could not describe that dress. I almost didn't want my mother to make it; I was afraid that she would ruin it, and I couldn't bear the disappointment.

I was taking Home Economics and Mother took me material shopping when I was to start a new project. I always left her at the broadcloth table and walked among the bolts of silk and satin. I loved the shiniest and brightest; the sheer, the swirling; taffeta, chiffon with sequins, dyed fur. Mother would come fetch me. *That's not very practical, dear. You can't machine wash silk. Don't you think that's an awfully large print for a skirt? Wouldn't you rather have dotted Swiss?*

I didn't want dotted Swiss. Or corduroy or broadcloth. Or a machine-washable skirt with a small flowered print. I wanted black and glitter and hot pink and a fake tiger-skin cape.

She would pull me over to the pattern counter. *I am NOT paying $5 a yard for something you can't even put in the washing machine for you to learn how to sew.* We would sit on the high stools, Mother flipping summarily through the pattern books. I would hardly be through the first section before she would be through every book they had.

She would urge me on. *You don't really want that empire waist, do you? I am NOT going to set those sleeves in for you.* But, I wouldn't be looking at the dress. I was looking at the way the whole picture made me feel: the way the model looked, and her hair and jewellery, the way she tossed her skirt and glanced over one shoulder. How did they look like that? Were they born that way?

Mother would interrupt. *That is not appropriate for your age. Where on earth would you wear such a thing? Why are you looking in the designer section? Why are you looking at Vogue? You should be looking at Simplicity.* But I didn't want a pattern if I didn't like the picture.

Of course, Mother ruined the dress. First, she replaced the rhinestones with a strip of the material. Then, she lengthened it and closed the slit in the back. I hated it. I didn't know which alteration made me the angriest, but the dress was now a sickly relation of its cousin in the Paris boutique; it looked like something from the shopping mall.

And I was angry that Mother was all wrong for it, with her drooping arms and pointed elbows, her sloping shoulders. She hunched slightly, and the material that was supposed to flow down fell out from her body, making her look even more flat-chested than usual. Anybody could tell that she never knew what to wear, didn't know how to 'make the most of herself'. I hated her for thinking that she was being so daring to wear this dress, and for knowing and yet ignoring that it was all wrong, for trying without hope to be sexy and fashionable.

'You look pretty, Mom,' I said.

'Thank you, dear,' she said flatly. She was too used to being disappointed for it to bother her much.

We went out to the living room and she called my brother. His door opened and the whole hall was flooded with a smell like the boys' gym at school. He shuffled towards us and stood in the doorway to the living room, his head hanging, his hands in his pockets. He always looked as if he were waiting for somebody to step on him. His hair was long and greasy and over his mouth were some patchy dark hairs he thought was a moustache. He was going to have to shave and get a hair-cut before our father got back if he didn't want to catch hell.

Mother looked at him a few seconds and then sighed, deciding not to say anything about his appearance. When our father wasn't around, she didn't like to disturb the peace. She said mechanically, 'You can eat anything you want but clean up your mess. The number to the theatre is by the telephone. The Ashlands are at home if you need them. Lesley is to go to bed at nine. Yes, Lesley, at nine. Read her a story. One story. No, you may not stay up and watch television. I do not care if it is Saturday. Nine o'clock means nine o'clock.'

She sighed again and opened the door. 'Nancy, if you let any kids into this house—'

'We won't,' I said, exasperated. I had been through that with her about a million times that day.

She draped the shawl over one arm and took her car keys out of her bag. My brother was looking at the floor. I kept my eyes level with her thin shoulders.

We stood there for a minute. I could tell she wanted to say something else but couldn't think of anything to say. Finally, she said, 'And no fighting.'

I didn't bother to answer. My brother and I hadn't fought for over a year.

She stepped out onto the porch. I wished she would hurry up and go, but she stared at us as if she was trying to decipher through our blank faces what mischief we were plotting. She sighed, and finally, in the weary, slightly pleading voice she used when she was tired of being a parent and didn't really care any more what we did, said, 'And *don't* burn the house down.'

Now, this was an extraordinary statement. It was the first time she had admitted frankly that she could do nothing about our smoking; that however much she carped, and however much my father beat us, she knew the minute we were alone, we would light up. It meant, I know you're doing it; just don't let me find out.

My brother and I kept our faces completely expressionless at this new cynicism. As she closed the door, we both raised our eyebrows in amazement. We watched her start the car and pull out of the drive-way. Lesley ran off to the kitchen, but we waited, listening to the car drive down the street, and turn at the end of the block. We could just hear it continue towards the highway that would lead Mother to the city.

'*Al*right!' I yelled, going to the kitchen.

'Do you have a joint?' my brother called.

'Yeah, sure,' I said sarcastically. 'I have a whole pound.'

Lesley was sitting at the kitchen counter, devouring a box of Oreos in the fashion she liked, which was to break them apart, and first lick the white middles out. I looked at her with disgust, ready to berate her for her childishness and the mess she was making, but she gave me such a fearful glance that I did not bother. I heard my brother putting on a record in his room, and I yelled, 'The Stones!' I mixed myself a glass of chocolate milk. We no longer pilfered the liquor cabinet; my parents marked the levels on the bottles. After a moment, I heard Led Zeppelin at top volume.

My brother came back to the living room with his cigarettes and ashtray. We opened all the windows. I took one of his cigarettes and we both lit up.

Lesley said from the kitchen, 'I'm going to tell.'

'You do,' I said, 'and you're going to bed at nine.' She resumed eating her Oreos calmly. 'Is Mother's door closed?' I asked my brother. He was sitting on the back of the sofa next to the open window. He nodded.

I turned on the television with the sound down and then sat on the other end of the sofa and read the TV Guide while I smoked. '"Some Like it Hot",' I read between puffs. 'With Marilyn Monroe, Tony Curtis and Jack Lemmon. 1959. Directed by Billy Wilder—' My brother ignored me, playing an invisible guitar to Led Zeppelin, with his cigarette hanging out of his mouth.

'Marilyn Monroe!' I said. 'Don't you want to see Marilyn Monroe?'

'Who's Marilyn whatever?' said Lesley.

'God, Lesley,' I said.

'Well, who is Mara-whatever?'

'Forget it. You're too little to understand.'

'I am not.'

'You are too. At eight o'clock. Don't you want to see Marilyn Monroe?'

My brother shrugged. 'Sure.'

'I am not too little.'

'You are too. Shut up or you're going to bed at nine. I'm not even sure if you're old enough to see this movie.'

Lesley started to whine, so I told her she could to shut her up. My brother still pretended that he didn't care whether he saw Marilyn Monroe or not, and I decided not to tease him about it.

It had been around my twelfth birthday that our cruel taunts, fist fights, and nasty tricks quite simply ceased, without fanfare or discussion. I had, in a few months, shot up nearly three inches, and was suddenly almost as tall as he; no longer was he so clearly my superior in a fight. I was about to go into the sixth grade and he, the seventh, junior high.

He had always been big for his age, and a bully; the kids at his elementary school were terrified of him. But in junior high, he wasn't the biggest around. There were older kids. And, it wasn't enough anymore to be just big. Strength was less important than the ability to run, to manoeuvre, to talk the right way, to carry yourself the right way, the way that said, *Don't fuck with me*.

My poor brother. He was lazy and actually a weakling. He could beat me Indian wrestling, but only just. He was flabby, uncoordinated and a slow runner.

The kids from sixth grade who went to junior high with my brother all seemed to spurt up and fill out that year. They spent the first part of seventh grade getting him back for all they'd taken in elementary school. Then, they left him alone. He kept on eating and getting bigger and flabbier. He had acne. He never brushed his teeth, which were yellow and looked like a lab experiment. He took showers, but somehow always smelled, and his hair looked like it hadn't been washed in years. He had only one friend, a boy who avoided him, and girls ran from him in the hall at school.

My first year in junior high, kids would ask me, 'Hey, is that weird guy in eighth grade *your* brother?'

He would marry a timid, neurotic and miserly girl who was terrified of strange inevitabilities, hoarding food, hiding money.

She would keep him in a steady job and off drugs. My mother would be grateful, never say a word against the girl, count her blessings. My brother would be large and silent, moving crated washing machines and refrigerators from a factory floor into waiting trucks day after day, going home for lunch. He would lurch about, an enormous cripple; the men would leave him alone, not testing the strength of his bulk, speculating on the cause of his limp.

The news came on the television. While the anchorman mouthed in silence, Led Zeppelin shrieked in the background. Then a reporter in front of the White House appeared and talked into a mike, his hair blowing in the wind. After a minute the camera cut to a man talking from a podium with the President's seal on it. We watched, smoking.

Some film clips were shown of soldiers in the jungle and then a map with arrows. I wondered idly how many planes crashed in Vietnam. A few a week? A day? I wondered what the chances were of getting shot down. I imagined a plane spiralling, then disappearing into velvety green, and a parachute bursting open, then floating down. How long would it take to notify the family? It might take weeks because of the jungle. Maybe they didn't tell the family right off, hoping they'd find the guy. Maybe they didn't even send out search parties for crashed planes. At least, they wouldn't if it crashed in enemy territory; it would be too dangerous. I wondered how much money the family got if the pilot was shot down and never found. Would it be enough to live on?

'How much money does the family get if your plane crashes and you're killed?'

My brother took a long drag. 'Nothing that lucky ever happens to us.' After a minute, he added, 'Anyway, he doesn't fly a fighter plane. He wouldn't get shot down. He flies transport planes.'

I knew my brother was right, but I still paused for a moment to imagine all of us in black, being photographed by the newspapers. I would be standing out in front, tragic and beautiful with a black veil and somebody would discover me and I would go to New York and become a model and make so much money that I could buy Mother anything she wanted and take her to the theatre and to French restaurants and go to Europe, just like the Crispens.

I had baby-sat for the Crispens once. Mother drove with me to their house, which was downtown and had an electronic iron gate. Inside, my first impression was that everything was in shades of white: the marbled hall, the two sofas, the numerous, stuffed chairs, the carpet. After a few minutes, I saw small, delicate wooden tables, Persian rugs. On the walls were paintings of pink and blue nudes with enormous rears climbing into bathtubs. I held my mortified gaze stiffly from these, knowing I would blush if I looked at them.

Mrs Crispen and my mother went upstairs, and her daughter, a girl of four or five called Anna Maria, came down shortly afterwards. She was wearing a pink pinafore. She had exquisite features, large eyes, white skin, glossy hair. We looked at one another, and our ages melted into insignificance; I saw us stripped to some fundamental sum of what we each had and did not have, of privilege, money, choices. Instinctively, I looked away until she had descended the stairs; I knew already that my defences against females like her were small, essential, and had to be guarded closely.

Mr Crispen followed his daughter down the stairs. He was not handsome, but he was elegant, and his face was sharply angled. He was so unlike any American man I had ever seen, he could have been of a different race. He was putting on gloves. I had never seen a man wear gloves before. He thanked me for staying with Anna Maria, as if I were doing him a great favor. Then he said, with a vague wave, in his strange, wonderful accent, 'Please make yourself at home.'

I never found out where he was from. When I could have asked, later, I did not. Swiss, Belgian, French? He had come over after the war. He had been orphaned. He was a DP, a Displaced Person, Mother had told me. I pictured a war-torn little boy with a Dutch hair-cut, in ripped lederhosen wandering past heaps of rubble, eating out of garbage cans, making his way to a port, stowing away on a ship, emerging onto the deck after days in the hull, the Statue of Liberty on the horizon.

He made his money in the construction boom, Mother had said.

They left, Anna Maria and I still facing one another. She examined me with a sort of benign curiosity, sensing inferiority and intimidation. Then, without a word, she went over to one of the white sofas and, with proprietary nonchalance, sat down and began to bounce up and down. I watched this and saw that she was at once establishing her right to do as she liked, and putting me at ease, telling me that the marvels she lived around were, after all, merely *things*. Things she used every day. Things I could use, too, for the moment. I watched her.

After a minute, she stopped bouncing and said, 'We're not alone.' I did not reply. 'Cook's downstairs. She lives there.' Then I saw that she was not only telling me that I was not in authority here, but also that I had been brought along merely to keep her company.

'Do you want me to read you a story?' I asked with icy politeness.

'No, thank you,' she returned. 'I will show you my room though if you like.'

It was as large as our living room. In the middle was an enormous creamy lace canopy bed, and against one wall, a polished, heavy dressing table, covered with a lace ruffle. In her closet were rows of starched dresses with Peter Pan collars, bows, lace cuffs and below, dozens of shoes, each pair in a box.

But the best thing in the room was the mural, which covered one entire wall. It was of a little girl on a swing which was attached to the overhanging branch of a tree by ropes of woven flowers. Behind the girl was an enchanted forest with trees and birds and animals. The little girl was swinging out, her legs straight, toes pointed, hair streaming long behind her, dress billowing in the wind. I looked at it for several minutes before I realized that the painting was of her, Anna Maria.

That was when I knew that I would never be precious, to anybody.

'Some Like it Hot' started, so we turned off the music and turned up the television. Marilyn Monroe looked drunk throughout the whole movie and slurred when she talked, but in a sexy way. It was hard to believe that she was after all only a female, of the same stuff as I. I thought she looked like an alien, or something that had been made up by special effects, like the idea of the perfect movie star.

The movie was very confusing. The men in the movie leered at her, as if they desired her and yet wanted to harm her. She was supposed to be the epitome of femininity, and yet she existed in opposition to every virtue women were supposed to have – modesty, chastity. Her near-nudity embarrassed me, not only because I knew it was immoral in the way *Playboy* was immoral, but because it was so acceptable. There seemed to be some special rule for Marilyn Monroe, which made it alright for her, but not normal women, to flaunt herself indecently.

We had a photograph of a woman who looked a lot like Marilyn Monroe. My brother had found it in a box in my parents' closet. When I was ten, I thought she *was* Marilyn Monroe. In the photograph, my father had his arm around her. They were at a party, somewhere overseas. Europe, Asia; I never thought about it; he was just 'overseas'. The woman wore a long dress, very low cut, and trimmed around the top with fur. Her shoulders and breasts looked as if they were perched on this bed of fur. Some people were standing around them in the photograph, holding drinks and laughing. My father was looking down the woman's cleavage with a stupid grin on his face.

During the commercials, we raided the refrigerator and made popcorn. Lesley fell asleep about nine o'clock, but when we tried to move her to bed, she woke up and made such a fuss that we left her on the floor in front of the television. At the end of the movie was the 'public service announcement', a voice which demanded reproachfully, 'It is ten o'clock. Where are *your* children?' We always replied to this, 'Out smoking and drinking and screwing around!'

I checked the TV Guide but the late movie did not interest me. I didn't feel like staying up, so I went to bed, leaving Lesley asleep on the floor and my brother smoking in front of the television.

This was the night my brother had the accident that gave him his limp.

Because of the accident, he would miss some school. He would begin to fail and eventually drop out. Then, he would start taking drugs in a serious way. One night, he would lurch down the middle of a major highway, against traffic, his pockets filled with pot, speed, LSD, waving his arms and shouting at the cars.

There would be a way to get a first offender's reprieve, which was to enlist. But the army would refuse to take my brother because of his leg, and he would go to jail for nine months. After jail, he would get married.

The accident happened like this:

From the middle of nowhere, I am jolted awake. The ceiling light jerks me up and then, immediately, my sister leaps screaming onto the bed. She jumps up and down on the bed and on me. I almost slap her, but then hear her disordered words: bathroom, shower door, glass, cut, blood. I push her aside and run out.

My brother lies on the tiled floor, propping himself up on an elbow. He is dressed. He looks up, calm, a little dazed, embarrassed, as if he knows something has happened, but he is not sure what. He is ineffectually wrapping a dirty bathtowel around his leg. Blood is spreading through the towel with steady progress.

The shower door is gone. Everywhere is glass, shattered into large and small pieces. Bright blood trickles down the cabinets and walls and on the toilet, and is all over the floor, mixed in with the glass. In the toilet is piss, my brother's urine.

My brother is wedged between the shower stall and the cabinet under the sink. The toilet is inches from his head. I have never realized before how small the bathroom is. He is wrapping the towel closer around his leg, looking at me confusedly. He seems to be waiting for me to do something.

'Let me see,' I say, kneeling carefully in the glass. He smells and I blanch slightly. Then I lift the towel. The calf is sliced open to the bone in two bloody trenches, each about ten inches long. One starts near the knee, the other lower down, ending at the ankle. All around are more cuts, glittering with glass dust, the blood clotting and matting the hair on his legs.

Pure panic seizes me. I know I have gone pale and cannot move. I look at him to see if he understands how serious this really is, and he stares back at me dumbly. Then I realize, he is stoned. He would have to be stoned to have fallen back with such force through the shower door. I ask him what he has taken; he denies that he has taken anything. I think, *I will never get through this. I will not cope. He will bleed to death*. Here is the crisis Mother has always warned about. Here it is: an emergency. The middle of the night. Nobody at home. Nobody but me, and I have to do something. I freeze.

A moment passes. My brother watches me. 'I'll get someone,' I finally said, backing out of the bathroom. I see the bleeding again, swelling, engorging the towel and am afraid he will die while I am gone. I find some clean towels and make a kind of tourniquet. Then I run out.

I run out of the house in my nightgown and across the next door neighbors' wet lawn and drive-way to the Ashlands' house. I ring the doorbell over and over again, without stopping, and bang on the door at the same time.

Mrs Ashland, in her dressing gown, her head wrapped in toilet paper, comes to the door, listens, tells me to go back and wait, and calls to her husband as she shuts the door. I obey, relieved to have directions to follow, to have an adult taking over, to have done what I should.

As I run back across the grass, I collide with my sister right in front of the next door neighbors' house. I shake her by the shoulders. 'What the hell are you doing here?'

She begins to cry. 'I was getting the neighbors.'

I am livid at her insubordination. 'What do you think I was doing?' I shake her harder.

'I don't know,' she cries pathetically. I slap her. 'You stupid idiot! Did you wake them up?'

'No!' She holds her face.

I push her down onto the grass and then yank her up by one arm. 'Get in that house. You know Mother says they're trash. How dare you go to them? Don't you think I know what I'm doing?' I half-pull, half-drag her to the house. 'Get in there and shut up. Do you want to wake up the whole neighborhood?'

I send her to bed and go back to my brother. He is holding the tourniquet, and now looking scared, like a wounded animal. I flush the toilet, replace the blood-soaked towels, help him sit up. We are both embarrassed now, by this intimacy, this touching; our indifference to one another has become our bond since we have quit fighting; we have passed from the fierce love and hate of childhood and into the mutual contempt of adolescents. We know this closeness is thrust upon us by sheer chance, as much as our sharing of the same parents. We share nothing, except the desire to shed this life; we know that we are already strangers who meet, touch, care only because of this present moment.

Mother has left her cotton housedress on her bed and her sandals on the floor, and I put these on. I glance at myself in the mirror. My face is white and my lips red. My hair is a mess and I pull Mother's brush through it a few times. I feel strangely excited.

Mr Ashland comes and we carry my brother to the car and put him in the back seat. Then Mrs Ashland comes and takes Lesley back to their house. I am afraid that she will try to make me stay behind as well, and am prepared to defend my right to go to the hospital, but neither object when I climb into the car.

I tell Mr Ashland in an efficient voice the name of the nearest hospital and the theatre where my mother is. He nods without comment. When he turns in a different direction than the hospital, I say, 'Hey, you're going the wrong way.'

He says, 'That hospital doesn't have an emergency room.'

'Oh,' I say. It dawns on me how limited my role actually is in this. After a minute, I add conversationally, 'Well, wouldn't you just know. An accident just had to happen with my father overseas and my mother at the theatre.' Mr Ashland smiles a little at me but doesn't answer.

Mrs Ashland has called the hospital to tell them we are coming, and when we drive up, there are two nurses waiting with a hospital bed on rollers. They don't seem very concerned, which shocks me. Even when they lift the bloody towels from my brother's leg and see the cuts, they chat cheerfully, like the school nurse used to when we would fall on the asphalt. I get madder and madder at this indifference, and am about to tell them that they'd better do something fast before my brother starts to bleed to death, but then, he is gone, rolled away through some swinging doors. I follow and am left in the bright, dirty waiting room.

There are some children there, one with an ear-ache and one with a burn, not very bad, and some old people. After a few minutes, some policemen come in with a man who is drunk, bleeding all over his head and yelling about his wife, calling her a bitch and saying he is going to kill her. The nurses, who march around like military sergeants, warn him that he will go straight to jail if he doesn't shut up. He tries to grab one of them, and she twists his arm so hard that he cries out and begins to whimper like a dog.

A Mexican comes in holding a cloth around his hand and he can't speak English and all the nurses are yelling at him at the top of their voices, trying to make him understand. The lady next to me asks me what was wrong with me and I tell her about my brother. She tells me that her husband had convulsions and she doesn't know whether it was epilepsy or a stroke.

Then I remember: what if he has taken some drugs? Should I tell them? Such a betrayal is nearly equal in import to the risk of his death. I stare at a nurse sitting behind the desk, writing. Then my mother walks in. She looks stiff and white. Her make-up lays on her face like a transparent mask. I can see the bags under her eyes that she had covered with a special make-up and her skin hangs down as if she is very tired. I try to say something to her, but she walks right past me and to the nurses' desk. I am dismayed. She isn't happy that I've done something right for a change, that I have handled an emergency. She has grimly assumed responsibility for this; I am now of no importance.

I watch her go through the swinging doors.

After a long time, she comes out again with Mr Ashland. She stares at me for a minute as if she does not recognize me. She looks very small in her dress, as if I am looking at her at the end of a telescope. Her dress and make-up and teased-up hair stand out like a costume; underneath, she looks like she usually looks: tired and fed up.

She continues to stare at me and I wonder if it is that I am wearing her dress – she hates me to touch her things. Or, maybe it is that I have come to the hospital when I should have stayed at home. Or maybe she knows that my brother is stoned. Then I wonder, can she be in shock? That would have been the way a mother in the movies would act.

I briefly imagine Mother being paged at the theatre and then dramatically rushing into the hospital, her black dress in a swirl. Two gentle nurses would guide her to where her handsome son lays bleeding to death, and she would take his hand and gaze tenderly into his eyes.

She sighs, deciding not to mention whatever it is she is mad about. And, I know she has rushed over because that's what mothers have to do, even when their sons are smelly, have yellow teeth, take drugs. She is not in shock; she will take care of everything now.

She says, wearily, 'Mr Ashland will take you home.'

When we drove up, the front door was open and all the lights were on. Standing inside were Mr and Mrs Crispen in their evening clothes. We walked in, and the Crispens and Mr Ashland spent about ten minutes politely disagreeing about who should stay and clean up and wait for my mother. Finally, the Crispens won and Mr Ashland left.

Mrs Crispen said, taking off her gloves finger by finger, 'Let's just see if we can't clean this up a little for your mother.' Mr Crispen followed her down the hall and I came last.

'Well!' said Mrs Crispen. 'When you kids have an accident you certainly know how to do it!' I laughed a little to be polite, and watched her. She was wearing a green taffeta dress, gathered at the waist and with a neckline like a heart. I wanted to see if she was really going to start cleaning up all that glass and blood in that dress.

Mr Crispen surveyed the bathroom. He did not appear embarrassed; he seemed to be considering things.

'What we need is a bucket and some rags,' said Mrs Crispen with forced heartiness. I stood there, entranced. I had never been around the Crispens alone before. I wanted to study them.

Mrs Crispen had changed from the days when she was Mrs Jackson. She was blonder and thinner. I had heard Mother tell Mrs Ashland that she had had a boob-job and I tried to see if I could tell the difference. She had done it, Mother said, because they went to the South of France on vacation and the women there go topless on the beach. Mother had said this in a odd way, as though it were funny but kind of embarrassing and not very surprising. After all, she seemed to say, that's the Crispens.

The telephone rang and I went to answer it. Mother asked me where Lesley was, and I told her. Then I said, 'The Crispens are here.'

She groaned. 'What are they doing?'

'We're cleaning up the glass,' I said, even though nothing had been done yet.

'Oh God,' groaned Mother. 'Tell them to stop immediately.'

'Mother says to stop immediately,' I called to the hall.

Mrs Crispen came and took the phone from me.

She said, 'Virginia . . . Don't be silly . . . How is he? Well, thank heavens . . . No, no, don't worry . . . We won't . . . Of course not . . . You just do what you have to and . . . Alright . . . Yes . . . Bye-bye . . .' She put the telephone down. 'Your poor mother.'

Mr Crispen had left the room and now returned with a bucket and some rags. He began to pick up the larger shards of glass and put them in the bucket. Mrs Crispen bent down to help him.

Then she turned a little toward me, still bending over, to pick up a piece of glass that had flown out of the bathroom and onto the hall carpet. Her hair had fallen forward and across the side of her face, a perfect blonde curve, coming to a point on her cheek. Her neckline gaped open a little, and I could see the edges of her bra.

She said, 'Well at least your brother waited till the end of the last act to have his accident!' I didn't say anything.

'Your mother,' she went on, 'certainly enjoyed the show.' She looked up at me as she shook out the contents of the rag into the bucket. I suddenly felt very tired and wanted them to go. I knew that Mrs Crispen felt sorry for my mother for being married to my father and saddled with us while she was married to rich, European Mr Crispen. And I knew that there was nothing I could do about that. I wanted to tell them that they didn't have to clean up my brother's blood and the glass, that I could take care of it myself, that I didn't need their help. But my part in all this was not to decide; I knew I would have to wait until eventually they would leave.

When I was in high school, the Crispens got divorced. Mrs Crispen, my mother said, 'came out of it very well.' But a year later, she found out that Mr Crispen had hidden a lot of money from her in Switzerland. When she tried to sue him for some of it, the judge ruled against her.

When my mother warned me about the perils, the awful responsibility, of adulthood, I knew already that the risks I would undertake, and the damage I would live with, not only from childhood, but collected at every stop ahead, would discourage me, but not for long. I had already seen the women I would never be.

The memory of Mrs Crispen faded with her divorce, as though she had again transformed. Into what? I never found out. What I remember best from that night is not Mrs Crispen, nor her daughter, nor even my mother, who, like us children, were only appendages, who could be discarded, ruined, protected as others saw fit. It is Mr Crispen, the displaced child who made dreams come true, whom I remember best.

Dark Hour

Philip MacCann

Philip MacCann was born in Manchester in 1966. He has been a critic for *The Guardian*, and his collection of short stories, THE MIRACLE SHED (Faber and Faber), was published in 1995.

Dark Hour

One day Gera walked in to Silver Palace but I wouldn't look up from *Lethal Weapon*. I was sad because I didn't have money to play. Exhaust got in from the street. He went to the corner. My brother was there in a green shadow at a game. His arse went tight when he banged the buttons. They talked about the game. I stood about, then I watched Gera go. He walked with the chink of new bullets. Cars were jammed outside. I didn't get on with him. A minute later my brother walked out. I leaned against a glass front and watched a game.

When Dano came back home I was sitting with some mates at the dry stream at the flats. 'You're wanted,' I told him just for a doss.

'Am I?'

A picture drifted past my face of my old one shouting and clasping the air in front of her face. She said if Dano got caught up she would batter him. I had a promise to watch him but that was just a load of bollocks because Dano would kill me if I ratted and anyway I don't give a bollocks. He started going. Then this is me: 'Gis somethin'?'

'I haven't a penny, John.'

'Ah go on.'

'I swear.' He balanced on a bike wheel that was lying there. The warm afternoon made you kind of sick. We watched my mates passing a robbed Walkman. He was thinking. The sky was like a black blanket. 'D'you know what I was thinkin'?' he said in a low way. 'D'you wanna make somethin'?' He stepped over the mud. I went with him. 'D'you wanna do a job for us?'

'I don't mind,' I said.

'I'll tell you later,' he said. 'Right?' I bobbed my head. He went on to the tarmac and up to the flats. Then I sat about dossing with my mates. A Honda Civic went by but it was making a lot of smoke.

Later me and Dano crossed the road and leaned on the railing outside Silver Palace. Not as many cars were there. I hung over the railing and tried to yawn in the stillness. 'D'you wanna go robbin' with us?' he said. 'Just come along and watch.' A shadow came out.

'What do I have to do?' I said.

'Nothin',' he said. 'Just trust me.'

'I know.'

I flopped off the railing. We started walking. I wasn't going to trust him. I was just tagging along for a minute to see. We wobbled in bruised windows. Diane and Sharon passed us and he nodded. We walked to the top of the road. We stopped at the old fountain. 'Here?' I said. We sat down.

'He'll be here in a minute. That's him!' said Dano.

'Who?'

'We'll go for a spin, right?'

'Where is he?' We walked along the road past the parked cars until Dano stopped. An old car opened its door. Dano looked round. He said to get in the back. My stomach was a bit dizzy. 'Where are we goin'?' I whispered.

'It's cool. Quick.' I got in and he got in the front. The car took off but the traffic was jammed.

'So,' said the man. It was an old fellah. 'You okay back there? Haven't I seen you before some place?'

'He's kind of shy, you know,' said Dano. 'He doesn't really know about it. Well, he knows about it . . .' Dano lit a smoke for us.

'We'll just go for a spin,' said the man. 'What age are you?' Dano got the window open a small bit.

'Fourteen,' I said and the man said, 'No you're not!' The cars were slow and they didn't really talk and I yawned.

The man pulled the car into the grounds of a church and parked it at the back. He twisted round. He blinked at me and went: 'Well, you see there's . . . I'll tell you the truth.' He sighed. He leaned closer. 'Well,' he said. Then his hand went on my leg. I looked at Dano who shook his head tinily. The man spoke in a kind way. 'Would you be able to tell me . . .' He thought for a minute. 'Can you be a good young fellah?' I caught Dano's eyes again and they glanced away blinking. The man's hand went back and forth on me for a bit and he asked me questions. I had a horn.

'Is this what I have to do?' I asked. The man's eyes looked at my legs.

He went, 'I was thinking . . . Would you like to make something?'

I thought. 'Not really,' I muttered.

He smiled at me. 'A score?'

I looked out the window. There were houses and clouds. 'I don't really want to.'

'Ah he will, Ken,' Dano said. 'The next time.' The man looked all over my face and shook his head. Then his head nodded. Then he went back in his seat in a happy way.

'Home sweet home?' he went.

'Yeah.' The church bells started clattering.

We started driving. The traffic trickled. He asked Dano was I upset now.

'No he's not. Are you?'

'What?'

'Are you upset?' Dano laughed.

I didn't know so I said to the man, 'Can you get the full clock out of this?'

'Yeah. More.'

Dano went: 'D'you like him or d'you not like him?'

'Like him,' I said. And I added, 'I have another friend now. I'm happy.'

'He knows Gera and all,' Dano told me.

'Do you?'

'Gera's a very good friend,' said the man.

I thought I should say, 'Ah, he's dead on so he is. He has a nice personality, d'you know?'

We were getting near to where we had got in the car. 'You'll do it with him, won't you?' Dano nodded to me.

'When I get to know you,' I said. 'It's just, you're new.'

The man pulled in. Dano said, 'Tomorrow?'

The man nodded. 'Will you do that thing, Dano?'

'Ah, it's cool,' Dano cut him off. He got out and let me out. 'Nice one, Ken,' he said and slammed the door.

'Bastard,' I said to Dano as we walked back in the brown air. He handed me a fiver. 'What's that?' I took it.

'For goin' with him, you dope.'

'You said you were robbin' him!'

'I want to rob his *gaff*!' He was loud. 'I need someone with me.'

'Well it won't be me, that's a *fact*.'

'I was gonna explain about him, John,' he said. 'He's a queer.'

'Why didn't you then? Cos I wouldn't have gone, that's why!'

We went into the flats. A tyre was burning in the court. 'Don't flash that,' he mumbled. Dano is a dirtbird and his face looks like a dog.

My old one got me up the next day while I was thinking of the man wanking Dano. She came into our room and said, 'Where's Daniel?' I said how was I supposed to know. I was in a hurry to get out. Everything was all over the kip in our gaff. 'Do I not have clean shorts?' I shouted to my old one.

Here's her: 'How am I supposed to know?'

'Fuck off then.'

I got on my clothes. Then I went out and crossed the road. I just leaned on the railing outside Silver Palace and waited for Dano because I hadn't the money to go in. I was disappointed because it was a gloomy day. I smelled the dust and I was tingling. A minute later Dano came up the road with a can of Lilt. We started walking up to the old fountain. There were Porsches and all parked. I looked at us in their dusty windows.

Dano said, 'Watch him, right? In the gaff. He could try anything.'

'I better not have to do anything,' I warned him. Because I was only going along for the money.

'Don't be stupid! I'll be there.'

'How are you gonna rob him?'

'How do you think?' he said flattening his jacket against his chest. I looked at it. I got a bit worried.

We went and sat on the fountain again. There was rubbish in the fountain. I went, 'How much do I get?' but he didn't know how much was there. Our flats were leaning against the sky. The colour of the sky was called buff. The sky was slipping into your head. My hands were grubby. I hated them. I took my comb out and raked my hair. I couldn't get it to sit right. Then Dano stood up. 'Don't make a bollocks of it, Dano.' We walked along by the cars again. 'I don't know about this.' The car door opened. Dano looked round and we got in again.

'So?' said the man.

'The gaff,' Dano said to him. 'If you want. It's up to you.'

The man turned his head round to me. 'Will you do it? Just for an hour?' I didn't speak. 'Eh? Good-lookin'?'

I made my face go bored. 'So are you,' I said. Dano smiled at that. 'I thought you were gorgeous the first time I seen you.' The man blinked. 'Why d'you have that moustache?' I said. 'Is that real?' The man started the car and started driving.

We drove past old markets that were bricked up. I saw tiles and walls with layers of old paint. A bit later he said, 'Not long now.'

'Your gaff?' I thought I recognized where we were. Soon there were big cylinders for gas behind the houses. The sky was muddy. He parked on an empty street. I was tingling and kind of tired of it.

'Now,' he told us before we got out. 'Just don't whisper.' We got out. He took keys out. We stood while he opened a door on the side of a boarded-up shop. A dog wagged its tail. I whispered to Dano had he got the smokes. Then we went in. There were stairs. The man closed the door and we went up into a flat. He locked the door of it. 'Right,' he said and smiled. It smelled of socks. Dano used the jakes. The man poured a cup of milk and asked did I want a drink. His hand brushed past my arse.

'Nah, it's cool,' I said. 'Dano, light a smoke.'

I went into the jakes after Dano. I didn't know what to say

to Dano. He puffed into my ear, 'Go along with it for a minute. Then you can tell him to fuck off.'

'What?'

'Relax, will you.'

We both went back in. I was bursting to giggle, then Dano said to the man, 'I was gonna ask you for eighty. Him sixty and me a score.' The man was leaning against a surface. I was thinking if the man kissed me I had Lilt on my tongue.

'It would have to be forty,' he said and sucked his lip in.

Dano nodded at me and went, 'Yeah.' The sun was falling on the surface. The man asked Dano to go into the bathroom. Dano asked for something to do there. The man looked around. 'Even give us somethin' to draw with,' said Dano.

'Where's he goin'?' I said. The man gave him a notebook and coloured pens. 'Why're you goin' in there?'

Dano gave me the smoke and said, 'I'll be in the jakes,' then he went.

The man sat on the bed. My heart started to kick. He asked would I come over. I said what did I have to do. I finished the smoke. He nodded. I went over. He said, 'Do you mind?' He put his hand on my shoulder in a sad way.

'Don't care,' I said and shrugged my shoulders. He lifted up my jumper. He pulled it over my head.

'You haven't much on.'

I looked at the jakes. 'Where's Dano?' I asked.

'In the bathroom,' he said in a playful way as he took off my cross.

'Is he?'

'Yeah.'

I nodded.

'I'm just the luckiest man in the world,' he said. 'You know that?' The cylinders were close to the window. He sat me down and lifted my foot on to his lap and took off my runner. 'Smelly feet.'

I asked did I have to get stripped. He had a pimple on his neck. He pulled down my tracksuit bottoms. I went along with it. I had a big horn. I said I was a bit nervous. His hand went back and forth on my leg again. His hand was cold.

'What's your name again?' he asked.

My tongue made a tutting noise and I went, 'Nobody.' With a smile he asked could I come off. 'What?' I said.

He stood me up. 'Turn round,' he said. Then he pulled my shorts down. I was afraid of someone coming into the gaff.

'Dano won't come out, will he?'

He shook his head and patted his knee. I had to go on his lap. His fingers went up and down twiddling me. He gave a big sigh. He said how cream my legs were. His hand was grey. The lace curtain put a shadow on it. He said I could come every day after school if I wanted. 'Is this it?' I said. His other hand rubbed my back.

'Have you never done this before?'

I said, 'Yeah.'

'Dano said,' he said, 'you knew about it.' He pressed my nose. I sort of felt sorry for him. 'You don't?'

'Do you like sex?' I asked. He closed his eyes.

'Like it?' He was at my dick again. His throat swallowed. He shook his head. 'I . . .' he said. He stared at my face. He made a soft laugh. 'I fucking love you.'

It went quiet.

'I love you too,' I mumbled. I heard my stomach. I needed a piss. He was wanking me too much. I was afraid of pissing on him. I was going to ask him to stop. I was going to ask if Dano did this with him. Then all of a sudden I got a thrill all over. I heard him breathe, 'Good boy.' My head was kind of against his arm. He stopped rubbing my dick. I looked at it. 'What's that?' I said. He pulled me close. 'Is that my spunk?' I said. There was a nice smell like rubbish from outside. He was looking at me. He used a tissue and wiped it off my leg. He rocked me on his knee for a bit. 'Can I go now?' I said. He pressed me closer.

'Well I . . .' he said.

The curtain was twitching. I jumped up. 'Will I get dressed?'

He watched me start to get dressed. 'Could you not . . .?'

'What time is it?'

He got up and grunted, 'Okay.' He came back with a tenner and scratched my leg and smiled. He put a finger on his lips. He whispered, 'Don't tell Dano.' I took the tenner and shoved it in my shorts. He went into the jakes. It was bright and we could go and play loads of games. Dano came out. I was a bit embarrassed.

'Where's me stockin'?' I said in a messy voice. I didn't look at him. The man came and took his keys.

'Youse ready?' he said. I tied my runners fast. Dano put the notebook down. He had drawn a young fellah sucking a big nodger. The man tore the pages out and stuffed them in Dano's pocket and said, 'You know not to talk. Or whisper.' I remembered about my cross and I put it on. When he was sure we were ready he opened the door and we went down the stairs and outside. A milk bottle top blew along. Then we got into the car and drove home.

When he stopped the car he said, 'Can I see youse next week?'

Dano said, 'Yeah.' He handed Dano forty. 'Nice one,' Dano said and opened the door. We got out into the woozy light. We gave a small wave as the man drove off.

On our way to the amusements Dano didn't say anything but I said, 'I'll get him shot.' The traffic fumes were kind of sweet. I said give me my money because I was broke. Dano gave me a score. Litter was twitching on the surface of the road. I took a piss behind a billboard.

I started spending my tenner and Dano didn't know. I was going to save something for my old one but we were pouring it into the machines. We were happy in the amusements. We were standing in the green light banging the buttons when Dano said with a shrug, 'There was nothing to rob . . .'

I went, 'That's life.'

'Don't start goin' up to that queer on your own!'

'Fuck off, I won't,' I laughed.

The Great Leonardo

Erica Wagner

Erica Wagner was born in New York City and lives in London, where she works as a freelance journalist and editor. 'The Great Leonardo' is in the early stages of adaptation for the stage by the opera and physical theatre company Opera Circus.

The Great Leonardo

His heart was pounding now, like it always did just before he went out into the ring. He had imagined he would get used to it: that his palm, curved around the handle of the thin black whip, would cease to sweat, and that his chest would cease to feel constricted by the glittering silver leotard. He had always dusted his armpits with talc; shifting from foot to foot he felt the wet mineral slippery on his skin. He inhaled, flexed his arms, watched the muscle bunch like the back of a dolphin curving through water. Muscle he'd made, a penance, after peering, that first day, into the dim stinking gymnasium that looked a fit place for atonement. It was filled with twisted black and steel machinery, straps and iron weights, racks whereon he could stretch his thin white body into something new. At first, he did not know what to do. He watched the others, would not speak or ask, but saw them buckle their strong shapes into the instruments and pull, push, lift. No one met his eyes, and he was glad. It hurt, and he was glad. Thus was Adam made, he thought, built out of the dust. I will build myself. I will begin again.

It was a cold day, it was February, the first time she came into the church. He remembered her red nose, her red earlobes, and her fingers, when she pulled them out of her woollen gloves, delicate as spines of silver birch. She had opened her purse awkwardly, her cold hands clumsy, pulled out a coin and put it in the wall-box: it clattered loudly for there were so few beneath it. He smiled as he stood at the back of the church, a dust-cloth in his hand, the sleeve of his cassock pushed up; but she did not. She did not see him. She walked quickly to a pew at the back and sat very still, her eyes on the altar, gripping the pew in front of her. She did not remove her coat. After a while she knelt, and leant her forehead on her hands. It was a broad forehead, square and very white, the hair pulled back off her face with a plain black band; an Alice-band, it was called, and she looked like Alice, with her grave face and straight back, her delicate hands and small feet. All these things he had noticed, as he stood by the altar, and found himself thinking it was as if he had never really seen anyone before, as if he had been blind.

But had he? He thought of some of his other parishioners and what they looked like: Mrs Arnold, with her thinning, dyed hair (always a little grey at the roots) and spectacles resting on her bosom, anchored to her body with a thin gold chain; Mark Andrews, his bright face leached of colour by his wife's recent death, towing his three small children dutifully, carefully, as if they might break or be snatched away as his wife had been.

No. He knew them well. And yet here, kneeling at the back of the church on Wednesday afternoon, was a woman he had never before seen and yet in whom he suddenly saw the meaning of the words he had known all his life: *in our image, after our likeness.* He stared at her – her head was still bowed – and held the dust-cloth very tight. Her shoulders rose and fell, a sigh or a sob, he did not know, and then her head came up and she saw him. He must still have been smiling, for now she smiled back, a tentative, momentary flutter.

He turned and walked quickly into the vestry.

The smell was just the same as when he was a little boy, only stronger. His father used to take him to the circus every year; there was a troupe that came each spring and set up their tent on the village green. It wasn't a very big circus, they didn't have elephants or lions, but it was a circus nonetheless, and he had loved it. There were white horses with sparkling bridles that trotted sedately round the ring while girls with taut, muscular thighs danced easily on their broad backs; there was a trapeze, and a tightrope, and a Polish family who traversed the air above the ring, back and forth, up and down. His father bought him candyfloss and peanuts and they sat rapt, afraid for the Poles and their feats of daring, laughing at the clowns, admiring the horses and the pretty girls. And all afternoon there was a smell of sawdust and sweat, of the horseshit the clowns with their big brooms could never quite clear away, and of people packed too close together, their homes, their lives, all crammed in under the hot lights in the tent. He had loved it. His mother had not liked them to go; she thought it was wicked. She had told him, he ought to confess it on Sunday, confess going to the circus; but he never did. He knew it was not wicked; he did not want to give it away.

His mother was long dead. He could not have faced her now. And yet the circus scent in his nostrils called up her stern face, much easier to remember now she was so far gone. Perhaps she would not even have recognized him with his new, thick brown body, his hair slicked back and his blue eyes rimmed with kohl. This will make you look fierce, Lina had said, leaning over him, the soft black pencil pressed between her fingertips; open your eyes wide, look up. He had looked up high so that he could no longer see her, her white breasts blossoming from her tight sequined bodice. He had blushed, and then thought, it does not matter anymore what I hold in my head, it is all mine.

And the man said, The woman whom thou gavest to be with me, she gave me of the tree, and I did eat.

He began to wonder who she was and where she came from. She visited the church often, but never on Sundays; he had scanned the congregation for her serious face and never saw it. Only in the afternoons, on weekdays, sometimes with a shopping basket over her arm which she would lay down by the door of the church as if it would be a profanity to bring it any farther in. He wondered if it would be; he did not think so. He had never thought of it that way, but was sure that she did.

He did not speak to her for many weeks. He knew that he ought to, for he knew that she was troubled. He was a good priest, a caring priest, and he recognized what he saw in her: her eyes too bright as she gazed at the altar, the fingers white-knuckled, clenched together with wrists pressed down hard on the wooden pew in front. He should go up to her as she stood by the collection-box (she always stood there for a few moments after she had pushed in her coins, indecisive, it seemed, as to whether to go or to stay), touch her arm, say, can I help you, my child?

But he could not. It was not that he was afraid, he could not call it fear; he just – could not. It pleased him when she came in: when he saw her, he would breathe a sigh of relief. Then he would place himself as far away from her as possible, in the opposite corner of the church, walking quietly, looking over his shoulder to catch glimpses of her bent head. It was clear that she did not wish to speak to him – did not wish to see the priest, he corrected himself. Not yet. He wondered if she would – surely she would – and then wondered what he would do.

He knew nothing about her. Only her little, thin hands, the small feet in plain shoes and slim ankles in thick stockings. He thought they were slim ankles; but he had not much experience of such things. He liked the sound of the two words together: slim ankles. The brown hair pulled back from her forehead, always the same, with the black band, no earrings, no jewellery that he could see. He wondered if she wore a cross at her throat. No make-up. Her face, below the wide, wise forehead, was not particularly pretty; the eyes were deep set and a little too close to the nose for what he knew was considered beauty; but her mouth was kind, relaxed, more relaxed than the rest of her, and a fine rose pink. Peering through the gloom of the church, he thought he could see the faint traces of lines around it; he guessed she was about his age.

He did not think of love, and he did not think of sin. He watched her face as he imagined he would watch the face of the Mother of God, should he ever see it. Her pale skin glowed in the light, in the faint flicker of the candles by which she knelt. He felt wonder.

Across from him, on the other side of the tent, they were rolling out the cages, one by one, linking them together to form a train of ferocity. It was quite dark in the wings, he could not see very clearly, but he could make out the shapes in the cages, moving, twisting in their small spaces, opening their jaws and pressing their fur against the bars. As they came closer to him, the note of the smell changed slightly, darkened with civet. He closed his eyes and inhaled. It was a splendid, dangerous smell, unlike anything else he knew. It was more a texture than a smell, so vividly did it conjure up the feel of thick fur – gold, orange, black, silver-spotted – of the slick blunt teeth and saw-toothed tongues rasping against his skin. He loved this: the hot scent in the moment before they met. He welcomed it, took it gratefully into his lungs. He knew they sensed his presence as much as he did theirs, and it made a vivid bridge between them, across the tent, across the ring, waiting for the moment when they would speak to each other and touch each other. At that moment, when the cages were opened, the ranks of seething, fidgety people became still, watching his glittering smoothness move so easily among the huge beasts. They would think, he has tamed them with his whip and his strength, but he knew that was not so. For in the ring, the love between them grew into a great searing sun that almost singed his flesh, hotter than the fiery hoops through which they leapt at his command. It was not so different from the old love, of incense and altar and velvet; it was only a new mystery. The sweat trickled down between his shoulders as he watched the clowns roll about the ring, run up and down in the dimness of the audience. It was almost time. The ringmaster was adjusting his brilliant coat, pulling on his tie, clearing his throat. In their cages the cats waited.

My God hath sent his angel, and hath shut the lions' mouths, that they have not hurt me.

In the end, of course, she came to confess. He was sitting quietly on the other side of the screen, reading in the half-light, wondering if anyone would come. People rarely did. Yet Mass was well attended; well, times change, he thought. Though it was not so long ago that he was young, and they all went to confession, his friends, his parents, their friends. He had enjoyed it, in a way. He had, in any case, never found it difficult. But then, he reflected, he had never really done anything wrong; and he could recall the priest chuckling as he gave him a few Hail Marys to say. Sin was never something of which he felt he had an adequate grasp. He wondered if that made him a lesser priest.

He was reading the gospel of St John, because he liked the voice of Christ that he heard in it, human and mystical all at once. That was how he imagined Him. A man you could sit down to dinner with, could laugh with and feel his arm solid around your shoulder, and yet who might at any moment say the most extraordinary thing, the thing that would change your life forever. It might be a little sly, it might be a little riddling, but if you thought hard enough you would come to understand.

If he read this gospel, he thought, he would understand. He read it carefully, moving his lips a little, practically whispering, with the image of the woman – who he now called Mary in his mind – just in front of him, floating in the darkness. The deep eyes were like shadowy beams before him, boring into his flesh and causing him a nameless anguish. He could not find the sin, although he knew it was there. It must be lust, he thought. This is the sin of lust. He tried (he could not do it for very long) to imagine himself and the woman in a room, a room with a bed, where they were naked together, making love. He tried to imagine her voice crying to him, wanting him, and himself hot, burning, as he had been sometimes, pressing his skin against hers, her small breasts beneath his palms. He could go no farther than that. It was not that he felt horror or disgust; he just could not go on. It was not in him. So he thought, perhaps it is not lust: and then the vision of her seemed holy. But he was afraid to discover that lust might wear a cloak of holiness. Michelangelo had painted the serpent with the torso of a beautiful woman. Such things were well known.

I said therefore unto you, that ye shall die in your sins: for if ye believe not that I am he, ye shall die in your sins. Then said they unto him, Who art thou? And Jesus saith unto them, Even the same that I said unto you from the beginning.

The ringmaster strode into the ring, long steps in his high shining boots. He was a good man, the ringmaster, a man with faith. His name was Arthur Smith. He had had faith in the hollow-eyed, strong-bodied man who had come to him one day saying he wanted to be a lion tamer. He had not laughed. He had looked down at his big red hands and nodded his head.

'Don't call it that anymore,' he had said.

'You don't?'

'No.' He looked solemn, appraising. 'Don't go down well. This cruelty business. All the fuss. You know. Working with the big cats, that's what we say now. Cat Men, that's what they call them.'

'Cat Men.'

He had told Arthur Smith that he had been a priest. Arthur Smith did not look surprised, but then, he did not seem the kind of man who would be surprised at anything. He had looked him up and down and then taken hold of his arm and squeezed.

'D'you get muscles like that being a priest?'

'I haven't been a priest for a while,' he had said. He did not look into Arthur's eyes.

'Well. Muscular Christianity, I suppose. Why cats, then?'

He said nothing. He had not known. He had only wanted, been certain.

Arthur had been silent for a minute or so. 'Funnily enough, we're having a spot of trouble with our man. Don't say I said. Nerves, you know. Happens to the best of them. I like your face. Priest, you say? Go get yourself a broom, man, do a little sweeping. Get a little closer. Take care. See what you think.'

It seemed a long time ago, that afternoon. He had told no one else of his previous occupation, and believed that Arthur had kept the information to himself. He discovered that in circuses, people didn't ask. Many of them had grown up in the life and knew nothing else, but the others, drawn from the outside edges of life, appreciated discretion. Slowly, with cautious smiles, they had taken him in. He had, they said, a gift, and gifts they respected. The then Cat Man's nerves got worse, and he started drinking more and more. One morning, he was gone, and he left the glistening leather whip on the bed of the priest.

Now Arthur Smith moved swiftly into the tight circle of white light that swung out to meet him. He raised his hat; swung his arms; smiled, and bowed.

'Ladies and Gentlemen!' he called. 'Ladies and Gentlemen!

The moment you have all been waiting for! What more can I say? He needs no introduction. Ladies and Gentlemen, I give you The Great Leonardo!'

A little hop off his toes and he was running into the light, his arms wide, his chest wide, his legs pushing him gracefully out into the centre ring, seeing the cages out of the corner of his eye roll to meet him. The clowns and roustabouts pulled the barred train into a semi-circle behind him as he bowed deeply, before and behind, his head nearly brushing the sawdust on the ring floor, his face set still and stern. The crowd – from here they looked like dark bubbles on the surface of turbulent water – shouted and whistled and clapped, twirled their little torches to make small arcs of spinning light.

The Great Leonardo let one arm drop slowly to his side and brought the other hand to his mouth, one finger on his lips, in an exaggerated gesture for silence. There was whispering, shuffling, giggles, and then quiet. He never spoke during the course of his act; the previous Cat Man had been hard of hearing, and had trained the animals with a series of gestures and claps. He had, however, spoken to the audience, told them of dangerous acts of daring, of the extraordinary skill of the animals, warned them of what was to come. The Great Leonardo did not open his mouth.

When he was a priest, his congregation always left the church whispering among themselves. What a beautiful voice he has, they said, so deep and musical. He had always known that this was so. He had liked to hear himself intoning the words of the service, in English, in Latin, letting his sermon (and how well he writes, they said, so simple and clear) roll off his tongue. Like wine in his mouth. He liked to begin his sermons with a reading from the Psalms, simply because he liked to feel the words resound in his head, floating over his palate, ringing the small bones in his ears. *In thee, O Lord, do I put my trust: let me never be put to confusion. Deliver me in thy righteousness, and cause me to escape: incline thine ear unto me, and save me. Be thou my strong habitation, whereunto I may continually resort: thou hast given commandment to save me; for thou art my rock and my fortress.*

So now that he had escaped, he was silent. He abandoned his priestly vanity and became a thing of movement only, dwelling in his body only. It seemed fitting. His self was something entirely new, unrecognizable, and it was right, he thought, that he should find a new and different voice. And after all, to his real audience – the great sleek cats – his beautiful solemn voice would mean nothing at all.

He clapped his hands twice. The roustabouts jumped to the front of the cages and turned keys in locks, six locks, six doors, six cages, six cats. The doors opened in a repeating curve, the roustabouts slipped out of the ring, and the cats glided out of their cages to sit in a circle around him. The audience began to applaud, and then, recalling his gesture, rustled quickly into silence.

There were two tigers, Sheba and Konrad. There were two leopards, called Silver and Gold because of their coats: Gold a leopard like any other but Silver seeming bleached and paled, his spots dark grey against his whitish coat. Orion was a black panther with knowing eyes like emeralds set in dark velvet. Roland, tawny-bright with powerful shoulders and wide splayed paws, was a lion. Roland sat at the centre of the circle, looking out over Leonardo's shoulder. He was smaller than both Sheba and Konrad, who sat to either side of him, and yet it was he who commanded the most respect, who made the audience sigh and shudder. His movements were slow and dignified, and he seemed to act entirely of his own accord. His mane was thick, his fur gleaming under the lights. The Great Leonardo stood, a still centre in the breathing circle of blood and bone. Closing his eyes, he heard a tail twitching on sawdust, the rasping squeak of a yawn. He imagined the mouth that made it, peaceful and terrible all at once. Muscle quivered under skin. He raised his hands high, clapped once, and the circle opened and moved.

The door clicked open; he heard the sound of cloth moving against cloth, and then the creak of wood as she sat down on the seat. He knew, straightaway, that it was a woman who had entered the confessional; the anonymity of this office, he had very swiftly learned, was of a limited kind. Smells, speech rhythms, breathing patterns, all these were easily recognized. He did try not to notice such things; but he could not really help it. But he supposed it was the idea that was important:

the small dark box, the little screen between the sinner and the priest creating a new identity for both.

He smelled plain soap, and heard a slight sigh. He felt the pressure of a body leaning against the wood of the confessional; she would be leaning on his shoulder but for the planks between them. He recognized nothing, neither movement nor scent. He was sure it was her. His hands grew cold and he clutched at his Bible, snapping it shut. She jumped. He swallowed, hoped that his voice would not break when he had to speak.

'Bless me, Father,' she said softly, and stopped. The voice was nondescript. No accent. Perhaps a little deep, deeper than he had expected. A little trembling in the 'a' of 'Father', and then an anxious pause. He remained silent, waiting for her to finish the form. His mouth was dry; but he did not wish to clear his throat. He did not want to frighten her.

'Bless me Father for I have sinned,' she began again quickly, almost running the words together. 'It is a long time since my last confession . . .' The quiet voice trailed off, leaving the threat of tears in the air. He heard her breathing, imagined the harsh surface of her brown wool coat rising and falling too quickly.

What would it be that she had to confess, what sin? He realized, quite suddenly, that he did not want to know. Like lantern slides he saw projected in front of his eyes the images he held of her in his mind: the dark bent head, the narrow shoulders, the luminous eyes (in the darkness of the church he had never learnt their colour) gazing at the altar as if it offered some healing, some answer.

Doubt and confusion struck him like a wave of the sea; he was tossed in the surf, his lungs filling with water, lost between the sand and the sky. He pressed his body against the wooden back of the confessional to stop himself shaking, and gripped his Bible until he began to lose feeling in the tips of his fingers. He did not wish to know her sin, he could not offer her anything, he would not say the right words. He would say to her, come out with me, talk with me, let me see the colour of your eyes, and is your name really Mary? He would ask to hear her speak: *My soul doth magnify the Lord, And my spirit hath rejoiced in God my Saviour. For he hath regarded the low estate of his handmaiden: for, behold, from henceforth all generations shall call me blessed.* He would watch the rosy mouth make the words of Mary over, make them for him. And that would be wrong.

He managed to speak, a little. 'I am sorry, my child,' he said, and clattered his way out of the confessional, the airless little box, sliding on the stones of the church to reach the vestry where he wrenched his shoulders trying to undo the back buttons on his cassock. He had it over his head, had torn his collar off, before he remembered that he had no other clothes in the church. He stood still in his underpants, shivering in the cold coloured light streaming in through the pretty pointed windows that pierced the thick walls.

His predecessor had called himself Rufus, that was all. And no one had ever called him anything else outside of the ring: it suited him. Rufus had not been a particularly adventurous animal trainer; the act he had devised with his six cats was nothing very unusual: sitting up, rolling over, leaping over each other, jumping through hoops, jumping through flaming hoops. Only the leopards would do that, work with the flames. Rufus had said that tigers had a terrible fear of fire – it had been something to get them to stay in the ring with it – and as for Roland, well, he probably would have done it but he'd never wanted to risk that beautiful mane. The priest, leaning against the cold steel bars of one of the cages, had nodded agreement. He had watched Rufus carefully, had charmed him, had been an acolyte. Had gone out and bought the bottles of gin that Rufus was beginning to need, had not always asked to be reimbursed. They had both known what was happening. It was the only way.

There was little difference between the two men's acts, except for the silence. It is almost impossible to retrain big animals, animals that are not inclined to be trained in the first place: he had seen how difficult it had been for Rufus to make even the tiniest of changes. But The Great Leonardo was never bored or frustrated. He felt such absolute joy at being in the ring, alone, dancing with soft-furred death, leading them quietly through their paces. Feeling their love. There was a moment, near the end of the act, where The Great Leonardo would stand still, at the edge of the ring, as if he had forgotten what came next. He would turn to the audience, shrug. And the cats, arranged on their barrels, would watch him intently, willing him to come forward, or so it seemed. Finally, black Orion would leap from his perch and trot up to him, his thick tail held up like an ink stroke, and butt his head against the hand of The Great Leonardo, the corner of his soft mouth dragging against the skin so that the teeth grazed against his knuckles. He would sit, and look up with his chrysoprastic eyes, the pupils narrowing to slits as they faced the light. He purred. Like a cat by a hearth, he purred, rumbling, thunderous, deep in his throat, and the audience would whisper and ripple. And Ah yes, said the nod of The Great Leonardo. Ah yes; thank you, Orion: and he patted him on the head like a good child. They would trot back together to the centre of the ring, companions. And they were his companions, all of them.

He knew the act so well now that he barely needed to think about it. He could watch it going on before him, and feel the splendour of the animals around him, each a different size, a different texture, affecting him in a different way. It was, he admitted, a sensual pleasure, having them around him, and at first he had felt some guilt. And yet his heart was moved by so great a love for them that he felt it could not be evil. The love filled his body and his mind until everything else, all his past life, vanished utterly, and brought him peace, a peace he had never felt standing in the altar, giving out the bread and wine. Then, he had always been fearful, afraid of he knew not what – until she had come into the church and given a shape to his fear. With his strong arm he raised a silver hoop and watched them leap, Silver, Gold, Konrad, Sheba, Orion, Roland, moving the air around him, with the bending grace of trees in wind and the terrific strength of ocean, sucking the fear from his soul. They were the seven stars in the sky. They were seven alike.

Now he stood at the side of the ring; now Orion came to fetch him, as always. He walked with long, loose-hipped strides, trying to feel that his pace matched Orion's, his fingers just brushing the dark fur. Orion leapt back onto his barrel, and Roland jumped down, coming forward to stand by The Great Leonardo.

It was the end of the act. He had never liked it very much, but the audience did, and so he kept it in; it was easy enough. He leaned forward, and stretching out his arms brought his hands quickly together to his mouth, index fingers raised. Then slowly brought them out to the side again. His gaze was intense: absolute silence. The crowd, a dim sequence of shapes and circles, settled again in their seats. Their torches did not flicker. Their sweet smell hung in the air like a tapestry, woven in with the circus scent, a rich curtain around him. He let one arm drop so it rested on Roland's mane; grasped the fur with his fingers. He lowered himself down to his knees and faced the lion. They were eye to eye.

What did Roland think of his face? He always seemed to be gazing at it just as intently as his trainer stared at him. Roland had eyes the colour of antique gold, flecked with black and brown, and fur the colour of wheat shining in the sun. His broad nose was bent like a boxer's, and the fur there was thin, close over the bone, and scarred with a pattern of scratches like the lines of a map. Thick, wiry whiskers sprouted from beneath the nostrils, quivered in the air. The tongue rasped out, once, revealing the teeth which always protruded slightly – pearls resting on the black lip – to their full length. The yellowing canines were nearly an inch and a half long, and one of them, at the bottom, was gold. Roland was not a young lion. His breath was heavy and meaty, intoxicating. The Great Leonardo reached out, touched the lion under the chin, in the hollow between the bones where the flesh was soft and supple, and the lion opened his mouth wide.

For a second, The Great Leonardo peered into the yawning pinkness of the mouth, a mouth dappled with teeth and shining with saliva. He could see the opening of the throat. Then he shut his eyes, and turning his head a little to the side, slipped it easily into the lion's jaws.

The audience gasped. They always did. Though he could barely hear them; rushing breath surrounded him, and spilled into his ears and nose. He held himself very still, let the teeth scrape gently against his cheek. He reached up and stroked the tawny fur of the neck.

And then someone screamed. He could hear that easily enough: a hysterical, keening note that sounded as if it would tear the tent to pieces. Impossible to tell if it was a man or a woman. He felt the cats become uneasy, shift, grow confused, slope off the barrels and circle. Another scream. Someone else? He could not tell. His hand still on the neck of the lion he went

to ease himself gently out, but found the jaws had stiffened.
Beneath his palm the lion's pulse quickened, jarring against
his own. Breathing. Pushing. A growl. And then he saw her
again, her sweet, serious face, more vivid than ever, the eyes
(he saw now) a deep sea-blue. Wet with tears, staring at the
altar, and himself, trembling with his dust-cloth, hovering at
the back of the church, the black cassock burning his body, the
collar too tight around his throat, pulled tighter and tighter until
he could not breathe, could only watch her staring and weeping,
the salt tears beginning to flow down her cheeks. *And at the
ninth hour Jesus cried with a loud voice, saying, Eloi, Eloi, lama
sabachthani, which is, being interpreted, My God, my God, why hast
thou forsaken me?*

Roomkeepers

Robert Cremins

Roomkeepers

'A few individuals in the middle ranks of life,
inhabiting a part of the town where the population was
poor and crowded, had daily opportunities of knowing
that many poor creatures who were unable to dig and
ashamed to beg expired of want and were often found
dead in the sequestered garrets and cellars to which
they had silently returned; they resolved therefore to
form a society for the purpose of searching out those
solitary objects.'

> Warburton and Whitelaw
> *A History of Dublin*, 1818.

It was Christmas Eve afternoon, and although I had been back
in Dublin only a matter of hours, I found myself on Grafton
Street collecting money for the Destitute Roomkeepers Society.
I'd been nudged into this by a friend from Trinity College, Justin
Kenny, whom I'd met in the baggage reclaim area of the airport.
I hadn't seen him since the previous Christmas Eve – the first
holiday home for all of us who had graduated and emigrated that
summer; we'd met here on the bustling pedestrianized street.
Justin had been collecting; it had looked like cold work. But
now, despite the temperature, I was delighted to be standing
in the middle of Grafton Street. Out of the river of shoppers
came the faces of schoolmates, college acquaintances, ancient

flames, and sentimental enemies, so many like myself beginning another brief homecoming. All of them gave something.

I chatted and shook my can and took a sip every so often from the miniature bottle of whiskey that Justin's father, the gregarious marshal of the collection, had given each of us to fight the cold. Nearby, carolers were belting out Beatles songs. The Christmas lights festooned above our heads and the blaze of commercial light on both sides of the street dispelled the murk of the afternoon. The one uncomfortable moment had been when an old tramp had come up and asked for *a few quid* from my can. Justin had warned me this delicate situation might arise: you were not allowed to instantly redistribute donated money. I pointed out Mr Kenny, telling the tramp that the gentleman would give him information on how to apply for assistance from the society; he melted back into the crowd.

I had just finished talking to a friend of my sister when I saw Corbin Sharkey. He saw me too.

'Hey, it's Pete Prendiville!'

His accent was American, not that Corbin had ever sounded very Irish. The old firm handshake.

'You've gotten thinner, Pete.'

'Working for a living,' I shrugged.

He nodded sagely.

'But you, Corbin. You haven't changed, not exactly. Just become . . . more like yourself.'

He was delighted by this, but I hadn't meant it as flattery. A Sharkey adage from college days had come back to me: *If you want to make a million dollars, you've got to look like a million dollars first*. Back then, Corbin had been worthy of the figure of speech; now, in his presidential overcoat, silk paisley scarf, and gleaming loafers, he could very well have been a real millionaire.

Smiling, he looked at my badge – it said simply *Roomkeepers* – and peered into my open-top can; it was half-full, or, as I imagined he saw it, half-empty.

'Quite the Robin Hood,' he said.

'Yeah.'

I nodded towards Bewley's.

'Listen, do you have time for a coffee?'

He looked at his gold watch gravely for a moment, then smiled warmly.

'Of course.'

Justin was close by and I told him where I was going.

'You remember Corbin, don't you?' I said.

Corbin smiled warmly at him. Justin nodded back formally.

'Let me take your can, Peter,' he said.

I handed it to him, and Corbin and I walked into Bewley's. The ground floor was crowded.

'Mezzanine,' Corbin said.

'Sure.'

We walked upstairs to the more expensive level and got a window table.

'A large pot of Java coffee and two apple danish,' Corbin told our waitress, *then* turned to me for confirmation.

Yes, he was more like himself than ever. I confirmed.

There were many questions I wanted to ask him. He had not been back last Christmas – too busy in America – and although I had an address for him and he had an address for me, we had not been in communication, writing not being a priority for our generation.

In college we'd been unintense friends. He was slightly older and a touch avuncular, introducing me to the music of Thelonius Monk, his discarded girlfriends, and the word *impresario*; Corbin was going to be an impresario, or already was if you took into account the profitable dance club he ran in the sweaty basement of a Dame Street bar on a Thursday night; he was generous with passes for his friends. Now it seemed he was fulfilling his ambition in New York, running an Irish-flavored café-club in the East Village.

'So how's Saints and Scholars these days?'

'Ah, so you've heard about my little place!'

'Naturally. My father sent me the cutting from *The Irish Times*.'

'Oh, yes,' he said nonchalantly. 'I heard they did a piece.'

'Is it true about Bono pulling pints?'

'Yes,' Corbin said shyly. 'That was true.'

'And Daniel Day-Lewis playing the piano?'

'That too!'

'Where are you living now?'

'Oh, in SoHo. I'm renting a loft. May buy it in the new year.'

He talked about its spaciousness and the art he was filling it with – the work of yet-to-be-discovered Irish painters and sculptors living in the Bronx and the Lower East Side. Our order arrived. When the waitress put the bill down between us, I remembered having paid for most of the coffees we'd drunk together as undergraduates, sometimes because Corbin claimed he had nothing smaller than a twenty-pound note on him.

'So how's Paris!' he said.

'Paris is great.'

'Where are *you* living?'

'Oh, in a studio apartment . . . near Père Lachaise cemetery.'

'Last I heard you were teaching in some language school. Still there?' he smiled.

'Yes.'

'Not much money in that!'

'No.'

'So why not open up a school of your own and make some *real* money? Paris is a great place to spend it!'

I sighed.

'It's not as simple as that, Corbin.'

'Yes, it *is*,' he said, knocking on the tabletop for emphasis. 'It's very simple. Tell me, what's the difference between you and those guys who *do* open those little schools and laugh all the way to the Banque Nationale de Paris?'

I had no answer; all I could think about was swapping the metro for a taxi, the twentieth *arrondissement* for the first, and my shady neighbourhood café for *Les Deux Magots*. Luckily, he treated the question as rhetorical and continued:

'People are just so unaware of their possibilities, Pete. Look down there, for example.'

Below us on Grafton Street were the collectors of the Destitute Roomkeepers Society, still points in the streams of people.

'How much do you guys expect to collect today?'

I shrugged.

'I believe the figure last year was about twelve thousand.'

'Twelve thousand! On *Christmas Eve?*'

Some of our neighbours glanced at Corbin. He leaned forward and said confidentially:

'If you get anything less than twenty grand it's a *disgrace*.'

I pushed down the plunger of the cafetiere.

'And how would you go about things differently, Corbin?'

He thought about this, then leaned back and held out his hands expansively.

'Let me show you! Let me collect . . . That wouldn't be a problem, would it?'

I had thrown down a challenge, I realized. I would have felt foolish now trundling out an excuse. It would have to be arranged.

'Oh, no,' I said, 'I'm sure it wouldn't be – the more the merrier!'

'Great!'

Once we were done, Corbin picked up the bill.

We made our way slowly across Grafton Street to where Mr Kenny was standing guard over the yellow buckets that collectors filled with silver; the bulge in his jacket was formed by paper money. I introduced the new volunteer as a friend of mine and Justin's from college – Mr Kenny was happy to give Corbin a can and a badge. As soon as he had it pinned on, Corbin dived into the crowd.

He was extraordinary, something between a restaurateur and street-preacher – stopping people, shaking their hands, whispering visibly witty things into their ears; berating, exhorting, proclaiming:

'Dispose of that disposable income! . . . We've got people freezing in this town! . . . Don't forget what Christmas is all about! . . . Be your own miniature Santa Claus! . . . Help your fellow roomkeeper!'

People began to stop to watch him perform. One of them was Justin.

'Who gave Sharkey a can?' he asked me.

'Oh . . . your father did.'

Shaking his head and tracking Corbin as he moved through the crowd, Justin said:

'I don't like his style.'

'But look at the amount of money he's collecting!'

'Huh,' Justin grunted, and went back to his soft sell.

Shoppers were soon queuing up to give Corbin contributions. After twenty minutes, I saw him heading over to Mr Kenny. I followed. The contents of his full can cascaded into one of the yellow containers. Mr Kenny slapped him on the back, knelt down, and started plucking out five- and ten-pound notes. He looked up at me and said:

'Your friend here is quite an asset!'

Corbin was beaming. I nodded at him.

'Yes, he certainly is.'

My can was quarter full.

Corbin went back into the thick of the crowd again. I stepped into it, too, and started to say *Help the Roomkeepers, please!* a little louder.

After a few minutes, I stopped hearing Corbin's ringmaster voice. He was nowhere to be seen. I began to get anxious. I told myself to have some faith, however, and concentrated on my collecting. Twenty minutes later, he reappeared. His can was full again.

'Corbin! Where did you get to?'

'Oh, lucrative side streets, and back into Bewley's.'

' . . . For another coffee?'

'No. To collect money, of course.'

'But, my God, you can't do that! We're not supposed to . . . I'm sure we're not. Didn't they throw you out?'

'Nope,' he said, smiling. I was very discreet.

' . . . Fine, but I don't think you should tell Mr Kenny.'

'I won't; I'll just show him this.'

Corbin took a folded piece of paper out of the can and handed it to me. I unfolded it. An Allied Irish Bank cheque. *To: The Destitute Roomkeepers Society, One Hundred Pounds only*. The cheque was signed by a dissolute member of the Senate.

'Excellent work!' I said, handing it back.

'Stay here, Pete. I'll be back in just a moment.'

Once again he went over to Mr Kenny, and got another warm reception. I glimpsed an expression of relish on the organizer's face. Corbin came back over to me as promised, empty-handed.

'Well, Pete, it's been fun, but I have presents to buy in Brown Thomas.'

'You'll be coming to Gleeson's tonight, won't you? Drinks are on Mr Kenny.'

Corbin nodded graciously.

'I'll sure try to stop by.'

Just as we were firmly shaking hands, that old tramp appeared.

'Der yeh are!' he growled at Corbin, raising a thick finger. 'Give us a few quid, or I'll get de guards on yeh!'

His face was red and his fingernails were blue. Corbin laughed.

'Go away,' he said loudly, as if the man were deaf, 'or it's *you* the police will be taking away!'

'I saw yeh!' the old man said, unperturbed. 'I was der too!'

'He's been drinking,' pronounced Corbin.

The man did smell, but not of alcohol.

'Wait a second,' I told him. 'What exactly did you see my friend do?'

'Oh for God's sake, Pete!' Corbin groaned.

'Mister,' he said emotionally. 'I was in de church. I was der cus I was waitin' for dem to take de straw off the baby Jesus in de crib – dey always do dat before the chisellers' mass – and der yer man was, kneelin' down and feckin' ten pound notes out of de can and inte his pocket!'

'I was praying, old man!'

I turned to Corbin.

'So you *were* in a church?'

'Yes, I was.'

'What church?'

'The one on Johnson's Court. What does it matter?'

'St Teresa's, Clarendon Street,' the tramp said authoritatively.

I remembered: in Johnson's Court – a passageway off Grafton Street – there was a side-entrance to Bewley's, and, opposite it, the side-entrance to a church. I had passed it countless times in my life, rarely noticing it and never going in, although I could never pass a church in Paris without checking out the interior for some aesthetic surprise.

I believed the old man. There was a horrible logic to what he was saying, a logic I was ashamed to comprehend.

Corbin remained unruffled. I did not. If there was trouble, it would not be forgotten that I had been Corbin's sponsor. I reached into my can and pulled out a ten-pound note.

'You must be mistaken,' I told the old man.

The ascetic image of James Joyce quivered between my fingers. I was doing the right thing for the wrong reason.

The old man studied the money, and then looked at us with contempt, the last survey of someone about to leave high ground. He took the ten pounds, and was gone. I looked around nervously to see if Justin or his father or anybody else had noticed me handing it over. But Grafton Street did not seem to have paid greater attention to this transaction than any other. Corbin Sharkey was staring at me.

'You shouldn't have given him a penny,' he said like a disappointed parent.

He began to walk away.

'Sharkey!' I called after him. 'Take off that Roomkeepers badge!'

He turned around, tapped the tin on his lapel, and had the last word:

'I think I'll keep it there, Pete. Shows I've made my contribution. Merry Christmas! Have a prosperous new year!'

L'Hotel Des Grands Hommes

Clare Morgan

Clare Morgan has published a novel, A TOUCH OF THE OTHER (Gollancz), and her short stories have appeared in, among other places, the British Council's anthology NEW WRITING (1992) and THE NEW PENGUIN BOOK OF WELSH SHORT STORIES (1993). Her work has also been broadcast on BBC Radio 4. She has just completed a Doctoral thesis on 1950s literature and visual art at Oxford University.

L'Hotel Des Grands Hommes

L'Hotel des Grands Hommes is an ordinary looking little French hotel on the far side of the Place du Panthéon. Three well-scrubbed steps lead up to it. Flanking the steps are two identical fir trees in white wooden boxes, so green and so identical you might doubt they were real except for the moist squares of well-turned earth in which each is planted, a rich dark red, particularly in the evenings when the sun slews down over L'Église de la Sorbonne and the whole square is filled with subdued ruby.

The hotel gets its name from the domed and decaying grandeur of the Panthéon itself, in which are housed the remains of famous men, of Hugo, Zola and the inimitable Voltaire. But one cannot say, though the hotel brochure claims it, that the best rooms overlook the Panthéon. All you can see from your window is a flat expanse of dressed stone, pale ochre in the early mornings, orange at midday, and the gangs of local children rollerskating on the pavement, with patches on the backsides of their trousers and an abundance of unkempt hair.

Marsha and Tony were staying in the Hotel des Grands Hommes by accident. Marsha had found it in a guide book she'd picked up at the *Bureau de Tourisme*, and was attracted by the name, and the fact that it was situated in the *cinquième*. They'd both wanted to get away from the *huitième* which was beginning to seem just a little pretentious now that Summer was coming and the real Parisiennes were making way for the tourists and you heard almost entirely American voices as you strolled, occasionally checking your reflection, past the elegant windows of the Rue Faubourg St Honoré.

The move made them slightly uncomfortable at first. The *cinquième* is very different from the *huitième* and they needed time to adjust. It was difficult to know what to wear. But perhaps they would have been uncomfortable anywhere. They had come to Paris for a holiday but also because there were things between them which needed to be seen to. They thought it would be easier to discuss in a foreign city those things it seemed impossible to contemplate at home.

Marsha and Tony were no longer in love. Perhaps they had never been in love. Perhaps love did not exist. Perhaps the only thing that existed was philosophy. You could tell they didn't love each other. He kept away from her and her movements, when she inadvertently got near him, were unnatural and stiff.

They were a prosperous looking couple, in a middle of the road way. They had recently made money and he was very involved in his business. She had that dissatisfied look that comes to some women. When they were in a restaurant he sat with his back to the room and she looked past him and generally they left early and walked through the dusk without talking, taking the long way back to the hotel.

On their third morning, the sun rose very gold over the dome of the Panthéon. They were late getting down to breakfast. Marsha had been slow in the shower and Tony had wanted to finish the final chapter of *Thérèse Raquin*. He rather liked the book. His view was, old Zola could put together a good story. That Thérèse. She was really something. But the parts about passion were well portrayed.

They took the lift all the way down to the vaulted basement where breakfast was served, and tried not to look at each other in the mirrors which covered the inside of the lift. As they got out of the lift Tony thought that Marsha was still a good looking woman. Marsha thought this morning they ought to talk. They sat down to their croissants in silence and felt uncomfortable in the empty room.

They began talking about Zola but it was difficult because Marsha didn't know *Thérèse Raquin*.

'There are some real brutish bits,' said Tony, putting a lot of butter on his croissant. Marsha had read *Germinal* and gave her opinion that Zola had a tendency to go over the top. A wrangle began between them, of no very great significance. Marsha was spirited in her own defence. She wrote a little, and had plans to produce the Great English Novel. She'd thought about taking a villa for a month. She knew that was what you had to do. Writers needed space. Maybe she'd take a villa at the end of this Paris thing. She shushed her husband who was talking too loudly and waving his hands. He held a piece of croissant in one hand and waved it in front of her. She told him they weren't alone and he quietened down. Two men were breakfasting behind one of the pillars. Marsha thought,

'Well, now we *can't* talk,' and was relieved. Tony began listening to the men's conversation in a quite uninhibited way. He pushed away his plate and lit a cigarette and pushed his chair back from the table. He asked the waitress in very bad French for more coffee. She brought it grudgingly, which annoyed him. The two men were American and one was interviewing the other. He listened for a few minutes, nodded a couple of times, pursed his lips, drank more coffee, and soon stopped listening, or listened only partially because half his mind was back home, and thinking about his business, and wondering how he could make sure his order books stayed full.

Marsha was in seventh heaven. When she thought about it afterwards going up in the lift she could hardly believe her luck.

'But didn't you *recognize* him?' she said to her husband, her voice pitching and tossing like a boat on a swollen sea. 'I mean, didn't you *hear*? Weren't you listening, for God's sake?'

She made a strange little noise when Tony said he hadn't been listening particularly. It was a little snorting noise, somewhere between incredulity and contempt.

'It was Carver, for God's sake. *Raymond Carver!* A real, live writer. *Everyone's* read Carver. My God, if only you'd listened! You can really learn something, listening to a man like that.'

Tony pooh-poohed it saying what could Carver tell him that

he didn't already know? But underneath he was annoyed. You couldn't often listen in on what somebody famous was saying. Marsha kept referring to it. They toured the Musée de l'Orangerie because Tony said it was small enough to get around, and right in front of Picasso's *L'Étreinte* Marsha said again,

'That Carver. The things he said about chaos. You'd be surprised.'

That night she told her husband she was going to take a villa straight after Paris. Nothing very much. Not too expensive. Something simple up in the hills. They spent the evening in because Tony had some calls to make. He needed to call America. Lack of progress on some deals there was scaring him. Marsha sat at a table in the corner and got out a pencil and paper and tried to write. It was some months since she'd written anything and the pencil felt odd in her fingers and the empty pages gave her a stretched feeling in her head. She thought she'd write a story, maybe call it *L'HOTEL DES GRANDS HOMMES*. It was a good title. If she handled it right, she could make it reverberate. She started it several times but it didn't sound right. She sat gripping the pencil and stared out into the courtyard. They had a bedroom which looked out over a small square courtyard. The courtyard was enclosed on all sides, seven storeys high. Across the courtyard, on the same level she was, someone was playing Brahms. The piano tinkled as if it were slightly out of tune. Marsha heard traffic revving in the distance and felt claustrophobic. She thought about how it would be when she was really writing. She'd sit by an open window on a terrace with the sun coming slowly towards her, eating up the shade. She wasn't sure what she'd write about. But that would come. There were so many things to write about. 'Order trembling at the edge of chaos.' Had Carver said that? She remembered it from somewhere. She felt happier than she had in a long time. There was so *much* to write about. She understood about chaos. She could write about chaos. As long as she was writing about it she could conquer chaos and be strong.

Tony finished on the telephone and asked if she wanted to go for a drink, but she said no. The next morning she got up early and spent an hour on *L'HOTEL DES GRANDS HOMMES*. Then Tony woke up and got out of bed and farted on his way to the bathroom and Marsha thought how white his body was, and decided not to write any more for the time being.

At breakfast the waitress was affable and Tony seemed good humoured. Carver was there on his own. He sat very still with his coffee in front of him and his shoulders hunched, staring at the table cloth.

'Why don't you go up and introduce yourself?' Tony said. 'You know – writer to writer.'

He said it just loud enough so that Carver would have heard if he'd been listening. But Carver gave no sign, and Marsha shushed her husband angrily. Later she wondered what it would be like to introduce herself to Carver. Maybe she'd do it. There wasn't any reason why not. And yet, when you got down to it, you couldn't possibly do it, not just like that, not go and introduce yourself out of the blue.

She didn't see Carver again that day. But the idea of introducing herself to him stayed in her head. It stayed with her while she and Tony went around the Panthéon. They could only go around part of it because it had been crumbling since the beginning of the century, and was in a bad state of repair.

'We could go up,' Tony said to her. 'There's supposed to be a great view from the walkway that goes round the outside of the dome. You can see everything. There's a great view of Paris. You can even see the Eiffel Tower. And I hear there's a tremendous perspective of Notre Dame.'

She liked the view of the city with its endlessly overlapping roofs. There was something perversely medieval about the tall eighteenth century houses and the ramshackle roofs. When the sun hit the roofs you could see it shimmering off again and everything was very white, there was a white behind the colours of things which was stronger than the colours themselves. In the streets where the sun couldn't get to, everything looked black in comparison. The window boxes punctuating this expanse of white and blackness looked like something which had been spilled.

'There's the Hotel,' she said to Tony, glad to have spotted it and in doing so to have got her bearings.

'I wonder if we can see our room? I don't suppose so. It's on the other side. I left our curtain not quite pulled back.'

They had to climb some narrow steps to get to the upper

walkway. Marsha was afraid of heights, especially when you were exposed, and she held onto her husband's arm. He said,

'Don't look down. You'll make it,' and let go of her as soon as they got onto the walkway. She didn't like the city quite as much this time. The view was too high. Everything took on a miniature look which unsettled her. The wind came from across the city in a shifting way. She moved from pillar to pillar, stopping a little in the protection of each one. They soon went down.

It was a long way down. The crypt was cool and the soft lights made it difficult for her to see after the intense directness of everything outside. That white colour in the roofs. That had been intense. Quite a few people were in the crypt and their footsteps echoed on the stone making a geometric sound. She stopped and bent down to look at the inscriptions next to each stone compartment. You could look through into the compartments where a piece of glass was set into the wall. Tony wandered off somewhere. In one compartment they'd put Zola and Hugo. She was surprised. She wouldn't have thought Zola and Hugo would have sat all that well together. Zola's stone coffin had nothing on it. Hugo's had a flag and a letter and some dried flowers. It looked rather ornate. She was drawn back to look at that compartment again on the way out. Some of the others didn't interest her as much. There were a lot of dead Generals.

From somewhere they were piping through profound music. It sounded like Wagner but she wasn't sufficiently into Wagner to say. On the way out was a benign statue of Voltaire. The wall plaque next to it seemed to be trying to make out that Voltaire was a defender of Catholicism. She said,

'Hey, Tony,' and Tony came round from the back of Voltaire where he'd been intrigued by the effect the fall of his cloak had, it was really amazing how those guys could make things out of stone.

'Hey, Tony. You know. This is crazy. Remember *Candide*? Was Voltaire an atheist or *was* he?'

Tony was in a fooling kind of mood, and struck up an attitude. It annoyed Marsha.

'Don't you remember how it ends?' she persisted. '*We should go and work in the garden.*'

Tony shrugged and said,

'Well. Maybe they got it wrong.'

A blue-jacketed official walked by and looked at them queerly. Marsha turned to Tony to tell him they ought to be going but he had wandered off.

The Wagner had stopped and Marsha became aware of how quiet everything was. A few people were still moving about the crypt, like bluish-looking shadows. Voltaire's benignity disturbed her. Surely you couldn't get it wrong about your own hero. Perhaps he had been a defender of Catholicism after all. Perhaps he hadn't been an atheist. She could understand that. You had to believe in something.

She decided, quite suddenly, that she would introduce herself to Carver. There was something about Carver. Tony came up to her again and took her arm and together they left the cool gloom of the hallway and went out into the bright sunshine. As they walked along, Marsha found the thought that she would introduce herself to Carver a consoling one.

Next morning Marsha and Tony woke up on opposite sides of the bed. They'd been out to a bad Italian restaurant and got rather drunk, and on the way back to the hotel they'd quarrelled. Marsha, making erratic progress from streetlight to streetlight, appealed for support to the darkness which was fixed over the city like a dome.

'I *ask* y',' she said, the edges of her voice rather husky.

'*You* ask me? You ask *me*!' Tony was at the gesturing stage. The quarrel had started over nothing, in the restaurant.

'Oh,' said Marsha. 'Oh.' She didn't know why she said 'oh'. She said 'oh' out of a sense, way out on a limb away from every other sense, of something cataclysmic. Her mouth made a little impregnable circle when she said it.

When they got back to the hotel Tony came out of the bathroom with a hard-on and Marsha pretended to be asleep. Sometime in the night, probably about three or four, Marsha woke up. The drink had worn off and everything seemed very bleak. She lay with her back to her husband, and thought about Carver. Then she thought about *L'HOTEL DES GRANDS HOMMES*. She knew she had to try and finish it before they left the next day. It would be impossible to finish it anywhere else. The atmosphere would be wrong, somehow. She lay awake for a while, feeling panicky, but keeping the panic down by breathing slowly, and opening and closing her hands.

They had a rather silent breakfast in the vaulted chamber. Marsha found the *confiture* too sickly. Carver was nowhere to be seen. Tony told her there wouldn't be time for her to work, they had to leave by 10.30.

'You know we said we'd head off down to Perpignan. Perpignan's a long haul.'

There was an artist down in Perpignan who Marsha had a yen for. She'd bought a little nude of his at the *Marché de Poésie* last time they were in Paris. She'd hung it in her dressing room back home in Baltimore and she looked at it every morning on her way to the shower. The way she'd hung it, the light really picked it out. The little nude had her arms raised, pinning up her hair. There was a lot of tension in her elbows. Sometimes it surprised Marsha she wasn't actually alive.

Marsha didn't write anything else but applied herself to the packing. By about ten everything was in and Marsha was pinning up the sides of her hair. She asked Tony if he thought it made her look more sophisticated and he said,

'I guess.'

Down in the lobby it took a long time for the clerk to prepare their bill. The Carver party was before them. Marsha nudged Tony and said,

'Look. That must be his wife.'

Carver's wife was about fifty, the same age as Carver, and had long brown hair loose to the waist except where it was held up over her ears with two bright red slides. She was deep in conversation with a young Frenchman. Marsha wondered if he was Carver's publisher. It must be really something to have a foreign publisher. She'd have a foreign publisher one day. The young Frenchman held Carver's wife's hands and they looked at each other and smiled a lot. Carver was sitting in the corner and looking out of the window and smoking. Carver's wife seemed very lively. They went outside and got a stranger to take their photograph. It was Carver's wife's idea. She had to call Carver twice before he'd come. In the end they stood together, the three of them, Carver's wife in the middle with her arms draped over both men's shoulders. It was an instant

picture and there was great hilarity when she discovered she'd
left her flies undone.

'Oh God!' she squealed. 'Just look at me!'

She planted an excited kiss on the Frenchman's cheek and her
lipstick came off and left a red impression there. Carver's wife
and the Frenchman went inside and sat in the corner talking
and laughing. Marsha thought, there was only one thing that
made a man and a woman talk and laugh like that. Carver stayed
leaning in the doorway, looking out over the Place du Panthéon.
It was a Saturday morning and there wasn't much traffic. It was
a dull day and the Place looked smaller somehow, without the
sun. Marsha stood watching Carver and Carver stood watching
the Panthéon. Tony paid the bill and said,

'Are you coming, Marsha?'

She said, 'Sure', and picked up one of the cases and walked
with her husband down the hotel steps and over to the car.

'That Carver sure looks miserable.'

'Doesn't he just.'

As Tony unlocked the car Marsha looked round and saw
Carver still standing in the doorway. He'd finished his cigarette
and his hands were hanging down by his sides. The light reflecting off the side of the Panthéon made his face, especially his
cheekbones, look bronze. Marsha felt very strongly she wanted
to go over to him. She waved Tony out of the parking space and
got into the car. The flags that decorated the upper walkway of
the Panthéon lifted in a cross wind then went limp. As the car
circled the Place and approached the hotel entrance for the final
time, Marsha hoped Carver would still be standing there. But
as the two green trees in their neat white boxes came into view
she saw, with a disproportionate sense of sorrow, that Carver
had gone.

Disillusionment of Ten O'clock

Suzanne Cleminshaw

Suzanne Cleminshaw was born in Boston, Massachusetts, in 1964, and raised in Ohio. She moved to England in 1990 to attend the UEA Creative Writing Course. She now lives in Norfolk and is writing her first novel. Her stories have appeared in NEW WRITING 3 and Faber and Faber's FIRST FICTIONS.

Disillusionment of Ten O'clock

The houses are haunted
By white nightgowns.
None are green,
Or purple with green rings,
Or green with yellow rings,
Or yellow with blue rings.
None of them are strange,
With socks of lace
And beaded ceintures.
People are not going
To dream of baboons and periwinkles.
Only, here and there, an old sailor,
Drunk and asleep in his boots,
Catches tigers
In red weather.
  Wallace Stevens

Memories are like viruses. They infect whole families. I should know. I have been earning money as a bartender at weddings at the country club this summer. My friend Casey and I do it. We had to provide our own tuxedos and wear them, but the girls really go for them. And around one in the morning, it never fails, some red-faced uncle comes up and says he wants to take over the bar and that we should go dance with his nieces. There are always nieces. They all go to Mount Holyoke or Bryn Mawr and they have pinkish indentations across the bridges of their noses from the glasses they removed just before the wedding. Glabella is the word for it – the space between your eyebrows. It sounds sort of sexual and sort of like an isle off of Italy. Just knowing this word makes these spectacle-less girls somewhat charming – knowing that they are probably more aware of their glabellas than girls with twenty-twenty vision.

I'm studying the classics in college. When I tell parents this at the weddings they look at me kind of strange, but also as if it's noble, like I joined the Peace Corps or something. Like it's something they're glad someone is doing but relieved it's not their kids.

I have to finish a paper for Modern Poetry this summer. It's on 'Disillusionment of Ten O'clock' by Wallace Stevens. I got an incomplete for the course and the professor said he wouldn't flunk me if I get the paper into him by the end of July. I haven't written a word yet and this weekend is the fourth of July. My parents said they wouldn't ground me for the incomplete if I go to the library for a few hours a day to work on it. I sit in the reference section, thinking of the nieces and what they would look like sans taffeta skirts, sans glasses, perched on the dusty lectern that holds a mammoth Random House Dictionary, opened to the letter V. I never realized how interesting the reference section could be. I've been looking up the entymologies of words today. Virgin means man trap.

There are always stories being told at weddings. After a few glasses of wine everybody remembers stories. Families have their own Greek tragedies but they usually run along the lines of family accidents. The time Matthew got his hand smashed in the car door on the family vacation, the time the McKnights' poodle scratched Missy's cornea, the time Uncle Bob got a suction cup dart stuck to his forehead at Jenny's birthday party, the time Peter stuck an unstrung pearl up his nose. I guess this is the only common ground for all these cousins who haven't seen each other for a couple of decades. One of these wedding planner books was left on the bar one night. The first line of the page it was opened to said, 'Place distant cousins further away at tables in the nearest row on the far left or right.' Second cousins are a lot like Greek characters. They are the ones that send your family these long tragic mimeographed letters at Christmastime telling you about cousin William's operation and cousin Bette's imprisonment. There are a lot of Hecuba-types amongst second cousins.

Where Streetsboro Road begins, at the exit off of Highway 77, there is a Moo Shu Chinese restaurant with a plastic pagoda out front, the Atomic Bar that looks like a set off a sixties motorcycle movie and the No-Tell Motel with a flashing pink and black neon sign of a winking cat. Then there's a trailer park, with all these rusty trailers sitting on pavement. You never see anyone outside of them and it makes me think of those places up north where whales go to die. Then there's a stretch of road that's just marshes on either side that developers always want to landfill and build on but environmentalists protest because there's some muskrat that will go extinct if they do. After a few miles of these marshes the road gets all windy and overhung with huge trees that stand at the edge of the road like obedient dogs. There's a stoplight at the end of all these trees and this is where Ridgewood starts. Past the stoplight are eighteenth century houses with plaques in front of them telling you how old they are. They are all painted white and have black shutters and there is a brick sidewalk out in front of them. Further along are shops contained within more eighteenth century houses – there is Haddie H. Halpern's, a women's dress shop where there are huge stuffed pigs with gold rings in their noses under all the dress racks and velvet cushion seats in the dressing rooms. My mom used to take me in there before my voice changed. Once I saw Mrs Cutter run out of Haddie H. Halpern's in just her slip to talk to her husband who was standing on the sidewalk. She's very pretty. Further on there are lots of gift shops with things made out of glass and wood in the windows and antique shops with Amish quilts and old clocks. There are also a ton of real estate offices and the women who work in them are always marching up and down the sidewalks wearing suits of red or green or yellow depending on which real estate company they work for. They look like brand new items in a hardware store. You take a right just past the gazebo where there are band concerts and ice cream socials in the summer and you're on Ogilby Drive. You go past Ms Dimmer's house, who has hair the color of flat champagne and wears silk robes all day out in her grape arbor and is pretty crazy – for instance, she can't stand the word 'succulence' and as kids we used to hide under her bushes and chant 'succulence, succulence' until she banged open her shutters and flung wineglasses of water out at us. I've felt pretty bad about this lately. The houses get bigger as you drive further down Ogilby – there is Mr Mastrioni's house that has gates and who everyone says works for the Mafia and whose son told our class that they bury their victims face down so they can't haunt the killers, but he might have said this just to get popular. Further on is Mr Huxley's, who owns sports cars that sit in the driveway with grimacing grills and back ends that lift up in the air like the rear ends of mating baboons. You turn left at Mr Huxley's and then you are on Treelawn Avenue. Here the houses are large and sunken in among big elms and maples – the houses and trees on Treelawn seem to have some sort of communion, there is something pachydermish about them. If they were alive, they would be slow-moving and powerful and unaware of what is scurrying about at their feet. If you turn right into the driveway of 154 Treelawn, you are at my house. It is large and white with green and white striped awnings over the windows. I used to eat pears under the Oriental plum tree in the front yard and pretend I was in China.

Casey is majoring in pre-med at Columbia. I grew up with him here in Ridgewood. He's always been into obscure diseases of the mind and body. Like in sixth grade we both pretended we were missing our left arms, which made lunch and scooter dodge ball in gym difficult. Then in tenth grade he put on that he had 'Tourette's Syndrome' and screamed 'Fuck you cunt' at the principal's secretary. He got ten consecutive Saturday detentions, but the teachers still liked him because he's so brilliant and all. Like he could probably figure out this poem in one hour and write twenty pages about it in the next but I'm basically pretty ethical about these things. In fact, I think I'd like to be a poet. I'd never tell Casey that, he'd think it's 'fruity' and not lucrative enough. You can be sure all the uncles know how lucrative Casey's profession will be – the nieces are marched up to him in an unending procession. Casey's goal is to have some obscure tropical disease named after him.

Why do the words in poetry sound so different than words on billboards, in advertisements or coming out of the mouths of people you know? The word purple in this poem sounds different from purple in everyday life. Purple in real life is a Crayola crayon, my father's deep purple leather chair, the ink they stamp on fresh meat. Purple in the poem sounds like it comes from some other place, far away from crayons or grapes, somewhere where it exists on its own, purely purple, without having to inhabit an object.

The uncles all hang out at the bar. Most of them are large with shoulders like bridges but there's always a little one stuck in among them like a sneeze. They are at that obscure stage in life – in between yelling 'Hey Dude' to their friends and wearing black socks and brown shoes down to the beach. They all bore each other like mad, choking back yawns like snakes swallowing mice, but they try to rise above it by acting boisterous and describing the hips on a new secretary with hand motions in the air.

Around twelve I was dancing with one of the nieces. There were all these little kids running in and out amongst the dancing couples like stinging nettles, and then I saw Mrs Cutter. I hadn't seen her since I saw her in her slip outside Haddie H. Halpern's. She wore this dress with purple and yellow flowers on it, but the fabric was kind of see-throughish and when she moved, the flowers seemed to go from solid to liquid and back again – like they were freezing and melting and then freezing again. I've read that the Greeks got their idea for the shape of their vases from the shadows of women dancing on a sunlit wall. 'What are you majoring in?' the niece asked. I watched Mrs Cutter as she disappeared behind a row of black tuxedos. A little kid ran by and nearly knocked us over. 'What are you majoring in?' the niece asked again once we got our balance. She had this brand new notebook feel to her. I caught sight of purple and yellow in between black suits. 'Huh?' I asked. 'What are you majoring in?' I couldn't get sex off my mind for the rest of the night. All the big vases in the room starting looking like Venuses of Willendorf.

It's hard to think poetic thoughts in Hudson. I'm not just procrastinating. I think you need a clean fall of vertical light on everything – clean blue, clean white, clean curves, clean angles. In Hudson there is too much bric-a-brac. There are cupolas and shutters and door wreaths and flowers. Tons of flowers. Did the Greeks have flowerbeds? I can't imagine it. Geraniums are like caged animals. Geraniums are a hindrance to the mind.

I remember seeing Mrs Cutter one winter. She was in front of me at the traffic light in a blue convertible. Its top was down. And it was snowing. Just a light snow. There was a pinkish glow to the flakes from the red light. The snow was falling gently upon Mrs Cutter's bare head – almost as if someone was placing each one there in some sort of arrangement.

At the Ridgewood Public Library there are glass cases full of objects at the entranceway. There are Indian head nickels and Mrs Maddie Cohasset's widow's ring, which is onyx and opened part way to show the piece of hair off her husband's head who was killed in the Civil War, an indentured servant's document with the red seal of the King that looks like melted red licorice. And there's this big soup tureen, with painted Chinese pagodas and trees and little people moving over bridges and a typewritten card under it that says, 'This soup tureen was used in the service of luncheon to Mrs Mamie Eisenhower when she visited Ridgewood in 1965.' It's kind of creepy and Egyptian – all these artefacts of Ridgewood. It's like no one is sure the past actually ever occurred so they have to prove it by displaying all these things in these glass coffins. All these commemorative plaques and historical items in Ridgewood get on your nerves after awhile – you start to feel like you're living in one big sunken Spanish galleon.

Later on that night, the night Mrs Cutter was at the wedding, I saw her out by the pool. It was drained, I guess because they were going to clean it, and the lawn chairs were sitting aimlessly around it like bison panting around an empty watering hole. I went up to her and said hello. 'Don't you love aquamarine?' she said, looking down into the pool. 'Yeah, I guess so.' I didn't really know what to say. 'Not just the color. The word. Aquamarine.' She sat down at the edge of the pool and let her feet dangle into it. 'Aquamarine,' she said into the pool, and it echoed a bit. Her voice sounded like a clear stream running over smooth pebbles. I sat down next to her. I tried it. 'Aquamarine.' It sounded great. I realized it must be my favorite word. When you say it, you can feel yourself submerging into its complex turquoise depths, bubbles rising at each consonant. And I wasn't even drunk. Mrs Cutter must have been reading my mind because she looked at me and said, 'I'm not drunk.' 'I didn't think so,' I said, even though I guess I did. She kicked her feet against the pool wall and the flowers on her dress danced around. I wanted to ask her something but I couldn't think of a question. Someone called my name and I remembered I was supposed to be working.

'None are green / Or purple with green rings / Or green with yellow rings / Or yellow with blue rings.' I used to picture blue rings coming out of President Nixon's mouth whenever he spoke. Watergate was on television all the time one summer when I was little. It was on all day long and then at night too. I'd be in bed and I could hear President Nixon's voice on the television downstairs. I'd picture the blue rings rolling outwards from the television set. They never seemed to dissipate like smoke but wheeled behind the furniture and up the stairs to spin like tops in the corner of my bedroom. It's funny how language can be a force like electricity or gravity – the way it pulls on you, how it can cause chemical changes, blushes, yawns, shivers.

Mrs Dawson came up to me tonight. She used to babysit for me when I was little. She got stuck on the subject of how I used to suck my thumb. About how I was eight years old and still sucked my thumb. Of how I put my left thumb in my mouth and then rubbed my nose with my left index finger. She demonstrated this. All the uncles laughed. Then Mrs Dawson wanted me to demonstrate how I used to do it. She said she tried to put oil of cloves on my thumb to get me to stop, but nothing, absolutely nothing could stop me. She reminded me of my sister's music box that played 'Blue Danube' over and over unless you closed its lid. She plants rows of geraniums in front of her house.

'From whence hast thou come and whither thou goest?' Socrates reminds me of the uncles at the weddings. He is always nosing into other people's business, wanting to dredge up their pasts and corner them about their futures. I wouldn't want to get into a conversation with Socrates. People at weddings are always asking you, 'What are you going to do?' It is a terrible question. It gives you this unsettled vertigo feeling. I wanted to be a Pony Express rider when I was little. I remember seeing an old ad for riders in a history book. It said you must be willing to risk death daily, that you needed to be young, skinny and an expert rider, and that orphans were preferred. Who could resist this? But I guess as you get older you start worrying about breaking your legs and stuff. Heraclitus saw organisms as storms of fire, but everyone seems to simmer down after awhile. There's some guy, Boris Ulla or Olla, who is a fish frightener. He frightens salmon. It's true. These domesticated salmon don't learn fear in the laboratory they are raised in so Boris has to teach them to be frightened before he releases them into a natural stream. This is what Boris 'does.' I wonder what the uncles are afraid of. They don't seem to be frightened of anything – they have the same elephant attitude as their trees and houses. But I don't think they would be Pony Express riders.

'The houses are haunted by white nightgowns.' I have looked up haunted in the dictionary. It means to visit often or continually, to recur repeatedly, supposedly frequented by ghosts. There is an upright Steinway in the corner of the library that I think is haunted. It bears the inscription: 'Played by Sir Robert Winston on his visit to the United States, April, 1940.' It is made of cherry wood and depending on the light, I can see different figures traced in the grain – they have the motility of clouds –

first Oriental men pulling carts, then plum trees with laughing branches. Because it is humid, the piano gives off a deep brown smell, the smell of shadows. Plants communicate through smell; they can warn each other of poisons and insects. I wonder if inanimate objects can do the same, hot rocks in summer, the insides of old pianos, suitcases in closets, books packed together tight. I wonder if everything is haunted, if everything is talking behind our backs.

About two in the morning the parents leave the reception. They are slightly drunk and swaying in front of their newly polished cars shining under the streetlamp like huge metallic Junebugs. This desolate look sometimes flashes across their faces, like they have arrived after a week's train journey only to find an empty station with a broken timetable. But then I guess they think 'tomorrow' and they put their car keys in the lock. I sometimes try to picture the bride and groom in the hotel room later that night. I never completely imagine the ACT, but I see her on the bed, cocooned in her white stockings, and him, lit by the supermarket light of the bathroom, his tuxedo tie undone and hanging around his neck like two black goldfish, his mind thinking the Far Eastern thoughts of a new husband.

The library has the smell of old school buildings. You wonder if learning gives off a smell. The librarian is this man with long fingernails. You can hear him flipping through books. Clip, clip, clip. He has an unnatural skin color because he is never out in the sun. He reminds me of those phosphorescent jelly-like things you find under old piers at night that no one knows the name of. But I like him. There is something foreign about him, even though he's American. It is interesting to watch him move – the cuffs of his trousers lift up to cling to his socks for a moment and then drop down against his shoes. It is funny how a detail like that can make you feel for a person.

This poem makes you notice colors more. Purple grapes, purple nights, blue towels, blue gardens, yellow skies, yellow eyes, green celery, green salamanders, red stop signs, red nail polish, white houses, white tennis shorts, white lawn chairs, white cake, white wedding dresses. Casey once told me that there is nothing perfectly white in nature.

I keep thinking about Mrs Cutter out on that sidewalk in front of Haddie H. Halpern's in her white slip. The mica in the sidewalk was sparkling and it made it look like her feet were sparkling too. She was angry. You could tell by the way she was standing that she was angry. It was a very sunny day. I could see the shadows of her legs under her slip. The ancients thought that anger could be a form of art.

I went walking through the neighborhood last night. It was late and all the lights were out. Everyone was asleep. You wonder what these people dream about. That line about baboons and periwinkles has really gotten to me. It's been running through my mind all week. It's been like a mosquito buzzing in my ear. 'People are not going to dream of baboons and periwinkles. People are not going to dream of baboons and periwinkles.' These lines are like checkmates in chess or something. They just leave you stranded. All the lights were out down our street. I thought of all these people turning their pillows over to the cool side. My mother used to tell me to turn my pillow over whenever I had a nightmare, because then I'd get the good side. I still do it sometimes, although I don't have nightmares much anymore. It was so quiet on the street. It's strange to think of everyone going into their own private trance every night. It's like everyone's diving into their own private grotto and then they resurface in the morning and have their coffee and get in their cars and go to their offices without a thought about the strange place they just came from. I read that under the Sahara desert are all these small seas and rivers, where all these multi-colored and unknown fish live and swim.

One of the uncles got extremely drunk last night. Casey and I found him in the hallway leading to the kitchen. He was walking as though the hallway had stairs. Casey got a hold of his shoulders and led him over to a chair. 'Come on, sugar shoes,' he said real gently. Casey and I are used to dealing with drunks. 'Life is a series of endless yellow hills, young man,' the uncle mumbled at Casey's fly. Uncles start to talk in proverbs by the end of the night. Casey and I call them the 'Unclilian Dialogues.' One of them stayed in my mind though. 'The man who asks many questions may seem stupid for a moment, but the man who asks no questions stays stupid all his life.' The thing was, the uncle who said this said it in such an exclamatory way – you could tell in the way he said it that he thought in exclamation points rather than question marks.

Your body is always lagging behind your thoughts. I sit in the library and my thoughts go zooming, but pretty soon my body drags them back down to the hard yellow wooden chair I always sit in. Casey is always saying we should get back to our limbic system, the ancient reptile brain, and think fierce wild animal thoughts. He usually makes this point in reference to one of the nicer-looking nieces, but I think it would be a good idea all around. Casey is also into how our bodies are full of memories. He's always pointing out aspects of people that he feels fell behind in evolution. Some uncle has a gibbon hand (an elongated palm and short fingers), another orangutang arms. He says there are vestiges of evolution all over our bodies, the third eyelid at the corner of our eyes, the muscles used for smiling being once the muscles used for snarling. They seem like price tags left on clothing. Most of these people at the wedding are Protestant, but most of them would say they believe in evolution. I don't think they really believe in it though. I don't think they believe that they are animals.

Weddings are like painting a scenic background against LOVE. The background really starts to overshadow the original intention if you ask me. I can't believe how thick these wedding planner books are. We used to have a print of Fragonard's 'Progress of Love' in our bathroom. I used to think this was what 'love' was – blue gray trees in the background haunting roses in the foreground. Everything gets so concrete as you get older. When I was eleven Casey told me that having an orgasm was like a dozen great sneezes all at once. It ruined it a little.

Mrs Cutter was in the library today. She knows the librarian.

He was looking something up for her in the card catalog. Click, click, click. I could see the part in his hair as he leaned over the file. It was all crazy and jagged and meandering like a South American river. He said something to Mrs Cutter and blushed and she laughed. Her laugh sounds all shiny and new like patent leather shoes. He helped her get all these books and then she sat down at one of the long yellow tables and looked at them. I don't see many married women in the library. Or men. Usually just students and children. I was going to go up and talk to her, but she seemed so absorbed. She had a little notebook and a pencil and she was writing a lot. After a few hours she left and I went over to the table she was sitting at. I could smell her perfume. The books were all about gardening. 'Horticulture and You.' 'Basic Pruning for the Beginner.' I closed the one that was still open on the table and looked at its cover. 'Petunias and Geraniums: Happy Bedfellows.'

I have decided to look up each word of the first line of the poem, 'The houses are haunted by white nightgowns', in the dictionary. If I can just make the words concrete then maybe the meaning will follow. But it just ends up making a new poem:

> A particular person or thing
> By how much
>
> Or a building to live in, a shelter
> To cover
> and exist,
>
> and visit often or continually,
> repeatedly occurring and
> supposedly frequented by ghosts.
> Near
>
> and following in a series
> in another dimension.
> Having the color of pure snow or milk
> A light colored part,
>
> Pale, wan, like a loose gown
> worn to bed by women or girls.

You realize, though, that you could look up all the words in the first line and get all their definitions, and then look up the definitions of those words in the new line and then look up those definitions, ad infinitum. It gets you dizzy just thinking about it. There is no end. It's like a mirror facing a mirror. I drove by Mrs Cutter's house today. She was out in the front yard. She was out there talking to her housemaid. She had white gardening gloves on and a white skirt. But you couldn't see her legs through it. All around them were cartons of red geraniums.

A Silver Christening Mug

Sarah Gracie

Sarah Gracie was born in Bahrain in 1961 and grew up in England and Scotland. She has won a number of awards for her short stories and has recently completed a collection. She is now working on a novel and living in New York City.

A Silver Christening Mug

Of all his dreadful colleagues, whom Lubowicz considered a bunch of emotionally retarded, dangerously repressed and unrelentingly snobbish middle-class Oxford academics, he found Porbright the most difficult to deal with. Porbright seemed to be the epitome of the breed; or rather, the exaggeration or caricature which occurs when the outsider of a club devotes his whole life to becoming an insider.

Porbright had arrived in Oxford on a Rhodes scholarship shortly after the Second World War, a first from Canberra in his pocket, a proven track record in rugby, and an insatiable desire in his loins to conquer that world that had been too much for his bankrupt and emigré father. With a giddy swiftness, he set about losing his nasty Australian twang, the cheap and unpleasant cigarettes, the oversharp blazers and ties. He acquired a reputation for the finest plus-fours in Oxford, became a master of etiquette, and cultivated membership of a multitude of dining societies and flatulent clubs.

In time, he became more of an 'Oxford chap' than the Oxford chaps themselves. He became the institution's conscience, the sort of spiritual *primum mobile* of his college. It was to Porbright that people went when they wanted to check up on the exact wording of the Latin grace for the feast of St Swithin; to Porbright that they went when they wanted to know the correct form of address for a lesser cousin of the royal family, or the Baroness of Sutherland. And it was to Porbright they went when they wanted to discuss any little matter of college business, such as the allocation of rooms, or the deployment of a legacy from the city. So profound was his transformation that he ingested the language of his chosen home, and spoke it more fluently than its authors. It was Porbright who composed the Christmas address, and scribed the college bulletins, such masterpieces of erudite and infantile wit as could only be penetrated by one who had spent at least twenty years absorbing the Biggles slang and classical references of Eton after-the-match teas and Master's sherry parties on summer evenings on the long college lawns.

And Porbright's life, occupied in this fashion, was a happy one. He was fulfilled, successful, satisfied. In time, he acquired, as a finishing touch to his portrait of himself, a deep plummy bass which succeeded in intimidating undergraduates from the North or young academics who had come up through the state schools. He married the daughter of a former Conservative Cabinet minister. And he acquired a long wonderfully polished rosewood pipe, from which this bass, replete with billowings of smoke, would boom out to the terror of young students of Tacitus and Pliny; for Porbright taught, of course, the gentleman's subjects: Classics and Ancient History.

Lubowicz, a Polish Jew by origin, who had come from Israel to work in Oxford, could not say when his loathing of Porbright had first begun. It had been going on for several years now, and had become one of those institutionalized obsessions, those incursions of madness into the flat landscape of the everyday, which you no longer examine.

If pushed, Lubowicz would have said he hated the man's pomposity, his pretentiousness, his vaunting, vacuous and obscene pride. The gnawing snobbery which was at the very vitals and heart of the man, driving him ever on to further peaks of folly. And then, if questioned further, he would have added more quietly that Porbright might be a fool but he was also dangerous. That he might be a caricature of something, an antediluvian obsolescence, but that it was not so very long since the good old heady thirties – apparently the romantic core of his value system – when he would have been a member of clubs where no Jews nor blacks nor women were allowed. That he was a believer in Empire, and that it was a great disappointment to him that he had to relinquish the system of race distinction for that of class distinction in making his day to day judgments about people. And that of course he was one of those historians who consider it in very bad taste to try to prosecute old Nazis living peacefully in Britain fifty years after the events they are accused of are over and all decent gentlemen have come to a polite agreement to drop the subject.

Generally, Lubowicz's hatred took the form of avoidance. Porbright was too powerful a member of college to have as an open enemy; so he engaged in the only thing possible under the circumstances – flight. He avoided high table dinners where be might be forced to listen to Porbright's booming drone, or contemplate his magnificent profile slowly turned for everyone's inspection, where the similarity between its chiselled splendour and that of his great hero, Alexander the Great, could not possibly be missed by anyone except those ciphers of the classically illiterate, who unfortunately seemed to have been worming their way through the college portals over the last few years. He avoided the college quad as much as was possible, and especially on those days when Porbright would do ostentatious perambulations there with visiting dignitaries. He cut his attendance at college meetings to a bare minimum, and avoided those most dull of Oxford parties, where Porbrightianism – complete with small armies of aspirant new members booming and guffawing, flexing twenty-year-old calf muscles clad in the thickest of tweeds, dropping Latin phrases as regularly as a hen drops turds – might be uncontrolledly rife.

The policy worked in the main, and his irritation level was kept to a minimum. But then one day – it was a clear bright autumn day, with golden trees and fresh white clouds scudding high across a blue sky, a day in which you forgot about college and college matters – Lubowicz's policy of containment was overturned with one fell blow; a blow which struck him down into an abject position of dependence and overturned that delicate emotional homeostasis of hatred and superior detachment which had taken him so long to achieve. The long and the short of it was that

Lubowicz fell of a ladder, cricked his back, and Porbright rescued him; thus placing him in a position of indebtedness which he found completely intolerable.

Lubowicz fell while trying to hang up a painting in his college room. He was at the top of the stepladder when it slid away from him and he was left without so much as a picture rail to hang on to. Porbright, going past at the time to visit his friend the bursar to discuss the financing of a new Keasby bursary to keep 'young gentlemen at Oxford University in the style of living to which they are accustomed', heard the bang – 'prodigious' as he said afterwards – and came bustling immediately to the site of the accident. With great alacrity and energy, he took charge of the situation. 'Dear fellow! Dear fellow! Allow me!' Picking Lubowicz off the floor, where he was grounded in agony, he helped him drag himself to the sofa and covered him in some moth-eaten old college blankets. He ordered up his own doctor, a back specialist, and presided over the diagnosis and the prurient visits of half his colleagues, who loved, as Lubowicz well knew, nothing more than a sick bed (failing a death bed), as a relief to academic tedium, and the only thing left in life that still gave them a sensation of their own vitality. Then Porbright drove him home, despite protestations, and when Lubowicz tried to thank him, insisted on the whole thing being 'Gratis, my dear fellow, gratis. *Egregium sanctumque virum qui donet amico* and so on . . .' the meaning of which phrase Lubowicz did not know.

After he had recovered sufficiently to move around, Lubowicz determined to buy Porbright a large present to get rid of the unpleasant sensation of indebtedness he felt, and also the resentment at having been seen flat on his back on the floor, like a bug that can't turn over, and at having been buried by him, with whatever excuse, under a pile of stinking old blankets.

And he spent some time thinking what this present should be. At first he considered an artistic gift – a gift which would show his good taste and sober 'chappiness'; some fine old hunting print in a gilt frame, a picture of the college, or one of those old maps which were then the fashion, of Saxon or medieval Oxford. But the more he considered these, the more he found them too dull. God knows how many such things Porbright already possessed – they were probably something he had aspired to in some former life and rejected now as a sign of the tawdry culture of the nouveau riche. And Lubowicz wanted to give something a little striking, a little startling, as befitted his own more bold and striking personality, not something expensive and wholly unlovely, to be slid away into some dusty corner of bland English bric-a-brac.

He next thought of chocolates. He considered the fabulous hand-made chocolates of Gerard Ronay – he could go up to London and buy some – the exquisite sweetmeats with subtle striated colourings, and shaped in the form of shells and flowers and corals. He could buy a whole box of them, a complete set, monogrammed possibly in copperplate. A gastronome would find them a delight of course, an ultimate aesthetic experience, and would recognize the tastefulness and delicacy of the gift. But would Porbright?

When Lubowicz got to considering this, he became uneasy. He recollected those interminable meals after Latin grace, innumerable courses of crucified meats, deconstructed vegetables, and tapiocacized puddings, consumed beneath the arrogant gaze of former Masters, who stared down from their gilt frames with craggy features twisted in 'Socratic' contempt for things of the flesh. (Despite the spattering of port-shattered veins across their withered cheekbones.) No, Porbright would eat the most disgusting food with great relish, gustily praising the college kitchen. On second thoughts, the chocolates seemed a bad idea. He probably wouldn't realize what he was getting, and he might even think – here Lubowicz shuddered – that after all his help it was a bit of a shabby present.

After much heartache and anxious scrutiny, Lubowicz decided on a crate of champagne. The gift was a good one on several counts: it had an air of doing things in style, in a rather grand style, a style which Porbright would not hitherto have associated with Lubowicz; the champagne was fine if not ostentatious; and, unlike the chocolates, it carried its price tag with it.

So Lubowicz bought the champagne, and with a decided feeling of relief after all this time, and almost of exuberance, took it round to Porbright's room.

'My dear fellow! How charming of you!' Porbright greeted

him. 'But I just don't *drink* the stuff. Haven't been able to stand it for years – too fizzy you know. Affects the digestion. But a very kind thought, very kind. Really, you must take it away and drink it yourself, with some of your young undergraduate friends.'

He held his line, and couldn't be prevailed on to accept the champagne. He assured Lubowicz that getting the doctor was nothing, that he was paid princely sums to attend to his own, Porbright's, back, and so it made little difference to do a quick 'jiggery pokery' on the far more youthful back of Lubowicz. That Lubowicz must just accept the favour with his compliments, for what were one's colleagues for if they could not help one out of a jam, and that in short, if Lubowicz wished to express his thanks for so small a service, the best thing he could do would be to honour him with his presence at a small sherry party that he and his dear wife were holding for a few friends on the following Sunday evening.

Lubowicz could think of no excuses. He was in a fluster, deflated and bothered. He struggled back to his own room with the crate of champagne, which he promptly gave to his cleaner with an air of lordly unconcern; and then regretted it all afternoon, because the man probably wouldn't be able to tell a reasonable champagne from white Lambrusco, and the whole thing had, after all, cost more than a hundred pounds.

On Sunday, still in the same state of anxiety and dull resentment, he turned up for Porbright's party. It was just the sort of party he liked to avoid. A gathering of mini-porcs, as he called them in his mind. Twenty-one-year-old octogenarian buffers, the down still soft on their cheeks, and the ideology already as hard-wired in their heads as the feeding habits of a plankton. They were Porbright's acolytes; milky youths fresh from the playing fields of Eton, who, having served their apprenticeship of years of bullying, beating, buggering and browbeating, were determined now to enter into their manly inheritance.

Lubowicz found himself a corner over by the window and set in for some heavy drinking.

But he was disturbed in this occupation by Porbright himself, who came up in a resplendent new pair of tweed bloomers, and an air of magisterial patronage.

'Lubowicz, my dear fellow! How nice of you to come! And how's the back? A little better I hope. No twinges and creaks. No? Wonderful, absolutely wonderful . . . Now, you must come and meet Anthony Pantie, a very interesting young man, son of Pantie the minister for trade and industry. Studying classics, of course, like his father before him . . . up in '57, did you know?'

Lubowicz was directed over to the centre of the room where a short boy, with round glasses and an inveterately baby face, was delivering pronouncements on world politics to his fellows in a thin arrogant drawl, with an air of papal infallibility.

'Oh no!' thought Lubowicz, with a sinking feeling. 'This is going to be bad.'

But at this point he was saved by a sudden high-pitched scream in the garden outside the drawing-room, and the sight of two children running very fast across a flower bed. One was a girl, with long brown hair which flew out behind her, skinny legs, and a red dress; the other was a stout little boy, who was puffing obsessively as he ran and was pursuing her with something which he held tightly grasped in his right fist.

They disappeared from sight. There was a pounding of footsteps in the corridor, and they appeared, panting, in the doorway.

At the sight of the room full of guests, the girl, who was about seven and several inches taller than the boy, stopped abruptly in the doorway, turned and hit her brother behind her to stop him doing whatever he was doing. Then she began to compose herself into the picture of a demure young lady in a red dress with black patent shoes and a black velvet bow in her hair. She was only foiled in this effort by an air of irrepressible wickedness which flashed out from her large downcast eyes; and her ill-hidden sadism towards her brother.

'Ah Sophie – and Charles! You little savages, what are you getting up to?' said Porbright. 'This is a sherry party you know. There is a . . . ha . . . decorum . . . a certain decorum . . . ha ha.' He turned to Lubowicz.

'Lubowicz, meet my grandchildren – Sophie – and Charles.' He introduced them separately and ceremoniously, with great pride.

Lubowicz found himself looking into a pair of very large amber-flecked eyes, fringed by thick sooty lashes. The eyes looked up at him with sly curiosity, rested on him for a moment with the blinding attention of children, and then looked down again; there followed a small giggle as he shook her hand, a twisting of long pale fingers, and a shifting of the black patent shoes.

'And this is Charles,' Porbright boomed, bringing up little Charles, who had been standing watching his elders with wide eyes and an open mouth, and the seat of his trousers hanging somewhere down round his knees.

'But Charles!' he said as Charles came up, the round eyes still fixed on Lubowicz and a long tube of grey snot hanging down from a very tiny cold-reddened nostril.

'What on earth is *that*?'

Charles broke his gaze for the first time, and looked down now to where his grandfather was staring. Laconically, as if trying to study what it was that should produce the effect, he surveyed his own round dimpled fist, which held in its fat grasp a long pink wriggling worm.

Sophie gave a sniff and turned her head away on a long and perilously slim white neck. She asserted in a tone of chilly precision:

'He was trying to chase me with a worm. He's dis*gust*ing.'

Charles shifted his gaze to his sister and blinked vacantly several times.

'Charles!' boomed Porbright. '*Were* you trying to chase your sister with a worm?'

Charles blinked again, and looked around him. He had a baffled air, as if events were going out of his control, and he could not find a handle.

'*Were* you, Charles?' repeated Porbright.

Charles took a big sniff. The tube of snot shot up into his nose for a fraction of a second, and then reappeared again, in exactly the same position.

'She p-p-put a . . .' He sniffed again. 'She p-p-put a p-p-plastic b-b-bag—' Another big sniff. 'She said: "L-let's go down the g-g-garden and see wh-what h-happens if we put a p-p-p-plastic b-b-bag on your head."'

There was a small silence when Charles finished his deposition. Porbright stared at him for a moment, and then turned to Sophie, who had flashed her brother a look of pure hatred and menace, and then turned her head away at a severe angle, adopting an expression of icy and transcendent contempt.

'Is this true, Sophie?' said Porbright more gently, for Sophie was evidently a favourite with him. 'Is this true?'

She did not answer straight away, but remained standing, with her fine brow puckering in suppressed frustration, and her small chin, which was faintly receding, tilted in defiance.

'Is this true, Sophie my dear? Did you try to put a plastic bag on your brother's head?' Porbright continued portentously.

At this point something broke in Sophie. She gave a toss of her head, which made her long hair in its bow leap and fall, crossed her arms defiantly, and glowered down at Charles.

'He tried to hurt Nobody!' she asserted with great and self-righteous force. 'He deserved it. He tried to hurt Nobody!'

Everyone absorbed this piece of information. Then she continued in the same tone of righteousness. 'He pulled his wings to try and make him fly, and poked him with a stick and made him run until he fell over! It was *horrible*. And then he poked him in the eye with a blade of grass. He had no right to do that to Nobody! No *right*!'

The ferocity of the girl's opinion held everyone's attention for a while. Porbright, struggling now to keep his magisterial control, turned lumberingly round to Charles again.

'*Did* you do that to Nobody, Charles? *Did* you do that to Nobody?'

But by this stage Charles had had enough. He took one look at his grandfather's craggy and grandiose face bent down towards him, a sort of swimming look at the group of adults around him – all these mythical great giants arranging and disposing of the world in volcanic voices many feet above his head – and burst into tears. The snot jetted out of both his nostrils, and the worm fell out of his fist and on to the floor. Momentarily, the cocktail chatter stopped and people turned to stare.

'O my God. Humphrey, look! There's a worm crawling across the floor!' said someone.

'I do believe there is,' said someone else in a tone of mild wonder and pleasure. 'My golly, I do believe there is.'

'Oh . . . em . . . er,' said Porbright. 'Now Charles, now Charles, don't cry, dear boy. There's a good chap. Don't cry, eh, good little fellow. Stiff upper lip, eh . . . Mary! Mary!' he bawled for the child's mother, who came rushing from the kitchen.

Lubowicz meantime picked up the worm and threw it out of the window into the garden. He turned to Sophie, who was standing unaffected by her brother's tears, her expression of transcendent contempt, if anything, deepened.

'So who's Nobody?' he inquired conversationally, finding her rigour on the subject of tears rather intriguing.

Nobody was a small duckling, one of a litter of nine which had been born a week ago to Sophie's duck Jemima. Nobody had been born blind, with one leg shorter than the other and clipped stunted wings. He could not keep up with the others when they waddled after their mother, could not compete with them for food, and could not see his way to the water trough. So he had been christened Nobody by Sophie, and had been taken into her special care and attention.

'Oh yes!' asseverated Porbright, relaxing now that Charles had been whisked away by his mother. 'Nobody is a very special duckling. He is spoilt, I can assure you, quite spoilt. He has to have the best straw, and the best milk, the best grass and bowls of warm water to swim in. No one is allowed to harm him, and when he falls behind the others, Sophie picks him up and runs along and puts him first in the queue, just behind the mother.'

'Oh yes,' he continued, lighting his pipe and looking as mellow as Lubowicz had ever seen him, and almost human in his forgetfulness of self. 'Nobody has a fine life. Sophie makes sure of that. A fine life.'

Sophie, who had lost her chilly disdain during the course of the exchange and accomplished one of her instantaneous transitions from demure young lady to seven-year-old girl, now looked up eagerly into Lubowicz's face. 'Do you want to see him?' she asked with shy excitement.

'Oh yes, I would be honoured.' She gave a big smile, twisted her hands again, shifted her black patent shoes, blushed.

'Yes, you *are* honoured,' came Porbright. 'Not everyone is allowed to see Nobody. Not everybody by any means. Only Sophie's particular favourites.'

At this point Charles, who was having a horrible time – his buttons buttoned up so tightly his chin was pinched, his laces knotted, his trousers yanked up round his waist till they bit into his crotch, his face rubbed down with a flannel so vigorously his little nose was inflamed, broke free and interrupted. 'I want to come! I want to come! Can I come? Sophie? Can I come?'

Sophie considered this gravely. A frown appeared on her face. 'Only if you're not stupid,' she said eventually. 'Otherwise I'll never let you again.'

It was a fine frosty late afternoon. The sun was still shining in the beeches, in the hazel copses, on the fallow rose-beds. It polished the bright berries of hawthorn and holly and made them flash blood in their tawny thickets. The air was piercing, crystalline, and small skeins of starlings were unwinding across the sky, and then folding shut again into the topmost branches. Snitches of woodsmoke drifted across from neighbouring bonfires; and leaves were scattered, flame and organdie, not yet rotted. The world was in transition, on the brink of something. It held itself still and startling as a vision.

Sophie led the way directly to the copse of hazels at the bottom of the garden where a small hen hutch stood tilted against a tree trunk.

'In there,' she whispered, dropping on to her knees a few feet from the hutch. 'In there. They're all in there now. You can hear them.'

Lubowicz lowered himself on to his knees in the thick wet grass, and Charles, who had adopted him the minute they left the house, stuffing his hot little hand in his own, plumped himself down beside him. In his buttoned-up anorak and muffler, he seemed to throw off an amazing amount of heat. Lubowicz felt he was snuggled up against a hot little potato.

They all leaned forward carefully, and peered through the door inside the hutch.

Lubowicz could not see or hear anything to begin with. The

milky grey shadows of the interior were opaque. There was a strong smell of fowl-droppings, rather sweet and warm.

'Look!' whispered Sophie. 'Look! There they are! If you look like this, you'll see them.' Tactfully, she tugged Lubowicz by the sleeve, until he had adjusted his position to gaze at an oblique angle through the door.

Inside, he made out a darker density in the shadows, which he took to be a creature, surrounded by a thin bluish line, sinuous and soft. The line gradually took on the form of a duck, wing-tip to tail and neck, very fine, like a piece of calligraphy from a Chinese painting. It seemed huge, ruffled out and swollen. And he made out a jewelled eye, gleaming at him mistrustfully from the darkness.

'Now watch!' whispered his companion.

'Quack, quack!' she went sharply. 'Quack! Quack! Quack!' And scattered some crumbs of dried bread at the doorstep of the hutch.

Now Lubowicz's sense of hearing came alive. He was aware of a tiny series of sounds at extremely high frequency, almost too high for audibility; and in the same moment, was aware that these sounds had been going on for some time. Now they intensified, until they formed a swarm of noise, a multitude of tiny high-pitched cheeps, desperate, raw, almost terrifying in their insistence. There was a deeper answering quack from the mother. And then the line of Chinese calligraphy decomposed itself. A large ruffled shadow loomed up against the door. And suddenly, streaming out from all directions, flapping tiny unformed wings, with little beaks held fantastically ajar, came a multitude of clamouring cheeping tiny, soft creatures, thronging the door and stumbling into the light.

'You see!' said Sophie triumphantly. 'You see!'

Followed sedately by the mother, they swarmed on to the grass and began to peck up the bread. They followed the line of bread that Sophie had scattered, and stumbled over each other to get at it. Lubowicz was so absorbed in the ferocity of their greed, and its clamour, that he did not immediately notice the irregularity: a duckling that had been left behind, was still struggling to stand up, and was not getting any of the bread.

'That's Nobody!' said Sophie, ran towards him and gathered him into her palm. 'Nobody.'

'Nobody,' repeated Charles happily in the same reverent tone. 'Nobody. Nobody.'

'And they're so mean. Always shoving you out of the way, and trampling on you. I hate them.'

And she began to feed Nobody choice morsels of bread from the palm of her hand. He was so weak he could scarcely take them. His beak, with its tiny punctured breath-holes, waggled about aimlessly. His eyes were scarfed up with a film of bluish skin. And he flapped his wings continuously in an effort to give strength to his legs which could scarcely support him.

Sophie held him towards Lubowicz, and the latter stroked his head to please her.

'They always leave him behind,' she said, her voice full of confusion, as she addressed Lubowicz, and communicating to him the child's private universe of trauma. 'Always. They peck at him, to keep him away from the food. Even when there's lots of it. Even when there's lots. They drive him away from it, peck at him.'

She nuzzled herself to Nobody, and gave him another kiss.

Then she caught sight of the other ducklings, all falling into single file behind the mother, who was waddling off to the water trough.

'And there they go again,' she broke out. 'Leaving you last again.'

She ran behind the ducks and dropped Nobody into line directly after the mother, where he wobbled unsteadily on his feet, flapped his wings, stumbled, and began to be trampled on by the fast-succeeding others.

'But I'll make you first,' she said, bending to help him along. 'I'll make you first. Always.'

Lubowicz gave the duckling a week, at the most.

When he went back to the house, Lubowicz found himself much mollified by the whole escapade with the children. Sophie had invited him to her birthday party the following Sunday, when she would be eight, and he had accepted. Charles had trudged along with his hot hand in his, and offered him one of his most treasured possessions, a torn and sticky postcard of Diplodocus diplodocus, the dinosaur. And although they were now taken off by their mother for supper and baths, the glow they had created stayed with him. He felt much altered towards the whole party and Porbright in particular, who had unaccountably progenitured such charming children. What a stupid fuss about the present, he thought to himself. What a neurotic fool I have been.

And when he entered the drawing-room he gave Porbright a broad smile, as if to signify his approval.

'Ah Lubowicz, you're back! Well, my dear fellow, now Sophie has let you out of her clutches, I must get you into mine. I know you're a man of refined taste, a man with a love of the arts, so you must come and tell me what you think of my . . . ah . . . little collection.'

Porbright led the way rumblingly through the drawing-room, now thick with smoke and the voice of Anthony Pantie discoursing very loudly about how Israel must 'buck up its act' towards the Palestinians, to a small room which adjoined it. The room was cold and narrow and rather sombrely decorated in a thick hessian of olive green and brown. All over the walls, in elaborate gilt and mahogany frames, were paintings and drawings. They stretched from the floor to the ceiling, all shapes and sizes, colours and mediums.

Porbright now indicated them with a debonair flourish. 'My . . . ah . . . collection,' he said. 'Now, I don't want you to hurry, dear chap. Take as long as you like. I want you to examine them for me, so to speak.' He smiled coyly. 'And then give me your opinion – your true opinion as a man of the arts, mind you, one must never lie about these things – as to likeness, composition, chiaroscuro and so on.'

He rubbed his hands gleefully, and boomed as he moved towards the door. 'Now take your time, dear chap. Take your time.'

It took Lubowicz a little while to realize exactly what he was looking at, because he couldn't immediately believe his first intuition. But after surveying the whole gallery from top to toe, from the biggest oil painting placed above the fireplace, to the last little pastel sketch tucked in a corner, he could see that there was no doubt about it, no doubt at all. Every last one of them. Not a sketch, or a line, a dash of oil, or a smudge of charcoal, that was not devoted to the stupendous profundity, the classically noble Alexandrine profile, that king of craniums, Porbright himself.

It would have been hard for Lubowicz to say why what happened next in the room really happened. If he had had to track down the chain of causation, he would have muttered uneasily about the smoke and noise from the other room, how the fresh air perhaps had gone to his head, how he was drunk and his head was spinning. He would have mentioned a sudden memory of Porbright burying him beneath the blankets in his own room and booming 'Don't drink the stuff.' And then the arrogant drawl of young Anthony Pantie which penetrated easily to the cool room – 'Israel . . . the Jews . . . really must understand . . . don't play cricket . . . all that Moses and the mountain stuff . . . a superiority complex . . . whining self-pity . . .'

All of which Lubowicz might have been capable of remarking on himself at another time and in another language. But somehow it was the effect of it, the imperial arrogance of the voice with its drawling iterations, that same voice that had resounded in fly-blown offices in Cairo, Damascus, Jerusalem and carved up empires, that had boomed along the quays of Akko and Haifa with bureaucratic instructions that turned back ships from Germany. The portraits began to spin in front of him. The vacant and overweening features began to dislimb and disliver themselves. They split and curved and grew and writhed. The bloodshot eyes came running down towards him from the walls, coming to get him, to pulverize, to consume.

And caused Lubowicz, standing dizzy in the cool and shadowy room, to reach out his hand towards a softly gleaming silver mug standing beneath the portrait above him, and slip it unaccountably, without rhyme or reason, into his jacket pocket.

And that was when Porbright came back into the room, unable to wait any longer for Lubowicz's opinion; whisked him back into the main room, pumped him full of more sherry and insisted he give his views on his 'humble gallery', and also the Israel question being discussed so ably by young Anthony Pantie. Lubowicz, conscious of the mug in his pocket as if it were a tumour growing externally on his body in full view for everyone to see, suffered agonies of self-reproach and terror. He capitulated on the question of the gallery, and admired every piece. 'Yes, fine likenesses,' he heard himself say. 'Good compositions, yes, a powerful grasp of form . . .' And he allowed himself to be browbeaten by young Pantie, who was determined to be stern and stiff and not run away from this live Israeli in front of him – never mind that this Israeli had left his country some time ago and seldom went back – and bludgeoned into his head every last one of the world's scruples on Israel's treatment of the Palestinians. Lubowicz's head was dinning; the room was swimming; and his hands sweating.

Finally, he broke free, saying he must hurry home now for another appointment. He knew he should go back to the gallery, and deposit the mug, but when he got to the doorway, he heard voices inside. He thought briefly of just leaving the mug in the kitchen, the toilet, on a window sill, in the dining-room. But everywhere he looked people were milling around, and it seemed to him that they looked at him strangely, as if they could see right through him to his horrible tumour. Porbright came over and hovered boomingly by his side, his heart was pounding; he really must get out.

'Kind of you to come old chap . . . Don't mention it. Delighted to be of service. And if it plays you up again, don't hesitate to call.'

Then, just as he was leaving, from behind him in the hall, came a high clear voice. 'You will remember my party, won't you? I'm going to be eight. You won't forget?'

And looking up he saw Sophie, in a pair of striped pyjamas, swinging over the banisters, and smiling down at him shyly. Beside her was Charles, also dressed for bed and squatted down with his head stuck through the banisters. He was pointing repeatedly down at the crowd of adults, whom he seldom saw, from such a height, and found highly entertaining. 'There's one! There's one! There's one!' he was saying, pointing at one bright pink bald patch after another, and rocking with giggles.

'I wouldn't miss it for anything,' Lubowicz called up.

And then he was out again, the door closed, the fresh night air stinging his lungs, with only the reek of Porbright's tobacco and the bulge in his jacket to show he had ever been there.

It was not until he got back to the safety of his own flat that Lubowicz examined his plunder. Sitting down, for his heart was still pounding and his legs weak from the prolonged stress, he took out the mug and stared at it on the kitchen table.

It was a very fine Georgian silver christening mug; a tankard set on a faintly bell-shaped base like the cushion of a Doric pillar. It was decorated at base and rim with garlands of vine-leaves, entwined with nuts and fruits, and in the centre it contained the image of a bird of paradise, a lovely creature with a long plumed arabesque tail and its beak wide open in song. Lubowicz found it a beautiful object altogether, extremely handsome – with its chased silver, and the fine workmanship of its classical motifs. He turned it in his hand, enjoying its cool mass, and let it catch the light.

And as he did so he caught the thin hieroglyphs of an inscription. He bent closer. It was an elaborate flowing copperplate, with scrolls and loops like tiny dancing zephyrs, and letters that ran forward like a ship in full sail.

'To our darling Sophie,' it said. 'On her christening. May 14th 1985.'

It was clear to him that he should take this beautiful mug straight back to her. It was precious and lovely, and would quickly be missed. But how? Should he wrap it up and present it to her at her birthday party on Sunday. Saying . . . Saying . . . well, that it had got mislaid, that it had jumped into his pocket by purest accident, that it was an impudent cup, and didn't know its place. She would find that very funny. She would think it was a good joke. And she would understand it perfectly well, with the fine penetrating intelligence of children, which understands everything, while understanding nothing. And she would smile at him shyly, giggling, then take him by the hand, and invite him to play a game.

But then how was he to . . . ? The thought stung him so badly he jumped out of his seat and began to pace around the room. Oh no . . . Oh no . . . that was just not possible! Just not possible!

Not at all. My goodness, the talk of high table for the next five years! Oh yes, how many nasty little unspoken suspicions would it corroborate, those little suspicions that hang around like coiled snakes in the water tank of the supposedly liberal imagination. Oh no . . . Oh no indeed . . . And he imagined their voices. 'Did you hear the one about? . . . invited him to a party and popped a bit of silver in his pocket . . . helped him out with a crick in his back . . . walked off with the kitchen spoons . . .'

It was out of the question! And he was so disturbed by the sequence of images that he walked very fast up to the kitchen table, and brought his hand down sharply on its edge. Lubowicz now felt feverish. All the excitement had given him the shivers and he felt both dizzy and hectic, weak and energetic all at the same time. His forehead was throbbing. To keep himself warm, he lit a fire, and considered what he should do. Already the thought of discovery was sending cold trickles of horror up and down his spine. Porbright would know immediately that the mug had gone, he was deeply possession-conscious. And if he didn't, his wife would surely. From there it would be a small step to enumerating the few people who had been in that room, and from there it would take only an intuitive leap to arrive at him, Lubowicz. And then what? Lubowicz shuddered, and jumped up again out of his chair.

He couldn't take the property back. He couldn't send it through the post. That would compound the embarrassment. He couldn't leave it somewhere in the street for the girl to find, because, although she would be perfectly happy to find it in this manner – indeed delighted, to come upon it sitting up by a lamp-post in some obvious position, or on a little wall or a dustbin where someone must have put it just ready for her to be walking by – they would ask her where she had found it. And then they would know immediately that it was him. People guess that sort of thing. They make stunning dare-devil leaps across chasms of ignorance; he had often remarked it.

There seemed no possible avenue of escape. His thoughts, keeping erratic time with the leaping flames, whirled and tumbled and doubled back on themselves like fugitives in a dark alley.

Finally, he made a decision. Or at least, he did not make a

decision. The decision arrived in him, and communicated itself through his whole body before any other restraining force had time to act. He went over to the table, picked up the mug, and stoking the fire up to its maximum heat and making a kind of furnace with shovelfuls of fresh coals, he placed the mug in the very heart of the heat, and allowed it to burn.

It was a long time burning, an agony to watch. The flames licked about it, smoked and blackened it without altering the structure. Swearing, he bent forward, and taking up the ornamental bellows from the wall, began to pump oxygen madly into the centre of the flames. The heat intensified. The coals glowed redder. And finally, the flames took. The silver of the mug began to sizzle and snap. He saw large cracks appearing, and dark metal beneath. He saw the fine chased overlay peel away in ugly green slicks; and finally, he saw the thin fine lines of the inscription, 'To our darling Sophie . . . May 14th . . .' curl up, shrivel and disappear in smoke.

It was enough. Enough. The cup was completely unrecognizable. Turning it gingerly in the grate with the poker, he then picked it up, ran through to the kitchen and fetched out some newspaper. Very quickly, almost hysterically, he wrapped it up in wad upon wad of the sheets. He wrapped and wrapped until he had a large amorphous shape, a bale of paper. Then he went out on to the fire escape which led down the side of the house to the dustbins, and ran down the stairs. Lifting the lid of the first bin, he threw in his parcel.

It was pitch-dark now and very cold in the streets of North Oxford. Here and there soft yellow lights shone out of the dark, as if at each other, and up above them the colder fiercer light of the stars was scattered fantastically across the black heavens. Putting back the lid of the dustbin, Lubowicz stopped suddenly and was seized by a thought. 'Are you mad!' he almost hissed to himself. 'Are you completely off your head?' And everything he had just done whirled in front of his vision like a flow of hideously grinning carnival masks: alien and grotesque. He tamped the lid back tightly on the bin. 'You are mad!' he hissed at himself. 'Disgusting character! Insane!' And it seemed to him that all the yellow lights shining from the solid brick houses had turned into eyes; and that all those eyes were training on him, focussing on him, and that they would search him out, and see into the innermost core of his being.

Suddenly a cat leapt from a wall on to the dustbins. With a frozen ring, a lid slithered to the ground; the cat let out a yelp of outrage. With a start, and a burst of adrenalin, Lubowicz ran quickly back up the fire escape stairs, and slammed the door.

Why Not How

Jane Harris

Why Not How

Mum, can I get my Chuppa-chup lolly? Mum, how are we going on the bus, how? How are we going on the bus? Can't we not go on the train but? How not, mum, how can we not go on the train? Mum. Mu-um, can I get my Chuppa-chup lolly? Can I get my Chuppa-chup?

No, he couldn't get his bloody Chuppa-chup. And that was the last time she'd be telling him. So it was.

So the wee fella starts slamming the side of the bus-shelter with both hands, rattling the plastic, Bang! Bang! Ah-bang-bang-bang!, he goes, looking over his shoulder, checking out the folk behind. Bang! Bang! Ah-bang-bang-bang! Like that. But nobody's bothering their arse, by the way. Bang!

He was to cut it out that instant, she goes. Did he hear her? Did he hear her? Did he? That instant!

The wee fella's like that, starts scuffing his good shoe on the kerb, right?

Mu-um, he goes, the voice piping above the queue, curving up and away above the traffic roaring, a pneumatic drill grinding, a car alarm whining. The usual. How's there such a big queue, mum? Is all these people wanting on the bus, mum? Are all these people wanting on?

She's like that, rubber ear, kidding on she doesn't hear him. Right?

So the bus makes it to the stop. Doors open, swoosh! And she's like that, pulling him aside, smiling, right, nodding at the other passengers. Och, no bother, no bother, they were to go on ahead, not at all. Not at all. And would he hold still?

Mum, he goes, how did you do that? We were at the front, mum. How did you let they people on first? How, mum? How?

Because the nice people were in a hurry. Now would he look at the state of his hands. Would he? Would he look at the state of his hands?

But he's not interested in the state of his bloody hands, right?

How are they in a hurry, mum? he goes. How? How aren't we not in a hurry? Mum. Mu-um. How not?

She's heaving him onto the bus, pulling herself on behind.

He was to be quiet. Quiet. Could he not be quiet for two seconds?

How? How've I to be quiet? I can be. I can be quiet for more than two seconds by the way. I can.

Standing there, at the driver's cabin. The lip out.

See, mum. Mum! I can be.

So the bus pulls away, and she's lurching up the aisle like that, heading for a spare seat, trying to keep her footing, hold onto her bags and grab the wee fella's hand all at the once. Christ!

Mum, mum! Can't we not go upstairs, mum, please mum, please?

They went upstairs.

Can't we not sit up the front, mum? Mum, can we sit up the front?

They sat up the front.

Can I get my Chuppa-chup lolly, mum?

No, he couldn't get his Chuppa-chup lolly. Finito!

Oh the big sigh! He starts swinging his bloody feet back and forwards, kicking the wall of the bus below the window. Singing by Christ.

Watch out baby oo-oooh, 'cos here I come, ooh-yeah, watch . . .

Was he wanting a skelp? Was he? Was he wanting a skelp? Well then. He was to stop his nonsense.

So he stops the singing. Starts looking about. It's about

half-full. Goths up the back, old dears with shopping trolleys. The lilac perms and hair nets and that. The usual. One lassie's talking to herself. Laughing. The hair all matted. She's like that, counting on her fingers. Stops counting, rubs her hands like she's washing them. Starts again. Two, three, six . . .

Mum, is that lassie the full shilling? Is she, mum? Mum . . .

He was to button it.

But mum, that lassie's . . .

He was to turn round and button it.

But . . .

Would he just shut up! That minute!

Mum (whispers, right?).

She's like that, rubber ear.

Mum.

What was it now for god's sake?

Where are we going? Where are we going mum? Are we going up the town?

Yes, they were going up the town.

What for mum? Mu-um. What are we getting? Are we getting me something?

Yes, they were getting him something.

Aw, mum!

He's like that! Brilliant! Thinks about it a minute. Peeking over the back of his seat, just the eyes. The daft lassie's still counting. An old dear in a rain-mate gives him a wave, shows him her teeth. He's like that, opens and shuts his eyes, like he's expecting her to disappear. Then he sticks his tongue out at her.

Mum.

Rubber ear.

Mu-um. What am I getting? What mum? What is it? What am I getting?

Shoes. He was getting shoes.

Aw mum! Beezer! Mum, trainers, am I getting trainers?

He certainly was not getting trainers. He was getting school shoes.

Schoo-ool shoes?

He's like that. Sits back in the seat.

Mum, how school shoes? Am I going to school mum? Mum? Mu-um! When am I going to school?

The sooner the better, she says.

Aw.

So he leans his face on the seat, starts speaking into it, leaving wet marks on the leather, by the way.

Mum. Mu-um. How do we have to go to school, mum?

She didn't have to go to school. And *he* was to stop licking the chairs.

Can I get the lolly then?

No he could not get the lolly. And that was the last time she'd be telling him. So it was.

Up pops the conductor, leaning on the window to keep his balance. Sideburns and pale blue dots on the knuckles. The big rings. Wide boy. The full sketch. The wee fella staring at the sidies, while she's fumbling for their fares.

Mum, he's got bug-ladders. Mum . . .

That was enough. Enough!

Conductor's no bothering his arse but. Winking. Rips the tickets, gets off his mark.

Oh-oh mum. Mum! Mu-um! He's away with your mo-ney! Mum!

He was to give her peace.

Oh, the big sigh. Starts picking his shoe-lace.

Mum. Mum. How do you not have to go to school and I do?

Because.

Because how?

Just because. And it was why not how. Because *why*.

What? Why? How's that, mum? How's it why?

Because it was. It just was.

My lolly, mum?

He was to sit nice.

He sits nice a second, then spots something outside.

Mum, why's that man doing that?

What man was that?

She looks out. Check the wino in the kerb, the arm out-stretched, the can of Superlager held like a fucking trophy in his fingertips.

That man, that man out there, why's he doing that? Why's he lying on the pavement?

Perhaps because he was very tired.

Why's he tired mum? . . . Why don't you know? Can I get my Chuppa-chup lolly now? Can I? Mum, can I get my Chuppa . . .

Oh the big sigh. But she reaches into her pocket, gives him the lolly. He's like that, tearing off the wrapper, sliding it into his mouth. Sucking. In silence, by the way. Yes by Christ. Silence. Just the bus is rumbling, the traffic roaring, the road-works humming, a jumbo landing, the shop alarms whining, a busker wailing, somebody screaming, the drizzle streaming, the natives steaming. Silence. The bus whaling along till the driver, thinks he's bloody Nigel Mansell, or Christ knows what, takes a corner at speed. The wee fella gets thrown hard against his mother, like that, chokes on the lolly. She's like that, oh my godfathers, worried, rubbing his chest.

Was he alright?

Uh-huh, he says.

He was alright.

But how did it do that, mum? How?

Because the driver was going too fast.

But the bus nearly tipped over, it nearly tipped over mum. We could of been killed, mum, couldn't we? We could of been killed, isn't that not right?

Could *have*, could *have* been killed, she says. It was have. Have.

The bus nearly tipped over, he goes.

Yes, she goes, sometimes buses did tip right over and people on top were killed. Especially small children because they got thrown from one end of the . . .

Oh look mum! Look! Quick!

He's shouting, right, jumping up and down. Drawing attention. Christ! Pointing out the window with his bloody day-glo lollipop.

Mum, mum! There's the church we went to when you got married! Mum! Over there!

Jogging her arm with a sticky hand.

The church we went to when you got married . . . how's that

enough? How? How've I to be quiet? Have I to be quiet for two seconds? Have I? Have I to be . . . ?

He was to be quiet for two seconds.

She's staring out the window, the jaw clamped, the face like fizz. So he sucks the lolly, makes the stick wobble up and down in front of his nose. Then he yawns. The bloody thing drops out on the front of his anorak.

Ttch! Och . . .

Sorry mum.

He picks it up, starts painting his lips with it, smearing them with the sticky sugar, licking it with his tongue. The tongue bright green. Coats his mouth. Starts plastering the lolly across his chin and upper lip.

Mum, look. Look, mum. Mu-um. I'm putting on lipstick so's you can give me a kiss, mum, look.

So she looks. The whole bloody mouth covered in syrupy saliva. A grey-green drool down his chin. Glistening slavers running along his jawline, dreeping onto his good clothes. And he's yawning.

Mum? I'm sleepy. Can't I not get a cuddle?

Not with that face on him he couldn't. No he could not. No chance.

So he snuggles against her, the big serious face, by the way. Aw.

Mum?

Oh the big sigh. But she finds a hanky, holds it up to his mouth.

Have I to spit, mum?

He was to spit.

He's like that, pushing a wee gob of froth onto the hanky with his tongue, the face screwed up. She scrubs his skin till it's shining. Puts the hanky at his nose.

He was to blow.

The wee fella shuts the eyes, breathes in, jerking the head back.

Blow. Not sniff.

He tries again, manages a wee snort. She dabs the end of his nose, screws the hanky back in the pocket.

Now can I get a cuddle, mum?

Now he could. Yes.

So right, the lolly still in the fist, he stretches out both arms, wraps them round her neck, hiding the face in her collar. Stays there a minute, then speaks into her hair.

I'll miss you if I go to school, mum.

She would miss him, too, she says. So she would.

And she strokes his neck with her one free hand. The eyelids droop, close. She shuts her own eyes, rocking back and forwards, his breath against her throat, soft and rhythmical, like. Holds him till it's time to get off. Gets to her feet, careful, bracing herself against the seat, the shopping bags over her arm. She takes the stairs one at a time, right, hanging onto the balustrade with one hand, the wee fella, fast asleep, propped on her hip, the lollipop tangled in her bloody hair.

Casper

Harriet Braun

Harriet Braun was born in London in 1968 and studied Drama at Bristol University. Her short play, *Love Me Tender*, was recently produced at The Finborough Theatre and she is currently writing a feature film for British Screen.

Casper

The trunk arrived today. It's perfect, C.C.F.T. embossed on the front in gold. A little ostentatious, I know, but Casper will be pleased. He probably won't show it of course; he's so spoilt. He'll just say something like, 'Yes, very good, Smithers, put it by the window,' throw a glance at it and carry on reading. But he has to be allowed his arrogance. It becomes someone of his station. It simply wouldn't do to have him fawning over a trunk now, would it? Casper is destined for great things.

I'm very pleased with the trunk, but there's a long way to go till we're ready for school. It's so exciting. I'm really starting to see the possibilities. I run my hand across the lettering: Casper Cuthbert Fotherington Thomas. I still don't know if I'm entirely satisfied with the surname; it may be a little clichéd, but I had to make a decision. I was getting impatient. I ponder for a while, then get so excited that I take off all my clothes and lie across the trunk in a manner befitting Casper, one arm lazily propping up my head. I need the other free, obviously. 'Leave it over there, Smithers,' I say, as I'm about to come. At orgasm I despair over the declining standard of servants.

The hair isn't right. What beautiful hair, such a pretty little girl, people used to say. I remembered that and in my arrogance hung onto it. Fair hair down to my shoulders. It's also been useful in attracting the right types. Some very butch women still gravitate towards the merest hint of femme. But I'm bored with that. It's so hard to keep a casual encounter . . . casual. 'Will I see you again? Can I have your phone number?' Very irritating.

There was one woman who had possibilities. 'What do you fantasize about? What turns you on?' she said. I realized that my distraction during our brief sexual encounter must have been evident, but at least she had the guts to ask. I thought about it for a moment, mulled it over. 'Oh I don't know,' I said, eventually, in a manner which indicated the conversation was closed. The fact of the matter was, when faced with the opportunity of articulating my needs, I'd realized I didn't know what they were. I only knew they weren't being met.

That was date four. On date five she said, 'I think I'm falling in love with you.' I nearly choked. There was no date six. I haven't been close to anyone for years, it's a little late to start now.

But I'm grateful to her. She was the catalyst. The direct nature of her question forced me to look at myself and, in doing that, I made my find. It wasn't the first time I'd been concerned by my relation to things sexual. Lust has always been something to be satisfied quickly; someone catching my eye, a flicker of interest, a fuck. Urgent, fast, and once over, nothing, save for boredom, and a sense of frustration. A desire for something more, something else.

What do I fantasize about? Now there was a thought. Not a great deal really, but maybe, just maybe . . . I set myself something of a project, a quest to find the desirable. Initially there was the usual mundane and uninspired array of genitalia floating across my mental landscape. But that didn't answer my question. So for a few days I tried new images, anything I thought might turn me on. It was like browsing through a book shop hoping to hit upon a good read. Nothing, until one day a brief image that aroused such an overwhelming feeling of the illicit, I was overcome. It wasn't something new, but something old, very old.

I was eleven, in the cinema, drawn into a world that bore no similarity to my own, save for one thing. In this depiction of public school and cricket matches, dorms, fags, chums and aristocracy, something went on that struck a chord. Something that inspired the same warm feeling I got when hiding in my sister's cupboard watching her undress, or stealing furtive glances at my schoolfriends in the changing rooms after netball. In this film, boys fell in love with boys. I'd discovered I was not alone. I used my pocket money to go back to the cinema again and again until the film was no longer playing. Yet its departure didn't quell my desire to climb into the screen and join in.

It didn't stop there either. I was soon to discover that there was more. One day in my uncle's house I came across a book. It was lying face-down by the side of his bed; the words 'homosexual love' on the back cover. I'd heard my mother use this phrase in hushed tones to my Aunty Ellen. I wasn't entirely sure of its meaning, but I knew it made me feel guilty. I'd ease off on hiding in my sister's cupboard, and try to stop imagining what the women in *Little House on The Prairie* looked like with no clothes on.

The book that I'd come across was *Maurice*. On first finding it I only allowed myself the briefest glance. I felt that if I was even caught in close proximity to the word homosexual it was enough to secure my immediate disgrace. On going home I became completely preoccupied with it. The book, like the film before it, filled my thoughts. On my frequent visits with my mother to Uncle John I took to sneaking away and taking the book off the bookshelf. Then, with heart pounding and sweaty palms, I'd leaf through, looking for – I didn't know quite what. The sensation this inspired was, at the same time as being terribly frightening, almost unbearably sexy. It was on one of these occasions that I found the reference to the unspeakable act of the Greeks. Horrified, the full import of my illicit activities occurred to me. I realized that I might be an unspeakable.

Had my Uncle John been an Aunty Joanna, and the book *The Well of Loneliness* and not *Maurice*, well, who knows? As it was, to my knowledge, I was the only unspeakable female ever. In order to be able to indulge in unspeakable activity, I needed to be a boy, preferably aristocratic, and attending public school. I was in something of a quandary. Now, fourteen years later, a long buried quandary has re-surfaced.

I've been sleeping with women for a number of years, but when the point came that I could acknowledge my unspeakability to myself and others, it was a little late. I hadn't fumbled at parties, forged juvenile relationships: things I'd once heard described as 'practising for marriage'. If you've stood outside the window for long enough, it's silly to imagine that on stepping in you will no longer feel cold. I can only ever see intimacy, after the initial lust has been satisfied, as a clawing intrusion; embarrassing, unnatural almost. Until now that is, until the emergence of Casper.

Casper is getting his hair cut today. He's been in existence for a few weeks. I've hardly been able to wait to get home from work in order to play around with my new-found friend. As with anything though, excitement can be short lived. I need pastures new. It's not enough to crawl into bed at night to thoughts of dormitories and illicit meetings in the games cupboard, delectable though those things are. Casper wants to walk and talk. Casper wants to wander around my bedroom. Casper wants to own things, and now Casper has his very own school trunk with a tuck box inside it. As yet though he has no haircut and no clothes to speak of. Casper the nudist just won't do! Although he does have a lot of fun with his trunk. He finds it very exciting to get up in the middle of the night and indulge in a naughty piece of tuck. So exciting, that sometimes Casper sneaks back for another packet of Rolos, at great danger to himself. Casper's housemaster is very stern and doles out beatings like Smarties.

It has not escaped my notice what a good time Casper could have getting his hair cut, yet this poses something of a problem. You see, ordinarily I'd go to a hairdresser, but that simply won't do for a public school boy. I've spotted a barber just down the road. I've walked past it a few times but have been too scared to go in. It's not the loss of my hair that bothers me any more – in fact I positively relish the prospect – it's the questions that might be asked. What am I doing getting my flowing tresses cut off in a barber? Will the barber not find this a little odd?

Yes, that's right, I say, I'm in a play. I'm playing the part of a boy in a play and I'd like an Eton crop. Casper is going to have a haircut to match his school. Only the very best of schools for Casper. The barber chats about the amateur dramatic production of *My Fair Lady* that he's in. I'm bored, but I don't show it. Casper is far, far more vicious than me. Oh, the damned proletariat, thinks Casper. Why, oh why do I have to suffer this bumbling idiot? I'm shocked; I'd never think such a thing, but at the same time Casper's naughtiness, his blatant snobbery, is ever so arousing. I think about exactly what Casper would do in this situation, as I stare into the mirror, watching the hair fall away from my face. I know that Casper doesn't suffer fools lightly. Casper would bury his face in a book after having given the barber a disdainful look. I get wet simply thinking about it.

Clutching my play excuse close to my chest, I leave the barber and head for Keats, the school uniform store. I'm on a roll and don't want to lose the impetus. I feed the same line to the shop assistant and, unfortunately, she finds the whole idea most intriguing. How much money do I have in my budget? What's the play? When's it on? Can she come and see it? I hadn't really anticipated any of this. I tell her not to worry about expense and am as evasive as possible about the rest. I'm surprisingly offhand and bossy as she brings me different variations of school uniform to try on. Is it possible that this is Casper being a naughty boy again? He's really coming into his own these days.

When she goes to see to another customer I stand and assess myself in the dressing room mirror. My hair now flops lazily over one eye. I run my hand across the unfamiliar texture of the short bristles on the back of my neck. I'm sporting the items Casper has settled on: black slacks, a black blazer, a white shirt open at the collar, no tie. The lack of tie is an indication of his rascal devil-may-care attitude to life. Fortunately, I'm skinny, with no chest to speak of. Casper looks in the mirror and likes what he sees. He's an arrogant little so and so, but I grow fonder of him by the minute.

He rests his head against the wall and stares at himself; a petulant look comes across his face. I know what's bothering Casper. He's had a tiff with his new-found friend, Ted. He's pained. He shuts his eyes and thinks about Ted. Then he opens his eyes and looks at himself thinking about Ted. Yes, a dashingly tragic figure, he thinks. The love that Casper and Ted share is so pure, so sweet. Something he's aware he could never achieve with a woman. He thinks about yesterday evening when they punted down the river. Talked about how nice England is and how tea is the best drink, walked across daffodil-filled, moonlit fields, and other such romantic-poet-type activities. He's filled with longing. Oh Ted! he thinks. No, maybe, Oh Edward! No, definitely Ted; it has a better ring to it. I leave the dressing rooms a few moments later and purchase the items. I've never wanked in a shop before.

By the time Casper and I get home he's also the proud owner of cricket whites, bat, and ball. He rushes over to his trunk and packs them away neatly, then, almost immediately, gets them out again and puts them on. I stare at Casper in the mirror. He really is a fine figure of a man. He knocks a few mock shots into the mirror. 'I say, chaps,' he calls out to his friends, 'fancy a knock-about in the nets?' Then he hits the ball around the room a bit, like the boisterous young scally-wag he can be at times. He does this until the people downstairs start banging on the ceiling. Oh, how damned tedious life is, he thinks, as he flops down on the bed and daydreams about Ted.

Casper is becoming demanding, taking up more and more time. Casper thinks it's tedious that I have to go to work. He wants to stay in and compose love sonnets to Ted. He's rather proud of his poetry, particularly yesterday's effort, which, it has to be said, moved him more than a little:

Oh Ted.
How I love your head, Ted
and Ted, isn't tea the best drink?
Don't you think?
Ted.

So of late I've been indulging him a little and phoning in sick. I've developed a mysterious and prolonged stomach complaint. It's the kind of thing I can imagine Casper having. He's a delicate sort, the refined type. Too delicate almost for this world, so he's choosing to live in it less and less, which suits me fine. He's feeling particularly bad of late, for a very good reason. Yesterday he had a run-in with his friend Perkins. Their relationship has always been turbulent. Perkins thinks Casper is a bit of a rotter and has no time for what he terms his 'self-indulgent melancholia'. Perkins fails to notice Casper's inner fragility.

The run-in was in my bedroom. Casper was leaning nonchalantly against the window staring into the middle distance. He looked dashing, if I might say so myself. It's something about the way the light catches his hair, frames the fine line of his jaw. He does this often, especially when fretting over one of his many rows with Ted. It was his morbid attitude that prompted Perkins to tell him off.

'I say, old chap,' he said. 'Why don't you get a grip. You'll be leaving school soon and putting all these silly crushes behind you.' As you can imagine, Casper was absolutely beside himself. How wrong could Perkins be? Their love, a silly crush!

'What rot! Don't you understand, old man,' he said. 'I'm never going to love women, never!' Casper and I are aware of the irony, but we try to ignore it. In fact, this is a favourite moment of ours which we return to again and again. I have now incorporated a cigarette which Casper can drag on moodily. It makes him all the more petulant and lovable.

I've realized, of late, that although Casper and I are having a good time, he would benefit from some company. I've never felt more myself than when I'm with Casper, or happier, but I can't help wondering if there's someone else out there, someone just like him. It's time for Casper to meet the outside world. Casper wants to act on this idea straight away. But how exactly?

Casper has a plan. He's searching through the personals in a gay magazine, looking for inspiration. Exactly how to introduce himself? It's a dilemma I'm familiar with: having wandered around for years, scavenging for clues, looking for ways in which to recognize myself, I'm nothing if not diverse.

Eventually Casper picks up a pen and writes:

Lesbian boy seeks chums for public school fun.

Addictionary

Melanie Danburg

Melanie Danburg was born in Texas in 1969 and educated at the University of California. She married the writer Robert Cremins after completing the UEA Creative Writing course in 1993. She is currently at work on her first novel, and is expecting a child in September 1995. She lives in Houston.

∫

Addictionary

Walter Reynolds, historian, had intended to stick with Alexander Hamilton, statesman, throughout. He was determined to show it all: the intrigue, the romance, the blackmail. The passion of the man. The deceit of the woman. The life of post-revolutionary Philadelphia.

(W. Reynolds relating his research's raison d'être:)

'I'm engrossed with the idea that Alexander Hamilton was pulled into the affair with Maria Reynolds. It's obvious that the Secretary of the Treasury was an easy target for blackmail in the Philadelphia of 1791. His social standing and vulnerability were equally high. I'm questioning how much the mudslinging newspaper war between Hamilton and the followers of Jefferson was a cover to distract the public from character sullies. And I believe it was. I believe in the purity of Alexander Hamilton and the demoralizing influence of Maria Reynolds, family connections aside.'

The demise of Walter's dedication to his work happened to coincide with the rise of his friendship with Freya Hirsch, bookseller. Their climb had been leisurely at first, a day's outing: a browse and a chat in her academic book store. Enthused by their friendship, he started dropping by daily to discuss the new facts that contributed to his thesis. She kept an eye on the latest history publications, giving him inside information on academic publishing in Philadelphia. Anything 200 years old was invaluable to him. They flirted intellectually. He was smitten. And when, finally, he was at the point of writing, she waited casually to hear about his pen-to-paper work. She expected him to ask her advice about organization, focus, potential publishers. But he was silent. For Walter Reynolds' good intentions had slipped away. It all started with <schism>. Then, after that first regression down to <schist>, the dictionary gradually eroded his interests, his thoughts, everything about him. Noah Webster, lexicographer, had managed to surpass Freya Hirsch, bookseller, in Walter's estimation.

(Walter's shamefaced sidetracking soliloquy:)

'I was in the final stages of my research, and I was planning the progression of my monograph. Everything was orderly, my thesis proven, my notes supportive, the correct quotes ready for the correct paragraphs. I only needed the final outline to organize my structure before I began the actual writing. For some historians, this is the easiest phase, the most captivating aspect of research. Personally, I prefer the initial rush of enthusiasm for a project, the delight of going through documents in search of vital information. At any rate, I was ready to finish up this particular project and I devised a title for the work. I called it: *Schism or Diversion?: Alexander Hamilton's public war with Thomas Jefferson, viewed in light of his private liaison with Maria Reynolds*. It was at this stage that I found I simply couldn't spell the word <schism>. There are a few words which have affected me thus, notably: cinnamon, imbecile, and gazpacho. I'm sure there are others, but these are three that remained, from youth, unspellable. And now, I was forced to add another, more vital word to the list. I was compelled to look it up every time I needed it. After a few days my pocket dictionary opened to it automatically.'

Enough. His words go on and on. His point was that he'd lost that spark of passion about his work, and he was basically ready to wander off with whatever project came along next. So, in came the dictionaries. How did the dictionaries affect his attitude? It started with just the occasional word catching his eye. All of those fascinating, unfamiliar combinations that guide the dictionary reader through the alphabet. Okka. Sciolistic. Minacious. Cystotomy. Paleography. Flyte. Rhizopus. All the way from A to Zymurgy, in the 'Second College Edition' of *Webster's New World Dictionary*. He gradually descended into the dense red book, spending the hours he should have been devoting to his thesis, instead counting words. He came up with absurdities.

(From pages penned '~~Skhi~~ Schism or Diversion – Thesis Notes') 'What were Hamilton's goals in perpetuating the quarrel with Jefferson? How should I qualify my theory that he was trying to quell the rumors about Maria Reynolds with publicized ~~quarolus querolos~~ querulousness? – There are eighty-eight entries in the pocket dictionary for <Q>. The best ones after <querulousness> are <quinsy> and <Quonset hut>. I have a quinsy now. I have never seen a Quonset hut, as far as I know.'

And with Walter on the words, he couldn't stop. He couldn't leave them alone. Here Freya Hirsch truly entered into the picture. He turned to her in search of Webster's *Grammatical Institute*. This tome was the first attempt by an American, the notable Noah Webster, to define English as a language for the new nation. It was a ten day wait for the order to arrive, and in the meantime Walter was to dedicate himself to the completion of the Hamilton essay. It had originally been planned as a hundred and fifty page investigation of the interrelationship of the newspaper wars and the Reynolds' blackmail. Already he had reduced it to seventy pages, at most: barely an acknowledgment of the work he'd put into the research. And in the end, Walter did little to produce his pedantic pamphlet other than writing a short paragraph, crediting the role of Hamilton in his original distraction.

(Walter whitewashing the waning of his work:)
'Much of my new enthusiasm began with Hamilton, himself a man of extensive vocabulary. I've consulted *Webster's* sporadically while reading Hamilton's letters and papers, when I needed to clarify passages like: "I have often heard that

authors in England, or their booksellers for them, when they find their books do not sell according to their wishes, hire some garretteer to write against them – then publish a reply to his own lucubrations – and so go on, objecting and replying, until the attention of the public is drawn towards the book, and thus it is brought into demand." Actually, <lucubrations> isn't in my pocket dictionary. But <lubber> is: a clumsy person.'

Walter needed to be cut off, to be controlled in his fancies. But the hiatus, while he waited for the book, didn't calm him. He began to feverishly question Freya Hirsch about words, looking through the complete OED she kept in the register showcase. His lengthy visits and frequent compliments piqued her interest. She wanted to know if he needed the Webster in some connection to Hamilton. Both men were, after all, Federalists. Perhaps Webster had contributed to Hamilton's diatribes in the *Gazette of the United States*? No. Then perhaps he had written to Hamilton with advice about how to handle the affair with Maria? No. Surely Webster didn't include subversive diatribes against the Jeffersonians in his own work? Of course not; the *Blue-Backed Speller* (Part I of *A Grammatical Institute of the English Language*) was published in 1783, a full decade before the controversy began. So why the sudden shift in focus? Why Webster?

(An affronted answer to Freya's axiomatic apple of discord:)
    'Why should I persist with Alexander Hamilton? When he got involved with Maria Reynolds he was veering from the path that drew me to him in the first place. Admittedly, I was initially fascinated by Hamilton; but the precisely controlled, adamantly ambitious man risked his sterling reputation in his flagrant flirtations. Noah Webster had no such flaws. He did not deliberately misconstrue the words of imagined foes; he worked to create a national unity for Americans. He rejected the aristocratic systems of England and brought education to the thousands of students wondering what the new national identity would mean to their futures.'

That last bit of Walter's was a lie; an attempt to justify his own retrogression by praising the virtues of a man he, as yet, knew little about. He simply got carried away with the novelty of language. Tragically, the *Speller* was delayed at the distributors, but he frittered away the time by reading Freya Hirsch's dictionaries and writing her love missives. He wanted her to be amazed at his own way with words. And she was fittingly flattered. In his previous diatribes about the Hamilton thesis, she had concluded that Walter didn't know what he was talking about. So going up a new path might not be such a big mistake. And maybe his study of the lexicographer would help de-antiquate his own language.

(Wally's longing love letter to lively, laudable Freya Hirsch:)
'My dear Miss Hirsch,

You must forgive my audacity in dispatching this unrequested letter. My missive's mission is to relate the visions I have of you: a veritable paragon of pulchritude. But it is not simply your extraordinary beauty which inspires me whilst penning this epistle. Oh, no! Indeed, your fair visage, though paramount in arousing my interest in you, is secondary to the diurnal joy I feel in contemplating your achievements as a trader of books and, in many senses, as a vessel of culture for all Philadelphia. Your shop is spoken of as an avenue for the attainment of lofty preoccupation and, as you will surmise from my position as an academic, this is a matter I deem to be of the utmost importance. I sincerely desire that my palpable devotion to you will not weigh heavily upon your conscience. I ask for no more than permission to continue my regular encounters with your exquisite character. With all good faith, I remain,

　　Yours, Walter Reynolds.'

Walter's profusion of passionate <P> words amused Freya Hirsch, but the visits to the book shop gradually became calls on the OED, not the bookseller. While this freed her up to deal with the paying customers, she began to feel used by the errant historian. He blocked access to her cash register without attempting to entertain her with the etymology of expressions like <manse>, <sacerdotal>, and <gawk>. His pedantic chuckles no longer preceded the phrase, 'Miss Hirsch, have you encountered this word before?' Her ire led her to withhold Webster's *Grammatical*

Institute, Part I, once it had finally arrived. And when she did present Walter with the volume, he neglected to thank her, ignoring the attached bill for the special order fee and rushing back to his apartment. He still hadn't surfaced in time for their date the next evening.

(Walter's 'shopping list,' from the *Speller*'s Table XXIX – 'Of Herbs, roots, Plants, Fruits, &c.':)

'Tur nips	po to toes	car rots	peas
beans	beets	rad ifh es	fpin ag*e*
cab bag*e*	caul ly flow er	ar ti choke	af par a gus
let tuce	en dive	cel e ry	parf ley
purf Iain	cref fes	for rel	on ion
gar lic	fhal lots	leeks	thyme
fag*e*	wa ter mel on	mufk mel on	cu cum ber
pum kin	fquafh	go *u*rds	fern
tu lip	vi o let	pink	gil li flow er
fen nel	dill	par fnip	fmal lage
hyf fop	faf fron	ap ples	pears
cher ries	plums	al monds	peach es
figs	wal nuts	cheft nuts	fil berts
rafp ber ry	bil ber ry	ftraw ber ry	goofe ber ry
grapes	cit rons	or an ges	rai fins
lem ons	tam a rinds	wheat	rye
corn	bar ley	oats	grafs
row en	flax	fpik*e* nard	mul len
dai fy	liq uor ice	plan tain	dan de li on
pen ny roy al	el e cam pane	far fa pa ril la	

— also frozen pizza, milk, tofu, soda, and salsa.'

While normally, in an investigation, Walter produced copious notes on his fanciful theories, his reaction to the *Grammar* was simply to dog-ear the pages whose lessons most appealed to him. He did occasionally do more than shop for the common fruits that Webster indexed. He also copied out the tables, from 'words of three and four letters' to 'words of five syllables, accented on the fourth.' But writing 'cir cum lo cu tion cir cum val la tion cir cum vo lu tion' was not aimed at impressing those who read and publish historical works. ᵂWas it the fear of going broke that snapped Walter out of his rhythmic reverie? Or was he driven back to the bookseller, eager to share his joy in the tables and lessons? Did Freya Hirsch actually worry about Walter in his little apartment, dissolving in the vat of vocabulary? Was there a mercy mission from the skirted sibyl, on pretense of an unpaid bill or the availability of a Webster work? Well, whether she took pity upon Walter or he pulled himself away from the *Grammar* in search of the history of one of Webster's words, a consultation with his beloved Freya did occur.

(Walter waxing whimsically on Webster/from Table XV – words of three syllables, accented on the first:)

'To an i mate the for ci ble ap ti tude of this cor di al gen tle man is to in ti mate that to ren o vate the rhet o ric was a per qui site for par ti san el o quence. He ro ism was haz ard ous in the change a ble peas ant ry, so se ri ous crit i cism of ob du rate man u script(s) was lau da ble.'

Freya Hirsch's reaction to Walter's transformed lingo – from formal phrases to stilted tricrotics – was to demand accountability from him. What was the point of his absorption in Webster? Would he produce anything from it, or merely babble on about irregular pronunciations and accented vowels? Where was the proof of erudition which he had asserted to her, before losing himself in this blue-backed book? And why bother so much with language if there was no context for it? The emphasis upon nonsense had compounded her changing opinion about Walter. The historian was startled. He hadn't been aware that Freya Hirsch cared overmuch about what he was doing these days. Would she approve if he veered back towards the traditional? If he devoted himself to his essay on Noah Webster's influence in colonial America? Maybe, said the bookseller. Maybe so.

(Walter trying to wean himself from Webster's words/from Table XXVII – short vowels inadequately divided:)

'Op po si tion to my e bul li tion has led to an ad mo ni tion to produce a com po si tion on the rhet o ri cian. It is a pro pi tious and aus pi cious fru i tion to my pe ti tion, on con di tion that I show con tri tion for de fi cient co mmi tal of ca pri cious vo li tion. And I must please Freya Hirsch.'

Walter determined that if even Webster's pocket dictionary didn't include Noah Webster in the indexical 'Hall of Fame of Great Americans,' he should bring the man to the attention of the world. And it was true that there was a dearth of material about him; even the brief *Encyclopedia Britannica* entry on Noah suggested that there needed to be a major study of the man and his goals. Did he intend the influence that he achieved? Was he ambitious for himself or for the new country? Was it revolutionary fervor or insightful genius? But these were the same questions Walter used to ask about Alexander Hamilton. Was history this repetitive, or was it just Walter who was redundant?

(Reynolds' return to ritual research rigidity:)
  'The directions in which Noah was headed aimed for a particularly American view of language. The *American Spelling Book* strove to create a uniform pronunciation for the populace, as well as to improve the educational system of the States. As he wrote in 1789: "As an independent nation, our honor requires us to have a system of our own, in language as well as government. Great Britain, whose children we are, and whose language we speak, should no longer be *our* standard; for the taste of her writers is already corrupted, and her language on the decline." To this end he promoted spellings like <honor>, without the useless <u>. He wanted to rid the language of British affectations. Admirable.'

But it wasn't long before Walter felt stifled by the stiffness of summary. Although he had Freya Hirsch actively supporting him – and she even went out to dinner with him weekly while he delved into Webster's *Dissertations* – he already missed his words.

(Walter's self-justifying surge of sensible speech:)
  'I am more interested in Noah Webster's way with words than his political goals. His wasn't a public life; he didn't present reports to Congress or write letters to George Washington. His

was a quest to organize language, to establish new meanings based upon the country's identity, to promote "the necessity, advantages and practicability of reforming the MODE of SPELL-ING, and of rendering the orthography of words correspondent to the pronunciation." It did have a lot to do with politics, but this fact simply makes it easier for me to undertake a study of the man and his life away from the political limelight. Noah Webster was a great patriot not because of his statesmanship, but because of his educational drive.'

Walter, pedantic side again to the fore, reflected upon his propinquity to the lexicographer. Should he move from Philadelphia to New Haven? Attain enlightenment from Webster's resting ground? Freya Hirsch bristled. He had removed himself from his sea of speech shibboleths on her account, suddenly reverted to them, and almost immediately spoke of moving. She denied that she would suffer inordinately from his departure, but she had made an effort because he so patently needed someone to do so. She expected some gratitude. But Walter was carting about an Amtrak timetable as if he might disappear at any moment. And this he did.

(Freya's finespun falderalian farewell from Walter/a selection of Table XII:)
  'Doom whom bloom noon prove noose. Choose lose. Who coo two touch botch. Book look. Good should could would soon shoot proud wound. Sprout doubt word, burst thirst flood her worth. Flirt dove, love drop. Swap track tough. Fail fair where they feint brain. Train state straight. Great spake shape, more prose. Known folks rove, none home. Roam globe sworn. Course source know right fight. Smile. While pride guide deep, keep peer read, lead dream. Dear pure, your view true. Use praise phrase. Fond strong once done. Pledge friend. Walter.'

The Effigy

Jacqui Lofthouse

Jacqui Lofthouse's first novel, THE TEMPLE OF HYMEN, was published by Hamish Hamilton in May 1995. Born in 1965, she grew up in Basildon. She studied Drama and English at Bristol University and has worked as a radio producer and actress. She now lives in London where she teaches creative writing at City University and is working on her second novel.

The Effigy

On January 19th 1729, the dramatist William Congreve died. He bequeathed his estate to his mistress, the Duchess of Marlborough. In order to minimize gossip, he made her husband, Francis, second Earl of Godolphin, executor.

As it was widely believed that Congreve's relationship with the Duchess had been platonic, the will seemed eccentric. But the Duchess grieved openly for Congreve, and as a result many stories circulated about their relationship. Some said that she secured a life-sized waxen statue of him which she worshipped or treated in an unnatural way.

YOU SPEAK to me, Madam, but you do not hear my voice. Each day since the funeral, I have been with you, and at night in your bed-chamber I watch you sleep. I try not to look at Godolphin. His presence disturbs me, more than you may imagine.

I was a man of wit, dear Henrietta, but what am I now, without my tongue or my pen? My words are nothing but self-pity and vexation. Because I have neither the luxury of an audience nor the comfort of friends, I am at liberty to express myself as I please. For the first time, I am not obliged to be charming.

Yesterday, once again, you had the physician attend to my gout. He unravelled the bandages that swathe my feet, prodded the afflicted area, shook his head grimly and wrapped me in fresh dressings. Then he looked at my eyes and, seeing no improvement, said he could do nothing for my cataracts. Foolish man! Does he not recognize that I am no longer blind? I see very clearly now. Nothing escapes me.

They have heard about me in the town, it seems. Did you believe that you could keep this to yourself? It is all rumour, of course. Nothing that can be substantiated. I trust you have paid your servants handsomely to remain discreet. Yet the word has spread. They talk of me at Drury Lane and in the chocolate houses. 'Mr Congreve lives!' they laugh. 'He has risen from the grave and is alive and well in St James' with the Duchess of Marlborough.'

Did you not think of my reputation, Henrietta, when you thought to breathe life into me? Do you think that any man, however great his fame, can survive this ridicule? Hear me, my love; do not gaze at your reflection. Will it always be thus? That I am here to comfort you when you grieve for me, but when I wish to speak you will deny my existence. Am I to be your doll and nothing more?

Lady, you invented me. I did not ask to live beyond the grave. I certainly did not wish to be resurrected in St James'. Take me to Wills to see Pope and Berkeley. Perhaps they will rejoice to see their friend returned from the dead.

Ah, you turn toward me now, disarming me with your beauty and I can no longer rail. You put your hands to your hair, releasing the pins that hold it. It falls around your shoulders, pale chestnut red. I do not believe I have ever seen you look so lovely. Who would have thought it? That the dead man sees better than the living. Even before my eyes deteriorated, when we both were younger, you did not have this air of naturalness. You do not truly believe I am here, my love, I understand that now. You do not know that I watch you, and so you have no art. I have never seen a woman without art. Even Mrs Bracegirdle . . . I apologize . . . but you do not hear me, so why should I not speak of my former love? Ann Bracegirdle could have been my wife; but a gentleman cannot marry an actress. And Arabella, my singing Angel. She made every place alike heavenly. I had thought to meet her again in Heaven, but it was not to be. You have arrested my journey there.

I try to understand you, Henrietta, but my heart overflows.

You did this because you love me, because you cannot bear to part with me. And yet . . . was it also to taunt the Earl, your husband? Could you not let him be, dear Godolphin, dull as he is, and give the last years of your life to him? Is my Duchess so spiteful as to wish him eternal cuckoldom?

When I died, you could not bear to let me go. My soul desired to meet the Almighty, but your grief was too much. I could not desert you in your hour of need. I thought my funeral would release me. It was not the funeral I requested, but I forgave you even that. A quiet occasion, I had said, without the least ostentation. But you had me buried as if I were your Duke, in the nave of Westminster Abbey; in your family plot, so that you may join me hereafter. I felt myself carried above the heads of Bridgewater, Cobham, Godolphin, and Wilmington. It was not a fitting end. But soon, I thought, there would be silence. Yes, in those final moments, before my soul departed, I had doubts. I was afraid that all our human hopes may be but dreams; ephemera. Vain creatures to trust that we will be saved, not just returned to dust.

Don't look at me so, Henrietta. That dummy you stare on is not me. A waxen effigy indeed. You stroke its wig – how touching. But it is not me, I tell you. Your dabbling has brought me back, but I do not reside in that ridiculous figure, though I reside with it. Does it look like Congreve, the greatest Comic Dramatist of the age?

Do I boast? A dead man must be allowed some pleasures. I could have called myself the greatest Tragedian also. Do you remember? 'Heaven has no rage, like love to hatred turned.' You used to say that Mrs Bracegirdle was the woman of whom I wrote. 'Nor hell a fury like a woman scorned.' You liked to mock her.

'William, shall we go through to the dining-room?'

Ha! You speak.

'I believe Joseph has prepared Quail and Partridge. Will you sup this evening?'

Madam, I come from the spirit world. Would you have me be corporeal?

'I shall ask Francis to carry you. You are too weak to walk. Oh, that fool Arbuthnot, why can he not cure your gout?'

I would walk, I assure you, if I could, my love. But lately I have discovered that I prefer to float.

'Let me look at you, William.'

Look at a dummy, Madam. The man himself has gone.

'Perhaps I should powder your nose?'

I have no nose, Henrietta! Have you lost your senses? I cannot believe that this is the woman I loved. What? You apply rouge to the monster? You kiss its forehead. Horrible.

'Have I made you too like a fop, Sir? I hope not. I would you were a Mirabell and not a Witwoud.'

Me? A Witwoud? This is too much. If I am a Witwoud, I would call you Lady Wishfort. You would not like that, my dear. No, you must stop this nonsense. My plays are for the stage, not for your bed-chamber. You should not make a fop of me after my death. I was ever a man of fashion and good manners. An indolent man perhaps, a disappointed man, in spite of my fame. But never a fop.

'Ah, Francis. Where have you been? Poor William's gout is bad. Could you carry him through to the dining-room?'
'Yes, my love. Of course.'

What kind of a man is this, who will bear this waxy burden? Can you call him a husband? A man who secured his office only through marriage and attends the House of Lords only in order to sleep.

I see the servants trying not to snigger at this sight; a husband, bowing beneath the weight of his dead rival. His horns should grow excessive long now.

'Where should I set him down, Henrietta?'
'In his usual place, Sir. I am surprised that you ask.'

Could it be, Duchess, that he wants me gone? Or that he hopes you will set the fat doll in a corner, out of his sight?

'Would Mr Congreve like potatoes?'
'Yes, Mrs Waters.'

Do you not think it strange, love, that they question nothing? They allow you to speak for me. Do you not wonder what they make of it?

'Can you fill Mr Congreve's glass, Tom?'

And what must young Mary think? I see it in her eyes. My mother has gone mad! It does not escape her, in spite of her tender years. Even Godolphin seems different today. He is brooding.

'Why are you silent, Francis? Is the meal not to your liking?'

You see it also. But perhaps you should not ask.

'I was thinking of the will, my love.'
'Yes, Francis.'
'The whole town is talking of it.'
'His was indeed an unusual bequest.'
'That he should leave his estate to you?'
'I cannot imagine what he was thinking of.'
'They say that he had a great many poor relations, and some say a son by Mrs Bracegirdle.'
'Sir, I will not have you defame him. Mary, have you finished your meal sweet heart? Good. Mrs Waters, could you take Mary to the nursery?'

Mrs Bracegirdle indeed. That he could think of it and not look closer to home.

'And that you should squander the money so!'
'I am a rich woman, Francis. I have put aside three thousand pounds for Mary. What else should I do with the remainder?'
'I do not presume to tell you that, my love. But that you should frivol away seven thousand pounds.'
'You think my necklace and earrings extravagant?'
'Yes, dear. I do.'
'And do you not find my jewels becoming?'
'I have not seen you wear them, Henrietta, but I do not think that even Mr Congreve here would approve of your improvidence.'

'Perhaps we should ask him. Mr Congreve, Sir. Do you think me reckless for spending your legacy on diamonds?'

My love, I have seen you wear the diamonds. I have seen them scatter light about your face and neck. I was transported, Henrietta. Their mineral glow catching on your apricot flesh. The candles burned dimly, they were down to the very stubs. I was not angry then. I did not ask to be released, because my Heaven then was in your eyes. The diamonds become you, love. At the heart of a diamond lies a star, so in that necklace is our little universe.

'He does not reply, Madam. Could it be that Mr Congreve has lost his tongue?'

'Francis. I beg you. Mr Congreve is exceedingly ill.'

'And pray, what is that disease whereby one loses one's ability to speak?'

'He has not lost his speech, Sir, he merely rests.'

'Well might such a corpulent man deserve his rest.'

This is outrageous. He never dared mock my figure whilst I lived.

'I cannot listen to you, Francis.'

'Perhaps it is time you did listen, Henrietta. Mr Congreve, I fear, lives no more. Mr Congreve, Madam, is in his grave.'

I had not imagined the good man could be so bold. He should have come to this before now. My Duchess rises. She colours. She stammers.

'Sir, you ... I have not ... it cannot ... you offend our guest. Pray ...'

I see the tears form, jewel-like, in her eyes. Godolphin suffers to see her so. His remorse is apparent but he cannot reclaim his words.

'Pray, Sir. Leave us alone.'

'No, love, let us sit down.'

'If you will not leave us, Francis, I shall retire to my chamber.'

Is she to leave me here with him? This is not kind of her. But she turns and exits without looking behind.

'So, Mr Congreve! It is time that you and I entered upon a discussion, man to man.'

Man to spirit, rather, you should say.

'What, Sir, do you propose I do now?'

Why do you ask me? The worms are at me, Godolphin. They gnaw my brain.

'What do you make of her strange attachment to you?'

More than even you divine, Sir.

'I have made a mistake this evening, that much is certain. Yet should she always triumph over me in this manner? Am I to have no respect?'

Sir, you are as mad as she to address a dummy. And you will never gain her respect.

'Nobody doubts that she was faithful to me, William. They are puzzled by the will. You were indeed a good companion to her, but why should she construct this "thing". It is more ugly than the original, if that is indeed possible.'

Worse and worse. And yet, Sir, not so ugly that I could not cuckold you.

'Methinks the man himself was fatter still.'

You loved me in life, Francis. Oh, that her tampering should come to this.

'If I could only know the truth!'

The truth is worse. It will burn your heart away. But you do not listen. You turn to the fire. Still I will tell my tale, for if I do not speak, I cannot rest.

After death, Francis, all is not simple. I imagined that when release finally came, the decisions made in my lifetime would seem clearer; that I would see the error of my ways. Before I met Henrietta, I thought of myself as a moral man. Do you remember this?

'From hence let those be warned, who mean to wed;
Lest mutual falsehood stain the bridal-bed:

For each deceiver to his cost may find,
That marriage frauds too oft are paid in kind.'

Yet I could not live according to my words. And I love Henrietta still. Wife, husband, it comes to nought. It is only love that has substance.

I am evasive of course. I delay the truth. But the truth, Sir, is the fact that you always denied. Your daughter is not your daughter. You do not start? How you would if you could hear. She was conceived in an adulterous bed. We made the beast with two backs, Francis. We were prime as goats, as hot as monkeys, as salt as wolves in pride. Is this the candour you require? Your Mary is not your Mary, nor has she ever been. Does your green-eyed monster rage now? Moll Congreve they christened her once, but you did not believe them. You saw her plainness and knew her to be a Godolphin.

And am I proud of my success? That all the town talks of the oddity of my will yet none suspects me? It was a clever turn that, to make you the executor. It removes suspicion. And so, all my property, my envied books, my portrait, my plate, my diamond ring, all will go, eventually, to Mary. And if you were to look closer at the famed diamond necklace, you would see how my initials are carved upon the back of every collet. So when Mary inherits that, she will carry me with her, all her life. I admit, I did not play fairly. But I love your wife.

'Sir, my lady desires to see Mr Congreve.'

'Alright, Tom. Tell her Mr Congreve seems to have recovered. She can wait on him here. I will retire to the library.'

Alone now; waiting for my Henrietta. Will she come with a light step or will she rail and frown? Alas, she has suffered for me, and yet I think I have the greater complaint. Oh, this loneliness is overbearing. How long can I continue thus? Another week? A month? A year? I would not be immortal long. It pains me to see Henrietta's grief. She does not show it; she smiles on the effigy as if it were me, and yet I see by the cast of her eye that she is not deceived. She is delaying her pain. And so long as my image remains, she will continue to suspend her sorrow.

Indeed, I guess right. For here she comes, all lugubrious.

'William, my dear. I have been thinking. How can I express what has passed through my mind?'

Easier than I can, Henrietta, that much is certain. Take your fingers from the waxy face. It may melt beneath their heat.

'I have been thinking on Francis' words and I know them to be true. You do not live, Mr Congreve. I have been deluded.'

I do not live – no indeed – and yet I do exist.

'But though I know these heavy eyes, these fine brows, to be but wax and horse-hair, I feel you here, my love. I feel you with me.'

She sits in the lap of the dummy and kisses its ashen face. It is more than I can bear.

'Can you remember, William, when my brother died of the small-pox? You did not know me then, yet in your poem, I became Amaryllis, my brother, the Marquis, became Amyntas. It made me love you. You pitied me, though you had never seen my face.
"Tell me, thou Sun that round the world dost shine,
Hast thou beheld another Loss like mine?"
It was a great loss indeed; I felt that I should never recover. Yet this is greater. My grief o'ershadows any sentiment I ever felt before. Oh, William, it is as if my heart is being crushed.'

My Henrietta. I cannot mock you now. I cannot leave you neither.

'I had a mother once. I loved her and yet she could not understand me. I remember when I first became acquainted with you and your friends from the Kit-Kat Club. She did not like that. I had lost all shame, she said, and the company I kept was corrupting my morals. And so we became estranged. I lost my mother, William, but I gained your love.'

I am not proud of that. You have not always treated the old Duchess as you ought.

'Shall we go to the bed-chamber? I cannot lose you yet. You must stay with me for a while. Tom! Where is that wretched boy? Tom! Ah. Could you bring Mr Congreve through to my chamber?'
'Yes, Ma'am.'

My Duchess walks ahead, the thick silk of her skirts skimming the passage-way. I see her reflected endlessly in the mirrored walls. Her step is sombre. How heavy it is to be mortal.

Behind her, Tom struggles with my figure.

'What are you doing, child? Hold Mr Congreve steady.'

What's this?

'Don't drop it, Tom. Hold on!'
'I can't, Ma'am. I can't keep hold of it.'

I am dazzled, Henrietta. I feel as though I see, suddenly, through the eyes of the effigy. I am hurtling toward the glass. My head clashes against silver, and shards of brilliant light shatter around me, a million broken pieces. But it is not just the mirror that is splintering. It is I, Henrietta. Your doll has broken.

'William!'

I am still here, my love. I see the effigy; pieces scattering across the floor. An arm is in three parts; the head has rolled clean off. You cannot speak. You stare at the bloodless carnage. And I too am affected. I cannot stay, Henrietta. I feel myself dissected. I am being pulled away. My soul is torn apart.

And you bend down, trying to gather the pieces. I see, but it is already less clear, like the beginning of my blindness. My vision is fragmented. I see only a part of you. Your face I see still; its sudden ghastly pallor. And your hair, the only red tincture that remains in my vision. You are vanishing, Henrietta, diminishing before me. You do not cry out. It is the silence that strikes me. You dissolve, my Duchess, you evaporate. The world of flesh is drawing away. There is nothing substantial remaining.

'Thence by a soft Transition, we repair
From earthly Vehicles to these of Air.'

Our love cannot be contained in wax, Henrietta. That is all I know.

Cutting

Martha Perkins

Martha Perkins was born in Maine in 1971. 'Cutting' is an extract from her first novel, FALLING TREES, which she wrote while at UEA.

∫

Cutting

The Ramsey brothers don't care what the weather is. In the fresh snow of the morning they put on the same clothes they always wear when they work, wool pants that have splinters and bark and wood chips nearly sewn into the fiber, a thermal shirt then a thick plaid or chamois shirt, their insulated, waterproofed Bean boots, a down vest and a fluorescent hunting cap and their chopping mitts. They look nearly identical every Saturday when they walk into Cook's variety to get their thermoses filled with coffee, and the only difference this morning is that the younger of the two, Lonny, sets a case of Miller on the counter with his thermos. His brother pays for it, annoyed with each dollar bill he slides from his wallet. The owner doesn't care too much about age unless it starts getting people in trouble, and Lonny's a good boy, up at 7 on a Saturday even. There's nothing suspicious about it, really: two boys out working in the woods all day probably get thirsty. Let 'em do what they want. So Lonny heaves the case into the back of the truck next to his chainsaw and packs some snow around it; his brother stirs eight packets of sugar into his thermos with his feet hanging out the truck door. He crumples the packets and lets them fall into the slush of the parking lot before wrenching the door shut. The door reads *Ramsey Brothers* and below it in big letters: DURGINTOWN. Lonny painted on the letters the afternoon after the truck failed inspection, thought he'd be cute with the *Brothers* stuff even though it's Pete's company. It doesn't stop them from taking it where they want, though, farm truck and all. The only reason it failed is the brakes and the frame, one too worn and the other rusted out more than just a bit. When they drive it at night their feet go cold from the draft in the rusted floor.

They've been working in the woods behind the orchards, clearing them out of the hardwood first, then all the chip wood and scrub. Lonny only works on the weekends and on days he doesn't feel like going to school. The Ramseys have a skidder sitting out by the piles of trees, but they haven't been able to get the damn thing to start in the last two weeks. Might be something wrong with the fuel intake, the pump maybe, but Lonny doesn't know a thing about it. His brother tinkers most hours of the weekend with the engine, reading the repair manual for the CAT 450 in the front seat of their farm truck, smoking cigarettes. He reads then he tinkers then he reads some more. The thing's almost seven years old, but they've only had it for a year. Got it for a song at an auction up in Jay; one of the mills had their private logging operation bought out. Lonny wishes he'd done more work down at the garage, because then he could sit all day messing around with stuff. Instead he has to go out and fell the rest of the trees on the lot they've been paid to clear. They're getting fifteen-hundred to clear the lot, well, Pete's getting it, plus whatever they can make off selling the wood. At this point, Lonny thinks, they'll be lucky if they don't have to put all of that into getting the skidder fixed. His brother, though, is determined to do it himself. It just ain't smart, he says, to pay someone to do something you can do yourself. Waste of money. So it's been sitting there for a week, collecting soft layers of snow with each passing night.

When Lonny gets his gear out of the back of the truck he sticks a few of the beers into his vest pockets. Instead of heading out to the back of the lot right away, he decides to file the chain on his saw. He has to ask Pete to get up for a minute, to pull the truck seat forward. Neither of them can find the file in the mess of oil rags and beer cans and paper bags from Kentucky Fried Chicken and Burger King. Christ, I was wondering where that was, Pete says, lifting up a rusted maul. Probably in the glove compartment, Lonny interrupts, slamming the seat back down.

The rifles clatter against the window rack by the force of the seat; Pete gets riled and gives a 'careful with those' look that Lonny tries to ignore, ducking his head in close and sliding his hand in between the twenty-year-old owner's manuals and receipts. All he can find in the glove compartment is the old one, rusted and worn; it won't do much good. His brother finally gives in and lets him use the brand new one, the one that's in his tool box with the tools that he doesn't let Lonny use either. Lonny has a habit of letting things sit out, getting rusted or lost or just plain fucked up. Lonny doesn't try to do it, it just happens that way. Lonny knows his brother's going to sit there and wait until he's done filing so he asks him right then if he wants to go out that afternoon. Where you want to go? Maybe we could sit on Hanson's ridge for a while. I could check to see if they've been coming through there. Yeah, maybe, Pete says, skipping to the back of the manual to see what page the injectors are on. If I can get this new line finished by two, we'll go out there for a while and see what we can scare up. Lonny slides the file away, pulling the chain up further and sliding the file into the grooves down the line again. It's like grinding down teeth, rasping them to a fine, sharp curve. It doesn't even take him ten minutes to get the whole thing sharp as a whistle. If there's one thing Lonny takes care of, it's his saw.

His brother's got the fuel line detached and hanging out of the belly of the skidder by the time Lonny trudges out into the woods. Lonny's got his saw, an ax, a maul and a small dirty red gas can that's got his chainsaw fuel already mixed. The beer cans *ting* against each other next to his thermos, and when he gets out to where he was yesterday, he takes out the cans and packs snow around them at the base of a tree. Cold in half an hour if he's lucky. His hangover needs one, but if there's something Lonny can't stand, it's warm beer. He twists the cover off the little tank and makes sure it's close to full before he gives the cord a hard yank. The saw whines high and fast until Lonny turns the throttle down. He looks around and decides to clear up some of the trees he cut yesterday, so he stands at the raw yellow end of a pine and works his way down to the tip, cutting off the branches as he goes. On the bigger trees he has to work his way down one side, then up the other. His brother listens to the variations in the whine. You got to be aware of the woods, he always tells Lonny, you got to be careful of any changes. As long as the whine ebbs and flows, he knows Lonny's OK. If he heard the saw go silent, like if it was just idling on the ground, he might worry that something's wrong. It's not like he doesn't trust Lonny to do his work, Christ, it's not that. It's just that after you've seen a man who's been hit by a saw that's kicked back, you don't ever forget it. He did have to run out once, when he and Lonny were working separate, to make sure he was OK. He'd heard the saw go silent, and he heard Lonny yell, and it didn't take any more than that, he ran through the woods so fast, the blood pumping hard enough to make his neck hurt, and when he got there Lonny'd only caught his shirt in a tree that was falling, the dummy didn't notice till the tree took him down with it. They laughed and Pete helped him up, but it didn't stop him from feeling shaky the rest of the day. Lonny could have been hurt, falling with the saw in his hand, it could have been terrible. But his brother doesn't like to think about it. The saw whines and whines its way through the cold dampness of the mid-morning sun.

It takes him nearly four hours to get the old fuel line off and the new one back on again, but in the middle of doing it he's decided to change the fuel filter, so he's had to drive down to the garage out on Route 126 to get a new filter and a can of diesel to soak it in. By the time he gets back Lonny's sitting in the seat of the skidder drinking one of his beers. Didn't know you took off, he says, when his brother climbs out of the truck. I gotta get some more oil for my saw, I think it's in the back. His brother leans over and looks, and there's nothing there except his tool box, the diesel, and his oil. Have some of mine, he says, chucking it up to Lonny. Lonny reaches out but misses, and the plastic bottle bounces off one of the skidder tires and sinks into the snow. He jumps off the skidder and grabs it, heading back out into the woods. Thanks. His brother grabs the filter off the seat and the can of diesel and starts on the skidder again, pissed because Lonny knew full well he didn't have any oil, and that he didn't come right out and say he didn't. They could have picked some up this morning if he'd wanted to. Pete gets tired of paying for Lonny's stuff; he's not a kid anymore, he's almost eighteen years old and sure as hell old enough to be responsible for himself. His wife doesn't like Lonny staying at the house too much either, but there ain't a whole hell of a lot he can do about that, is there, with their parents moved down to Florida permanently. He knows, and he tells himself when he starts getting angry at Lonny, that he's an alright kid, and he works hard. He'd never be able to get anyone better to help him on the weekends, not round here. Right, so he's a bit careless sometimes, maybe even a bit of a sneak. He'll grow out of it, his brother thinks.

Lonny pops a new can open after he sets the oil down by his ax. His head's beginning to clear up and he feels ready to build up a sweat. It's an hour before their lunch break, and he hopes that Pete will want to go back into town to get sandwiches. He doesn't feel like going home today, he'd rather get a grinder at Cook's and eat it back out here. Lonny knows how to play it: tell Pete something will save time and he'll be doing it before you know it.

The peculiar sound of a high whine and a low diesel rumble comes from the direction of the skidder. Lonny wonders whether he finally got the thing to run. If he did, it means Pete will be in a good mood for the rest of the week. You never know with these damn engines though, diesels are tricky. You may get the bastard to run all afternoon but it may die for a month after that. It doesn't sound too good though, there's obviously something wrong with it still. The sound stops. Lonny yells out:

DID YOU GET IT?

The trees and the snow stretch out the silence.

NOT YET.

The woods feel clean, the way the sound moves back and forth. The leaves soak up so much of it in the summer, with rustling and the birds, but in the stillness of winter, in the emptiness, the woods become an echo.

Lonny sets down his beer and with a good hard yank the saw fills up the silence, then subsides to a quieter grumble. Lonny unbuttons his shirt before walking out to the edge of the lot with the saw in one hand, his beer in the other. The stone wall marks the end of the lot, but it also lines off a gully that runs alongside the edge of a steep knoll. He lays his saw, still running, on one side of the wall, and climbs over. In the gully there are fresh tracks, some pawing marks. One of them is pretty big by the size of the hoof, the others could be spike horns, females maybe. He sets his beer down in the snow before clambering his way up to the top of the knoll. Every ten steps he slides down a bit on the leaves and has to grab hold of a sapling to stop himself from going all the way to the bottom. When Lonny gets to the top he scares a rabbit from the clearing, and it scurries off into the underbrush of some low bushes. From here he can see the ridge, with his hand over his eyes; the sun is strong against the new snow, it hurts unless he pinches his eyes to little slits, shades them from the glare. He can't see anything from here but he's sure they must be going through. Lonny slides back down the knoll on his butt, soaking the bottom of his wool pants. He doesn't care though because it makes him feel like a kid. He wonders how it is that he doesn't act like a kid more. Fucking jobs and bills, isn't it. As he climbs over the wall he remembers that he's supposed to take Stacy to the movies tonight. Not only does he not have any money, but he hasn't asked Pete yet if he can use the car. Shit. Maybe she won't want to go, he thinks, but then he remembers that she wanted to see that new Disney movie, christ what is it, that cartoon one in the fucking ocean or something . . . Lonny laughs. The things I go through to get laid, he thinks. Lonny feels bad for thinking that way, betraying things that they've said to each other . . . but Stacy doesn't care all that much, she knows they're not serious, like sure, OK, they don't go around jumping into bed with anyone else, but it isn't all marriage vows and kids and a house either. Stacy's sister has that and her life sucks. That's what Stacy always says.

Lonny picks up the saw and wonders how he's going to ask Pete for money and the car tonight. Christ, maybe he should just tell Stacy that she should pay for once. I'm not the Bank of America, for christ's sake. He starts in on the saplings near the wall, cutting each one down in a matter of seconds. Sometimes he thinks that maybe he should see other people, because sure, he likes Stacy but sometimes she's just not all that fun to be with, kind of a bitch really. She wants to go to Florida during February vacation, and somehow she's gotten it into her head that they can go and stay with Lonny's parents. Never mind the fact that neither of them have money to get there and back. Every time she brings it up it means there's going to be an argument. She never liked his parents when they lived here, and now she wants to march right down there and act like she does. They don't exactly have a soft spot in their hearts for her either, especially after she went and got pregnant. It makes Lonny angry to even think about it; he starts taking swipes at the saplings with the saw, cutting off branches in mad swings before severing them at the base. It was dumb of him, really, to even tell them. Then you got to marry her, his father said. But that wasn't what she and Lonny wanted. When she told Lonny, she didn't say Lonny, I'm pregnant, she said, Lonny, I've got to have an abortion. She didn't want to consider the options. Christ, she didn't even tell *her own mother*. Instead Lonny drove her in and waited three hours and drove her back. She looked pale and sick to her stomach the entire way. Lonny was afraid that she was going to throw up in his brother's car, or that she'd start bleeding on the seat or something.

Lonny hears the horn on the truck and cuts the chainsaw off; it's one o'clock. His brother sits in the front seat smoking when Lonny emerges from the woods. Lonny points at the skidder, So what's the diagnosis, is it going to live? Pete takes a long drag, then scratches the back of his head in annoyance, letting the smoke slowly ebb out of his nose. Well, it'll run alright, but it's making some damn noise now. Yeah, I could hear it, Lonny says, setting his saw and ax in the back of the truck. Your sister in law's making us hamburgers for lunch, he says when Lonny gets into the truck. Lonny hates it when Pete calls her that. Pete doesn't think Lonny shows her enough respect. Lonny shrugs: Sounds good to me. He wonders how he's going to ask Pete in front of Denise for money and the car. When they get to the house there's a note on the counter and the hamburgers are in neat little patties in the fridge. Denise's sister up in Lewis Falls needed a baby sitter for the afternoon, Denise'll be back by dinner. Pete reads the paper in the living room while Lonny cooks the burgers in a frying pan, and they eat them off TV trays, each with a big bag of chips. Lonny likes to watch TV when he eats, and this afternoon there's fly-weight boxing on from Miami. There's a Cuban beating the shit out of a black guy. Pete looks up from the paper to watch because Lonny keeps saying JESUS CHRIST every time the black guy takes another punch. That guy has got balls, Lonny says, I'd be lying on the mat by now. CHRIST ALMIGHTY. The black guy takes a slug to the face and there's blood everywhere. The ref stops the fight and holds up the Cuban's arm on a technical.

When they finish Pete grabs the plates and puts them by the sink. He runs a little water into the frying pan and adds some soap: if he doesn't do at least this much Denise will be livid. Come on, let's get moving. Lonny's switched the channel to a Planet of the Apes movie, and he's standing in front of the TV, trying to catch as much of it as he can. Yeah, alright. The picture collapses to a bright white dot in the center of the TV.

On the skidder there's a note left on top of the front tire, held in place by a rock. Jorowski wants to know how long it will be before they're done. Looks good so far, he writes, in parenthesis. Pete takes the note and drops it on the front seat. What's he want? Nothing, just wants to know when it'll be cleared. Oh. I'm going to come out with you for a while, Pete says, grabbing his own saw from the truck bed. I've had enough of that thing for one day. Each carry a chainsaw in one hand, a rifle in the other. When they get out to the back wall they both crack a beer and sit for a minute, drinking. D'you check the ridge? Well, I looked round noon, but it was so damn bright I couldn't see much. There's tracks all over the place though. Pete drinks fast, just like it's water, so he crumples his can when Lonny's half-finished and gets up to look in the gully. Lonny wants to go so badly that he says exactly what Pete wants to hear: That big bastard's still around, that's for sure. Yeah, Pete says, leaning over the wall. You want to walk up to the ridge and back, see if we see anything? Lonny finishes his beer in a few gulps and gasps: Sure. They grab the rifles from where they're leaning up against a tree, and check the clips in each. Shit, Lonny says, give me a couple of yours if you got any extra, there's only one in this. Pete slides his finger into his clip and pops out a few of the lead-tipped bullets. That thing needs to be oiled, Pete says, watching Lonny shove the loaded clip back into the rifle. Yeah, I know. This's the one dad won in that pool, remember that? Pete nods. Jesus, you'd a thought the old man'd won a holiday around the world by the look on his face. Yeah, well you should have seen mom when he called, Pete says. That's what he made it sound like, being all mysterious and whatever. She thought he was bringing a brand new car home. He really likes to disappoint her, you know. Pete looks out across the woods at all the trees cut and stripped. He thought he was getting a really good laugh. Lonny looks down at the ground, half-listening, nodding.

Instead of climbing up the knoll they decide to walk the length of the gully to where it opens up into a wide valley. Following that means they'll come up the back side of the ridge, just the right place to surprise one. They walk slowly, being careful where their feet land. The snow hides all the twigs and dead branches, but that doesn't stop them from letting out a good crack when a big one is stepped on. The tracks run all the way up the gully, so there might be something in the clearing, they don't know. Pete carries his gun in his right hand, lets it angle down to the ground like his father showed him as a kid, but Lonny likes to carry his up and ready, like he's in a war and somebody's aiming to ambush them. It makes Pete nervous, having the barrel pointed up diagonally, in his direction, so he steps behind Lonny and walks on the other side of the barrel. He'd say something to Lonny but he feels like there's only so much you can tell Lonny before he just starts ignoring you anyway. Ten years puts a lot of sense into your head, Pete thinks, I probably did the same shit-stupid things when I was his age. At the clearing there's nothing there but a rabbit which Lonny takes aim at but doesn't fire. The rabbit runs so fast it's as much sound as motion, a blur across the snow. When they get around to the full length of the ridge, there's nothing there either, only traces. Some must have bedded down there for the night because there are patches near the bushes which are bare, dry. We'll have to come up in the morning, Lonny says, tipping the snow off the bushes with the tip of his barrel. Yeah, Pete murmurs, maybe next week . . . I'm not coming out here on a Sunday anymore. Pete surveys the valley, and the edge of the orchard that can be seen just on the other side of the knoll. Already the sun's getting cold, distant. He lights a cigarette with a wooden match and puts it out by dropping it into the snow.

The match lets out a dull, short-lived hiss. Well, let's do another hour and call it quits. The brothers walk back to the lot, with the same strides pacing out the ground, one rifle aimed down, the other cocked up.

Adventures in Capitalism

Toby Litt

Toby Litt was born in 1968 and grew up in Ampthill, Bedford-shire. He studied English at Oxford. From 1990 to 1993, he lived in Prague. He is currently working on a novel and a book of short stories.

Adventures in Capitalism

It Could Have Been Me and It Was

After I won the Lottery and jacked in my job at the Lab, I decided, in a spirit of scientific enquiry, to spend a year and a day believing everything the ads told me. *Coke* was *it* and *Pepsi* was *The Choice of a New Generation*. (I was 32 and so wasn't really sure if that meant me.) 'A Year in Fairyland,' I called it, 'The Place Where All Your Dreams Come True.' They'd been telling you (me) from since before you (I) were (was) born that if you (I) just did exactly what they said, you (I) would become 'The New You' ('Me'), so I (on your behalf) decided to obey them (Them).

Before: After:

(Eugh!)   (Phwoar!)

At the end of the Fairytale Year, I would judge whether I was substantially any happier than I would have been at the end of Just Another Year. Somehow, I doubted it. Almost immediately, because I live in London, travel by tube and because it was summer, I got *Heatbusters* to fit some air-conditioning in my flat. 'Phew! Thanks *Heatbusters*. We needed that.' I drank *Grolsch* and joined *Dateline*. I *too* could find love. My first date, Lauren, who worked in qualitative Pharmaceutical Market Research in Putney, was lovely. But I drank so much *Grolsch* during the first half of the evening that, during the second, I metamorphosed into *The Human Whoopee Cushion*. Lauren told me that a man with my unfortunate problem should seek medical help. But as Lauren wasn't an ad, I didn't believe her. You see, I'd also decided, about two weeks in, that I'd have to stop believing people. So when my mother phoned up and said 'Hello,' I didn't believe her; I said, 'Who are you?' and she said, 'Brian, I'm your mother,' and I said, 'No you're not,' and put the phone down. This continued for several days until I managed to buy a new flat. I informed *Dateline* of my change of address but not the crazed woman pretending to be my mother. My next two *Dateline* dates were disastrous: I fell in love with both of them. I'd had to. If the ad said I *too* could find love through *Dateline*, then I could. Maria worked for a company that supplied *VoiceMail*. I soon had *VoiceMail*. Mandy worked as a receptionist in a Harley Street practice. I soon had no appendix. In the meantime, of course, I was spotting other ads in which I couldn't not believe. I bought loads of stuff. One Friday evening I sat down to watch *Eurotrash* and the next day I had to go out and buy a Fiat *Punto*, two Renault *Clios*, a Volkswagen *Polo*, a Citröen *Xantia*, some *Monster Munch, Crunchy Nut Cornflakes*, a Cadbury's *Twirl* and a pack of *Wrigley's Spearmint Gum, Andrews Antacid Indigestion Tablets* (which came in quite handy after I'd eaten the *Monster Munch*), *Colgate Bicarbonate of Soda Toothpaste* (which overcame the ill-effects of the chewing gum), a large box of *Tampax* tampons and a pack of *Energizer* batteries. I had breakfast at *Burger King*, where a *Whopper* was definitely on the menu, and lunch at *McDonald's*, where the *Egg McMuffin* was not to be avoided. I also made enquiries about the issue of *PowerGen* shares, took out several *Personal Pension*

Plans, opened an account at *The Cooperative Bank* and joined both *WeightWatchers* and *The Territorial Army*. On the next day, Sunday, I bought *The Sunday Telegraph*, which necessitated a further glut of purchases, the most embarrassing of which was the full set of *Birds of the British Isles Heirloom Thimbles*. At this point I almost gave the whole thing up. One evening, when I was out at *WeightWatchers*, Mandy accidentally heard the message that Maria had left on the *VoiceMail*. Maria was thanking me for the *Diamond Ring* I had just sent over to her via *UPS*. That got rid of Mandy. Unfortunately, Maria had left her parents' number in her message (she had gone down to Devon to ask their permission to marry me), Mandy called them up, told them everything, and that got rid of Maria. I lost 10lbs in two weeks, mainly thanks to *The Territorial Army*. The next three dates that *Dateline* sent along were Teresa, a Bicycle Courier who really wanted to be a nun, Maxine, a Dental Hygienist who was a transsexual, and Sarah, a nun who couldn't decide whether to become a Bicycle Courier or a transsexual. I suggested she give Dental Hygiene a try. My life became busier and busier. As well as all the *Dateline* business, there was the Culture (a hundred must-see and unmissable films, plays and exhibitions), the Investments (*PEPs* and *High Interest Savings Accounts*), the Insurance Policies (*Life, Health, Car, Home*), the Cigarettes (*Silk Cut, Marlboro, Embassy Mild, Benson and Hedges*) and the Properties (Soho loft, Surrey Tudor, Scottish castle, Slough repossession). I was soon skipping *WeightWatchers* meetings and trying to forget I'd ever joined *The Territorials*. I started to wear dark glasses and to walk round looking at my feet, which was cheating, I know. But something big was coming up. Sooner or later, I realized, I would have to stop deceiving myself. I was being hugely inconsistent. I had to get away. I needed a break. I needed a holiday. *The Territorials*, who had started leaving frankly abusive messages on my *VoiceMail*, would have to go stuff. Florida. EuroDisney. Israel. Dublin. Malta. The whole world competed for my body and my cash. In the end, I decided to go out the next morning and obey the first travel advert I saw. I slept badly, dreaming of the thousand places I might have to visit: I arrived at *Pontins* in Welshpool, took a daytrip to the Wailing Wall, got lost in the Galapagos, was mugged in Central Park and finished with some Après-Ski. In the morning I got up, drew the curtains and immediately saw a very scrappy ad on the side of a double-decker bus. It was for Beijing, so to Beijing I went – although I missed several flights on my slow and gradually more and more overladen trip through Heathrow. By the time I found *AirChina* Check In, I had stocked up on perfumes and cameras and extra luggage and towels and novels and the newspapers. They wouldn't allow most of it on the plane, so I had it posted back to Surrey. It could rot on the lawn. During the flight I was able to really relax for the first time in months, though I did feel obliged to get pissed-up on the *Duty Frees*. You may think me stupid, but it was only when I arrived in Beijing and stepped out of the airport that I realized I wasn't able to understand a single one of the many ads I saw. *Hotel* was the only word I could decipher. Going back into the airport would be an act of conscious will. I would be deliberately overriding my ad-obedience, which intended me to have a holiday in Beijing. All I could do now, therefore, was have a holiday in Beijing. I checked in to my *Hotel* and started buying things, mainly cans of *Coke*. For a day or two I tried to decide whether learning Mandarin would also be a disobedience. I decided it would. I had six months left in China, then. And after that, who knows? *The Territorials* would probably have me Court Martialled the moment I set foot in Blighty. And as for *WeightWatchers*, I hardly dared think. There was nothing else to do. I was stuck. One day I took a walk away from the *Hotel*, hoping that I would see an ad, any ad, telling me to go on holiday in Surrey or London or even just England. There was nothing. Deng Xiaoping. Televisions. Smiling faces eating rice. I carried on walking. Wide pale streets full of people riding bicycles. I was lost. I couldn't go back to the same *Hotel* as before unless I got lucky and saw an ad for it. But I never did. My luggage, including my dictionary, faded behind me as I was pinballed around from foreign *Hotel* to foreign *Hotel*. Some law of chaos led me gradually north, out of the city. A month had passed. I was a different, bearded, shabby, raving man. I had started to have dreams in which I was a *Monster Munch* monster. I lost my passport, somehow or other, but, thank God, not my *American Express Card*. I found myself in a *Hotel* from which I seemed unable to reach any other *Hotels*. I waited in the lobby for days, hoping for a copy of a foreign newspaper or magazine. Anything. Even *Rolling Stone* would have done. If I had read *Rolling Stone*, I would have had to enroll at the *American University* and to do that I would have had to travel to Michigan or Malibu or somewhere. But nothing happened to help me. I put the 10lbs back on, plus. Two months passed and then the woman claiming to be my mother arrived. I couldn't explain to her that I still had three months of my experiment left. She wouldn't have understood. Mothers, true or false, never do. But, bless her, whoever she was, she had a crappy novel with her and in that crappy novel was a complimentary bookmark. By taking out a year's subscription for the *Reader's Digest* (unavailable, as yet, in China), I was able to maintain my pride and consistency. Just. I returned to England with my pseudo-mother, looking forward to receiving my free *Clock Radio*. When we arrived in Heathrow, there was something an incident. Here, in the Clinic, with a fortnight to go, they have learnt to prevent my escape bids by forbidding me television, newspapers, magazines and any glimpse of buses or taxis. Instead, Doctor Chandra lends me copies of the *Autograph Edition* of the *Complete Works of Charles Dickens*. Every time I finish one, he gives me the next. I am currently reading *Bleak House*.

Mr Kipling

Mr Kipling, as you no doubt already know, makes *exceedingly* good cakes; and has done now for about as long as most of us can remember, though it was, in fact, only 1967 that he first came to public notice. What I would not expect you to know is that Mr Kipling is the best friend I have in the world. We correspond. I write to him, almost daily now, telling him of the small travails of my small life, and he replies, under a pseudonym, politely denying that he exists. He is so kind. He claims that he is merely the invention of an advertising executive, established in order to humanize a rather soggy line of cakes and biscuits. He only admitted this after a very long while; before then, he thanked me for my letters, and was afraid that he couldn't help, but was glad that I enjoyed his products. He sometimes even sent me a token. I have them, framed, up above my desk. It is a 'quiet country retreat' I have here. In fact, there is an orchard out back not dissimilar to the one in which the apples for Mr Kipling's Bramley Apple Pies are picked. There is a village postmistress, who is the 'bane' of my life. She looks like a rabid wolf and, I am sure, steams open my letters. Her name is Miss Blood. My neighbours, on the left side, dress their children in Christmas jumpers and, during the summer, walk around in rather less than was considered proper in Mr Kipling's day; on the right side, I have the dairy farm: Mrs Jones is constantly threatening but never delivering children. I live alone and am trying to get some money from the National Trust to repair the roof. It is thatched, but has not been redone since the Jubilee, when a rather shoddy job was made of it. Thatched roofs have never done particularly well under Labour governments. At four o'clock every afternoon, just as Noël Coward would have it, everything 'stops' for tea. Mr Kipling is with me in spirit. I always pour him a cup and put a little treat on his plate. Some people would say that surely by now Mr Kipling must be rather tired of eating his own cakes, but I believe that – given the prestigious circumstances (the oaken walls, the cheery log fire, the sympathetic company) – Mr Kipling could always be prevailed upon to partake. If not, then he is a different man from the one I take him for. Yesterday, it was his Battenberg Treats that I did justice to; today, Saturday, the Glazed Fruit Tartlets; tomorrow, I have not yet decided. Perhaps the Lemon Slices or perhaps the Almond. They know me of 'old' in the Village Shop, and tell me whenever Mr Kipling is preparing an innovation. 'Oh, he's harmless enough,' I heard Mrs Poon say, as I left the other day. I wonder how anyone could ever think Mr Kipling capable of harm? There was a new girl. Miss Ogbuku. I think she may diminish the pleasures of shopping. Mrs Poon anticipates me in everything, and I hope she is not thinking of retiring. Mrs Poon is only middle-aged. She does not attend church. Mr Kipling does. Mr Kipling is a High Anglican, like myself. I suspect, though, that he has more of an inclination towards Rome than I do. The occasional overuse of cinnamon in his Mince Pies tells me so. Who cannot be sensible of the lure of further incense and plusher robes? A more august tradition and a bloodier roll of honour? But I will not desert the church of Betjeman and Larkin. And Mr Kipling will never, I trust, go to Rome. I have in my letters warned him off Jesuitical dinner parties and other Popish dabblings. I believe I have made him fully aware of their dangerous allure. Such a distinguished convert, no doubt, has great attractions for them. In a way, if Mr Kipling were suborned, it would undermine the constitutional position of the Church of England. I don't quite know how, but it would. Mr Kipling does not take Earl Grey tea, being more desirous of robuster flavours; and to take, as he does, 'Three sugars, please' in that Queen of Teas would inevitably lead to suspicions of effeminacy and, indeed, of Sodomism. No, Mr Kipling has his three heaped teaspoons in a small china cup of fine but strong Assam. I can't stand the stuff myself. We pipe smokers have a phrase for what happens when the accumulated tobacco finds its noxious way into the mouth, we call it Arab's Armpit: that is how Assam tastes to me. Mr Kipling does not smoke a pipe; he likes a long cool cigar, and I always make sure to have some in. Mr Kipling is a widower, totally devoted to his culinary craft. Mrs Kipling, sadly, died a number of years ago. They met during the Blitz, when she was the prettiest girl in the shelter, and he the dashingest man. They were happily married for 30 years. She supported him through his early struggles. She never cooked. It was a great grief to him when she passed away. He went through one of his darker periods. I like to think that the Rich Chocolate Tart is his posthumous tribute to a passion whose strength he hardly realized until it was too late. There is certainly something mournful and even gothic about this creation. A requiem in chocolate. Mrs Kipling is with the angels now, looking down upon Mr Kipling and blessing him and his work. I often pray to Mrs Kipling to intercede for me when, as it does, temptation overtakes me. The Own Brand Devils dance before my eyes and the Discount Demons whisper. Of course Mr Kipling's cakes are more expensive; it is because they contain love and compassion and, even, grief. I believe Mr Kipling would be the ideal man to provide flavoured wafers for the Mass, if such a measure were ever introduced to encourage new worshippers into our churches. His every recipe is a homily, his every baking, a prayer. That he makes Angel Cakes is hardly surprising. It is a great joy to him that his many nephews come to visit him at Christmas. He sometimes can be prevailed upon to put on his Santa Claus costume. The Mince Pies which he proffers during the festive season are his own humble offering to the Lamb of God. How integral they are to so many people's celebrations! On Christmas Eve, I always raise a glass of sherry to Mr Kipling, for his sterling efforts yet again in providing the larger part of the nation with their yuletide fare. It is a heroic yet humble achievement, recalling his experiences during the Blitz. I believe we may even have fire-watched together, once or twice.

Please Use a Basket

You know me, I'm the Boots *Please Use a Basket* girl. I stand beside the door in your local Boots, eight or ten of me, wire baskets stacked up to my tummy: unexceptionable, sisterly, happy to be of service; brunette, sparky-eyed, about 4'9". The girl-next-door, only made out of cardboard. My nametag reads 'Mrs L. Timmins', but that's not my real name. My real name is Rebecca Llewellyn. You know me – you've probably even accepted my offer of a basket, once or twice. We know each other – we know each other well enough to ignore each other. Don't worry. I don't mind. I'll still be there the next time you shop with us: sisterly, brunette, about 4'9". I will always be happy to be of service. Do you like the way I'm dressed? Do you like my white labcoatish uniform with its discreet navy trim? Does it make you trust me just that little bit extra, as if I were a doctor or a nurse? It should do – if it doesn't, there'll be hell to pay in Marketing. Because, you see, I'm not just a young woman called Rebecca Llewellyn; I'm not just that person who turned up to a photostudio in Battersea one July morning; I'm not just the daughter of Michael Llewellyn and Angela Sexton; I'm not just an image exposed onto Kodacolor Gold. I am a company policy decision. I am the ultimate expression of Boots self-image. I am a capitalistic device. You yourself must have thought of it at least once. When you decide to *Please Use a Basket*, you almost always end up buying more; if only to kill the pathos of the single item in the vast spatial yearning that is a Boots wire basket. (Wire for the baskets is no accident, either: that simple grid provides all the other customers with the exact co-ordinates of your poverty.) It's simple, but it works. I must therefore please, averagely. No one must find me in any way offensive. (I have not yet mentioned that I am white – but that is because you probably haven't even thought about it. I must please the majority, and minorities are called that for a reason. I am addressing an assumed majority in which Mrs Smith outnumbers Mrs Patel – an assumed majority in which Mrs Smith is white and Mrs Patel isn't.) Perhaps I am not quite as nice as I at first seem. Perhaps trustworthy young women like myself were employed in certain places half a century ago. You know me, I'm the Auschwitz *Please Remove Your Clothes* girl: unexceptionable, sisterly, happy to be of service; brunette, sparky-eyed, about 4'9". A little like Uncle Michael and Aunt Angela's daughter, Rebecca. Only made out of cardboard. And now you think I have ruined my point by overstating it. And I probably have. But the problem with fascism is, according to some, that it can only accurately be called fascist when it is no longer any use to call it anything. When I joined the SWP, about a year after that July morning in Battersea, I didn't realize the true threat of fascism. I was coming out of Boots one evening after work. All day I had been on the checkout with Marge and Mavis. Even though I'd dyed my hair cherry and changed it to a really short bob, people still recognized me as the *Please Use a Basket* girl. 'It's you, isn't it? Over there – it's you.' The young woman selling the *Socialist Worker* was just like me – brunette, sparky-eyed, about 4'9" – only she wore vegetarian Docs, calico and a Donkey Jacket where I wore Clark's, a labcoatish uniform and a Debenham's raincoat. She smiled at me, in between shouts. I bought one of her newspapers, though I really wasn't sure what it was. We started having a really good chat. I told her how fed up I was, working at Boots. We went for a coffee. I told her I was the Boots *Please Use a Basket* girl. She called me a 'tool of the capitalist hegemony'. She explained what hegemony meant. Instantly, I recognized that she was telling the truth. She had the forms with her, so I signed up. What I'd realized was that, if anyone else was to change, if the capitalist hegemony was ever going to be smashed, then the Boots *Please Use a Basket* girl had to be in the vanguard. I had been selected, selected from hundreds, as an image acceptable to the masses. I myself had been mass-produced – there were now literally masses of me. I was a crowd, a mob, an army. But I was an army lined up against myself. I was the fascist oppressor – but I knew that I was made of cardboard and that I couldn't speak. Rebecca Llewellyn now began her campaign against the Boots *Please Use a Basket* girl. I resigned from Boots, after seven years, sending a letter of explanation to all the senior management. 'Your cardboard representative, your ubiquitous symbol of hegemony is now against you,' I wrote. 'You have created me till I outnumbered you.' Nancy helped me with the letter. Nancy is the name of the girl who sold me my first copy of the *Socialist Worker*. We live together in a Battersea squat, just round the corner from the photostudio. We go on rallies and demos together. Last year we went on the big anti-fascist march round the East End and got into a fight with Combat 18 and the BNP. We also went to Reading and Glastonbury. Nancy's lovely. Her regular patch is by the tube station; mine's outside the Boots where the old Rebecca Llewellyn used to work. So now, even as I stand inside, warm under fluorescent light, eight or ten of me – *Please Use a Basket, Please Use a Basket, Please Use a Basket, Please Use a Basket, Please Use a Basket, Please Use a Basket, Please Use a Basket, Please Use a Basket, Please Use a Basket, Please Use a Basket* – I also stand outside, alone, in the weather, shouting, '*Socialist Worker! Socialist Worker! Socialist Worker! Socialist Worker! Socialist Worker! Socialist Worker! Socialist Worker! Socialist Worker! Socialist Worker! Socialist Worker!*' And no one recognizes me anymore.

Cosmetic

Though enabled by money, I was created by myself. Even Max, my chief surgeon, will admit to that, won't you, Max? What you see before you – man, woman, child or beast – is *all* of my own choosing. I didn't even look at the catalogs. They are skilled craftsmen, but they have no imaginations. What limits them is the human precedent. Anime and Manga mean nothing to them. Disney was a holiday destination. At some point, before money, dreams began; after money, dreams met their easy enactment. Objections were made on the grounds of 'nature' – is anything more ludicrous? What is nature? Windows were pointed through: lawn, hedge, cows. A brief lecture, to her, on the centuries of genetic manipulation that lead to the contemporary model of bovinity. I revealed to Dr Schubert the intimacy of metal and grass: no blade, no mower, no lawn. My point, and then my money, was taken. Dr Schubert pleaded 'conscience'. That, I realized, was the thing more ludicrous. 'Aquinas!' I shouted after her. 'Jerome!' She did not look back. Max produced the catalogs. I disposed of them and produced Marvel and DC. Max took a walk beside the lake. I think he was thinking about nature. I think that is what is called conscience. I think he was trying not to think about money. 'You want it, you got it!' His glasses steamed up as he entered the room. A constant 45°C. We celebrated with hot chocolate in the limo and vodka in Geneva. I paid. Despite my unnatural objections, I enjoyed the lawns. Cows, I despise, unless *à point*. Perhaps I should mention the mountains. Perhaps not. I discovered a rather marvellous *savetier* and everything was ready. Lights, absence, pain. Bandages, mirror, pleasure. We had begun. I had my old nose mounted, after freeze-drying. Restructuring, we had decided, though Max at first had doubts (financial worries, I presume), would be inhibitive. 'Begin afresh,' as my father said, after my first custodial sentence. My mother did still exist, around Opus 1. But after one too many sorry phonecalls, I had that matter taken care of. We even sued the car company. Opus 2: lights, absence, pain. Eyelids. An in between fact, but deserving. Opus 3 (I can give dates, if you wish: 8 31 99): l-a-p. I always wanted cheekbones, even back in Boredom, US. Mangan cheekbones, with a slight overhang (beetle or Beatle?). Max was having problems with his wife. They had a daughter who found my file. She was my first post-Op fan. Max found her a place, at very short notice, in a Viennese boarding school. His wife moved away to be closer to her. Long nights of Max's Bourbon and Max's tears. Opus 4: lips. Is there any relation more intimate than man and surgeon? (To this day the monster gets called Frankenstein and Frankenstein is popularly considered a monster.) Lovers we may, indeed, penetrate; but rarely do we alter them. If so, only haphazardly. The winebottle, smashed, slashed. A club in Rio. Carnival. My chinos were ruined. I would like, at some point, to call myself an absolutely modern man. Opus 5: the new nose. Opus 6 (Xmas): a correction to the new nose. Opus 7 (Easter): chin and nose, again. Max's apologies became quite tiring. This time, my Bourbon. His daughter had a boyfriend. Swaddled, I attended the Inauguration. The First Lady was ravishing. She thanked me personally for my endorsement. When I walked into the forests, alone, and followed the grass highways beneath the ski-lifts, I still picked up the winterlost coins. There were mountains. I tried to think of a use for the lake. My butler committed suicide quietly, without mess or a fuss. I therefore returned to the same agency for his replacement. I rate loyalty among the highest of the virtues. Opus 8: nose iv. Routine, though, this time. About 7 further on it, Max said. Perhaps 8. When one starts to keep a diary, one immediately becomes adolescent again. I maintained a secret correspondence with Max's daughter. 15. She was very fond of horses and cocaine. I tried to warn her off horses. Opus 9: nose v and cheeks ii. I promised to marry her, when she grew up. This was not enough. I promised to relieve her of her virginity during the summer holidays. She seemed satisfied. June. July. There was a Goya retrospective in Prague. One of my companies bought out another of my companies without either of them realizing it. I think that might stand as a definition of wealth. Opus 10: lips ii. This was not strictly necessary, but I thought it might provide an excuse not to kiss the prospective daughter. I kept my word, though. The nurse who interrupted us has, I believe, just opened her third beachfront bar in Malaysia. I am an absolutely modern man. Opus 12: nose vi. Golf. Opus 13: nose vii. Sometimes I lie awake at night and wish I could lie awake at night more often. There was talk of Madison Square Gardens. 'Patience is a virtue,' as my father said (to the judge) after my fifth custodial sentence. Opus 14: nose viii and ears.

Why did I leave them so long? Dumbo. Max's daughter went back to Vienna for an abortion. She couldn't wait to tell her schoolmates. At least it put her off horses for a while. The first snows. Opus 15: nose. Between October and February: Opuses 16, 17 and 18. Mostly nasal. Completion could, at last, be discussed. Madison Square Gardens were informed. Bruises permitting. The First Lady would be delighted. August. Opus 19. The finishing. Almost. *Coup de? De quoi? Théâtre*, of course. MSG. MonoSodiumGlutamate. An artificial preservative. I am not forty. I am 20. Thoroughly modern me-me. Opus 20. Second thoughts on the nostrils. All the time I was on junk, I never got a cold. Taking Concorde is like taking bad cocaine. The foetus was on the cover of the *Enquirer*. It had my nose. My new nose. It was a girl. America: lights, absence, pain. New Year's Eve. Millennial. A different kind of theatre. 'I am one of the lost,' as they used to say, once. The metropolis that is my identity was jerrybuilt (indeed, my wetnurse was from Karlmarxstadt) about a central abandonment, a Nagasaki of the ego: there will always only be failure, within and about me both. You do not believe that, I hope. I never could stand the sound of laughter. The President will be assassinated. Geneva, Manhattan, Tokyo.

Acknowledgements ∫

Rose Tremain: 'Will and Lou's Boy', from *The Garden of the Villa Mollini*, © Rose Tremain, published by Hamish Hamilton, 1987.

Ian McEwan: 'Solid Geometry', from *First Loves, Last Rites*, © Ian McEwan, published by Jonathan Cape, 1975.

Clive Sinclair: 'A Moment of Happiness', from *Hearts of Gold*, © Clive Sinclair, published by Allison and Busby, 1979.

Kazuo Ishiguro: 'A Family Supper', from *Firebird 2*, © Kazuo Ishiguro, published by Penguin, 1982.

Hernán Lara Zavala: 'Iguana Hunting', (trans. Andrew Jefford) from *Sudden Fictions*, © Hernán Lara Zavala, published by W.W. Norton, 1989.

Jonathan Holland: 'An Afternoon in America', from *First Fictions 11*, © Jonathan Holland, published by Faber and Faber, 1992.

Anthony Sattin: 'The Holiday's Over in Old Alexandria', © Anthony Sattin, 1995.

Andrew Cowan: 'Terminus', from *Looking for the Spark: Scottish Short Stories*, © Andrew Cowan, published by Harper Collins, 1994.

Deirdre Madden: 'Killing a Pig', from *Remembering Light and Stone*, © Deirdre Madden, published by Faber and Faber, 1992.

Lynne Bryan: 'A Regular Thing', from *Envy at the Cheese Handout*, © Lynne Bryan, published by Faber and Faber, 1995.

Glenn Patterson: 'Flag Day', © Glenn Patterson, 1995.

Anne Enright: 'Felix', from *First Fictions 10*, © Anne Enright, published by Faber and Faber, 1989.

Louise Doughty: 'A Whore's Vengeance', from *Success Strikes Twelve*, © Louise Doughty, published by Fontana, 1990.

David Rose: 'An Ugly Night', from *At the Stroke of 12: Winners of the Ian St. James Awards*, © David Rose, published by Harper Collins, 1989.

Mark Illis: 'The Day the House Fell Down', © Mark Illis, 1987.

Kathy Page: 'Woodsmoke', © Kathy Page, 1994.

• Acknowledgements

D. L. Flusfeder: 'Eight Published Works by Donald Cousins', © D. L. Flusfeder, 1995.

Suzannah Dunn: 'Sisters', from *Darker Days Than Usual*, © Suzannah Dunn, published by Serpent's Tail, 1990.

Denise Neuhaus: 'The Crispens', from *First Fictions 11*, © Denise Neuhaus, published by Faber and Faber, 1992.

Philip MacCann: 'Dark Hour', first appeared in *The New Yorker*, © Philip MacCann, 1994, from *The Miracle Shed*, published by Faber and Faber, 1995.

Erica Wagner: 'The Great Leonardo', from *The Word Party*, © Erica Wagner, published by UEA, 1991.

Robert Cremins: 'Roomkeepers', © Robert Cremins, 1995.

Clare Morgan: 'L'Hotel des Grands Hommes', from *New Writing 1*, © Clare Morgan, published by Minerva in association with The British Council, 1992.

Suzanne Cleminshaw: 'Disillusionment of Ten O'clock', © Suzanne Cleminshaw, 1995.

Sarah Gracie: 'A Silver Christening Mug', from *New Writing 2*, © Sarah Gracie, published by Minerva in association with The British Council, 1993.

Jane Harris: 'Why Not How', © Jane Harris, 1995.

Harriet Braun: 'Casper', from *Mafia*, © Harriet Braun, published by UEA, 1993.

Melanie Danburg: 'Addictionary', from *Mafia*, © Melanie Danburg, published by UEA, 1993.

Jacqui Lofthouse: 'The Effigy', from *Mafia*, © Jacqui Lofthouse, published by UEA, 1993.

Martha Perkins: 'Cutting', © Martha Perkins, 1995.

Toby Litt: 'Adventures in Capitalism', © Toby Litt, 1995.

Extract from *The City*, from COLLECTED POEMS by C.P. Cavafy, translated by Edmund Keeley and Philip Sherard, edited by George Savidis. Reprinted by permission of The Hogarth Press and Princeton University Press.

Extract from *The Crucible*, by Arthur Miller © 1952, 1953, reprinted by permission of Greene & Heaton Ltd. and Penguin USA.

Extract from *Disillusionment of Ten O'clock*, from COLLECTED POEMS by Wallace Stevens © 1923, 1951, reprinted by permission of Faber and Faber Ltd. and Alfred A. Knopf Inc..

The Garden of the Villa Mollini

ROSE TREMAIN

A new collection of stories from the author of
THE SWIMMING POOL SEASON

'Her talent at its best'
Susan Hill

'Professional, ingenious . . . genuinely witty'
Martin Seymour-Smith in the Financial Times

'A quintessentially English writer – her work has a
charm and finesse, a civilised irony'
Robert Nye in The Guardian

'The stories have a strange, fairy-tale quality: the
simple, beautiful prose, the sense of inevitability, the
use of allusion and metaphor to suggest undercurrents
of disturbing portent'
Selina Hastings in The Daily Telegraph

'An expert at conveying the kind of apparently
inconsequential detail that might be the moment of
definition in someone's life'
The Times Literary Supplement

'A skilled writer deftly turning her hand to different
situations'
Vogue

'A collection full of gems'
Country Life

SCEPTRE

The Colonel's Daughter
and other stories
ROSE TREMAIN

At the moment that Colonel Browne is standing in the shallow end of the swimming pool of the Hotel Alpenrose, preparing for his late afternoon dip, his daughter Charlotte, carrying a suitcase, is getting out of her car back in England, preparing to rob the ancestral home. It is not just another day: it is the culmination of hundreds of days, hundreds of disappointments and misunderstandings, and thousands of very small lies . . .

'Rose Tremain goes from strength to strength. THE COLONEL'S DAUGHTER is a winner . . . a riveting and satisfying read'
Grace Ingoldby in the New Statesman

'A true writer of fiction . . . A writer whose every book has been a pleasure'
The Scotsman

'Demonstrates a wry talent and considerable fertility of invention'
Christopher Wordsworth in The Guardian

'Dialogue and offbeat humour are spot-on'
Elizabeth Berridge in The Daily Telegraph

SCEPTRE

Telling Stories 4

The Best of BBC Radio's Recent Short Fiction

Edited by DUNCAN MINSHULL

Twenty entertaining and stimulating new stories by contemporary writers are presented in this fourth selection of the best short fiction found on BBC Radios 3 and 4. With settings ranging from Czechoslovakia to Hong Kong and subjects from geese to ghosts, here is a wonderfully rich and varied feast of fiction.

Clare Boylan	Joanna Trollope
Stephen Amidon	E. Annie Proulx
James Hamilton-Paterson	Michèle Roberts
Allan Massie	D. J. Taylor
Susan Johnson	Frederic Raphael
Roy Heath	Janice Galloway
Christopher Hope	Geoff Nicholson
David Hartnett	Philip Hensher
Tom Drury	Helen Simpson
Jane Gardam	Robert Cremins

$\int$

SCEPTRE